NO SAFE PLACE

BOOK 1 OF THE COST OF SAFETY SERIES

EMME ROSEWOOD

ROSEWOOD CREATIVE HOUSE LLC

Written by Emme Rosewood.

ISBN: 979-8-950453-00-7

For my husband

Thank you for supporting me long before I was ready to share this book with the world.

CONTENT ADVISORY

This novel contains mature and potentially distressing themes including:

Domestic abuse and intimate partner violence

Emotional abuse and controlling behavior

Gun violence and shootings

Threats, intimidation, and stalking

Organized crime and corruption themes

Child endangerment and custody-related conflict

Infidelity and marital breakdown

Psychological trauma and identity loss

Surveillance and paranoia elements

Alcohol misuse

Death and traumatic violence

Strong language

Sexual content

Dark romantic suspense themes

Recommended for mature readers.

Chapter One

The House of Hawthorne

Dean

The kitchen gleamed like something out of a magazine. Brass fixtures polished so bright they caught the overhead lights, dark stone counters that reflected back at me like black water, a ten-foot island lined with stools that had never once been pulled out by family. Outside, somewhere past the manicured hedges and quiet sidewalks of our neighborhood, a siren wailed and faded into the distance. Just another Chicago night reminding you the city never really slept.

Vicky had gotten everything she wanted in this place. Designer finishes. Custom cabinetry. An open floor plan meant for donors and judges, people who never think to ask where the money, or even the man behind it all came from.

Me? I'd built it. Every cut, every nail, every piece of wood trimmed to fit. My sweat still lived in these walls. But standing there, running my hand along the already perfect countertop, I couldn't shake the feeling that the house had never actually been mine.

A soft grunt pulled my attention.

Lila squirmed in the corner bassinet, her fists batting at the air like she was trying to fight invisible demons. Her face flushed red, tiny lips pulling tight before she could work herself into a full cry.

I crouched down, my knees popping. "Easy, peanut. You don't have to win the fight. Just breathe."

Her legs kicked, restless under the blanket. I tucked the edge tighter around her chest, brushed a finger over the fuzz of her hair. The powdery and faintly sweet smell hit me. Pure. That smell could quiet the storm in my chest quicker than bourbon ever had.

She blinked up at me, gummy mouth still working on nothing, eyes too big for her head.

"Dean!" Vicky's voice cracked across the air from the dining room. Sharp. Precise. Over the clatter of dishes. "They're folding the napkins wrong. Can you handle it?"

I looked at my daughter, her wide eyes fixed on me like I was supposed to have all the answers.

"Yeah," I muttered, pressing a hand gently against her blanket. "Two minutes."

I stood, shoulders already tight.

Victoria Hayes, my wife and one of the rising names in the District Attorney's office, stood framed in the dining room archway. A slim silhouette cut sharp against the glow of the chandelier. She wasn't tall, but at five-four, she had always known how to take up space without raising her voice.

Her black dress skimmed her hips in clean, deliberate lines. The kind she favored for events like this: practical and polished all at once. Half her warm blonde hair was still pinned up with silver clips she hadn't had time to remove, catching the light. I remembered helping her practice speeches in this same room once, back when neither of us had imagined evenings like this would become routine.

Her brown eyes swept the space with cool precision, as her eyes moved over the table settings, the glassware and the placement of every chair with quiet position. She lifted one manicured hand and gave a small but efficient gesture towards the caterers finishing their rounds. The kind of signal they understood meant she was watching, her expression saying more than words ever could: *hurry up, and don't mess it up.*

For a moment she stood perfectly still, taking it all in. Then she smoothed a hand over the front of her dress, composure settling over her like armor.

"They're folding them in halves," she said, her voice clipped. Not quite irritation, more like urgency. "It's supposed to be thirds. The symmetry photographs better. This isn't...casual."

Tonight couldn't be casual. Not with half the city's legal ladder climbing through our front door. Assistant state's attorneys, judges, donors; people who would decide whether Victoria Hayes was just promising or inevitable.

I followed her gaze to the dining room table. Crisp linens. Silverware straight enough to pass inspection. It already looked better than anything I'd grown up with. But I stepped forward anyway, picked one up, and refolded it slow enough for the staff to catch on.

"Like this?"

Her shoulders eased a fraction and her face softened for the first time all day. Not a smile, exactly. But close enough. "Exactly like that."

She moved on before the moment could settle as her heels tapped toward the bar being assembled in the next room, voice shifting into that calm and efficient tone she used when she needed things to happen fast.

I caught the flicker in one of the caterer's eyes. Relief. Maybe gratitude that I hadn't made things harder, that I'd spared them another round of corrections. I refolded two more napkins, just so they could have the pattern clear, then left them to it.

Back in the kitchen, Lila had worked herself into a tiny but tired cry. I scooped her from her carrier, her weight solid and warm against my chest. Her head tucked beneath my chin like she already knew the spot. Her tiny fingers gripped the fabric of my shirt. I rocked on my heels, swaying without thinking. The rhythm had become instinct in the past three months.

Outside, the hum of delivery trucks idling the quiet street with voices rising and falling, as cases of wine and crates of glassware disappeared through the front door. The house hummed with movement, like a stage before the curtain lifted.

"You should already be dressed," Vicky said from behind me.

I turned. Vicky had come back into the kitchen without me noticing, diamond earrings catching the light as she paused near the stove. She adjusted the clasp of her necklace in the oven's chrome reflection. Her movements were quick. Practiced.

"We're already running behind," she said, glancing toward the hallway where voices carried in waves. "The nanny's here. You don't have to do everything."

I pressed my lips against Lila's head before answering. "She needs one more feeding before bed."

A quiet breath left her. Not quite frustration. Not quite surrender. "She'll be okay," Vicky said. "That's why we brought someone in for tonight."

"She settles easier with me," I said. My voice stayed even, but my arms tightened around my daughter's small body without meaning to.

Vicky's gaze lifted, catching mine in the oven's reflection. For a second, she just watched us swaying, the tiny fist curled into my shirt as Lila's cheek rested beneath my chin, as I fed her.

The faint line between her brows deepened, then smoothed again as she looked away. She didn't push it further. I kept rocking. Lila's grip loosened as her eyes fluttered closed as she finished her bottle. The tension in my chest eased with hers.

The house around us grew louder with the first guests began to arrive. Trays clinked somewhere near the entryway, laughter rolled down the hall in polite bursts, and a low pulse of bass vibrated through the floor as someone tested the sound system.

I knew every inch of this place. I'd cut the lumber myself, sanded the cabinets until the grain felt like silk beneath my palms, and laid tile long past the point my knees stopped complaining and just went numb. Tonight, it all gleamed under soft lighting and careful stagging, transformed into something meant to impress the people who could elevate Vicky's career.

When the nanny arrived, I carried Lila upstairs before anyone could offer to take her. I caught the brief glance Vicky sent my way, measuring, distracted, already moving to the next thing. But she didn't stop me.

The nursery smelled faintly of sawdust and paint. The last room I'd finished before she was born. I laid Lila gently into the crib and rested my hand along the railing, waiting until her breathing settled into a slow and steady rhythm.

Downstairs, the living room had been remade while I was gone. Candles flickered along the mantle. Glassware caught the light in sharp, glittering rows making the bar sparkle. Servers in black vests moved through the space with quiet efficiency. The place looked perfect. Designed. Controlled.

And for the first time that night, I felt like an intruder in my own house. Like I was stepping into a version of my own life that no longer quite fit.

By the time I reached the bottom of the stairs, Vicky was already at the center of the room, a glass of champagne balanced easily in her hand like it belonged there. She spoke to the bar staff with quiet efficiency, indicating placements with the rim of flute while the jazz trio set up in the corner.

She noticed me without turning. "You disappeared."

"I took Lila up."

A small pause. Then she nodded once, already shifting her attention back to the flow of people and movement around her.

I looked down at myself. Dark slacks and a white shirt rolled to the elbows. Good enough for most rooms. Just maybe not this one.

"For tonight,." she added, finally facing me, "you should change."

She crossed the space before I could answer, setting her glass aside. Her fingers moved to my collar, quick and practiced, smoothing the fabric like she'd done it a hundred times before. The brush of her knuckles along my throat sent an unexpected current through me. Her perfume lingered; sharp floral layered over something colder, more expensive.

"This is important," she said quietly. "Half the county board will be here. Donors. People who decide what gets funded and what doesn't.

"Since when are we hosting them?" I asked.

"Since I need their support on an appropriation bill." She gave the collar one last final adjustment, eyes flickering up to meet mine before stepping back. "And then, I'll be in D.C. the rest of the week."

That made me blink. "D.C.? You didn't mention that."

A faint crease touched her brow. "I thought I did." Then it smoothed away, replaced by the composed expression she wore when rooms started filling. "Federal strategy meetings. I am catching the red eye to D.C. after the reception."

Before I could sort out what I felt about this, the doorbell chimed. Then a knock followed, voices rising in overlapping greetings as the first wave of guests stepped inside

The house filled fast. Coats brushed polished wood, as bursts of cologne layered over the rosemary and seared meat drifting in from the kitchen. Laughter rose and broke the high ceilings. Polished shoes clicked across the tile and hardwood in restless rhythms. Judges. Assistant state's attorneys. A detective I half-recognized already working his way toward the bar. Rick Garcia, I think.

I stayed near the edge of the room, bourbon anchoring my hand, watching it all like a man who knew the script but didn't rehearse the lines.

"Dean." A familiar female voice cut clean through the noise.

I turned, and almost didn't recognize her.

Jenna Alvarez a few feet away, dark curls pinned back in a way that probably took more effort than she'd ever admit. Out of uniform, she looked...different. Softer around the edges, maybe. Or maybe it was just the dress, deep navy and fitted through the waist, heels that made her nearly my height. She'd always been solid and grounded. The kind of presence that intimidated a room. That hadn't changed.

"Well, I'll be damned," she said, breaking into a grin. "You clean up alright for a civilian."

I let out a breath that might've been the first real one all night. "Still running point on everyone who walks into a room, Alvarez?"

"Someone has to." Her eyes flicked over my shoulder, already clocking exits and the invisible currents that never stopped moving. Cop instincts didn't clock out for cocktail hour.

She leaned in slightly. "You hiding or just pretending to host?"

"Little of both."

"That tracks."

She turned and lifted her chin toward a cluster near the bar. "Mark! Get over here. You're not going to believe who Vicky managed to drag out of retirement."

Mark Sullivan pushed through the crowd a second later, broader than I remembered, suit jacket already hanging open like it had offended him. His tie sat slightly crooked, dark blonde hair shorter now, hiding the streaks of gray filling in. The promotion sat on him differently than the badge ever had. More weight. More responsibility.

"Shit," he said when he saw me. "Look at you. Thought you'd vanished into contractor witness protection."

"Lieutenant Sullivan," I said, raising my glass. "Didn't realize you still spoke to the working class."

He snorted and pulled me into a quick one-armed hug that thudded solid against my ribs. Familiar. Grounding.

"Don't start," he muttered. "I spend all day getting yelled at by people who think promotions mean I suddenly know what I'm doing."

Jenna smirked. "He doesn't."

"For the record," Mark added, "this place is insane. You built all this?"

"Yeah."

He whistled low. "Hayes doesn't do small."

Before I could answer, another voice cut through the hum of conversation. This one was older, sharper, carrying something that made the back of my neck tighten.

"Dean?" a man's voice cut through.

Jenna's eyes flicked past my shoulder automatically, already assessing whoever had managed to get that close without being noticed. Mark followed her glance, then gave my arm a quick squeeze.

"We'll let you play host," he said.

"Try not to get into trouble without us," Jenna added, already turning back toward the bar.

I watched them disappear into the current of suits and polished laughter before facing the man who'd spoken.

Jonathan Turner stood a few steps away, looking almost exactly as I remembered him. Same steady presence. Same quiet way of taking up space without demanding it. He wasn't tall, maybe five-ten, but built like an most men who spend their days behind desks and their weekends fixing things that didn't really need fixing. His brown hair was neatly combed, though a few strands had already escaped the effort, and his equally brown eyes held that steady, unremarkable warmth that always made people underestimate him. The charcoal suit fit well but sat stiff across his shoulders, like he still hadn't decided whether he wanted to be in a room like this.

We'd known each other more than half our lives. College. Early jobs. Bad apartments and cheap beer and the promise that someday things would look different.

"Long time," he said, gripping my hand. His smile was warm, familiar. The kind that had carried me through more rough nights than I liked to admit. "Hell of a place."

"Yeah," I said. "Good to see you, John."

Then my gaze shifted past him. Bella Turner stood just behind his shoulder, near the edge of the crowd.

Something in my chest tightened without warning.

She held herself with a quiet kind of confidence that didn't need attention to exist. At five-seven, she had a curvy, graceful figure that the soft green dress only hinted at. The dress moved subtly when she did, catching the light in muted flashes. Nothing flashy. Nothing forced. Just deliberate. Her dark red hair fell in loose waves that framed her face, half pinned back in a way that looked graceful. And her eyes were meticulously lined and shaded to deepen the natural ocean blue and moved through the room with calm precision taking in people and the rhythm of conversations.

When those eyes landed on me, even for a second the noise around us seemed to dull at the edges.

"Dean," she said, offering a small nod.

"Bella." My voice came out lower than I intended.

John clapped a hand lightly against my shoulder. "You really built all this?"

"Most of it."

"Man." He let out a soft laugh. "Victoria really put you to work."

As if summoned, Vicky appeared beside Bella a moment later, moving smoothly through the crowd. Her smile shifted into place the way it always did in rooms like this: warm, polished, and welcoming without giving too much away. "Bella, I'm so glad you could make it," she said, leaning in for an air kiss near her cheek. "You look beautiful."

Her gaze flicked briefly to me. "Don't you think so, Dean?"

I swallowed against the tightness in my throat. "Yeah. She does."

Bella's smile was quick, almost private, before John guided her toward a growing circle of spouses near the windows. Within seconds, she disappeared into the movement of the room, leaving behind the sound of glassware clinking and the burn of bourbon in my throat. The room swelled with sound as the night settled in. Music threaded through conversation as glassware chimed softly on passing trays. Warm air carried the scent of citrus peel and roasted herbs. Somewhere near the windows, someone laughed too loudly at a joke that hadn't quite landed.

Vicky moved easily through it all. She had always known how to command a room without appearing to try. One hand curved around a champagne flute she barely drank from, the other brushing sleeves, greeting donors, anchoring conversations before drifting on to the next one. Her dress followed in clean, fluid lines. Every movement measured without feeling rehearsed. I fell in to the role I knew best. Smiling. Pouring. Offering introductions when needed. Making sure no one waited too long for a refill or a place to stand.

It was my house, but it sure as hell wasn't my party. Tonight, it belonged to the version of our life she was building.

Every so often, through the shifting currents of voices and music, I caught the sound of Bella's laugh. Not strategic. Something softer. Real. Light. Unfiltered. And it pulled at me harder than I wanted to admit.

She stood near the far side of the room now, speaking with a group of spouses who leaned in as she talked, drawn in without seeming to understand why. She didn't look uncomfortable. If anything, she looked present. Like she knew how to exist in rooms like this without letting them shape her.

Seeing familiar faces here helped more than I expected. Mark. Jenna. A few others who had known me long before polished floors and catered dinners. It reminded me this night wasn't entirely foreign territory.

Still, my attention kept drifting back toward the green shimmer of Bella's dress moving through the crowd.

Mark appeared beside me again, already reaching for a bourbon before I could offer. "Not bad, huh?" Mark said, tipping the glass toward the room like he was evaluating a crime scene.

"Depends on who you ask."

He snorted. "Come on. This place? These people? You're hosting half the damn county in your living room."

"I'm pouring drinks," I said. "She's hosting."

Mark followed my line of sight as Vicky paused near the windows, leaning in to listen to something the treasurer was saying. She laughed softly, one hand resting lightly on his arm before she moved on to the next conversation without missing a beat.

"She's doing more than hosting," he said. "Her name comes up a lot downtown."

"Good or bad?"

He gave me a sideways look. "You fishing? Or do you actually not know?"

"Both."

Mark took a slow sip, considering. "She's sharp. People notice that. Judges like her. She doesn't waste time. Doesn't play scared." He tilted his head slightly. "There's talk she'll move up faster than anyone expected."

I watched Vicky accept a glass she wouldn't drink from, already pivoting toward another cluster of donors.

"Federal?" I asked.

"Eventually. Maybe sooner than that if she keeps pushing the right cases."

"Is that what this is?" I nodded toward the room.

"Part of it." Mark shrugged. "Appropriations. Probably influence and optics. Chicago runs on relationships whether anyone admits it or not."

I huffed a quiet laugh. "She always was better at that part than me."

"You were better at kicking down doors," he said. "Different skill set."

For a second, we stood there in the noise, watching the life I'd helped build move around us like it didn't need either of us to understand it.

"She happy?" Mark asked finally.

The question landed heavier than I expected.

"She's...busy," I said.

Mark didn't push. He never did. He just lifted his glass slightly in Vicky's direction.

"Well," he muttered, "whatever she's doing, it's working."

By the time the first course was set down, a dull pressure had already begun to gather behind my eyes. Too many conversations layered over one another. Too much champagne clinking against crystal. Too many practiced smiles held just a second longer than they needed to be. I kept moving anyway. Nodding. Refilling glasses. Answering questions like I'd memorized the lines ahead of time.

The judge across from me leaned back in his chair, loosening his tie. "Hell of a spread, Dean. You should be proud."

"I am," I said. "Vicky's been planning this for weeks."

His wife leaned forward, pearls swinging softly as she studied the room. "But you built this home, didn't you? The woodwork, the floors...all of it?"

"Most of it." My hand slid along the smooth back of the chair without thinking, fingertips tracing the grain I still knew in my heart.

Vicky stepped in smoothly before the conversation could stall. "He won't say it himself," she said her tone warm enough to carry across the table. "You should have seen it when we bought it. Bare studs. Concrete dust everywhere. Dean turned it into something we could actually live in." Her fingers brushed lightly against mine beneath the table, brief and grounding. She shifted her attention toward the county treasurer beside her, already drawing him back into conversation.

I took a slow sip of my bourbon, letting the burn settle in my throat as the noise of the room rose again.

Three seats down, Bella leaned forward, listening as someone launched into a story about a bowling ball used in an evidence bust. Her laugh broke free a second later. Clear and easy, the kind that didn't seem designed for rooms like this but somehow filled the space anyway.

I realized I was watching her before I could stop myself.

Maybe she felt it. Maybe she was just used to reading a room. Her eyes lifted, finding mine across the table. For a heartbeat, everything else softened. The music and conversation. Then she looked away, quick, like the moment had caught her off guard too.

John never noticed. He was already deep in a debate with a detective about overtime budgets.

A waiter stepped in to clear our plates. Across the room, the jazz trio eased into another song with soft notes floating just above the hum of conversation.

"Dean," Vicky's voice cut cleanly through the hum of conversation, firm enough to reach me without drawing attention. "Can you see that the wine keeps moving? Table three is already empty."

I pushed my chair back with a nod. "Yeah. Got it." The movement felt like relief. Something to do. Something simple.

The waiter passed me a fresh bottle, and I moved from guest to guest, topping off glasses while conversation drifted past in half formed pieces. Trial schedules. Zoning rumors. Even someone arguing quietly about who's been passed over for a committee appointment.

Near the doorway to the hall, Jenna stood with a man I didn't recognize. Her posture angled just enough to suggest she wasn't entirely off duty.

"...telling you it's not just street crews anymore," she was saying under her breath. "This one's organized. Warehouses, shell deliveries, burner accounts. Someone's backing it."

The man frowned. "Feds?"

"Maybe. Or someone they haven't named yet." She shrugged, already sounding tired of the conversation. "Either way, if that shipment actually came through the port like they think, we're going to be playing catch-up for months."

I kept walking before they noticed me listening.

Across the room, Vicky lifted her glass slightly in silent approval as I refilled another table. The jazz trio slipped into a slower number, brass notes curling through the warm air.

For a moment, the night almost felt manageable.

Bella's voice reached me again as I circled back toward their end of the table. Quieter now.

"It's not just about selling houses," she said, her hand swaying slightly as she spoke. "You're helping people picture a life they haven't lived yet. The space makes a huge difference. How it feels when you walk in. What you think might happen there."

I paused mid-pour before I even realized I'd stopped moving. The words settled somewhere under my ribs, heavier than they should have.

Across the table, Vicky was already leaning into another conversation, her laugh warm and bright, drawing a new cluster of attention without seeming to try. She had always understood how rooms worked. How to move through them. How to shape them into something useful.

I forced my hand steady and filled another glass.

Bella looked up then, catching me standing there. For a second neither of us spoke, as our eyes caught again. She offered me the faintest smile, like she understood I'd heard more then I meant to.

I broke the moment first, turning away before it could settle into something harder to ignore.

The rest of the evening began to soften at the edges. Plates appeared and disappeared. Coffee replaced wine. Conversations shifted from strategy to stories.

A hand clapped lightly against my shoulder.

"Hey."

I turned to find Mark already shrugging into his jacket, tie loosened like he'd finally declared defeat.

"Calling it?" I asked.

"Lieutenant's privilege," he said. "Plus, if I stay any longer someone's going to try to recruit me for a fundraiser."

I huffed a quiet laugh.

He studied my face for a second, longer than most people would have dared tonight.

"You good?"

"Yeah."

He didn't look convinced. "It's almost over," he said, nodding toward the thinning tables. "Hang in there."

His gaze flicked around the room. "Where'd Alvarez go?"

"Haven't seen her in a while."

Mark grunted softly. "Figures. Probably got pulled back into something. She can't help herself."

He extended his hand, then pulled me into a quick one-armed hug before I could take it.

"Don't disappear again," he muttered.

"Wasn't planning on it."

He gave the room one last sweeping look, then headed toward the door, already shifting back into cop mode as he moved through the crowd. By the time the last guest finally drifted out, a dull ache had settled into my jaw from how long I'd kept it tight.

The house bore the quiet evidence of the night: crumbs scattered across polished wood, abandoned glasses catching the low light, and candles burned down to uneven stubs. I loosened my tie, rubbing the back of my neck, when I noticed Bella standing in the doorway with her coat draped over her arm.

John was nowhere in sight.

"He's got an early morning," she explained, like she followed my thoughts. "I told him I'd find a ride later." Her gaze moved slowly across the room, then back to me. "Do you need help?"

The answer rose automatically. Habit. Pride. But my shoulders felt heavier than either of those.

"Yeah," I admitted. "I could use it."

We worked in near silence at first. Bella stacked plates with careful efficiency while I scraped leftovers into the trash. The soft clink of silverware and the steady hum of the dishwasher filled the space between us. One by one, the candles guttered out, leaving behind thin ribbons that smelled faintly sweet in the air.

"Hell of a night," she said after a while, folding a napkin into neat thirds. Her tone stayed light, but her eyes searched my face.

"It wasn't really mine," I muttered, as I rinsed another glass, watching water bead and run over the surface. "I never wanted anything like this."

She gave me a look, half-curious, half-knowing, but didn't push. Just nodded and stepped closer to gather another stack of plates. Our hands met when we both reached for the same fork. Warm skin against damp fingers. Neither of us moved away right away.

Upstairs, Lila's cry cut clean through the quiet. I pulled back first, drying my hands on a towel. "I'll get her."

"I'll finish here," Bella said.

By the time I returned with Lila pressed against my chest, already drifting back to sleep, Bella was blowing out the last candle on the table. The room sank into shadow, smelling faintly of wax and wine. For the first time all night, everything was still.

She slipped her coat on but didn't head for the door immediately. Her gaze lingered on the baby tucked against me.

"She's beautiful," Bella said softly.

I kissed the top of Lila's head, feeling the steady warmth of her small body. "Yeah. She is."

For a moment we just stood there in the dim light, surrounded by the quiet remains of something that had taken so much effort to hold together. With Bella beside me, even just clearing dishes in the dark, the house didn't feel quite as empty.

Chapter Two

SHATTERED QUIET

Bella

The house still smelled heavy with beef and rosemary. Beneath it lingered the faint smell of candle smoke, wax cooling in uneven pools on the table. My heels clicked against the tile, too sharp in the quiet. The dining room looked wrecked with crumbs scattered across polished wood, tipped glasses catching the low light, and napkins slouched into tired folds. More like the aftermath of a wedding than a dinner party.

I couldn't imagine putting on something like this. Not the planning. Not the performance of it. But then, Victoria Hayes had always known how to command a room. Even back when we were younger, she moved through people like she understood exactly where she was going and how to get there.

I stepped around a chair, careful not to snag my dress, wondering how she had the energy to hold court all night.

In the quiet, the house felt stripped of all its shine, as if it had been packed away with the guests. The lingering perfume and wine turning sour in the air. Dean moved through the rooms switching off the lights one by one until only the lamp in the foyer remained.

"Let me drive you," he said when he reached me. His voice was low, and steady. "It's late."

I almost refused out of habit. Instead, I nodded and crossed toward the bottom of the stairs where I'd left my coat.

Lila was half-asleep against his chest, her small face slack with exhaustion. He carried her carefully, instinctively, rocking without seeming to realize he was doing it.

He moved slower now than he had all night.

"I'll grab her bag," he murmured, as if raising his voice might disturb the fragile calm that had finally settled over the house.

In the foyer, the furnace rumbled to life, warm air pushing into the stillness. Bottles rattled softly inside the diaper bag when he swung it over his shoulder.

The front door opened before either of us reached it. Cold air swept in fast as a man in dark clothes stepped through the door.

Vicky crossed the threshold mid-conversation, phone pressed to her ear, a suitcase rolling behind her. Her heels struck the floor in quick, purposeful beats. She was already somewhere else, mentally and physically, moving through the space like it was simply another checkpoint in a night that hadn't ended, as she handed off her suitcase to her driver.

She paused just long enough to lower her phone and glance at Dean, without breaking her sentence.

"Text me when you land," he said quietly.

She nodded once, distracted. Her gaze flicking briefly to Lila before shifting back toward the driver waiting outside.

"Bye," she said. To the room or maybe to the moment. It wasn't clear.

The door closed with a dull finality. The brass handle trembling slightly in the silence that followed. Then she was gone again, swallowed by headlights and the low growl of the idling car.

I watched the door for longer than I meant to, half-expecting it to open again. It didn't. My coat felt suddenly too tight across my shoulders. I folded my arms without thinking.

"Where is she going this late?" I asked. The question slipped out before I could decide whether it was any of my business.

Dean shifted Lila higher against his chest. His mouth tightened slightly. "D.C."

The baby made a small, restless sound, rooting against his shirt. He began rubbing slow circles along her back, steady and automatic, like he was anchoring himself as much as her.

I dropped my gaze at the floor, because the silence settling between us felt heavier than the noise of the party had.

The garage was colder than I expected. The concrete held the night's chill, and my breath ghosted pale in the air as Dean flicked on the light. The overhead bulb hummed awake, throwing long shadows across tool-lined walls that still smelled faintly of oil and winter.

He unlatched the carrier and set it on the workbench for a moment, brushing his thumb gently over Lila's cheek. She squirmed, half-asleep. Tiny fists opening and closing in slow protest.

"C'mon, sweetheart," he murmured. "Can you hold this?" He said, turning to me as he nodded toward the diaper bag strap.

I slid my hand beneath it, keeping the buckle steady while he guided her into the seat. Our shoulders brushed, just enough to make me suddenly aware of how close we were standing. His warmth cut through the cold like a quiet shock I couldn't entirely blame on the temperature.

"There we go," he said, tightening the straps with practiced efficiency. Lila made one small sound before settling again with her fist tucked against her mouth.

He clicked the carrier into its base and gave it a firm, final tug. Then he crossed over to the wall and hit the garage door button.

The motor groaned. Metal panels rattled upward until the night spilled in. Dark and sharp and wide open.

We both paused for a heartbeat before moving.

He slid behind the wheel, adjusting the mirror out of habit. I closed my door, the sound echoing faintly in the cold space like a period at the end of a long sentence.

The engine turned over with a steady, familiar rumble. Dashboard lights glowed to life, washing Dean's face in muted blue. Gravel crunched beneath the tires as we rolled out of the driveway and onto the quiet street of Hawthorne Ridge.

The garage light snapped off behind us.

For a few seconds, there was only the hum of the engine and the soft rhythm of Lila's breathing from the back seat.

Then Dean's posture shifted.

"Bella..." His voice dropped. "You see that?"

I followed his gaze through the windshield.

Across the street, dark vehicles sat staggered along the curb. A black sedan and two SUVs. Engines running. Headlights off. Waiting.

My stomach tightened.

"Dean..."

He didn't answer. He was already moving.

The truck jolted into reverse, tires grinding hard over gravel as he swung us toward the street. The second our headlights cut across the road; the parked vehicles came alive.

Lights flared on all at once. Blinding white flooded the mirrors.

"Hang on," he said. The engine roared as he accelerated.

One SUV lunged forward, angling across the lane to trap us. Dean swerved sharply, the truck skidding before catching traction again. Trees and porch lights streaked past in fractured flashes.

Behind us, Lila woke with a thin, startled cry.

"Dean—"

"They're boxing us," he muttered, jaw tight. "Stay down."

The rearview mirror filled with headlights, closing fast. Another vehicle surged up alongside us, metal flashing under the high beams.

A sharp crack split the night.

Glass burst behind me.

For a second, I couldn't process the sound. Then cold air rushed in through the spiderwebbed rear window.

"Get down!" Dean shouted.

I twisted in the seat, instinct taking over, reaching for Lila's carrier. My hands shook as I unclipped my seat belt and climbed back to bend over her, shielding her small body while another shot rang out somewhere behind us.

The truck fishtailed again. Dean fought the wheel, forcing it straight.

The road ahead narrowed suddenly, streetlights thinning into darkness as he veered onto a service drive that cut along the edge of a forest preserve. Branches scraped along the sides of the truck, the world outside collapsing into flashes of shadow and light.

"They're still coming," I gasped.

"I know." His voice was raw now. Focused. "But they're not taking us."

Gravel sprayed behind us as the pursuing vehicles overshot the turn. One spun sideways. Another clipped the ditch, headlights bouncing wildly through the trees.

Dean didn't slow until the lights disappeared completely. Only then did he ease off the gas. The engine settled into a rough idle.

Dean dragged one hand down his face, breath still uneven. For a second, he just sat there, staring through the windshield like he was trying to force the world back into something that made sense.

Then he reached for his phone. The glow lit his hands, still shaking, as he hit Victoria's name without hesitation.

It rang.

Once.

Twice.

Three times, then straight to voicemail. He swore under his breath and pulled the phone away, jaw tightening.

"She might already be boarding," I said quietly. "Or going through security. They make you shut everything off."

He didn't look convinced. His thumb hovered over the screen for a second before he typed. The movements sharper now.

Call me. Something just happened.

He hit send harder than he needed to. The message whooshed into the silence.

Outside, the night pressed close against the windows. Silence rushed in. Thick and shaking. My lungs burned. Lila's cries softened into uneven hiccups beneath my arms. Dean's hands stayed locked on the wheel, trembling now that the danger had passed.

"You okay?" he asked without looking at me.

I nodded, though I wasn't sure he saw it.

"Dean..." My voice barely held. "What was that?"

He stared into the dark ahead, jaw set.

"I don't know."

But the certainty in his tone said something worse. Whatever this was, it wasn't over.

The night closed in around us. The dark road, steady engine hum, and the faint rhythm of my pulse still echoing in my ears. I stared out the window, but my focus kept drifting back to Dean's hands locked around the wheel...and the small rise and fall of Lila's breathing in the rear seat.

The cab smelled faintly of Victoria's perfume, sharp and expensive, like a presence that hadn't fully left. Beneath it lingered the softer warmth of milk and baby powder.

Dean's tension filled the space between us.

The truck itself was immaculate. Clean lines. Tools tucked away. Everything in its place. I didn't know why that detail stuck with me. Maybe because nothing else about the night made sense.

The silence stretched too long. Too heavy.

"Dean." My voice cracked on his name.

He didn't look at me. His jaw flexed once, like he was biting down on whatever answer he might have given.

"Who were they?" The words came faster now. "Why were they waiting outside your house? Why tonight?" My breath hitched. "Why was I even in the car when—"

"Bella." Just my name. Quiet. Steady. But it stopped me completely.

"Not now."

The finality in it knocked the air from my lungs. I pressed my palms into my knees, trying to stop the tremor in my hands. It didn't work.

Beside me, Lila stirred with a soft whimper. I twisted in my seat instinctively, but Dean kept his eyes fixed on the road ahead, shoulders rigid with concentration. I couldn't sit with the fear any longer.

My fingers fumbled for my phone. I nearly dropped it before John's name appeared on the screen. He answered on the second ring.

"Bella?" His voice was thick with sleep.

"Something happened," I said. My throat felt raw. "After the party. At Dean's."

He was awake instantly. "What do you mean?"

"Cars. Black SUVs. Someone shot at us." The word gun caught in my chest like glass. "They were waiting. They knew he'd be leaving."

Silence. Then: "Are you hurt?"

"No."

"And Dean?"

I glanced toward the mirror. He still hadn't looked at me, but the muscle in his jaw ticked. "He's here. And Lila. He's taking me home...I didn't know where else we could go."

Dean's eyes flicked toward me briefly in the reflection. Just long enough to remind me he was listening to every word. John exhaled. Hard.

"Bring them here."

"With the kids—"

"Yes," he said. "He's our friend. He's got his daughter. You don't leave someone out there after something like that. We'll figure it out."

Something inside me loosened at the word home. "Okay."

The call ended. I lowered the phone slowly, holding it against my chest like it might keep my heart from coming apart. Dean didn't speak. But I felt the change with the slightest easing in his grip on the wheel and his shoulders dropping a fraction.

Outside, the road widened into a long stretch of industrial parkway. Dark warehouses slid past. A distant freight train horn carried through the night. Lila sighed in her sleep. I watched the empty city blur by and realized how little any of us understood about what had just happened.

If whoever was hunting Dean had found him once...What was stopping them from finding all of us again?

Chapter Three

SAFE ENOUGH

Dean

Bella's house felt different the moment we stepped inside. Not hollow. Not edged with silence the way mine sometimes was. This quiet held weight. Only the faint tick of pipes settling in the walls, the low hum of a dishwasher running somewhere deeper in the house, and the lingering warmth of children already asleep.

It was the kind of stillness that came from life, not absence.

She moved ahead of me down the hallway. Bare feet soundless against the tile. My boots felt too heavy in comparison, tracking in grit I should have wiped off at the door. Lila shifted in my arms with a small, tired sound, and Bella slowed, glancing back.

"There's a room back here," she murmured. Even her whisper seemed careful, like she was protecting the quiet.

She opened a narrow door set into the far wall. The guest room carried a faint smell of cedar and dust. A metal-frame bed sat pressed against one side, quilt folded with practical neatness. Storage boxes lined the corners, of holiday decorations and old baby clothes. A vacuum leaned nearby like someone had meant to finish cleaning and never had.

Through the open bathroom door, I caught the outline of a claw-foot tub, pedestal sink, a single exposed bulb buzzing softly overhead. No mirror. No shower.

"It's not much," Bella said, setting the diaper bag on a scuffed dresser. "We mostly use it for storage. But..." She hesitated, brushing loose hair behind her ear. "It's private. And the windows don't face the street."

I stayed in the doorway a moment longer than necessary. Habit took over. Corners. Shadows. The cheap lock on the knob. The way the pipes ticked faintly behind the wall. Lila's weight shifted against me, warm and steady.

"It'll work," I said. My voice came out rough.

Bella nodded once, relief flickering across her face.

"The bed's not very big, but—"

"Big enough." I adjusted Lila higher, feeling her breath dampen the front of my shirt. "She'll sleep anywhere."

Bella offered a small, tired smile. "You both should try to rest. We'll... figure things out in the morning."

I dipped my head in thanks. Words felt useless. Too much sat behind them. My thoughts shifting between Vicky's sudden departure, the unanswered call, the chase, the realization that something had been moving toward us long before tonight.

Bella lingered at the doorframe, fingertips brushing the wood as if she might say more. Instead, she whispered, "Goodnight, Dean," and pulled the door mostly shut. A thin line of light stretched across the floor before fading.

I laid Lila carefully on the bed and eased open the straps of her carrier. She whimpered once, then curled into the quilt like she belonged there. I sat beside her, elbows braced on my knees, staring into the unfinished bathroom. The bare bulb hummed, casting a cold wash of light across chipped porcelain and exposed pipe.

Relief moved through me in uneven waves. We had made it out. She was safe. For now. But beneath it sat a harder truth, heavy and unshakable. Whatever had found us tonight wasn't finished.

I reached for my phone before I could talk myself out of it. Vicky's name sat at the top of the screen. My thumb hovered there for a second. Then pressed.

The call rang once. Then cut straight to voicemail. I stared at the phone like I could will it to change its mind.

She was probably still in the air. Or already in some windowless briefing room where signals didn't exist. That's what I told myself.

It didn't settle the unease sitting under my ribs. I hit redial. Same result. This time I didn't wait.

"Vic." My voice came out lower than I meant it to. Rough. "It's me. Call me as soon as you get this. I don't care what time it is."

I swallowed, eyes drifting toward Lila sleeping on the bed beside me. I ended the call before I said more.

The quiet rushed back in around me, thick enough to feel.

No notification. No response. Just the soft hum of the bare bulb and the steady rise and fall of my daughter's breathing.

I rested my palm against Lila's back, feeling the slow rise and fall of her breathing. For a moment I let my eyes close. Just long enough to pretend the night might settle into something normal.

It didn't.

I pushed myself up and wheeled the stroller Bella had brought in toward the corner. The hardwood creaked softly beneath my boots, the wheels rattling louder than they should have in the small room. Lila stirred but didn't wake. Her cheeks were still warm from the truck. Her skin carrying that familiar milk-and-powder sweetness that cut through everything else.

I crouched and opened the diaper bag. Two bottles. Four diapers. Wipes nearly gone. Enough to get through the night. Not enough for tomorrow.

The zipper rasped quietly as I pulled it shut, giving myself another second before the next problem demanded attention.

At some point I would have to go back. Slip into the house. Grab what we needed. Hope whoever had been waiting outside wasn't still there. But that was tomorrow. Tonight, this room was all we had.

The image of the vehicles outside kept surfacing whether I wanted it to or not. The dark shapes along the curb. The engines idling and headlights flaring to life all at once. No hesitation. No confusion.

They had known where I would be. And Vicky...

I could still hear the sharp rhythm of her heels crossing the foyer, the suitcase wheels dragging behind her. Her voice pitched toward someone who mattered more in that moment than anything else happening in the house.

One brief glance. Then the door closing hard enough to rattle the frame.

I had built that house with my own hands. Brick by brick. Board by board. We had talked about filling it with noise. With kids. With something solid enough to outlast the rest of the world.

And tonight, she had walked out of it without looking back. Left me standing in the headlights of something I didn't understand.

I pressed my hands flat against my knees and bent forward until the tension burned through my shoulders.

None of it lined up.

If they had been after me, they'd had the opportunity. Plenty of it. The driveway. The street. The turn onto the parkway.

They hadn't hesitated. But they also hadn't finished it. The thought came quietly. What if I hadn't been the target at all?

My stomach tightened.

Vicky had been leaving for the airport. She'd told me herself. Late flight. D.C. meetings. Tight schedule. The kind of plan anyone watching closely could have predicted down to the minute.

What if they had expected her to be in the truck? Expected me to be driving her. Instead, they'd found me. Bella. A sleeping baby in the back seat.

My mind started running through the cases she handled, the names that surfaced in late-night conversations she never quite finished, the way her phone had begun buzzing more often these past months.

How many people had reason to want leverage over her? Or worse.

I turned toward Lila. She slept curled in the middle of the bed, her breathing steady enough it barely lifted the blanket.

Something in my chest loosened at the sight. She didn't know any of this. Didn't care about politics or leverage or the kinds of promises adults made when they thought the future was simple. She needed warm bottles. Clean diapers. Someone who kept showing up.

A slow breath dragged out of me. I rubbed a hand down my face, stubble rasping beneath my palm, and sat back on the edge of the narrow bed. The springs creaked under my weight. The room smelled faintly of cedar and dust as the storage air clung to clothes and settled into the seams of things.

From somewhere deeper in the house came the soft rhythm of running water, the muted clink of glass. Bella moving through her kitchen. Then the steady hum of her refrigerator kicking on, filling the silence like background noise.

This place felt safer than mine ever had. Maybe it was the neighborhood. Lakewood Grove was quieter. Better lit. Less forgotten. Maybe it was the calm inside the walls.

It didn't stop the confusion from sticking to me like sweat. I leaned forward again, elbows on my knees, eyes fixed on the stroller.

"We'll get through tonight," I murmured. I wasn't sure if I meant her or myself.

Lila stirred, her tiny fist pushing weakly against the blanket before settling again. I watched that small movement until the tightness in my chest eased just enough to breathe.

Time passed. I didn't know how much. My phone sat heavy in my pocket, each minute making it feel heavier.

Eventually I stood, careful not to shift the mattress or wake her. I left the door cracked just enough to hear if she cried and stepped into the dark hallway.

The kitchen glowed faintly green from the stove clock. The house had gone still. Bella must have gone to bed. Without her quiet movement, the silence pressed closer.

I pulled out my phone and hit the first number that came to mind. Muscle memory. Two rings.

"Stone?" Mark's voice came thick with sleep. "Shit. Don't tell me the fundraiser's still going."

"Sorry," I said. "I need help."

That woke him faster than shouting would have.

"What kind?"

"We got run off the road. Armed. Multiple vehicles. My place is probably compromised."

A pause. Then a low curse. "You hit?"

"No. Baby's with me."

Another pause. He was fully awake now. I could hear him moving. "Alright," Mark said. "I'll start pulling traffic cams. Patrol logs. Anything that looks off. You stay put. Don't go back there alone."

"I won't."

"Good."

The line went dead. I didn't hesitate before scrolling to the next name.

It rang longer this time. When she finally picked up, her voice came through low and alert, not sleepy like Mark's.

"Stone?"

Relief hit harder than I expected. "Yeah. It's me." A pause. I could almost hear her recalibrating.

"Dean...I literally just saw you," Jenna Alvarez said. "You looked fine. What happened?"

We had spent years riding in the same car. Same shifts. Same bad coffee at four in the morning. When I'd put in my retirement papers, she'd been the only reason I'd hesitated. Leaving the job had meant leaving her watching my back.

"Things changed," I said quietly. "After you left." The line went still.

"Talk to me."

"We got hit on the road. Multiple vehicles. Blacked-out. Armed."

Her breath caught just enough for me to notice. "You serious?"

"Dead." Another beat. I could hear movement now. A drawer sliding open. The scratch of a pen. Jenna never listened to something like this sitting down.

"Anyone hurt?"

"No. We got clear. But my place is probably compromised."

"And Victoria?"

"Gone," I said. "Flight to D.C." That seemed to sharpen her focus further.

"...Okay."

I pressed on before she could ask the next question. "Can you run anything quiet? Plates. Patrol chatter. Dock cameras. Whatever you can touch without lighting up the board."

She exhaled slowly. "You don't make small calls, do you?"

"Not tonight." Silence stretched for a second. Not reluctance. Calculation.

"I'll see what I can find," Jenna said at last. "But Dean...if this is tied to her cases, you might already be in deeper than you think."

"I know."

"Keep your head down. I'll call when I have something."

The line went dead.

The kitchen settled back into its quiet rhythm: refrigerator cycling on, the green glow of the stove clock blinking steadily into the dark.

I slid the phone into my pocket. My fingers still twitched with the urge to call someone else, chase another angle, force the night into something that made sense.

There was no one left to call. Not at this hour.

I braced my hands against the counter until the tremor in my legs eased, then made my way back down the hall.

The guest room felt different now. Warmer. Lived in. The dry cedar smell had softened beneath the faint sweetness of formula and the damp wool of my coat draped over a chair. Dust still lingered in the corners where storage boxes pressed against the walls, disturbed just enough to hang in the air.

Lila's cry was already building when I stepped inside. It was thin at first, then sharp with urgency. I lifted her before it could wake the rest of the house.

The routine took over. Warm the bottle. Test the temperature against my wrist. Rock until the tension drained from her small body. Wait for sleep to take her again. Then start over. Feed. Rock. Settle. Repeat.

Every time her eyes closed, mine stayed open. The dark shapes of those vehicles lined up behind my eyelids. Vicky's heels striking tile. Bella's face lit hard by the first flash of headlights. The night stretched thin with it.

By the time pale morning light began leaking through the blinds, my shoulders ached from the hard chair and my vision blurred at the edges. The house remained quiet. Too quiet for a place that was supposed to mean safety.

I sat there with Lila sleeping against my chest and understood one thing with sudden clarity.

Stillness wasn't an option anymore.

Chapter Four

Watching the Street

Bella

I called out of work first thing, keeping my voice low so I wouldn't wake anyone else in the house. John had already bundled the kids off to school and daycare. The front door clicked shut behind him with a quiet finality that left the place feeling strangely hollow.

For the first time in years, it was just me...and Dean. Dean Stone. Our friend for nearly fifteen years.

The coffee had just started dripping when he appeared in the kitchen doorway.

He filled the space without trying. Tall and broad through the shoulders with the worn cotton of his T-shirt pulled tight across his chest like he'd slept in it. His head was freshly shaved, catching the pale morning light, but dark stubble shadowed his jaw. Exhaustion sat heavy around his eyes, dulling the sharp green I was used to seeing. He didn't say anything at first. He didn't need to.

"Thanks," he muttered when I handed him a mug. He took a long swallow before adding, "Lila barely slept."

Right on cue, she began fussing in the stroller parked near the kitchen table, her cry slicing through the quiet. I set my cup down quickly, a thought sparking. "Hold on — I might have something."

The linen closet still held the old wrap, folded into a neat square. The fabric was worn soft with use, edges fraying from years of being washed and tied and retied. I pressed it briefly to my cheek, catching the faint scent of baby detergent, before looping it over my shoulders.

My hands remembered the motion without thinking.

Lila quieted almost instantly when I lifted her,. Her small body settling beneath my chin with a long sigh. I swayed once, twice, feeling her weight go loose and trusting against me.

Behind me, butter hissed as it hit the pan. I cracked eggs one-handed, scraping the spatula along the skillet while shifting my weight to keep the gentle rhythm going.

Dean leaned against the counter watching.

"You even eat eggs?" I asked, glancing back over my shoulder. "You look like the type who lives on grilled chicken and protein shakes. Maybe broccoli if you're feeling reckless."

His brow creased like I'd genuinely confused him. "...Yeah," he said. "I eat eggs." The seriousness of it pulled a laugh out of me before I could stop it.

"Good," I said. "Because that's all you're getting."

The soft scrape of the spatula against the pan filled the space between us until Dean spoke again. Quieter this time.

"I made some calls last night." He turned the mug slowly in his hands, watching the coffee settle.

"No one's been able to reach her. Phone's off. No check-in from D.C. yet. It's like she just...disappeared after she left the house."

My stomach dipped.

"Maybe she's still in the air," I said automatically. "Or stuck in meetings. Those federal things can go late."

"Maybe." He didn't sound convinced.

"Mark and Jenna are already pulling what they can," he went on. "Traffic cams. Patrol chatter. Anything unusual around my block. They're keeping it quiet for now."

I blinked, frowning. "Who?"

He let out a rough breath, rubbing a hand over his face. "Mark is a lieutenant on the force and one of my closest friends. We basically grew into our positions together. Jenna's my former partner. Mark is making her the lead investigator on this now." His voice tightened. He glanced up at me then, something sharper behind the exhaustion.

"I keep thinking about how it went down," he said. "Those vehicles were staged. They knew when someone was leaving that house. They just didn't seem to know who was in the truck."

The spatula stilled in my hand. "You think they were after her?"

"I don't know." His jaw tightened. "But it makes more sense than them suddenly deciding I'm worth that kind of attention." He exhaled slowly.

"She's been working bigger cases lately. Talking less about them. More late nights. More travel."

The eggs began to brown at the edges, and I forced myself to move the pan again.

"And now she's unreachable," he finished. The words settled over the kitchen like smoke.

I pressed my cheek briefly against Lila's hair, letting the warmth of her steady breathing ground me while my free hand gripped the counter.

Dean dragged a hand down his face. "I didn't sleep," he admitted. "Between her waking up... and everything else. Just kept running it through my head. Trying to figure out who those guys were. Or who they thought they were getting."

He looked toward the window like the answer might be standing out there in the daylight.

"None of it lines up."

The eggs hissed in the pan, butter popping softly. Coffee bitterness hung in the air. I slid the food onto a plate and nudged it toward him. Our fingers brushed when he reached for the fork, his rough calluses against my skin, and I pulled back a second too fast.

Dean ate a few bites without tasting them, then set the fork down with a quiet clink. His palm flattened against the counter;

gaze fixed somewhere just past the tile. "I don't think I'm safe," he said finally. "And I don't know if Vicky is either."

I shifted my weight, rocking Lila in the wrap until her tiny fist loosened against my collarbone. "You're safe here," I said.

He shook his head once, already moving on. "I need supplies for her. Bottles. Diapers. And we shouldn't stay long. You've got enough going on without us camping in your kitchen."

"No." The word came out sharper than I intended.

His eyes snapped up.

I loosened the wrap slightly so he could see her face. Lila slept with her lips parted, hands curled in soft, unconscious trust.

"Look at her," I said quietly. "She's fine. We're fine. Let us help."

His fingers tightened along the edge of the counter.

"I don't want your kids dragged into this."

"They won't be." I forced a small smile. "If it makes you feel better, call in a patrol car. Park it out front. Flash some lights. Terrify the neighbors."

I meant it as a joke. Dean didn't smile.

"Okay." He was already pulling out his phone. His thumbs moved quickly across the screen. A moment later the faint vibration of an incoming reply buzzed in his hand.

"They'll be here in twenty minutes."

I blinked. "Dean...I was kidding."

He met my eyes, voice low and worn thin. "No. You weren't."

Something in my chest tightened. "Fine," I said softly. "Patrol car it is. But nothing's going to happen."

He didn't argue. He didn't agree either.

After a moment he leaned back, staring into his empty mug as if the answer might be waiting at the bottom. His thumb traced the rim again and again.

"I still need to get things for Lila," he said. "Formula. Clothes. Probably something for myself."

For the first time since the night before, he didn't look like the man who had driven us out of danger without blinking. He just looked exhausted.

"Take my car," I said. I shifted Lila higher and pressed a kiss to the warm crown of her head. "We'll move the car seats. You'll have space."

His reaction was immediate.

"No."

I stared at him. "Why not?"

He stepped closer, voice firm but controlled.

"You're not getting pulled any deeper into this than you already are."

The seriousness in his expression made my stomach knot. He wasn't angry. He was certain.

"Dean...it's just a car."

"It's not," he said quietly. "You've done enough."

There was no edge in his tone. No accusation. Just a boundary drawn clean and solid between us.

And somehow that scared me more than if he'd raised his voice.

The air outside was sharp and cool, still damp from last night's rain. Gravel crunched beneath my sneakers as Dean worked the latch on the truck bed, hauling out what little he had stored there. A toolbox. A duffel. Loose supplies that hit the empty side of the garage with dull, echoing thuds.

His sweatshirt stretched across his back as he moved. I could see the tension riding high in his shoulders, refusing to ease even in daylight.

"Here." I held out my house keys, the metal ring swinging slightly from my fingers.

He took them.

But instead of letting go, his hand stayed over mine for a beat. Warm. Rough. Solid. A brief squeeze that was grounding more than affectionate.

When his eyes lifted to mine, something heavy passed between us.

"Wait," I said before I could stop myself. "If you're...worried, we can stay on the phone. Just in case."

I wasn't entirely sure who I was trying to reassure.

His jaw shifted like he might dismiss the idea. Instead, he reached for his wallet, pulled out a business card, and scribbled quickly on the back with a pen from the truck console. He folded my fingers around it.

"If something goes wrong, you call this number," he said. "Tell them code one-twenty. They'll know it's tied to me. Give them my location. Don't hang up."

"Dean—"

"I mean it." His voice softened slightly, but the resolve didn't.

He unlocked his phone and tapped through a few screens before holding it out.

"I'm sharing my location with you."

The map blinked open in my hand. A small blue dot pulsed beside his name. He slipped an earbud in as I handed the phone back.

"I'll call you now."

A second later my pocket buzzed. I answered and set the phone to speaker until I could dig my own earbuds from my bag.

"Got you," I said.

His voice came through low and steady, like he was still standing beside me.

"Good. Just stay on the line."

I watched him climb into the truck. Fold himself behind the wheel. Pause for one last glance toward the house. Then he pulled down the driveway and disappeared past the hedges. The call remained open.

I stood there another moment, listening to the faint hum of his engine through the connection before turning back inside. Lila shifted in the wrap and I rubbed slow circles along her back, not entirely sure if I was soothing her or myself.

The house smelled like coffee and baby lotion. Warm and familiar, yet suddenly fragile. Her nearly empty diaper bag hung from the arm of the couch as I passed through the living room and headed upstairs. There were things to gather. Lists to make. Plans to form. Because if the last twelve hours had taught me anything, it was that nothing ahead of us was going to be simple.

The line stayed open in my pocket while I moved from room to room. I told myself I wasn't listening for the faint sound of his breathing on the other end. But I was. He had become a quiet pulse in the background; a tether I hadn't meant to reach for and couldn't seem to let go.

About half an hour passed before his voice finally came through the line, low and worn raw.

"I'm here."

I froze mid-step. One hand braced against the kitchen counter while I yanked the phone from my pocket.

"At the house?"

"Yeah."

His breath came heavy through the connection. I could hear the hollow creak of floorboards beneath his boots, the distant rattle of glass somewhere deeper inside.

"Everything looks...untouched," he said after a moment. "Lights still work. Tables exactly how we left them. Plates. Half-burned candles. Smells like beef and wine and stale coffee."

My stomach loosened a fraction. "You're sure it's safe?"

"So far." A pause. "The front door was still locked. No cars out front. No movement."

Something thudded softly in the background. A cabinet, maybe. Then his voice dropped lower.

"I'm checking the rest of the house."

A light switch clicked through the line. Footsteps. Another creak. Then a quiet curse.

"What?" I whispered.

"Nothing." He exhaled hard. "Just forgot how damn quiet it gets here."

His tone held something brittle under it now.

"You can hear everything. Every step. Every breath. Feels like..." He didn't finish.

"Like what?"

"Like I'm waiting for something to move," he said finally. "Or maybe I'm just worked up."

"You're not funny," I muttered, but when he let out a tired, genuine laugh, my eyes burned anyway.

"Relax. I'm good." Paper rustled. A drawer slid open and shut.

"Found Lila's paperwork," he went on. "Birth certificate. Hospital discharge stuff. I'm grabbing clothes. Diapers. Anything I can carry."

"Good." My fingers tapped restless patterns against the counter.

"Just...don't stay longer than you have to."

"I won't." His voice steadied as he moved, purposeful now, anchored in task.

"I'll be out before dark."

"Dean—" The word caught halfway up my throat.

"You'll tell me if something feels wrong, right?"

A beat of silence. Then, quieter than before: "You'll be the first to know."

Something inside his voice twisted at that. Something I didn't understand yet but felt all the same. I wanted to tell him to leave. To forget the documents and the clothes and just come back. But I knew him. He wouldn't.

"Just keep the line open," I said instead. My voice cracked despite myself. A soft hum of agreement.

"Wasn't planning to hang up."

Another door opened somewhere inside the house. Wood scraped. A drawer slid. Then his voice again, firmer now, locked into motion.

"Alright," he murmured. "Let's get this done."

I sank onto the couch with Lila pressed tight against my chest, the phone still warm against my ear.

Somewhere on the other end of the line, Dean moved through his empty house. Floorboards creaking/ Drawers sliding. The distant clink of something being set down too hard. The sounds wrapped around me like proof he was still out there. Still fighting his way back.

I forced myself to move. If I stopped, the fear would swallow me whole. At the hall bench I started building a pile of things that made sense. Extra towels. A stack of washcloths. Sam's old blanket with the worn satin edge he used to rub between his fingers when he was tired. None of it felt like enough.

I folded and refolded anyway. Shifted the stack. Adjusted corners that didn't need adjusting. The work gave my hands somewhere to go when my thoughts wouldn't settle. More gear. Bottles. Burp cloths. The spare pack of diapers I swore I'd shoved into the closet weeks ago.

I nudged the hall door open with my foot to check, but Lila stirred in the wrap. Her tiny body twisting against me with a soft, rising protest.

"All right, sweet girl," I murmured, rocking my hips as I turned back toward the nursery. "Let's get you somewhere comfy and quiet."

The room still held the faintest trace of baby lotion and lavender, leftover from the diffuser I'd forgotten to switch off. Sam's pale blue cotton sheets scattered with little moons were tucked into the crib. Not perfect. But soft. Safe. Enough for today.

I loosened the wrap carefully, easing her into my arms. She blinked up at me, lips pursing into that tiny fish-pout like she was arguing with sleep itself. My chest tightened. I bent closer, swaying without thinking.

"I know," I whispered. "I know."

Her lashes fluttered.

"I know you don't understand any of this." My lips brushed the fine brown hair at the crown of her head. She smelled warm. Milk-sweet. Completely untouched by the chaos that had swallowed the last twelve hours.

“You didn’t do anything wrong,” I went on quietly. “Sometimes things just...fall apart.”

The words surprised me as much as they would have anyone else. I kept talking anyway.

“Your daddy’s a good man,” I said, softer now, like I was afraid the truth might shatter if I said it too loud. “He loves you more than anything. He’s scared. He won’t admit it. But he is.”

Her tiny fingers flexed against my collarbone.

“And he’ll keep going anyway,” I breathed. “Even if it breaks him.” The last part caught in my throat.

I pressed my cheek against her head, drawing one slow breath before lowering her into the crib. Her arms twitched once. Then stilled.

In the corner, I wound the old music box. The lullaby spilled out thin and sweet, a song my own kids had fallen asleep to a hundred times. I stayed there until her breathing settled into a steady rhythm. My hand hovered on the rail longer than it should have. Then I forced myself to step back.

When I pulled the nursery door mostly closed behind me, the sigh that tore out of my chest was louder than I meant it to be. It sounded like something breaking.

“Thank you.” The voice made me jolt. Muffled but unmistakable. Vibrating from my back pocket.

“Shit.”

I yanked the phone free, fumbling to pull it off speaker. My heart stumbling hard against my ribs. I’d forgotten the line was still open.

"How much of that did you hear?"

Silence stretched long enough to make my stomach twist. For a second, I wondered if the call had dropped. Then his voice came through, low, rough, almost careful.

"All of it."

Heat rushed up my throat. My skin prickled like I'd been caught standing somewhere I shouldn't be. I pressed the phone tighter to my ear, eyes squeezing shut.

"Well," I said after a second, forcing steadiness into my voice, "I meant it."

He didn't answer, but I moved toward the kitchen anyway, bare feet whispering over tile. All I could hear was his slow and controlled breathing on the other end of the line. Present. I slid my headphones in and let the quiet settle between us. Not the heavy quiet from earlier. Not the kind that pressed on your lungs.

This one held. Like a rope bridge stretched across something deep and dark. Swaying, maybe. But still holding.

"All right," Dean finally breathed. His voice sounded scraped raw. "I think I'm done."

"You packed your stuff too, right?" I asked, reaching for the pot on the stove. The metal handle knocked lightly against the burner.

Silence. Then a sharp curse, bitten off under his breath.

"Shit. No. I was so focused on what she needs I didn't even think about that."

"Dean." I pinched the bridge of my nose. "Go back and grab your things. I don't know if they'll come back or not, but don't take chances. Clothes. Documents. Anything you don't want to lose."

A pause. The faint creak of floorboards.

"Yeah," he muttered. "All right."

Drawers slid open. Hangers scraped together. A hollow thump as something heavy hit the floor. Probably a duffel bag. While he moved through the house, I worked. Knife through onion. Board thudding beneath each slice. Oil beginning to hiss in the pan.

Ordinary sounds. Necessary sounds. They kept the knot in my stomach from tightening into something I couldn't breathe around.

Minutes passed. Maybe more. Long enough for the onions to turn translucent. Long enough for Dean's movements on the other end of the line to slow into a steady rhythm of packing and searching.

Then Lila's cry cut through the house. Sharp. Urgent. Impossible to ignore.

I dropped the knife into the sink and rinsed my hands fast, already moving toward the stairs with the phone pressed tight to my ear.

"Relax," I whispered, climbing two steps at a time. "I've got her."

I wasn't sure if I meant it for him or for the baby. He didn't answer, but I knew he was listening. I slid the phone back into my pocket as I pushed into the nursery.

Lila's little body was hot and rigid when I lifted her. Her face blotched red from crying. Her tiny fists balled hard into the fabric of my shirt.

"Shhh...sweet girl," I murmured, rocking her against my chest. "I know. I know."

Her weight felt both fragile and fierce at once, like holding something that could break or save you depending on how tight you held on. A few moments later the bottle sat warming on the counter. I tested a drop against my wrist, then eased Lila into the crook of my arm. She latched instantly, tiny sounds of relief filling the silence still hanging on the line.

"Better," I murmured, brushing my lips over the soft crown of her head. "That's better."

When she finished, I changed her quickly, movements automatic. A soft tune slipped from my throat without thinking: low, steady, something my kids had always fallen asleep to. It steadied me more than it did her. The line stayed quiet.

Then his voice came back. Lower. Closer.

"All right. I'm packed. Ready to go."

I froze. He must've been done for a while. He'd just been... listening. Listening to me move around his life. Listening to his daughter breathe. Then, softer still:

"I'm scared, Bella." The words landed heavy. "You're right. And I'd do anything to protect her."

My throat tightened.

"I know," I said gently. "But I need you to get back here in one piece. So take a breath. When you're ready...open the garage."

A long pause.

"From the windows it looks clear," he said. Unease threaded every syllable. "But I've got a bad feeling."

"Just come home," I whispered.

The line crackled. Then came the mechanical grind of the garage door lifting. A second later the engine roared to life. And then—

Shouts.

Glass exploding.

Gunfire ripping through the line in rapid, violent bursts.

"Dean!" My voice tore out of me, loud enough to bounce off the kitchen walls.

"I'm fine!" he shouted back, jagged with adrenaline. "Call that number!"

More cracks. Closer this time.

Metal screaming. Tires spinning.

I didn't think. My hands shook so badly I nearly dropped the phone as I killed the call, yanked the folded card from my pocket, and punched the number in with clumsy fingers.

It rang once. A steady female voice answered.

"Millbrook District Police. How can I help you?"

"Code one-twenty," I gasped. "Dean Stone. He's under fire. I'm sending his live location now."

Silence. Then the dispatcher's tone snapped sharp.

"Copy. Give me direction of travel."

"He just left his residence on Old Quarry Road. He's heading toward Millbrook. Shots fired. Multiple vehicles."

Keys clattered on her end. Voices rose faint in the background.

"All right. Units are already moving. Stay inside your residence. Do not open the door for anyone except uniformed officers. Do you understand?"

"Yes," I whispered.

The line went dead.

I stood frozen in the middle of the kitchen, phone still hot in my hand. Lila's small body pressed against my chest, warm and impossibly fragile. My whole body vibrated with it: the fear, the helplessness, the sound of gunfire still echoing in my ears.

Somewhere out there, Dean was driving straight through another ambush. And all I could do was stand in the quiet and pray that the next headlights turning into my driveway belonged to the right person.

Chapter Five

Running North

Dean

The first crack hit like a hammer.

The windshield bloomed white in an instant, spider-web fractures racing across the glass as shards sprayed into my lap and stung against my cheeks.

I ducked low, eyes barely clearing the dash, one hand choking tight around the wheel.

"Fuck!" The word tore out of me before thought could catch up.

I slammed the shifter down. The tires screamed as I punched the gas. The truck jerking backward out of the narrow concrete drive. Morning light flashed hard across the shattered windshield, blinding for a split second as the garage door rattled halfway open above me.

Gunfire chewed through the metal panels. Each impact rang sharp and hollow, sparks bursting bright in the dim space. The smell of hot steel and motor oil filled the cab, thick enough to taste.

I cleared the garage and spun the wheel hard, the rear tires fishtailing onto cracked asphalt slick from last night's rain.

Hawthorne Ridge stretched out around me. Tight rows of aging two-story houses, sagging porches and chain-link fences stitched together block after block. Someone's pit bull barked wildly from behind a rusted gate. A corner liquor store sign flickered half-dead even in daylight. Trash bags sat split open along the curb; yesterday's news already picked apart by crows.

It was the kind of neighborhood that pretended to be quiet. Until it wasn't. And right now, it definitely wasn't.

Two black SUVs blocked the far end of the street. Angled wide like barricades. Their doors hung open. Sunlight flashed off the rifles lifted to waiting shoulders as dark figures stepped out slow and deliberate, boots hitting pavement like they already owned it.

"Shit."

I wrenched the wheel left. The truck fishtailed across the narrow driveway and shot onto the street, tires shrieking over wet asphalt. In the rearview mirror the mailbox detonated into splinters, wood spinning through the morning light.

My heart slammed against my ribs, hard enough to blur the edges of my vision. The empty car seat jolted with the swerve, straps snapping against plastic.

For one brutal second my brain screamed Lila.

Then reality hit. She wasn't there. Thank God. That didn't stop the panic clawing up my throat.

Gunfire erupted again.

Rounds slammed into the body panels with dull metallic thuds. One punched through the bumper. Another obliterated the side mirror in a glittering spray that flashed once in the sun before disappearing behind me.

I ducked lower over the wheel. The sharp stink of burning rubber and hot engine fluid began to seep into the cab.

The phone buzzed violently on the console.

Jenna. Her name lit the screen like a warning flare.

"Not now," I barked, slapping it facedown onto the passenger seat.

My hands stayed welded to the wheel, sweat slicking my palms as my eyes worked the mirrors: angles and movement. Years on the job kicked in without asking permission.

Track threats. Find exits. Stay moving.

Sunlight flared behind me. An SUV surged into view, closing fast. They weren't letting this go.

"Not boxing me in again," I muttered.

I dropped the gear and hammered the gas. The engine roared back, violent and strained, and the truck lunged forward down the tight residential strip.

Street signs blurred past. Elm. Quarry. Pine Hollow.

Small brick houses streaked by on either side with sagging fences. Plastic toys scattered across damp lawns. A woman frozen on a porch clutching a coffee mug as we tore through her morning.

The world narrowed to asphalt, sunlight, and survival. Then another SUV exploded out of a side street. Chrome flashed as it swung wide to block the lane.

"No you don't—"

I aimed straight and clipped its rear bumper. The impact snapped the steering wheel sideways. The seat belt bit deep into my shoulder. Pain lit up my ribs white-hot, sharp enough to spark stars across my vision.

I fought the wheel back under control.

"Come on," I growled, slamming my palm against the dash. "Come on."

The radio crackled alive. Static first. Then a clipped dispatch voice cut through the chaos.

"Units in route. Last known on Quarry. Repeat. Code one-twenty in progress."

A breath tore out of me. Bella. She'd done it. Someone knew.

But the sirens were still far off. And the SUVs were still there as black shadows sliced through daylight in my mirrors.

If I slowed down...even for a second...I was dead.

So I didn't. I ripped the wheel into a narrow side road. The truck lurched hard, suspension bucking as it slammed through a stretch of cratered asphalt. Dust and grit exploded around me, sunlight turning the cloud into a blinding golden haze.

Branches clawed across the windshield. Dry leaves smeared into jagged streaks like something trying to reach inside.

"Hold together," I muttered, voice scraped raw, fingers strangling the wheel until the leather creaked.

The engine screamed in protest. Heat shimmered off the hood. I pushed the pedal down anyway. In the mirror, headlights surged over the rise behind me.

Still there. Still coming.

A sharp crack split the air. Metal shrieked as a round punched through the rear panel. The frame shuddered violently, vibration ripping up through the seat and straight into my spine.

"Come on..." I hissed.

The truck fishtailed as gravel spat from the shoulder. The dry drainage ditch blurred beside me. One wrong twitch away from rolling the whole damn thing.

I hauled the wheel back straight. Teeth grinding. Ribs screaming under the seatbelt.

They stayed glued to me. Two black SUVs tearing down the road like predators waiting for weakness.

I cut left harder than I should've. Tires howled. My shoulder slammed into the door. The world smeared sideways. Porches with summer ferns, crooked mailboxes, picket fences, and a kid's bike abandoned in wet grass beside a spinning yellow sprinkler.

Then the gunfire returned.

Muzzle flashes stuttered in broad daylight with violent bursts of white and orange. Each report slammed through me like the street itself was firing back.

"Think, Stone. Stay ahead," I growled, breath tearing loose. "Don't give them the shot."

Glass detonated beside my head. Wind roared into the cab.

Fifty. Fifty-five. Sixty.

The frame rattled like it might shake apart. My heartbeat chased the speedometer needle like it was trying to outrun death itself. Then—

Blue lights. Sirens tore through the chaos up ahead, sharp and rising. Relief hit like oxygen after drowning. The SUVs hesitated. Just long enough.

Their beams jerked sideways. Engines screamed as they split into driveways and side streets, shadows breaking apart under the flashing red and blue.

One final shot slammed into the trunk. The whole truck jolting from the impact.

Then they were gone.

I blasted through the intersection as two cruisers screamed past me, tires shrieking as they swung into pursuit. The road ahead stretched dark and endless. Heat shimmered across the asphalt. My lungs burned with every breath, ribs grinding like broken glass.

I didn't lift my foot off the gas. Couldn't. My hands stayed locked to the wheel long after the gunfire faded.

"Out," I rasped.

The green Lakewood Grove sign flashed past on the shoulder. Twelve miles. Bella's town. Then open highway swallowed me whole with empty lanes, blown glass rattling in the cab like loose teeth.

Out. But safe? Not even close.

The tremor in my hands wouldn't stop. Leftover electricity humming through muscle and bone. Every press of the pedal crushed more shards beneath my boot.

The console lit up again. Jenna.

I exhaled hard and answered. Her voice detonated through the speakers.

"Jesus Christ, Dean. You're alive?"

"Barely." A thin laugh scraped out of me. "Had a welcoming committee waiting at the house."

"Yeah, we know," she said fast. "Mark pulled units and cut them off. You owe him something expensive."

The knot in my chest loosened just enough to breathe. Of course he had. Mark had always had my back.

"Yeah," I muttered. "Tell him thanks."

The tires hummed steady now. Sunlight striped across my forearms through the cracked windshield.

Jenna spoke again, quieter this time. "How are you holding up?"

I dragged a hand down my face. Tiny shards of glass rasped against my skin.

"Driving. Breathing. That's about it."

A half-laugh slipped from her. Half relief. Half fear.

"Where are you headed?"

"You know I can't tell you."

"Yeah." Keystrokes clattered faintly behind her. She was already working angles. Running plates. Pulling favors. "Just... when you stop, actually stop. You sound wrecked."

She wasn't wrong.

The rearview mirror caught the empty car seat rocking gently with every bump. Its loose straps swung like accusations. My chest tightened.

"I've got somewhere," I said finally. "Somewhere they won't think to look."

She didn't argue. She never did when she knew my mind was set.

"We'll keep digging," she said. "Whoever's behind this, they'll make a mistake. They always do."

"Be careful, Jen."

"You too, Stone." Her voice softened. "You've got more to lose now than you ever did."

The line went dead. The cab sank back into quiet. Not peaceful. Not safe. The kind of silence that settles into your bones and stays there. The steady whine of the tires filled the space between my thoughts. I flexed my hands off the wheel. My joints cracked. My ribs flared sharp in protest. The seatbelt's bite still burning deep under the skin. Pain grounded me.

Still here. Still moving.

The highway stretched wide and blinding ahead, heat shimmering over pale asphalt as the sun dipped lower toward the horizon. Dust coated the hood in dull gray streaks, glittering faintly where shards from the blown rear window had scattered forward.

Every bump made them tinkle softly. Like broken wind chimes. It was an ugly kind of music to drive by. My phone lay face-up in the cupholder.

Bella.

Her name glowed bright in the dying light.

One swipe and I'd hear her voice. Soft and steady even when she was scared. Maybe Lila fussing in the background. Maybe that little coo she makes when she's settling.

My hand twitched toward it, but stopped. If I heard Bella now...if she said my name the way she does when she's trying not to panic... I'd break. And I couldn't afford that. Not yet.

So, I kept driving. Sunfire burning across the windshield. The world stretching bright and endless like it had no intention of letting me stop. The silence was worse than the gunfire. Bullets you could track. Predict. Dodge. Survive. Silence just swallowed you whole.

Vicky's heels striking tile. Lila crying in a stroller she never should've slept in. Bella's whisper, steady as granite: *He'll do anything for you. Even if it kills him.*

My jaw locked. I tightened my grip on the wheel until my knuckles went hot and numb at the same time. Blinked hard against the pressure building behind my eyes.

Then I grabbed the phone. Didn't think. Just hit Vicky's name.

It rang once. Twice. Then straight to voicemail. Again.

A hollow sound escaped my throat. Not quite a laugh, not quite a curse. I stared at the screen for a second longer than I should have, like I could force it to change.

"Damn it, Vic..."

I didn't leave a message this time. What was there left to say?

I dropped the phone back into the holder and drove harder into the falling dark.

By the time the first porch lights of Somerset Grove flickered into view at the edge of the trees, I felt scraped hollow. Neat lawns, trimmed hedges, quiet sidewalks glowing under warm streetlamps.

Raw down to bone. There'd be no sleep tonight. Not with the walls closing in. Not with the silence still following me.

Chapter Six

THE BLUE DOT

Bella

Lila kicked herself sideways on the mat in the living room, fists flailing until the dangling stars knocked together with soft, uneven chimes. I sat cross-legged beside her, phone balanced on my knees, the screen's glow too harsh in the dim light.

The little blue dot spun the same block near Dean's neighborhood. Loop after loop. Like an animal trapped with no way out.

My thumb hovered over the call button. One press. One word from him. That was all it would take to know he was still breathing. But if he was tearing through streets the way I imagined, the last thing he needed was me panicking in his ear.

Something wet slid down my cheek. I hadn't even noticed the tears starting until they blurred the map. Until Lila's warm cheek brushed mine when I scooped her up. Damp met damp. Shame flared hot and sudden. I wiped my face fast with the heel of my hand, tried to swallow the hitch in my chest before she could feel it.

I sat there staring, phone trembling in one hand. Three hours he'd been gone. Three hours of that blue dot blinking in and out of existence. Circling. Vanishing. Reappearing.

Two hours until the kids came home.

I needed to pull myself together before they walked in and saw me like this.

Lila yawned against me, her tiny jaw cracking wide, lashes fluttering until she sagged heavy. I kissed the top of her head and carried her upstairs. Phone still clenched in my palm. Thumb tapping the map like I could will the dot steady.

It was steady now. Southbound. A clean line instead of frantic loops. Coming closer.

I laid her in the crib, smoothing her blanket flat until the lullaby machine clicked on, soft music spilling into the room. She stirred once, then settled, chest rising slow and even. I stayed longer than I meant to, staring at the curve of her cheek.

At the blue dot inching closer to our street.

By the time the low rumble of an engine crawled into the driveway, my throat was raw from swallowing sobs that never came. I rushed to the window, phone clutched tight like it was part of me. And when I saw what pulled up, the air tore out of me in a hard, jagged gasp.

His truck lurched into the driveway, but it didn't look like his truck anymore.

Bullet holes peppered both doors. The back window was gone, glittering shards scattered across the bed like crushed ice. Something dark dripped steadily onto the pavement, spreading in slow streaks that looked too much like blood. One headlight hung loose, wires exposed, swaying with every rough vibration of the engine.

I was already moving. Downstairs. Through the kitchen. Into the garage. The door banged off the wall behind me, cold concrete biting at my bare feet.

"Dean!"

The truck door opened.

He climbed out slowly, shoulders hunched, movements dragging like gravity had doubled. His sleeve was torn wide, dirt and soot streaked down his forearms. For one breathless moment he just stood there, framed by the wreckage.

My body locked. Then instinct shoved me forward.

His head lifted at the sound of me. Something flickered across his face. Relief, maybe, but it was gone almost as soon as it appeared. His eyes dropped back to the ruined truck like it was easier to focus on metal than on me.

"There's already a report filed," he said when I reached him, voice low and measured, like he was reciting instructions he'd memorized. "They'll mark it as a crime scene soon. Don't worry."

My stomach twisted so tight it hurt. He saw whatever showed in my face because his tone shifted, softer now.

"I'm okay," he added quietly. "It looks worse than it is."

My throat burned. I nodded too fast. But the picture wouldn't leave me. John pulling into the drive. The kids spilling out. Their eyes catching bullet holes and shattered glass before they ever found mine.

Dean shifted, stepping subtly between me and the truck like he could block the whole morning from my sight. The sharp, metallic sting of gunpowder clung to him, thick enough to taste. His fingers flexed at his sides restlessly. Unsure. Like he wanted to reach for me and didn't trust himself to.

"Come inside," I whispered. "Please. Just...come inside."

"In a second." His voice was steady again. Controlled. He turned and walked to the back of the truck.

The tailgate groaned when he dropped it. He moved with slow efficiency, hauling out a duffel first, then another bag, setting them down carefully like each motion had to be thought through before his body would cooperate.

Routine. Survival.

He reached in again, pausing only once to brace a hand against the dented metal, head bowed like he was gathering whatever strength he had left. Then he straightened, bags in hand, and finally looked at me.

"Okay," he said.

We didn't speak while we unpacked the truck. Boxes hit the counters with dull thuds. Bags sagged heavy onto the tile. His boots tracked streaks of dust and dried mud across the garage floor and into the kitchen. The smell of engine oil and smoke followed us inside, seeping into everything. It clung to the air. To the walls. To my skin.

We left it all piled where it landed. Formula cans stacked crooked near the sink. Bottles knocking together with hollow rattles. Blankets spilling loose across the table. One duffel lay half-unzipped, shirts slumped out of it like limp arms after a fight.

Dean braced both hands on the counter. His shoulders were pulled tight and high, head bowed between them. His breath dragged in uneven pulls, loud enough to fill the kitchen. For the first time all day, he didn't look like a man holding the world together by force.

He looked breakable.

Something in me gave way. Before I could stop myself, I stepped forward and slid my arms around his middle. My cheek pressed into the damp cotton of his sweatshirt. He smelled like sweat and smoke and the sharp metallic bite of gunpowder, with the faint ghost of detergent underneath it.

Like he'd been dragged straight from a battlefield into my kitchen.

"I'm so glad you're okay," I blurted. The words splintered halfway out. Panic flared hot and fast and I scrambled to cover it. "For Lila's sake. I mean."

At first he didn't react. His body stayed rigid under my arms. Solid. Unmoving. Like he hadn't quite come back from wherever he'd been out there.

My chest tightened, bracing for him to pull away.

Then, slowly, his arms came around me. Strong. Certain. Pulling me closer until the line of his chest pressed fully against mine. I felt it then; the tremor still running through him. Fine. Constant. Like leftover electricity he couldn't shut off.

His breath hitched once against my hair. The tension in his shoulders eased by degrees. Every exhale draining another piece of the fight out of him. His jaw brushed the crown of my head. His weight tipped forward, not enough to crush me, but enough that I understood.

He was leaning. On me.

I didn't speak again. Neither did he. We just stood there in the middle of my kitchen, surrounded by bags and bottles and the quiet wreckage of what could have happened.

The silence between us wasn't empty. It was crowded. Fear. Relief. Gratitude.

And something sharper neither of us dared name.

For the first time since I saw that ruined truck roll into my driveway, the shaking inside me finally stilled.

Chapter Seven

Noise in the Kitchen

Dean

The smell of chicken filled the kitchen when the front door creaked open.

Skin crisped in the pan, edges spitting hot oil that snapped against the stovetop. Steam curled up into the low light, thick with garlic and salt. I didn't turn right away. I knew the rhythm of his steps.

John stepped inside, already tugging his tie loose. His keys hit the bowl by the door with a sharp metallic clatter that rang longer than it should have. He didn't look toward me. Didn't ask anything. Just moved straight past the kitchen like the space between us didn't exist.

The recliner groaned when he dropped into it, his weight sinking deep like the chair had been holding its breath all day waiting for him. The television flared to life. Game commentary burst into the house at full volume: whistles, shouting, crowd noise, and the squeak of sneakers on the court. The sounds bounced hard off the walls until the rooms felt tighter. Smaller. Like the air itself had nowhere to go.

I reached for the speaker on the counter. One press. The soft music I'd left playing cut off mid-note. Silence didn't follow. Only the television remained. Too loud and bright, filling every corner.

The kids scattered like they'd been shot from a slingshot.

Sam hit the kitchen first: a solid, reckless collision of toddler and momentum. He smacked straight into the fridge with a hollow thunk, bounced back on unsteady legs, and burst into wild, breathless giggles like pain was just another game. His brown hair stuck up in soft reddish tufts from his nap, bright green eyes blazing with curiosity as he immediately set off again, stomping heavy-footed across the tile like he was built to conquer it.

Chloe followed close behind, clutching her iPad to her chest like a life raft. Her small sneakers squeaked as she skidded to a stop beside me, brown ponytail already half-fallen out. She tilted her head up towards Bella, blue eyes wide and dramatic.

"Snack," she announced, tugging hard at Bella's sleeve like the word itself should solve everything.

Then Alex tore through the hallway. Eight years old and all elbows and knees, he moved like he hadn't quite figured out where his limbs ended. A crooked, safety-pinned superhero cape trailed behind him snapping against the doorframe as he misjudged the turn. He nearly clipped the chair leg, windmilled his arms in a panicked attempt to stay upright, then recovered with the fierce determination of someone who refused to admit gravity had almost won.

His brown hair flopped into his eyes as he sprinted past toward the living room, already shouting about something: levels, enemies, backup, ammo, and a boss fight that sounded like it mattered more than oxygen.

The house filled instantly. Footsteps. Voices. Laughter. Electronics chiming. The sharp scrape of plastic on tile. Chaos poured in with them, loud and alive and completely unaware that anything in the world had shifted.

Bella didn't yell. Her jaw tightened once with a small flex that disappeared almost as quickly as it came, but her hands were already moving. She redirected with touch and timing. Her palm landed on Sam's shoulder just as he tried to bolt past the table. A packet of crackers slid into Chloe's waiting hands. One sharp look sent Alex skidding back out of the kitchen before he even realized he'd been dismissed.

She worked the stove like muscle memory. Sauce ladled. Pasta tossed. Plates stacked in a clean line along the counter.

She placed Sam into his booster seat in one smooth motion, tray clicking into place with practiced efficiency. The second his bowl hit plastic, he plunged both hands in and smeared a fistful of red sauce across his cheek, laughing like he'd just discovered comedy itself.

"Sam," she said, voice soft but frayed at the edges, dabbing at his chin with the corner of a napkin. "Food goes in your mouth, not on your face."

He giggled harder and shoved noodles between his teeth with both hands.

Chloe and Alex hovered nearby, vibrating with impatience. Bella slid their plates toward them, and before I could even blink their iPads were glowing. Blue light washed over their faces. Forks lifted halfway, then stalled midair, forgotten in favor of whatever cartoon or pixelated battlefield had already claimed their attention.

She carried the next plate into the living room and set it carefully on the end table beside John.

"Thanks," he muttered. His eyes never left the screen. The crowd on the TV roared, loud and consuming, filling the house until there was no space left for anything else. He didn't reach for the food. Didn't look at her. Didn't even shift.

Two plates left.

Bella turned back to the counter. Knife scraping against the cutting board. Ladle dipping through sauce. The sports commentary droned over cartoon voices spilling from the kids' tablets. Sounds layered over sounds until they became a wall pressing down on the room.

I stayed at the island, silent. Lila's weight rested warm against my chest. My hand moved along her back in slow, steady passes. Up. Down. Again. Again. If I stopped, I wasn't sure what would fill the space instead.

Bella didn't look at me. Her shoulders stayed high and rigid. A curtain of hair fell across her cheek as she leaned over the stove. Her mouth pressed into a line so tight it looked like it hurt to hold.

The distance in the room stretched thin as wire. One more pull and something would snap.

She turned at last, a plate balanced in her hands. Her gaze skimmed mine without settling.

"What would you like?" Flat. Not cold, but not kind either. Just worn down to the grain. Like the question itself was another task on a list she'd been dragging behind her all day.

Bella standing there, scraped raw from giving everything she had to everyone in this house, yet still asking me what I wanted.

"I can do it myself," I said quietly, shifting Lila higher against my chest. "Let me just put her down."

She didn't argue. Just gave the smallest nod. Her eyes followed me as I walked down the hall.

My steps sank into the carpet, heavy and slow, like I was carrying more than the baby.

Lila settled into the playpen Bella must've set up earlier without a fight. I tucked the blanket around her, smoothing the fabric flat with my palm as if that could calm something deeper than wrinkles.

My hand lingered. One second too long. When I finally pulled away, the ache had already taken hold beneath my ribs.

"No fuss. She was tired." I kept my voice low.

Bella slid a plate across the counter without looking at me.

"Hopefully she sleeps better tonight."

I hesitated before taking it. The fork slipped awkwardly in my fingers.

"Thanks." The word felt thin. Not even close to what I meant.

She turned away before I could say anything else, already moving toward the row of cups lined along the counter. Juice poured. Plastic lids snapped tight. She stacked them with mechanical precision like she was running on fumes and muscle memory alone. Then she carried them out to the living room.

I stayed at the island, leaning hard against the counter, fork dangling loose while I listened.

Sam abandoned his plate the second the cup landed in front of him. Juice sloshed down his chin, dripping onto his shirt in sticky streaks.

"I wanted orange soda!" Chloe started whining as she crossed her arms, voice sharp enough to cut glass.

Alex mumbled a polite, distracted, "Thanks, Mommy," before disappearing back into his iPad. His fork hovered halfway to his mouth, forgotten.

Then John. Sprawled deep in the recliner like gravity had claimed him. One hand stuck out without even turning his head. Palm open. Eyes glued to the game. His brow lifted once lazily like words were too much effort.

"What do you want?" Bella asked. Her voice was flat. Scraped clean of softness.

"Another beer."

No sigh. No argument. No flicker of irritation. She just turned, grabbed a can from the drink fridge, and pressed it into his waiting hand. He cracked it open with a hiss of carbonation and didn't even glance at her.

"Just give her what she wants," he muttered, nodding toward Chloe. "Make her stop."

The fork bent in my grip. Metal groaned softly as the tines warped under the pressure. My jaw locked so tight my teeth ached. Blood pounded in my ears, drowning out the roar of the stadium on the TV.

Bella exhaled. Quiet. Sharp. Her shoulders folded inward like she was trying to take up less space. She didn't push back. Didn't defend herself. Didn't defend her kids. She just kept moving. Fading around him while he sank deeper into that chair like the whole world existed to serve him.

And he hadn't asked. Not once.

Not about the gunfire. Not about the wrecked truck sitting in his driveway like a crime scene. Not about the shattered glass glittering across the concrete or the dark stains spreading in crooked lines toward the drain.

Hell, he probably hadn't even noticed. Or worse...he had noticed and didn't care enough to ask.

My stomach turned.

This was supposed to be my friend. The man who'd stood beside me at barbecues and birthdays. The one who'd laughed over cheap beer while all the wives compared recipes and baby milestones.

And he couldn't spare a single damn question.

Not for me. Not for what happened today. Not for the woman running herself into the ground ten feet away from him.

Bella came back into the kitchen a minute later, silent, reaching past me for another soda. Her sleeve brushed my arm, light as a whisper.

I stepped aside immediately, careful not to touch her. But the warmth of her closeness stayed behind like a brand.

She cracked the can and slid it in front of Chloe. The girl took one sip, shoved it aside, and went right back to her screen. Not a bite of food touched. But the whining stopped.

Bella returned to the kitchen like nothing had even happened. Shoulders tight. Hands moving nonstop. Wiping counters that were already clean, stacking plates that didn't need stacking, scraping crumbs that barely existed, and rewashing plates that were already clean. She patched every crack in this house. Even the ones no one else could see.

My bent fork sat untouched on the counter. I couldn't lift it. Not with the rage sitting this heavy in my chest. Rage at him. At John, sprawled in that recliner like a king in a kingdom Bella built with her bare hands. Rage at the way she folded herself smaller and smaller just to keep the peace.

And beneath it...Something else. Something sharp. Dangerous.

"At least it's quiet," she murmured, setting a glass beside the sink. The words didn't sound like relief. They sounded like surrender.

The TV roared in the other room, announcers screaming like the world was ending over a ball and a line of paint. A beer can hissed as John tipped it back. The kids' screens chirped and chimed, high and relentless.

But in here...In here the air sat thick enough to choke on. I didn't answer.

My throat felt sealed shut, like anything I said would come out wrong. Too sharp, too honest, too insensitive, or too real. Something too close to the edge of something that would tear this whole house apart.

She brushed past me. Close enough that the faint scent of rose soap still clinging to her skin cut through the grease and tomato and stale gunpowder still stuck in my lungs. A drawer slid open. Silverware rattled, metal knocking against metal in quick, nervous bursts.

Small sounds. Sharp sounds. The rhythm of a woman wearing herself down one quiet movement at a time.

Up close, the strain around her eyes was impossible to miss. The tight pull at the corners of her mouth. The way she moved without really being present, like she was running on instinct instead of strength.

She didn't look at me directly. She didn't have to. She could feel it. The heat rolling off me. The storm I was barely holding in place.

My fingers found the edge of the counter. I gripped until my knuckles blanched, until the wood bit into my skin hard enough to anchor me.

From the living room, John let out a loud, satisfied belch.

My jaw locked so tight a dull ache spread up into my temples.

Bella's eyes flicked toward me. Quick but careful. Like she'd caught sight of the fire under my skin and didn't know if it was meant for her. She looked away just as fast, shoulders curling in tighter as she turned back toward the stove. Making herself smaller again. Safer. Quieter.

We stood there, side by side while the house drowned in everyone else's noise. But the silence between us...That was louder than all of it.

Chapter Eight

After the Dishes

Bella

Dean was still standing there when I glanced over. Plate in his hand, but he hadn't moved an inch. Like the food itself was some kind of puzzle he didn't know how to solve.

I leaned against the counter and pinched a piece of chicken between my fingers, popping it into my mouth just to keep busy. Grease slicked my skin. I wiped my hand on the dish towel, the fabric stiff from too many uses and too many nights like this.

"There's chicken, potatoes, green beans, biscuits, zucchini." My voice carried more exhaustion than I meant it to. "And if none of that works, there's still pasta and sauce. Or cold cuts in the fridge. Good sub rolls. Your choice."

"This is great," he said. Steady enough. But he still didn't move.

I frowned and reached for his plate, ready to load it myself just to end whatever silent standoff this was. "Okay. What would you like?"

"I got it." His hand tightened on the rim, pulling it back just enough to stop me. His eyes lifted to mine. Sharp, but not unkind.

"When are you going to eat?"

The question hit harder than it should have. My stomach twisted. Nobody asked me that. Not anymore. Not in this house.

I turned away fast, busied my hands at the sink. Let the faucet run over a plate that wasn't even dirty.

"Soon," I muttered. The word scraped dry against my throat. "I just need a minute."

I risked a glance over my shoulder. Something shifted across his face. Concern maybe. Or something heavier. Something I didn't want to look at too closely.

I dropped my gaze and scrubbed harder at porcelain that didn't need scrubbing.

"You should at least sit," he said, softer now.

Behind me came the faint scrape of metal as he finally started spooning food onto a plate. From the living room, John's voice cracked sharp through the house.

"Did you make gravy?"

My jaw snapped tight.

"Nope," I called back, sharper than I meant. "I knew I forgot something. But there is tomato sauce!"

His irritated grunt carried all the way into the kitchen.

The fork slipped from my fingers and clattered into the sink, the sound ringing louder than it should have. I sucked in a breath and turned my back on the whole damn room, rinsing dishes that were already clean.

"Here." Dean's voice. Closer now.

I turned. He was holding out a plate. Not his. Mine.

Chicken. Potatoes. A biscuit balanced carefully on the edge. Steam still curling up in soft ribbons.

I froze. For a second the kitchen felt too small. Too still. Like the house itself was holding its breath, waiting to see what I'd do.

I'd bet anything he hadn't eaten all day. And still he'd made me a plate first.

I wiped my damp hands on the towel and reached out, careful not to brush his fingers, though the warmth of him was right there, close enough to feel.

"Thank you." The words came out tight. Pressed against something lodged deep in my throat.

He just nodded. Calm. Quiet. Unreadable.

I carried the plate to the island and sat down. It was the first time I'd stopped moving since he'd walked in hours ago. The chair creaked under my weight. Only then did I feel the hollow ache low in my belly. Hunger I hadn't even let myself notice.

"Mama, I'm done!" Sam shouted from the living room, twisting in his booster seat until it screeched against the couch.

I sighed, stabbed one bite of chicken, then pushed back from the island.

"Okay," I said. But my voice came out thin.

By the time I reached him, Sam was already tugging at his cup, big eyes locked on me like I'd taken too long.

"More juice?"

"Sure, buddy." I slid his plate off the tray and set it on the counter.

Behind me, Chloe sat curled into the corner of the couch, arms folded tight across her chest. Her plate sat untouched beside her, except for the strawberries. The blue glow of her iPad washed over her face, turning her small features hard and distant, like she'd already learned how to disappear into a screen.

"Eat your chicken and I'll get you more strawberries," I bargained, my patience stretched thin enough to snap.

"For fuck's sake, just give her the damn strawberries," John barked from the recliner, never once taking his eyes off the TV. His voice cracked through the room like a whip.

My shoulders dipped before I could stop them.

"Okay," I whispered.

Not to John. Not to the kids. Just...to myself.

Back in the kitchen, I dragged the carton of strawberries closer. The knife knocked dull and steady against the cutting board. Slice after slice. Perfect. Automatic. Juice bled sticky down my fingers, sweet and sharp in the air.

Sam's cup was already tipped sideways on the tray. I rinsed it. Refilled it. Pressed it back into his waiting hands.

"Here."

He whined when I wiped his face, sticky palms shoving at mine, his eyes going glassy with sleep.

"Shhh," I murmured, brushing the cloth across his cheek anyway. "You're tired, buddy. I know. Just a little longer. Go play."

When I finally sank back into my chair, the plate waiting for me had gone cold. I speared a piece of chicken. Chewed. Swallowed. It landed in my stomach like lead.

Next to me, Dean's plate was already clean. His glass sat empty beside it. He hadn't moved from his seat, but the weight of him filled the kitchen anyway. Solid. Quiet. Watching. He didn't have to look at me for me to feel the steady pressure of his attention stretching across the island like heat from an open flame.

"Do you want anything else?" I asked, forcing brightness into my voice. It sounded thin even to my own ears.

"No." Flat. No rise. No fall. His face didn't change.

I forced another bite down. Then another. The food tasted like nothing. What I felt instead was the tension coiling in the air between us. Something sharp. Something I didn't dare hold his eyes long enough to understand.

When the clock clicked over to seven, I pushed my plate away. Still half full. My body moved before my mind could catch up. Dishes gathered in my hands. Ceramic knocked too sharply against ceramic, the sound brittle enough to make me wince. I carried them to the sink, the scrape of plate against steel ringing louder than it should have in the heavy quiet.

"Make yourself at home," I muttered over my shoulder.

The words sounded smaller once they were out in the air. Smaller than I meant them to.

I left him there. Alone at the island with whatever he wasn't saying.

The house still throbbed with leftover chaos. Blocks scattered across the rug. Toys overturned like casualties. Chloe's iPad shrieked bright cartoon voices into the room.

Sam sat in the middle of it all, stacking the same crooked tower over and over, knocking it down with slow, clumsy swings. His lids drooped. His limbs lagged behind his thoughts.

I scooped him up. He sagged into me instantly, warm and heavy, his head finding the hollow of my shoulder like he'd been searching for it all day. No protest. No fight.

The bathroom light buzzed faint above us. I ran a damp washcloth over his cheeks and his sticky hands, as the curls dampened at the nape of his neck. Soap clung to my palms. Pajamas tugged over pliant limbs that trusted me without question.

"Thirty minutes, Chloe," I called from halfway up the stairs, rocking him a little longer than necessary. "Then lights out."

"No! I want my daddy!" she shouted back, sharp and wild, her voice slicing straight through me.

I bit the inside of my cheek. Tasted iron. Ignored it. One fight at a time.

Sam's breathing slowed, deepened. I held him closer, letting myself feel the full weight of him pressed against my chest. His sighs puffed soft and warm against my collarbone. For once, I didn't rush.

I just stood there. Rocking. Stealing a few quiet minutes before the house swallowed me again.

In his room, I laid him down gently. Tucked the blanket snug beneath his chin. Wound the little music box until the lullaby spilled out, thin and sweet in the dark.

He rolled onto his side. Pulled the blanket closer. Asleep before I even reached the door. I lingered anyway. One hand braced on the frame, listening.

Breath in. Breath out. Steady. Safe.

When I stepped back into the living room, the sight stopped me cold. John was sunk deep into the recliner, shoulders heavy, eyes welded to the game. Chloe curled tight in his lap, small and fierce, both of them staring at the screen like it was the only thing that mattered.

Alex slouched sideways in the armchair, knees pulled up, iPad glowing pale against his face.

No one had moved. Not an inch.

I turned my back before the anger could climb any higher. The kitchen was safer. Pots scraped as I stacked them, lids snapping too loud, the refrigerator door thudding shut. I moved faster than I needed to, sharper. Every sound edged with something close to violence.

Clean-up was armor. If I stayed moving, maybe I wouldn't shatter.

"Do you want lunch for tomorrow?" I asked, not looking at him, raising my voice over the clatter.

"No." John's answer came flat. Dismissive. "I'll grab something."

Like I'd asked him for a favor. Like I'd interrupted something important.

My lips pressed tight. I sealed the Tupperware anyway. I already knew it would sit untouched until I threw it out days later, sour and forgotten. But the rhythm mattered. The illusion that I could keep this house running even when no one noticed mattered.

The greasy pan hit the sink harder than I meant it to. Water splashed up my arms. I dried my hands on the dish towel and turned toward the living room.

"Chloe. Bedtime."

Her head snapped up instantly, eyes wide and blazing. "No! I want my daddy!"

My patience had burned out hours ago.

"Chloe." My voice went thin. Hard. "It's time."

"NO!" She screamed it, fists pounding against John's chest.

"Just leave her," John muttered, louder now, but not for me. Never for me. His eyes never left the screen.

"It's a school night." The tightness in my voice surprised even me. "She needs sleep."

"Who cares?" His fingers twitched against the armrest, casual. Dismissive.

"I care," I shot back. "Her teacher will care when she can't stay awake tomorrow."

I crossed the room before I could second-guess myself and pulled the iPad straight from Chloe's hands.

She exploded.

A shriek tore out of her, raw and furious. Legs kicking. Arms swinging wild. Forty pounds of pure, unfiltered rage. Her heel slammed into my thigh. A fist caught my shoulder. Pain sparked white-hot under my skin, but I clamped her tighter against me anyway, jaw locked as I hauled her toward the hallway like a struggling wildcat.

From the recliner, John rolled his eyes. Just that. A flick of contempt. Like my fight was an inconvenience to his evening.

And beyond him, in the dim spill of kitchen light, Dean stood motionless. Silent. Watching.

His broad frame filled the doorway. Unreadable. But I felt the weight of his attention like heat against my back, taking in everything at once. Every sound. Every bruise. Every crack.

"You really can't let it go, can you?" John's voice followed us down the hall, sharp over Chloe's sobbing. "She likes me better. Maybe if you didn't run this place like boot camp, she wouldn't fight you so much."

The words landed low. Hard. Right beneath my ribs.

My chest tightened, but I didn't have anything left to throw back at him. Not tonight. Not with Chloe's fists still hammering my shoulder. Not with Dean's silence pressing in behind me like something dangerous and inevitable.

"It's a school night," I said quietly. Final. "She's five. She needs sleep."

I kept walking. Carrying her struggle like it belonged to me alone. By the time I closed her bedroom door, I felt hollowed out.

She'd cried herself quiet at last, curled tight under her blanket, lashes stuck together on damp cheeks. Getting her there had scraped the last thread of patience clean out of me.

The kitchen light felt too bright when I stepped back into it. I pulled a yogurt from the fridge, peeled the foil back with hands that trembled from more than just fatigue.

"Yogurt?" Dean's voice came from the island.

He hadn't moved. Same chair. Same posture. Elbows braced on his knees like a man holding a line no one else could see.

"She said she was hungry," I muttered, setting the spoon down harder than I meant to. "Go figure."

His eyes tracked every step I took, steady and unreadable. He didn't comment. Didn't question. And I didn't ask him to.

I grabbed Alex's pajamas from the back of the chair and walked into the living room. The TV blared as the light flickering hard across John's face. He barely blinked.

"Buddy, time to get ready for bed." I held the pajamas out.

Alex didn't look up from his iPad. "Mom... it's not even eight-thirty."

My jaw clicked tight.

"It's eight twenty-seven." The words snapped out sharper than I meant them to. My voice cracked across the room like something brittle breaking. "That's close enough. Now—" I shoved the pajamas into his lap. "—go change and brush your teeth."

The silence that followed rang louder than the TV. John muttered something at the screen. Low. Dismissive. I didn't ask what he'd said. I couldn't afford to.

My chest burned hot. I turned my back and grabbed the rag, scrubbing the counter like it had personally offended me. My wrist started to ache from the pressure, but I didn't stop.

"Mom?"

I looked up.

Alex had shuffled back in. His pajama top hung crooked over one shoulder, hair sticking up like he'd rubbed it raw. He held the iPad against his stomach like a life jacket.

"All ready." His bottom lip pushed forward, still soft with childhood.

"Good." My smile felt thin. Fragile. Like it might splinter if I held it too long. "Now say goodnight to Dad...and Dean."

"Goodnight," he mumbled.

John flicked a hand without turning his head. Dean straightened slowly in his chair and gave Alex a small nod. Nothing dramatic. Just steady acknowledgment.

Alex's shoulders eased a fraction. For one brief second, mine did too.

I walked him down the hall, the fabric of his pajamas swishing around his thin legs.

"Thank you for listening," I whispered, tugging him into me before he climbed the ladder to his loft bed.

He leaned over the rail and pressed a quick kiss into my hair. "I love you, Mom. Good night."

The words lodged sweet in my chest.

He rolled onto his side, blanket bunching under his chin. Sleep took him fast. It always did.

I stood there longer than I needed to, memorizing the slope of his small shoulders, the steady rise and fall of his chest in the dim glow.

I love you too. I whispered it to the quiet.

On the way back down the hall, I paused at Sam's side of the boys' room. He was curled tight in his crib, blanket twisted in both fists, mouth slack with dreams. I smoothed the fabric over him, listening to the faint mechanical hum of the music box drifting through the dark.

Then I eased the door shut. And just like that I went back.

Back to the sharp kitchen light.

Back to counters crowded with dishes.

Back to the mess that never seemed to end.

Chapter Nine

BEHIND THE LOCKED DOOR

Dean

By the time the clock crept past nine, she was still moving.

Dishes stacked. Counters wiped. Toys shoveled into baskets. Laundry thumped over in the machine down the hall. Every step looked mechanical now, like someone had wound her too tight and left her to run until the spring snapped.

Her shoulders dipped lower each lap through the kitchen. Her red hair had started slipping loose from the tie, strands clinging damp to her temples, catching the harsh overhead light when she passed.

I stayed planted at the island. Same chair I'd taken at dinner. A useless sentinel while she worked herself thin.

Lila's monitor glowed steady on the counter beside me, soft static threading under the constant roar of the TV bleeding in from the living room. Crowd noise. Announcers barking. John's occasional grunt cutting through it like punctuation.

My phone lit up twice against the wood. I didn't touch it.

I got up once to refill my glass. The tap ran cold over my fingers, grounding and pointless at the same time. Then I sat back down and watched her keep burning.

The longer it went on, the deeper it crawled under my skin. She carried the whole damn house on her back. Meals. Fights. Clean-up. Kids. Every loose thread tied off before anyone else even noticed it was fraying.

And him? Ten feet away in that recliner. Beer sweating in his hand. Eyes locked on the game like the rest of them didn't exist. King of nothing.

I'd seen them before all this. Before the kids. Before Vicky. Before the walls of this house felt like they were pressing inward. Back then they'd been the couple everyone watched. Laughing too loud at backyard barbecues. Arms always brushing. Inside jokes nobody else got. Bella barefoot on the grass, hair loose down her back, smiling like the world was something she could actually enjoy.

He used to look at her. Really look. Like she was the best thing that had ever happened to him. Now he barely noticed when she walked past. Now she moved through her own life like a ghost keeping the lights on.

She never barked. Never demanded. Never asked for help. Just kept working herself down piece by piece until even the light in her face looked dimmed.

And the worst part? I couldn't tell when it had changed. Or how the hell I'd missed it.

My jaw locked. Words crowded the back of my teeth, things I had no right to say. This wasn't my house. Wasn't my life to step into. But the silence gnawed like I'd swallowed glass.

When she finally sank into the chair beside me, it felt like watching something give way. Not dramatic. Just...collapse in slow motion.

Her arm dropped onto the counter. Her head followed, pressing into the crook of her sleeve. The breath left her in one long, empty stream. For the first time all night, she stopped moving.

"All done?" I asked, low. Softer than I'd meant.

"I think so." Her voice came muffled against the fabric.

She rolled her head toward me without lifting it, cheek flattened to her arm, eyes finding mine through the dim kitchen light. There was no guard left in them. No performance. Just bone-deep fatigue.

A beat passed. Then quieter, almost like she was apologizing for existing.

"There's no shower in your bathroom. If you want one, you can use ours. It's a walk-in." A small pause. A tired exhale that seemed to slip out without permission. "And...it's a hell of a lot cleaner than the kids' bathroom."

The corner of my mouth twitched. Not because it was funny. Because of the way she said it, like letting me into that small piece of her space cost her something she couldn't afford to lose.

"Thanks," I said. My voice came out rough. Dragged over gravel.

She didn't react. Her lashes lowered. Stayed there a second too long. When she forced her eyes open again, it looked like stubbornness was the only thing holding her upright.

I didn't fill the silence. Didn't crowd her. Just sat there and let the moment exist.

"Yeah," I said finally, sliding my phone into my pocket. "A shower sounds good."

I pushed up from the chair. My knees felt stiff from sitting there so long doing nothing. Watching. I rinsed my glass and set it into the dishwasher. The click of the door closing sounded louder than it should have.

Halfway down the hall, I stopped and looked back. She was still folded over her arm. Shoulders curled inward. Spine bowed like she was trying to make herself smaller inside her own life. For once, she looked fragile. Too small for the weight she carried every damn night.

No one else in that house seemed to notice. But I did. And I wasn't sure anymore if I could keep pretending I hadn't.

The guest room felt cooler than the rest of the house. Not just temperature. Something else. Like the air in here carried less noise. Less expectation. The furnace hummed steady beneath the floorboards, a low mechanical heartbeat, but the quiet wrapped thick around the walls.

Whole. Heavy.

Lila's playpen sat tucked into the corner, the small night-light casting a soft amber glow across the quilt. Shadows pooled gentle and still. She shifted once in her sleep. A tiny sigh slipping past her lips, her chest rising slow and even.

I leaned over the rail. My palm brushed the blanket. Just enough pressure to feel the warmth of her through the fabric. Real. Alive. Here. My lungs loosened for the first time all night.

The image of twisted metal and shattered glass flickered behind my eyes anyway. The smell of burned rubber still clung inside my nose, stubborn as memory. I swallowed hard and forced myself to focus on the steady rhythm of her breathing instead.

In. Out. Safe.

My duffel bag slouched against the wall like it had given up too. I crouched beside it, joints protesting, fingers fumbling through the mess until they closed around a clean T-shirt and a pair of sweatpants. Fabric soft. Familiar. Something normal to hold onto.

I tossed them onto the bed and dropped down beside them. Hard. The mattress dipped under my weight, springs creaking faint in the stillness. My elbows dug into my knees. My head fell forward into my hands before I could stop it.

The adrenaline that had kept me upright all day finally started bleeding out. My shoulders sagged.

For a second, I just sat there, breathing into my palms, staring at nothing. The burn that had simmered under my ribs all night came back full force in the stillness.

Him. Sprawled out in that recliner like the world owed him something. Beer sweating rings into the wood. Eyes locked on the game while she ran herself into the ground ten feet away. Shrugging when she asked for help. Rolling his eyes when she hauled their kid down the hall, screaming.

I rubbed both hands down my face hard enough to sting. Where the hell did my friend go? Because this guy…this hollow version sunk into that chair…wasn't the man I knew.

John used to be the one who showed up first. Stayed last. The guy who'd give you the shirt off his back without even thinking about it. I'd seen him do it, literally once, standing in a freezing parking lot after some idiot locked himself out in a T-shirt. John just laughed, peeled his hoodie off, and shoved it at the guy like it was nothing.

That was him. The man who hauled couches up three flights of stairs without being asked. Who drove across state lines at two in the morning because someone needed help. Who stood beside me through shit I wouldn't wish on anyone.

We used to be tight. Bowling nights. Bar tabs we could barely afford. Long stupid arguments about nothing that somehow mattered. Back when Bella laughed easy and leaned into him like the whole world made sense.

Back before kids. Before Vicky. Before everything got…heavy.

It had been what? A year since I quit bowling with him. Maybe a little more. Life got busy. People drifted. That happens. But this?

This wasn't drifting. This was like watching someone slowly rot from the inside out. And I couldn't figure out when it started. Or how I hadn't seen it coming.

I thought about the way he'd sat there tonight. The way he hadn't even asked what happened. Not about the car. Not about the gunfire. Not about the black smear of rubber and glass still staining his own damn driveway.

Not about me. Not about her.

My jaw tightened. Maybe he didn't want to know. Maybe looking too close meant admitting something was broken he didn't know how to fix. Or maybe he just didn't care anymore.

That thought hit harder than anything else. Not clueless. Not worn down. Willful. A man choosing not to see her.

I pushed to my feet, clothes tucked under my arm, and slipped into the hallway.

The house felt different up here. Dimmer. Quieter. The overhead fixture hummed faintly, throwing dull yellow light that flattened the walls. Kids' doors lined one side, cracked open just enough to spill soft sounds into the corridor. White noise machines and a music box winding down over the deep uneven breathing of sleep.

A blanket rustled somewhere. A tiny sigh. Life. Fragile and trusting.

My steps went soundless against the carpet as I moved past them toward the bathroom she'd offered. The hinges creaked when I eased the door open.

I stopped short. Didn't expect this.

It was bigger than mine at home. Warmer. Peach walls with a pink undertone that should've felt dated but didn't. White frames hung neat and deliberate: roses, lilies, pressed botanicals arranged like someone cared about how the space felt when you walked into it.

A double vanity ran the length of the wall. Her side was unmistakable. Makeup bag half-unzipped. Hair dryer tucked with careful precision. Bottles of perfume and lotion lined up like she'd placed them one by one, making order out of chaos.

The other side...Bare. Toothbrush. Razor. Nothing else. A man who slept here. Not a man who lived here.

My jaw tightened.

The shower filled the corner with a wide glass door clouded with old water marks. Inside, pastel tubs of scrubs and conditioners crowded the shelves. Labels peeling. Soap stacked like she'd replaced it before it ever ran out.

The whole room smelled faintly floral. Warm. Human. Her.

I set my clothes on the counter, stripped, and stepped into the shower.

The handle squealed when I turned it. Water exploded against the tile, steam rolling fast until the glass blurred the world into nothing. I planted my palms flat against the wall and leaned forward until my forehead hit cool ceramic. The spray hammered into my shoulders. Hot enough to sting. Hot enough to feel like punishment.

My ribs flared with every breath.

Gunfire still echoed somewhere behind my eyes.

Glass breaking.

Tires screaming.

Her voice on the phone.

Bella's face at the counter.

John not even looking up.

My fingers curled against the tile. And that's when it cracked. The first breath tore out of me before I could stop it. Sharp. Ragged. Catching halfway up my throat like it had teeth.

I tried to swallow it back. Lock my jaw. Force it down where everything else stayed buried. Didn't work. The sound came anyway, low and raw, dragged out of my chest like it had been clawing to get free for hours.

Everything hit at once.

Sitting at that counter all night. Jaw locked. Hands still. Watching her grind herself into dust while he barely shifted in that damn recliner.

The dishes. The screaming. The bedtime fights. The constant movement.

All of it hers. None of it his.

My chest heaved hard enough to hurt. My throat cinched tight. I drove both fists into the tile. Skin slipped under the spray. Knuckles squealed across wet ceramic, the sound too loud inside the glass cage.

How the hell does she live like this? The thought sliced clean through me.

How long has she been carrying this alone?

How does she keep standing?

How does she not just...stop?

The water pounded hotter. Harder. But the anger underneath burned hotter still. Anger at him. At John sitting there with his beer sweating onto the table like the world owed him comfort. Acting like her voice was background noise. Rolling his eyes when she dragged their kid down the hall. Shrugging at her exhaustion like it was weather he couldn't control.

My teeth ground together until my jaw trembled. And under that rage...Something worse. Something soft. Something I didn't want anywhere near me. Pity. Maybe. Grief. For her.

I shoved it down hard because I knew she'd hate it. She'd rather bleed than be pitied. It wrapped around my ribs anyway. Tight. Suffocating.

Steam thickened until the mirrors vanished. The bathroom blurred into nothing but heat and white noise. The spray hammered into my shoulders like it was trying to beat something out of me.

My head tipped sideways. And just like that, the world snapped back. Vicky.

Where the hell was she? Was she okay?

Black SUVs at the curb. Muzzle flashes sparking in the afternoon like something unreal. The sharp stink of gunpowder burning the back of my throat.

But that wasn't what stuck.

It was her. Heels striking the driveway in quick, clipped beats. Phone pressed tight to her ear. Walking away. Not running. Not panicking. Just...leaving. Like she'd already decided something.

My chest tightened as the memory sharpened.

She hadn't looked back. Not once. Not at me. Not at the house.

Most people would have. Would've hesitated. Vicky hadn't. Her shoulders were stiff. Her mouth set too tight. Eyes locked straight ahead like if she stopped moving for even a second, she'd fall apart. Or like she already had.

The way she'd said goodbye...Not see you later. Not call me when you get there. Just that flat little smile that never reached her eyes.

My stomach twisted.

What if she hadn't been saying goodbye for now?

What if she'd been saying goodbye for good?

My rage spiked so hard my vision throbbed.

What if she'd meant it?

What if she really had been saying goodbye...and just walked away?

My jaw snapped shut. I swung without thinking. My fist cracked against the tile. Pain bit sharp up my arm with bone slamming ceramic, knuckles stinging, skin splitting under the spray.

They could've killed her. My little girl.

The words looped, darker every time. Heavier.

Vicky, who once swore she wanted this life. Who stood in empty lots pointing at nothing and telling me where the kitchen would go. Who begged for children like it was the only thing that mattered.

And now? Gone. Left me holding a three-month-old and a target stamped clean across my back.

The rage cinched tight, a steel band crushing my chest. Heat roared in my ears until the bathroom blurred into steam and red haze.

I dragged both hands down my face, water sluicing off my chin. My mouth hung open under the spray like I could rinse the bitterness out of me. My breaths came jagged, breaking apart before they could fill my lungs.

I couldn't lose it. Not here. Not when Bella was down the stairs already worn to threads. Not when my daughter was asleep in her house, safe for the first time all day.

I forced my spine straight. Pressed my shoulders back into the punishing stream. Let it hammer the knots until muscle screamed and my pulse slowed by inches.

Steam swallowed the glass, erased my reflection until only a dark shape stood there. Someone I barely recognized.

The anger didn't wash away. It never did. It just settled lower. Sharper. Waiting.

Chapter Ten

Before Morning

Bella

When Dean disappeared up the stairs and the shower kicked on a moment later, something inside me finally gave out.

I sank onto the kitchen stool, my legs folding like they'd been waiting all day for permission. The hard wood of the chair bit into the backs of my thighs, grounding and uncomfortable. For the first time since morning, I wasn't moving. Not cooking. Not cleaning. Not negotiating. Just...still.

The kitchen hummed around me. Refrigerator buzzing. The faint hiss of the TV bleeding in from the living room. Water rushing through pipes overhead.

My hands felt heavy. Useless.

Without thinking, I reached for the iPad. The screen lit too bright in the dim kitchen, washing my face in cold blue. Just a few minutes, I told myself. A quick scroll. Something mindless. Something that wasn't tantrums or dishes or the sound of John's voice cutting through me.

Something to remind me there was still a world outside this house.

The screen lit too bright, stabbing at my eyes. Emails stacked up like bricks: showing requests, agents checking in, clients confirming, underwriters verifying details, and the office manager reminding me about deadlines I already knew were there. Each subject line felt like someone tapping me on the shoulder, whispering that I couldn't afford to slip. Not even for one night.

I started flagging names, scribbling notes with my fingertip across the screen so I wouldn't walk into tomorrow blind. Routes mapped out in my head. Which houses first. How long it would take to cut through traffic on the back roads. The rhythm steadied me. Numbers. Times. Addresses. Things I could line up neat and pretend I controlled.

A text bubble slid down across the top of the screen.

Tina.

I hesitated before opening it. Tina never texted just to text. She was a phone-call woman. Loud and direct making herself impossible to ignore. If she was messaging, it meant she'd already decided I wasn't answering fast enough.

Girl, you alive?

Another one followed almost immediately.

You've been quiet for two days and I don't like it.

My mouth twitched despite myself.

Short. Blonde. Five feet of southern attitude wrapped in designer flats and mortgage paperwork. Tina had a way of kicking down whatever door you tried to hide behind and then handing you coffee like she'd done you a favor.

A third message popped up.

Take a damn day off and let me buy you lunch. I mean it. Don't make me come drag you out that house myself.

I stared at the words longer than I meant to. Lunch. A day off. The idea felt so foreign it almost made me laugh. Days off were for people who didn't have three kids, a marriage hanging by threads, and a commission pipeline that could dry up overnight if they blinked wrong.

My fingers hovered over the keyboard. I didn't type back. Not yet.

Instead I opened another email. Flagged another name. Built another route in my head like if I just kept moving, even sitting still, nothing inside me would have to be faced.

But Tina's messages stayed at the top of the screen. Waiting.

My eyes blurred. My shoulders loosened into the screen's glow, the world narrowing to pixels and lists and the quiet hum inside my head.

I didn't even hear him come back.

"What are you doing now?" Dean's voice cut through the silence.

I jolted hard, the iPad smacking against my chest like I'd been caught stealing. My heart stumbled, breath snagging halfway in.

"Work," I said too fast. Too defensive. Like he'd found me doing something wrong instead of just...surviving. I swallowed, forcing steadiness into my voice. "Just catching up."

He stood there a second longer than necessary. Clean clothes now. Steam still clinging faint to his skin. His expression gave nothing away. No judgment, no curiosity. Just that steady, unreadable look.

Then he nodded once and kept moving down the hall toward the guest room.

The silence he left behind felt heavier than before. Like he'd taken the only solid thing in the room with him.

I set the iPad aside. The screen dimmed, glow fading into shadow, but the pressure in my chest didn't ease. From the living room came the flat drone of a late sports recap layered over John's uneven snoring. I tuned it out automatically, the way you stop hearing traffic after you've lived beside it long enough.

Tomorrow started now.

I pulled Alex and Chloe's lunchboxes across the counter. Lids snapped open with sharp little clicks that echoed in the quiet kitchen. Water bottles lined up. Pretzels shaken into Ziplocs. Juice boxes stacked like soldiers waiting for orders.

My brain spun faster with each movement. Alarm times. Shoes by the door. Backpacks packed. Permission slip. Chloe's library book. Sam's daycare bag. Hair combed. Teeth brushed. No room for mistakes.

Bread in one hand, deli meat in the other, I nudged the fridge shut with my hip—and nearly dropped everything.

Dean was suddenly right there. So close I hadn't heard him move.

The kitchen light caught the angles of his face, still damp from the shower. Clean cotton stretched across his shoulders. He smelled faintly of soap and steam instead of smoke and gunpowder now, but the memory of it lingered anyway.

My pulse kicked hard against my ribs.

"How do you do that?" I breathed before I could stop myself.

Dean leaned in the doorway, iPad tucked under his arm, his eyes steady on me. The kitchen light caught on his freshly shaved head, a faint sheen still clinging where the water hadn't fully dried. His shirt hung clean across his broad shoulders, fabric pulling tight over muscles that hadn't quite let go of the day yet. He looked steadier than before. Larger somehow. Filling the entryway like he belonged there.

But the raw edge was still there too. In his face. In the way he didn't look away.

"What are you doing now?" he asked again, lower this time, like the answer mattered more than he was willing to admit.

"Lunch." The word came out sharper than intended. I set the bread down harder than necessary. "Saves time in the morning."

My hands moved before my brain could catch up. Bread. Mayo. Knife sliding fast across crust. Muscle memory. Noise to crowd out the silence pressing in around us.

He didn't move. Just watched. Didn't let me vanish into routine the way everyone else did.

The weight of his gaze sat between my shoulder blades like heat. I bent my head, focused on lining up sandwiches in neat rows, pretending I wasn't unraveling one small thread at a time.

After a minute, he crossed the kitchen and dropped into the chair at the island. The iPad landed on the counter with a soft thud, like he'd never really left.

Something tight inside my chest loosened a fraction.

"Speaking of tomorrow..." My voice cracked before I cleared it. I kept my eyes on the bread, spreading mayo in slow, careful strokes now. "I've got showings lined up. The kids and I have to be out the door by seven-fifteen. Will you be alright here by yourself?"

"Oh yeah." His tone was easy. Quiet. Almost gentle. "Don't worry about me. I don't mean to be a burden. We won't be here long."

The knife stilled in my hand. The words hit harder than he probably meant them to.

"You're not a burden." It came out before I could stop it. Clean. Certain. I glanced up, and when his eyes met mine, something inside me softened enough to let a small smile slip free. "You can stay as long as you need."

He dipped his head once. No argument. Already opening the iPad. His fingers began to tap, steady and deliberate. The rhythm filling the kitchen alongside the hum of the fridge and the muffled drone of the TV from the living room.

It anchored me more than it should have. I kept moving. Sandwiches sealed. Baggies stacked. The fridge door closing with a quiet thump.

But the silence kept pressing until I cracked it open with the first thought that surfaced.

"Do you want coffee tomorrow?" The second it left my mouth, heat rushed to my cheeks. Too eager. Too familiar.

"I mean...of course you do," I rushed on, fumbling for a cover. "Who doesn't?"

He didn't look up. Just gave one small nod. Simple. Solid.

Somehow that was enough to make me smile down at the counter like I'd been handed something bigger than permission.

I pulled a bag of frozen fruit from the freezer, set it in a bowl to thaw. The oven clock glowed past ten, harsh green digits cutting through the dim kitchen.

Now that I'd stopped rushing, the weight of the day crashed in all at once. Every chore. Every argument. Every mile of fear and adrenaline. My arms ached from carrying everything. My throat burned from snapping at the kids. My chest felt bruised from holding it all inside.

"Okay." I brushed a loose strand of hair behind my ear, the motion automatic. A shield for how close I felt to cracking. "I think I'm off to bed."

I didn't wait for an answer. Didn't expect one. I turned toward the stairs, footsteps soft against the wood. Behind me, the quiet click of his keys shifting followed. And for the first time in longer than I could remember...I didn't feel like I was hauling the night alone.

Someone else was still awake. Someone else was holding a piece of the dark with me, even if it wasn't his to carry. Even if I knew he had storms of his own waiting just beneath the surface.

I was halfway up the stairs when his voice stopped me.

"Would it be okay if I made a couple calls out here?" His tone was low. Careful. Like he wasn't sure he had the right to ask. He nodded toward John, snoring in the recliner like a man welded to his throne.

I turned back.

Dean stood steady in the kitchen light, face unreadable. But the question itself carried something I wasn't used to. Respect.

"Yeah," I said after a beat, my hand lingering on the banister. "I can shut the TV off if you need. Or...the deck's fine too. Nobody around here to overhear."

He gave a single nod. Small. Certain. Gratitude showed more in the way his shoulders eased than anywhere in his expression.

"Good night," he said. His eyes caught mine before I could duck away. Steady. Too steady. Like he saw more than I meant to show.

"Try to get some rest."

I forced a smile that didn't quite make it to my eyes and turned before it could slip.

But rest never came.

The ceiling kept me company instead. Pale lines. Slow shadows from the fan blades turning just enough to remind me time was still moving. The sheets twisted around my legs no matter how many times I kicked them loose, cotton clinging like vines.

My mind refused to stop.

Tomorrow's schedule first. The drive. The showings. The lunches stacked neat in the fridge like proof I was still holding everything together.

Then tonight replayed sharper. The shouting. The eye rolls. The silence I kept swallowing whole.

And under it all, one voice I couldn't shut out. Dean's. Steady. Quiet. Telling me to rest...when no one else ever thought to.

John's snores dragged up the stairwell, harsh and mechanical, like a saw blade chewing through drywall. He hadn't moved. Hadn't budged from that recliner. It was his throne. His territory. His excuse.

Every rattling breath felt deliberate. Another reminder he was still there. Still taking up space.

When five-thirty came, it wasn't an alarm that woke me. It was drawers slamming open and shut in our bedroom.

Sharp. Repetitive. Too precise to be careless.

My eyes snapped open, though they'd never truly closed. Each slam landed like a message. If he wasn't going to sleep, I sure as hell wasn't allowed to either.

Gray morning light bled through the blinds, striping the ceiling in dull bars. I lay flat on my back, breath tight in my chest, resentment coiling deeper with every crack of wood against wood.

Heavy. Familiar. The kind of weight you learn to carry because setting it down was never an option.

Years. That's how long we've been doing this dance.

Chapter Eleven

Alive on Paper

Dean

The house went dead quiet once Bella's footsteps faded up the stairs. Not the kind of quiet that settles you. This kind pressed in.

TV chatter leaked from the living room in uneven bursts. The fridge hummed steady behind me. John snored in the recliner like a busted generator fighting to stay alive. A whole family under one roof, and somehow it still sounded hollow.

I checked the baby monitor again. Lila. Still safe.

Her chest rose and fell in that small, stubborn rhythm. The night-light washed her in pale blue, turning her into something fragile and untouchable. The only thing in this house that hadn't been worn down by noise or need.

My thumb hovered over the screen for a second longer than it had to.

Then I scrolled to Mark's number before I could talk myself out of it. He picked up on the first ring.

"Stone." His voice came through rough and awake, like he'd been expecting trouble. "Figured you'd be laying low tonight, not burning cell towers."

Vicky's face shoved its way in anyway. Lipstick too sharp. Dark brown eyes colder than the night she walked. Heels snapping across the tile like gunfire, each step clean and final. No backward glance. Not once.

The memory twisted deep in my gut.

The house we built came with it. Cabinets squared and leveled under my hands. Closets measured twice, beams hoisted into place until my shoulders screamed. Sawdust in my lungs. Nails bitten between my teeth. Every inch of that place shaped because she swore she wanted a family. Because she swore this was forever. And I believed her. I built her that house with my own damn hands.

Now I was sitting in someone else's kitchen with a baby monitor glowing beside me, a target stamped across my back, and nothing left of the promises she'd made.

"How the fuck do you square that?" I whispered into my palms before I realized I'd said it out loud.

Mark's voice snapped me back. "...you still there?"

"Yeah." The word scraped raw out of my throat. I straightened on the stool like posture alone could patch the crack running through me. "Yeah. I'm here."

He promised to keep digging. Promised to call if anything shifted. We hung up. The phone left my hand harder than I meant. It skidded across the counter and thunked into the backsplash, the sound ringing sharp in the too-quiet kitchen.

I braced both hands over my face and dragged them down slow, stubble rasping against my palms. The boil under my skin stayed right where it was.

The house hadn't changed. John's snores still rattled from the recliner. The fridge hummed steady. A late-night sports recap droned low from the TV. Ordinary sounds. The kind meant to signal safety.

Inside me, nothing felt safe. Confusion pressed in first. How she'd slipped away so clean. What part I'd missed. Where it had started to rot without me seeing it. Then the hurt. Sharp and constant. Like a nail driven straight through my chest. Underneath that, rage gathered thick and hot, threading tighter with every breath until it felt like it might split me open from the inside.

I told myself to listen to Mark. To try for sleep. To lay low. But every wet rattle from John's throat, every flicker of light from that goddamn TV felt like weight pressing harder against my ribs.

My pulse wouldn't settle. My jaw throbbed from clenching. Finally, I shoved back from the stool.

The duffel came with me, dragged across the tile in a rough scrape. I dug inside and hauled out my laptop. The plastic felt heavier than steel, edges biting into my palms. I flipped it open on the island. The screen's glow cut into my eyes, cold and unforgiving.

My fingers moved on instinct. Muscle memory. The secure link. The back door I'd built years ago. The one I was never supposed to keep. I typed slow. Deliberate.

Victoria Hayes.

Her name stared back at me in neat black type.

Employment records. Case lists. Trial notes. The address of the house I built her like some fucking idiot clinging to an idea that meant nothing now.

No activity. No flags. No jurisdiction changes.

I shifted to financials. Cards cross-referenced against gas stations, hotels, flights. Dead. Not a single swipe. Not a whisper.

The car? Last logged at a toll camera two nights before the party. Grainy still shot. Plate barely visible. Nothing since. No hits. No alerts.

Gone.

I leaned back, shoulders sagging. The blue light burning into my eyes until the letters blurred. People on the run always left something behind. A wrong turn. A charge they forgot about. A favor called in too loudly.

This wasn't sloppy. This was clean.

My fingertips drummed against the counter, sharp in the silence. Years of this work told me exactly what I was looking at.

Someone was covering tracks. Precise. Professional.

But another part of me, the part that still turned toward the empty side of the bed at night, couldn't line it up. Vicky in her heels, hair perfect, telling me she wanted a family. Telling me to build her a home.

And Vicky now. A ghost I couldn't pin down. Two women. One name. No way to make them fit.

I rubbed the back of my neck. The muscles felt like steel cable pulled too tight. The baby monitor blinked steady beside me, green light pulsing in time with Lila's breathing down the hall. Even. Calm. The only rhythm keeping me from coming apart.

My hand hovered over the laptop lid. Enough for tonight. Enough dead ends.

Then a flagged note blinked across the feed. Buried deep. I almost missed it.

My stomach dropped. I clicked. My name lit the screen.

Marcus Dean Stone.

Flagged. Two words beneath it. Hit. Alive.

The room tilted. I swallowed hard, staring until the letters sharpened again. Alive.

I'd seen those files before. Bodies tagged gang violence. Victims that didn't die right away. Victims meant to send messages.

Alive wasn't mercy. Alive meant time. Time to hurt. Time to break. Time for whoever ordered it to make their point.

My hand locked on the counter, tendons pulling tight under my skin. Breath tore ragged through my chest.

"Fuck." The word scraped out of me, raw enough to sting.

It had to be her. Didn't it? Her cases had been shifting. Gang prosecutions. Bigger names. Dirtier work. She'd joked once about needing thicker armor.

What if this was her armor? What if she hadn't just walked away...What if she'd set the board first?

Behind my eyes, the image slammed in. Men with rifles. Blades flashing. Hands dragging me down, holding me open. Carving until there was nothing left but a warning written in blood.

And all I could see was her face. The woman who once swore she wanted to build a life with me. The same one who might have just put a price on my head.

Then Lila. Not in front of me, but the memory of her. Curled in that playpen down the hall. One fist tangled in her blanket. Chest lifting slow. Safe.

For now. If they came here...If they came while I had her —

The rage went cold. Fear cut through me clean as ice. I could take the hit. Always had. Bullet or broken bones, that was part of the bargain. But not with her. Not with her breathing against my chest, trusting me to keep her whole.

That was different. That was impossible.

I slammed the laptop shut. The crack split the kitchen like a gunshot. From the recliner, John stirred. Snorted. Rolled onto his side and kept sawing through the night. Oblivious. A man in the middle of a war zone and he didn't even twitch.

I froze. Palms flat on the counter. My pulse hammered so hard it climbed into my throat. My eyes locked on the baby monitor, on that soft green glow pulsing in time with her breaths.

That thin line of light was her life. If they came through that door, it wouldn't just be me they took.

My chest cinched tighter. I couldn't sit still. Fear ran live under my skin, buzzing and sparking as if demanding movement. I flipped the laptop open again, fingers already moving before I'd decided to. Past the databases. Past the case files. To the feed I hadn't checked in months. Old cameras. Cheap ones. Hard-wired into a backup system I'd told myself I'd never need again.

The screen flickered. Grain bled across the image. Timestamp jittering in the corner. Driveway. Back porch. Street.

Then the footage jumped. Midmorning. Two black sedans rolled into frame. My gut twisted. Same make. Same build. Same low shine that had filled my rearview nights ago while adrenaline burned my lungs raw.

I leaned closer, knuckles whitening against the counter. Doors opened at the same time. Two men stepped out. Hoods low. Hands buried deep in pockets. No hurry. No nerves. They moved like they already owned the ground they were walking on, circling the house slow and methodical.

One pressed his face close to the kitchen window. The one I'd installed myself, leveling the frame until my shoulders screamed. For a second I could almost see his breath fogging the glass.

The other tugged once on the garage handle. Testing. Measuring. Then he shook his head. My jaw locked hard enough it throbbed. Every board I'd cut. Every nail I'd driven. Every wall I'd lifted into place had turned into nothing more than terrain on a map.

They lingered. Minutes stretching thin and brittle while I watched them prowl through the life I'd built. Then they slid back into the sedans and drove off. Like it meant nothing. Like they'd just completed a rehearsal.

I didn't realize I'd stopped breathing until the screen went dark. Hours later the feed lit again. Same cars. No hesitation this time. They went straight to the back porch. Hands flat against the glass. Looking in like they were already imagining where the furniture sat. Where the exits were. Where a man might try to run.

One crouched low. Hood slipping forward as he ducked under the deck, checking the crawl space like he expected to find me cornered there. Waiting.

My skin crawled. I sat frozen, teeth grinding, watching strangers move through the bones of my life like vultures circling something they already knew was dead.

Air stalled in my chest. The truth hit fast. Clean. I wasn't safe there. I would never be safe there again. Not me. Not Lila. Not with Vicky's shadow still stamped into the brass letters of the DA's office, stretched long across every streetlight in that town.

The house I built as proof of promises...was gone. The truth hit hard. Not like fear. Not like rage. Like a cinder block dropped straight through my chest.

I couldn't go back. Not ever.

The laptop clicked shut under my hand. The sound too final in the still kitchen. Something in me drained with it. The anger burned down to ash. Fear hollowed me clean. What settled in their place was heavier than both.

Exhaustion. It filled my bones like wet cement.

I pushed up from the chair. My legs trembled, knees stiff from hours locked in one position. The hallway stretched long and dim ahead of me, pulling me forward step by step toward the guest room.

The door creaked when I nudged it open. A night-light glowed soft across the carpet, wrapping the playpen in pale gold.

She stirred at the sound. A small whimper slipped from her throat, but she didn't wake. Just curled tighter under the blanket, lips parted, fist tucked beneath her cheek like she was guarding some secret dream.

I crouched beside her. My fingers curled over the rail until my knuckles blanched. Couldn't look away. Her chest rose and fell. Slow. Even. A metronome cutting through the chaos in my head, the only rhythm left in my life that still made sense. My throat locked. She was it. The last tether keeping me from snapping clean in half under betrayal...under rage...under the knowledge that somewhere out there my name was being traded like currency.

"You don't know," I whispered. The words barely existed outside my mouth. "You don't know what is going on."

My forehead dropped against the metal rail. Cool steel grounding me while my lungs scraped for air. But I made the promise anyway.

"I'll do anything to keep you safe," I muttered. Anything. And I knew what that meant.

If it came down to it...if the only way was to vanish...to let myself disappear until I was nothing but a ghost with no address, no face...then I would.

Better she grow up not knowing me than grow up hunted because she did. She deserved more than the war I'd dragged to her crib. Her breathing hummed soft and steady, pulling me back inch by inch from the edge.

I stayed there until my knees screamed. Until the ache forced me to move. Finally, I lowered myself onto the bed without turning on the lamp, without checking my phone, without giving my mind another second to start running again.

Exhaustion hit like a freight train. Flattened everything. My eyes closed.

And for the first time since Vicky walked out that door...nothing came for me in the dark.

Chapter Twelve

The Morning Rush

Bella

Mornings always started with John. Drawers slammed open like gunshots. His boots, or maybe just his feet, hit the floorboards hard enough to rattle the frames on the wall. The faucet blasted on, water hammering the sink like he was daring the whole house to wake with him.

Not an alarm clock. A warning.

“Daddy!” Chloe’s voice tore down the hallway, sharp enough to slice skin. “I want Daddy to take me to school!”

I pressed the heel of my hand to my forehead, already bracing.

“I’ve got work, Chloe,” John called back. Flat. Impatient. “I leave at seven. School doesn’t start until seven-thirty. Ask your mother.”

Her scream jumped an octave. Mattress springs shrieked under her kicking.

"No! I want you!"

I turned the baby monitor toward Sam's room just in time to watch him stir. A small whimper. Fists rubbing slow across his eyes. His head tipped toward the noise. No crying. Just wide, sleepy blinks, like chaos was the air he breathed.

I dragged myself out of bed. My legs felt packed with sand. My throat burned from a night that never really turned into sleep.

"Chloe," I called, sharper than I meant. "Enough."

She didn't even slow down.

Alex, at least, was still cocooned in his blanket, face buried deep. Soft snores puffing against the fabric. I nudged his shoulder. Nothing. Nudged again. Harder.

"Alex."

I stepped under his bunk bed and peeled the blanket down until the cold hit him. He groaned. One bleary eye cracked open. "Mom..."

"Up." I tugged the blanket lower. "You've got school. Don't make me say it again."

He rolled with a sigh dramatic enough to rival Chloe's meltdown, but then the grin came. Sleepy. Crooked. Enough to melt something in me I didn't have time for.

"Love you, Mom."

"Love you too." I pointed at the folded pile on his dresser. "Clothes. Now."

He grinned again, sheepish, hair shooting in every direction as he pushed himself upright.

I scooped Sam on my way past.

By the time we hit the kitchen, Chloe was still planted there, arms locked across her chest, lower lip pushed out so far, she could've tripped on it.

"I don't want you to take me," she snapped. Eyes hot with accusation. "I want Daddy."

The water bottle thunked into her lunchbox harder than I meant. The zipper hissed shut.

"Daddy's already gone," I said. Too sharp. "It's me or no one."

She stomped toward the door, muttering. I didn't ask what she said. I didn't want to know.

Sam had parked himself on the bottom stair, two fingers tucked in his mouth, eyes huge as he watched Chloe unravel. He didn't cry. Didn't fuss. He just...observed. Like he'd already learned tantrums were background noise.

I yanked Chloe's hair into uneven ponytails. Zipped Alex's backpack while he complained about math. Dropped to my knees to tie Sam's shoes tight enough they wouldn't betray him before lunch.

My voice bounced between them; sharp with Chloe, coaxing with Sam, clipped with Alex.

By the time I herded them toward the garage, my skull buzzed with the echo of it all. Shoes thudding into walls. Zippers snapping. Questions fired at me faster than I could answer. A morning that never ended. Just reset.

Dean's door stayed closed. No creak of boards. No low shuffle of movement. Maybe he was still asleep. Maybe he'd been up all night bent over that iPad.

For one quick, ugly second, I envied him. The quiet. The choice. I'd forgotten what that felt like.

I dumped the backpacks on the counter and grabbed a pen. The kids were already shouting from the mudroom, arguing over who got the front seat, sneakers banging against the baseboards.

I tuned them out and scribbled fast.

Dean

Passcode to the alarm system: 0214

Garage app login: 0358

Grocery delivery instructions taped to the fridge.

We'll be home by 3:30.

The pen hovered. My hand wanted to add something.

Good luck.

You'll be fine.

Sorry about last night.

I didn't. Instead I slid the note on top of his iPad and hauled my bag onto my shoulder.

"All right, let's go!" I shouted, steering Sam through the door while Chloe dragged her heels and Alex sighed like his life had officially ended.

Chapter Thirteen

DECLINED

Dean

I didn't crawl out of sleep until sunlight striped the walls. Sharp and unforgiving bands of gold that felt more like exposure than morning. Almost nine. Not real rest. More like my body had finally shut down and refused to negotiate.

The first thing I reached for was the baby monitor.

The small camera I'd propped up the night before still blinked steady green. On the screen, Lila's chest lifted and fell in slow rhythm, soft breaths puffing through the speaker like waves brushing shore.

Relief hit hard enough to loosen something deep in my spine.

She'd finally given in. After days of car seats and jolting highways and half-sleeps in strange rooms. No wonder she could breathe easy here. No engines. No gunfire. No tension humming through every wall. Just quiet.

By the time she stirred, I was already leaning over the playpen. She blinked up at me, lashes clumped from sleep, cheeks flushed warm. Her mouth twitched like she might cry, then settled when she saw my face hovering there.

"C'mon, kiddo," I murmured, scooping her up.

The diaper sagged heavy in my hands. My fingers felt thick, slow from sleep, but habit kicked in before thought could. Wipe. Tab. Fresh one snugged into place.

She yawned wide, whole body stretching like she'd been the one carrying the weight of the world.

"Hungry?" I asked.

She didn't answer, just rooted against my shirt while I shook the bottle together. Water sloshed. Powder dusted across my knuckles.

She drank slow. Eyes drifting shut between pulls like she trusted the world again. That trust sat heavy in my chest.

When she finished, she wriggled until I lowered her to the living room rug. Lila kicked hard, fists punching the air. Cooing at the spinning ceiling fan like it was the damn sunrise.

For a second...I almost believed we were safe.

I sank onto the couch, elbows braced on my knees, phone hanging loose in my hand. Blank screen. No word from Mark. The silence chewed at me. Turned the calm of this house into something jagged around the edges. My whole life sat suspended between breaths, waiting for the next swing. Waiting for someone to decide when the hunt resumed.

I thumped her rattle against the rug just to hear something louder than my own pulse. I needed movement. Needed purpose. Needed anything that didn't feel like sitting still while the world lined up its shot.

Bella had mentioned groceries. Said orders could be delivered. I started counting in my head. Diapers, down to a handful. Wipes, scraps. Formula, maybe a day if I stretched it.

Not good enough.

I carried Lila into the kitchen and settled her into the bouncer Bella had dragged out, straps snug against her belly. She kicked instantly, squealing, hands reaching for something that wasn't there.

I pulled open the fridge. Quarter gallon of milk. Two eggs knocking loose in the carton. Butter scraped down to a thin, glossy smear. The produce drawer stuck for a second before I yanked it open. Wrinkled apples. Carrots going soft at the ends. On the counter, the bread bag sagged in on itself. One slice left, curled at the edges.

"Fuck," I muttered.

I grabbed the notepad off the fridge, the pen scratching louder than it should've in the quiet.

Diapers. Wipes. Formula. Milk. Eggs. Bread. Fruit. Vegetables.

My hand kept moving. Faster than I could think. Filling the page like I was trying to outrun something.

By the time I stopped, it wasn't a list. It was weight. A full week of it. Everything she'd been carrying without a word. I leaned back against the counter, letting my eyes move through the room. Pans sat crooked in the sink, soaking in cloudy water. A thin film of grease clung to the air. Crumbs caught the light across the island, scattered and ignored.

I could see her in it. Shoulders tight. Movements fast. Smile stretched thin enough to pass. Just trying to keep everything from falling apart at once.

My palm dragged slow down my face. I couldn't fix the storm Vicky left behind. Not today. Maybe not ever. But I could do this.

I stepped forward, turning on the sink. Hot water surged, steam rising fast as it hit the pan. I could clean a dish. Cook a meal. Take something off her shoulders, even if it was just one damn thing. Give her something that didn't feel like another fight waiting when she walked through that door.

Across the room, Lila squealed, gnawing on a plastic ring until drool soaked a dark patch across her onesie. Her legs kicked like she was cheering.

"Guess we're cleaning today, huh?" I said, watching her grin around the toy.

She giggled, high and bright, like she'd already signed off on the plan. Once I'd decided, I couldn't sit still. I moved.

Her fussing came fast, little fists smacking the toy arch. Her cry climbing sharp until it cut straight through me.

"Alright, alright," I muttered, scooping her up.

Her face was blotchy from the effort, damp with tears, but she quieted the second her cheek hit my chest. The wrap Bella had left sat folded over the chair. I grabbed it, tried to knot the damn thing. The fabric twisted. Slipped. Again.

My jaw locked by the third attempt. On the fourth, it held.

I settled her in, snug against me, her tiny head tucked under my chin. Her breaths slowed into soft, hitching sighs, heat seeping through my shirt. Both hands free.

The day shifted. Still heavy, but workable.

I pulled the notepad closer and started writing.

Finish grocery order. Wash dishes. Wipe counters. Laundry piling by the washer. Prep dinner.

Give Bella one night where she didn't walk into another fight with the clock.

The pen scratched steady in the quiet, syncing with the low hum of the fridge. Action steadied me more than sitting ever could.

The stove clock caught my eye. Wednesday. Bowling night. The memory hit before I could shut it down.

The alley smelled like fryer oil and cheap pizza. That perfect mix of sweat and nostalgia that clung to every league night. Music thumped low overhead. Classic rock. John kept air-drumming between turns like he was headlining instead of waiting on a lane.

Bella was up next, her ball this ridiculous shade of pink she'd picked just to get under his skin.

"Watch and learn, gentlemen," she called over her shoulder, lining up her shot.

"Please," John snorted, already reaching for his beer. "You're about to bounce that thing off the ceiling again."

She shot him a look, tongue caught between her teeth as she swung back and let it go.

The ball clattered down the lane.

Bumper. Then the other.

Then somehow, a sharp ricochet that sent it straight into the pins.

Strike.

Her laugh cut through the alley, bright and unfiltered. "Ha! Who's bouncing now?"

John groaned, slumping against the ball return. "Beginner's luck."

"Keep telling yourself that," she shot back, leaning in to plant a quick kiss on his cheek.

I leaned back in my seat, beer loose in my hand, smiling before I could stop myself.

"Three gutters in a row, John," I said. "You sure you want to talk about luck?"

He flipped me off without looking, already reaching for another ball.

Bella didn't wait. She spun down the lane, arms thrown up in victory. The guys in the next lane cheered her on, and she turned back toward us, flushed and glowing under the flicker of neon, eyes bright and a little wild.

She dropped onto the bench between us, shoulder bumping mine. "You were saying?"

"Pretty sure you cheated," I said, keeping my tone easy, even if something in my chest had shifted half an inch.

She laughed again, breathless now, her hair slipping loose from the clip at the back of her head.

"You can't cheat at bowling, Dean."

"Then how'd you make it look that good?"

She rolled her eyes, nudging my knee under the table.

John didn't notice. He was already lining up another doomed shot, focused on the lane, the noise, himself.

But I noticed.

And right there, under the hum of neon lights and the crash of pins, I saw her. Not as John's girl. Not as the extra seat at league night.

Just Bella. Laughing. Loose. Alive.

That was the night I really saw her.

Twelve years ago. Young. Loud. Alive in a way that filled the room without trying.

The corner of my mouth twitched. I shoved it down and bent back over the list.

Groceries first.

I opened the app, loaded the cart: diapers, wipes, formula, milk, bread, vegetables, meat, coffee, snacks. The total climbed fast, numbers stacking higher with every tap.

Checkout. I punched in my card. Declined.

I frowned. Tried again, slower this time. Declined.

The knot in my chest pulled tight. I shifted Lila higher against me, already dialing.

"Name, please?" The rep's voice was flat, keys clacking in the background.

"Marcus Dean Stone."

A pause. Then: "Your card has been suspended due to suspicious activity."

"Suspended?" A short laugh broke out of me. "I'm trying to buy diapers."

"The system flagged multiple charges in a short span. Until we verify them, your card will remain suspended."

I pinched the bridge of my nose, heat building behind my eyes. "So what am I supposed to do? I need access to my money."

"You may withdraw cash in person at your local branch," she recited.

My jaw tightened. "What about a new card?"

"We cannot issue another card at this time due to the fraudulent activity."

"So, I've got money sitting there, and I can't touch it unless I show up in person?" I exhaled sharp. "Like it's 1985?"

"That is correct, sir."

Silence stretched. I could hear her breathing. Waiting.

I bit down on the next curse, jaw working until it hurt. "That's your solution?"

"I'm sorry for the inconvenience."

The line went dead. I stared at the screen, pulse hammering in my ears.

Against my chest, Lila whimpered. I rubbed slow circles over her back until she softened, her breathing evening out.

"Guess it's just you and me, kid," I murmured, voice rougher than I meant.

Another wall. Another piece of everything I'd built slipping out of reach.

I wasn't about to let Bella see me fall on my face. Not after everything she was already carrying. I dropped the phone onto the counter. It skidded and knocked against the laminate with a dull crack.

"Fine," I muttered. "I'll go to the damn bank."

The grocery order still blinked on the tablet. Total bold. Waiting.

I hit submit. This time it went through. Bella's card flashed across the bottom of the screen.

Her name. Her money. The weight of it landed hard. Shelter. Food. Space I didn't deserve. Patience she hadn't questioned. And now this.

My hand flattened against the counter, grounding, like I could press the guilt down through bone.

I'll make it right. Somehow.

My phone buzzed. Bella.

Running behind. Showings stacked. Might be closer to 5. Everything okay there?

I stared at the message a second longer than I should have. Still thinking about me. Even from the middle of her own chaos. I typed back quick.

All good. Got groceries handled. Take your time.

Sent. The words felt thin compared to what I owed her. I set the phone down and glanced toward the kitchen. Toward the sink and the counters, the list still sitting there.

But right now, there was dinner.

I pulled the fridge open and let the cold air wash over me. The light was harsh against my skin, spotlighting how little there was left to work with. A pack of chicken breasts thawing in their own juice on the bottom shelf. Carrots, soft at the tips, curled like they'd given up. Half a bag of rice shoved into the drawer's corner, grain dust clinging to the plastic. Not much. But I'd stretched less.

Lila grunted in her wrap, a restless little protest. I untangled her and set her down on the rug, the warmth of her body still clinging to my chest. Baby toys sat in a lopsided pile where Bella had left them. I lined them up in a row like soldiers at attention.

She went straight for the stuffed giraffe, smacking its ear until it flopped sideways. A gurgle followed, then a sharp, delighted squeal when the fabric cube crunched under her fingers.

"Yeah, that's better, huh?" I crouched beside her, steadying her when she tipped too far. She squealed louder, legs kicking, arms pumping like she'd just crossed some finish line.

The sound cracked something open in me. Loosened a knot I hadn't noticed until it slipped.

Back at the counter, I grabbed the carrots. Cold water hissed over them as I scrubbed away the dirt, cutting off the soft spots one by one. The knife thunked steady against the board, rhythm filling the silence. Every few seconds, I glanced back over my shoulder.

Lila was fine. Flat on her back, giraffe pressed to her cheek. Eyes bright and mouth working around a half laugh.

"Good job, kid," I muttered, turning back to the board. My hands moved easier now. Cleaner strokes. Scraps falling into a pile I'd deal with later.

I opened the chicken, trimmed away the fat, the blade sliding sure through the slick flesh. A bag of rice waited on the counter. I measured, rinsed, and set it to boil. The smell of starch rose quick, faint but grounding. Steam curled up from the pot, clinging to the air.

The counters would get wiped. The pans washed. Dinner would be waiting when Bella walked in, not hanging over her shoulders like another brick in the load she already carried.

It wasn't much. Hell, it wasn't enough. But today, it would be something.

Chapter Fourteen

SOMETHING WARM

Bella

By the time I turned into the driveway, the sky was streaked pink and gray, the kind of watercolor mess that should've felt calming. It didn't. My body was strung tight. My shoulders ached from the wheel. Teeth throbbing from clenching through traffic. Three showings back-to-back. Three kids dragging their feet at pickup. Three hundred deep breaths I never had time to take. All I wanted was five minutes without someone needing me.

I shoved the door open and froze.

The air inside the house hit me. Not the usual sour mix of stale cereal, dirty socks, and detergent clinging to a load left half-washed. This was...warm. Thick. Rich. Butter browned into something savory. Herbs. Rosemary, maybe, carried through the air. And under it, something sweet. Apples? Or something baking low and slow.

For one second, my brain stalled. This wasn't my house. Not the one I left this morning.

"Mom." Alex's voice snapped me back. He stood in the entryway, one sneaker already kicked into the middle of the rug. His backpack slipped from his shoulder and hit the floor with a thud. His nose wrinkled. "What is going on?"

"I don't know," I said, sharper than I meant. My finger jabbed toward the bag. "But pick that up. You've got homework."

He groaned like I'd asked him to haul bricks upstairs. "I just got home."

"Exactly," I said, voice flat.

He rolled his eyes, grabbed the strap, and stomped toward the stairs, muttering under his breath.

Chloe marched in right after him, already loaded for a fight.

"Daddy's not home yet, though," she announced, chin tipped high like she was delivering testimony. Her backpack bounced against her spine as she clomped upstairs and slammed her door.

The knot tightened in my chest. Always that line. Always the reminder.

I crouched in front of Sam, leveled a look at him without saying a word. He sucked harder on his thumb, eyes wide. Backpack still hanging off one shoulder. He studied me like he was waiting to see if the storm would break, while I slid his shoes off his feet. Then, quiet as ever, he started up the stairs. One step at a time. Careful. Watching. He didn't say a word. He never did when the air felt like this.

The stairwell went still as I reached the second floor. That's when I really looked around.

The counters weren't cluttered with half-empty bowls or sticky spoons. The sink wasn't drowning in pans. The floor looked...clean. And the smell of dinner was everywhere. Seeping into the walls, wrapping around me like a memory of some other house, some other life.

I blinked, my hand tightening on the strap of my purse. I hardly recognized my own home.

The dining table stopped me cold. Not buried under math worksheets and snack wrappers. Not the usual minefield of half-empty water bottles and mail I never sorted. Clear. Polished wood catching the overhead light. Plates lined up on placemats I hadn't seen in months. Silverware placed straight, like we were one of those families who actually sat down together.

Next to it, the baby swing creaked gently, that faint hinge squeak I'd tuned out years ago. Lila kicked, gummy smile stretching so wide it almost swallowed her face. She babbled like she'd been waiting all day for this moment.

And then: my kitchen.

Dean stood at the stove, sleeves bunched at his elbows, shoulders broad under the light. He stirred the pan like it was muscle memory. My counters, which were always sticky, always cluttered, gleamed. Bare except for neat stacks of clean dishes. The smell of herbs, garlic, and rice, layered and rich enough that I had to close my eyes for a second.

For the first time in forever, the house looked livable.

"Hi," I said, cautious, like a guest in my own home. My voice came out small, too small for a space that felt this full.

Dean glanced up. His face didn't break into a smile, not exactly, but something flickered quick and restrained. It tugged at something tight inside me.

I slid my travel mug into the sink, dropped Sam's sticky cup beside it, and stared. The basin was empty. No crusted cereal bowls. No leaning tower of pots and pans from the night before. No rogue spoons buried underneath. Just stainless steel. Clean enough to catch my reflection. I had to blink to believe it.

"MOOOOOM!" Chloe's scream split the ceiling. The window glass almost rattled with it.

My shoulders sagged. "What?" I hollered back.

"I can't find my iPad!" Her feet pounded the hallway like a herd of elephants.

Alex chimed in right on cue. "Mine's gone too!"

I closed my eyes, bracing for impact. Out of the corner of my eye, I caught Dean's mouth twitch, like he knew something I didn't.

I lowered my voice, leaning closer, catching the faint clean scent of soap still clinging to him. "What did you do?"

His reply rumbled low, meant just for me. "The iPads will be found after dinner."

Then, without missing a beat, louder: "Wash up and sit at the table."

Both kids skidded into the end of the hall, staring at him like he'd grown horns. Their eyes flicked straight to me, waiting.

I dried my hands on the towel, slow and deliberate. "Dean made us dinner, so he makes the rules. Do as he says, or don't eat." I shrugged.

Their groans hit in unison. Mutters trailing as they stomped toward the bathroom. Chloe's steps sharper, Alex's complaints dragging longer. The bathroom door slammed, rattling the floor.

"They're pissed," I said, a small smirk slipping through as I hefted Sam onto my hip. His sticky fingers patted my cheek like punctuation.

"I'm sure they are." Dean didn't look bothered. He lifted a pot, steam rising to frame his face, and spooned food onto plates he'd already lined up. Chicken, rice, vegetables. Efficient. Controlled. Like he'd done this a hundred times.

The ease in his movements made it look like he belonged here.

And when he laughed, low and quiet, it slipped under my skin and loosened something that had been wound tight for years. The weight didn't disappear. But for the first time in a long time, it shifted.

"Hi, sweet girlie," I murmured, bending toward the swing. Lila cooed up at me, cheeks pink, fists batting the air like she wanted in on the conversation. I brushed a finger across her cheek. Softness like that should've come with a warning. It hit too deep, too fast.

Sam squirmed down my leg, toddled over to crouch by the swing. His chubby fingers went straight for her toes, tapping at them like piano keys. He giggled at his own music.

"Gentle," I reminded him softly, crouching with him. "She's little."

His eyes snapped up to mine, wide and serious. Then he turned back, patting her foot slow. Exaggerated but careful. Testing the word I'd just given him. Lila squealed, bright and sharp. And for one breath, one fragile moment, the whole house stilled in the best way.

The kitchen wrapped around me in warmth and flavor. My stomach twisted, half from hunger, half from the strangeness of walking into my own house and finding it smelling like this.

I glanced at Dean, the words slipping out before I could second-guess them. "Smells good. Where'd you learn to cook?"

He set a dish of carrots on the table, steam rising in a pale curl. For a second his face softened, but then his jaw ticked. "Here and there. Mostly on my own. When Vicky worked late and I still needed to eat."

Her name settled heavy between us. His voice dropped quieter, rough at the edges. "I just don't understand."

The ache in my chest tightened. I wanted to reach for something to patch the silence, something that would make it lighter, but all I managed was a soft, "I'm sorry. For what happened."

Before he could answer, the hallway shook with pounding feet again.

"Do we have to sit at the table?" Alex asked, hovering in the entryway of the kitchen, that restless edge in his eyes already searching for an escape.

"Yup." Dean didn't even look up from the serving spoon in his hand. His tone left no room to argue. "Pick a seat."

My brows lifted, but I didn't push. Instead I waved Chloe and Alex into place: her on one side of the table, him on the other. Sam's booster I pulled snug against me at the head. The opposite end I left open.

Dean took it like it had always been his.

He carried the food in with a kind of focus I hadn't seen in this kitchen before, at least not from anyone but me. A bowl of rice pilaf steaming. Chicken that looked more like a Sunday dinner than a Wednesday night. And then: gravy. A whole pot of it.

A laugh slipped out before I could stop it. "You made gravy."

He rubbed the back of his neck, a flicker of something almost shy breaking through the steady control. "Figured I should cover my bases."

He set the serving spoons down, his hands hovering a second too long at his sides. His eyes flicked toward me, quick, bracing, like he wasn't sure how this was about to land.

I plated food for the kids on instinct. Sam's meat cut small, Chloe's gravy kept separate, Alex's piled high because he'd devour half and still swear he was starving. Finally, I scooped some for myself.

The first bite made me gawk at Dean. Tender, seasoned just right, the gravy tying it all together like he'd been cooking here for years. I swallowed, heat climbing my cheeks. "This is...delicious."

Dean's shoulders eased the barest inch. Relief flickered across his face so quick I almost missed it.

And then the kids chimed in, loud and over the top, forks clattering against plates. "Yummm," Alex dragged it out, already going in for seconds. Chloe stuffed a carrot into her mouth and muffled hers around it. Sam just banged his spoon against the tray, grinning like it was the best thing he'd ever tasted.

The table filled with noise I hadn't heard in years. The kind that wrapped around you, warm and full. Forks scraped, voices overlapped, laughter slipped in between.

Alex leaned halfway across the table, waving his hands wide like he was summoning an explosion. "And then when you mix the vinegar with the baking soda, it foams up like a real volcano—"

"Does it explode on the desk?" Dean asked, one eyebrow lifted.

Alex grinned, chest puffing. "Yeah. Well, kind of. It runs down the sides like lava, and everyone's like whoa!" He stretched the word long enough to make Sam giggle.

Chloe, chin propped in her palm, sighed like she'd been waiting forever. "At recess, nobody wanted to play my game."

Dean turned toward her, voice even. "What game?"

Her eyes lit instantly, hands flying as she rattled off rules so fast I lost track after the first two. Dean nodded like he caught every word, even adding a, "That sounds tricky. How do you win?" that sent her talking even faster.

Across from me, Sam leaned dangerously sideways in his booster, holding out a carrot toward Lila in the swing. "Bite, baby," he sing-songed.

Lila squealed, kicking her legs until the swing rocked harder. Her gummy smile flashing like he'd just told the best joke in the world.

"Sam, eat your carrots," I said, though the laugh in my throat softened it. He popped it into his mouth with exaggerated drama, chewing loud enough to make Alex roll his eyes.

For once, I didn't mind the noise. I wanted to sit inside it forever. It didn't feel like chaos.

It felt like...us. Like what I always thought my family would sound like.

When the last plates were scraped clean, Dean reached under the table and pulled out the iPads like a magician revealing his trick. "Earned these back," he said, handing them over.

Alex whooped, Chloe clutched hers like treasure, and Sam toddled after them, blanket dragging behind him as he dropped into the pile in front of the TV.

The music from Alexa kept playing, low and steady, softening the edges of the house. Lila fussed once, and I lifted her into my arms. Her cheek warm against my collarbone. She rooted until I guided the bottle to her mouth, her fingers curling tight in my shirt.

"I'll feed her," I said, settling back into my chair.

Dean nodded, already stacking plates. "I'll handle cleanup."

"I can do it," I started, guilt pricking sharp, halfway to standing. "The cleaning, I mean."

"Sit down, Bella." His tone left no room to argue. He flicked water onto the sponge and glanced at me over his shoulder. "You worked all day. I've got it."

I sank back down, the chair creaking under me. Lila's soft sucking was the only thing I let myself focus on. Her small body molded into mine, her breath damp against my shirt.

And I just...sat.

No rushing. No refereeing. No bracing for the next thing.

Just sat and watched Dean's shoulders move steady at the sink, water running, plates clinking in a rhythm that quieted the noise in my head.

By seven-thirty, the counters gleamed. Dishes lined in neat rows like soldiers waiting for inspection. Lila was heavy in my arms, her eyelids fluttering shut, her bottle drained.

"Thirty minutes until bed," Dean called toward the glow of the living room. His voice wasn't sharp, but it carried. Chloe flicked her hand in acknowledgment without looking up, and Alex murmured, "Yeah, yeah," already lost in his game.

I kissed Lila's damp hair and passed her over, reluctant but knowing she needed to be settled. "Here. Daddy duty."

Something softened in his face as he gathered her close. He didn't argue. Just nodded once, her head tucking under his chin like it belonged there, and disappeared down the hall.

I sank into the couch beside the kids, Sam curling into my side with his blanket clutched tight. His small body warm and trusting against me. My muscles loosened into the cushions, my eyes stinging from the relief of stillness.

For the first time all day, I wasn't moving. And I didn't want to.

Sam's soft whine started low in his throat; the kind that always meant he was getting tired. His fists rubbed clumsy circles against his eyes, damp and red from too much rubbing. I kissed the top of his head and pushed myself up, his little body melting against me as soon as I lifted him. One arm looped lazily around my neck, his head dropping heavy onto my shoulder. His soft hair tickled my cheek, warm and sticky with the day. Still clutching his blanket even after a quick wipe-down and diaper change, he rolled right over and snuggled into his pillow the second I laid him in his crib.

"Alright, Chloe." Dean's voice carried across the room as I stepped back in from the hall. Calm. Steady. The kind of tone that didn't rise, didn't demand, but left no cracks to push against. "It's eight o'clock. Your mom's putting you to bed now."

I braced for it. For the drawn-out "nooo," the stomp, the bargaining, the tears. Instead, Chloe slid off the couch, handed over her iPad without a sound, and slipped her small hand into mine.

"Come help me brush my teeth, Mommy," she said, her voice softer than it had been all evening. She tugged me toward the bathroom, her fingers warm and sure around mine.

The breath caught sharp in my chest. My throat tightened around it.

For the first time in a long time, I didn't have to brace for a fight.

When I came back from tucking her in, the living room felt different too. Not quieter. Just...easier. Dean sat on the couch, shoulder to shoulder with Alex, their knees almost touching. He wasn't crowding him, wasn't filling the space. Just there. Present. Alex's voice climbed high with excitement as he launched into an explanation about the game glowing on his screen. His hands moved in wide arcs, mapping out every step, every level. Dean leaned in just enough, nodding at all the right moments, asking a question here and there, like this had always been his place beside my son.

I dropped onto the opposite couch, phone in hand, thumb flicking across the screen without seeing a single post. My attention kept drifting back to the two of them. The way Alex's grin stretched wider the more Dean listened. The way Dean's posture stayed easy, patient, like this was second nature.

After a while, Dean's voice cut through, low and even. "Hey. I know you're having fun, but now it's your turn for bed."

I tensed, waiting. Alex always argued. *Five more minutes, Mom. Just let me finish this part.*

But he looked up, nodded once. "Okay, Dean."

Just like that. No groan. No flop of limbs. No fight. He set the iPad aside, leaned in for a quick one-armed hug, then padded off toward the bathroom.

I blinked, staring. "What did you do to my kids?" The laugh slipped out before I could stop it, tugging at my mouth even as I pushed to my feet to follow Alex down the hall.

Dean only shrugged, his eyes still on the paused screen like nothing unusual had just happened.

But something had.

I lingered in the hallway while Alex brushed his teeth, humming soft between strokes. No fuss. No complaints. No pleading for me to stand there and watch. Easy. Too easy.

And the truth pressed in, sharp and quiet beneath everything else tonight: my children were listening to him in ways they rarely listened to me.

I couldn't tell yet if that left me grateful, or terrified.

Chapter Fifteen

One More Favor

Dean

After Bella disappeared down the hall with Alex, I tossed my phone onto the cushion and pushed to my feet. I couldn't just sit there, not with the weight crawling higher in my chest.

The kitchen waited, quiet except for the hum of appliances, Alexa still thumping out a low beat. My slippers creaked against the tile as I crossed to the counter.

The kids' lunchboxes sat half-open, yesterday's crumbs clinging to the seams. I carried them to the island, wiped them out, and lined them in a row. Juice boxes stacked like soldiers. Apples rubbed clean against my shirt until they shone.

By the time Bella stepped into the doorway, the island looked more like a supply line than a kitchen.

"I don't know what snacks they like," I said, rubbing the back of my neck, heat creeping under my collar. "Didn't want to guess and screw it up."

She stopped short. Her brow pinched, her shoulders dipping like she'd dropped another weight she couldn't name.

"Dean, you don't have to do all this." Her voice wasn't sharp. Just thin. Worn. "This is too much."

I looked at her. Really looked. The dark red strands slipping loose from her ponytail. The tired pull of her mouth. The way her posture sagged like she'd been carrying the whole damn house alone for years.

My chest tightened, and before I could think better of it, I closed the space between us and wrapped my arms around her.

"I know," I murmured.

She went rigid at first, her hands caught between us like she didn't know where to put them. Then something gave. Her forehead tipped against my chest, breath catching uneven before she let it out slow.

I held her there. Steady. Until the pressure in my own chest eased too, like I'd been thrashing in deep water and finally found something solid under my feet.

The grind of the garage door tore through the moment.

She jerked back, arms dropping fast. My jaw locked at the sound vibrating through the house.

John. Earlier than usual. Never good.

It used to happen every Wednesday night. League night at the bowling alley. Bright lights, the crash of pins, the smell of cheap beer and disinfectant. The kind of place that should've felt easy. Fun.

But not for John.

The first sign was always his shoulders. Tight. Coiled. His jaw ticking like something ready to blow. I can still see the way he'd step up too fast, muscles jerking through every motion. The ball would hit the lane, drift too early, and thunk uselessly into the gutter. Again.

"Fuck!" The word would echo down the lanes, louder than the pins. Heads would turn. Bella would wince.

He'd snatch another ball off the rack and spin it in his hands like he could force it to behave. And when it didn't, when it slipped too heavy or stuck to his fingers, he'd slam it back hard enough to rattle the rack.

"Maybe try breathing next time," I'd joked once, trying to cut through it.

He'd shot me a look sharp enough to slice skin. "You mind your own game, Dean."

I remember Bella stepping in, always the one smoothing it over, her voice careful. "John, it's just a frame."

"Yeah?" He'd grab his beer, down half of it as foam spilled down his chin. "You think I don't know that?"

Then he'd storm off. To the bar, or outside, or wherever, leaving her there to clean up the moment. To smile through the embarrassment like it didn't sting. Like she wasn't used to it.

Half an hour later, he'd come back pretending nothing happened. Forced laugh. Glassy eyes. But the rest of us would still feel it, walking on eggshells, waiting for the next frame to set him off again.

Even now, years later, I can still hear it. The crack of the ball against the rack. The low muttering. The sound of him walking away when things didn't go his way.

Same storm. Different night.

When Bella stopped bowling with us, he'd storm out and not come back. Just like tonight.

I looked at Bella. That quick flicker across her face was impossible to hide and told me nothing had changed.

The air thickened, brittle as glass.

The door to the garage slammed hard enough to rattle the frames on the wall. Heavy boots crossed the floorboards, each step landing like he wanted the whole house to feel it. He didn't spare either of us a glance. Didn't look at Bella. Didn't notice the cleared counters, the kitchen smelling like real food instead of pizza.

The fridge door yanked open, bottles rattling. A hiss of caps twisting free. He tipped the beer back, drained most of it in three gulps, throat working hard. The bottle hit the counter sharp, rolled, and tapped the fruit bowl. Without a word, he stomped up the stairs. The bedroom door slammed.

Beside me, Bella let out a breath that sounded scraped from the bottom of her chest. Her shoulders slumped. Her hand dragging up and down her arm like she needed her own warmth.

I shifted closer. My voice came out low. "Want another hug?"

She gave me a look that hovered close to a smile, but it didn't land. "Better not when he's in a mood like this." Her fingers traced down her arm again. A tell I'd seen too many times before. A woman bracing for impact.

"I just have to make their lunches," she murmured, already turning toward the counter.

"Already done." I pushed off the counter, pulled open the fridge. Cold air spilled over my arms. "Well...kind of."

From the shelf, I set down the sandwich Lunchables I'd slipped into the grocery order earlier. Bright plastic packs lined up neat on the counter. "They can start making their own lunches."

Her brow arched, eyes flicking to the stack. A small nod followed, reluctant but real. "That...isn't the worst idea."

She started toward the living room, but paused halfway, her back angled toward me. "Did you get anything figured out today?" The way she asked made my chest tighten. Careful. Like the wrong answer might tip both of us sideways.

I sank into the chair beside her, the wooden edge biting into my palms as I gripped it. "No." My voice scraped out low. "Tried to rent a car. Failed the credit check."

Her eyes widened just a fraction. No judgment. No edge. Just listening.

"I reached out to my old precinct," I went on, words catching rough in my throat. "Got some information back. I think Vicky may have done something. Maybe made me look like a threat. Or at the very least, messed with my identity." I paused, like saying the rest would make it real. “My credit cards are frozen. I’ve got my debit card, but I’m scared to use it. If she’s watching, she could trace it. Or worse...shut it down too.”

The confession left me raw, heavier than when I’d started. My wallet felt like a stone in my pocket. I pulled it free, thumb brushing the worn leather, slid out a hundred-dollar bill. The edges were soft from years of folding.

“Speaking of which. The grocery order today.” I held it out to her, the bill unsteady between my fingers. “I couldn’t get my card to work. I owe you.”

She shook her head immediately, sharp but not unkind. “Stop. You got food for my kids and me. You don’t need to give me money for that.”

“Bella—”

“No.” Her voice stayed firm. Steady, but tired. “Besides, you’re out of work right now. Put it away.”

I wanted to argue. To tell her I wasn’t taking another handout. Not from her. Not when I was already crowding her house, her life. But something in her face, quiet and unyielding, stopped me.

I tucked the bill back. The wallet snapped shut as the sound landed heavier than it should have.

She exhaled slow. Her shoulders eased just a fraction, like she hadn’t been sure I’d listen.

The quiet between us wasn’t sharp. Just heavy. The kind that settles on your shoulders and dares you to speak. I couldn’t tell if it felt better having her know, or worse, knowing she had to carry it too.

John never came back out. Just the drone of his TV bleeding down the staircase, muffled enough to almost forget him. That night, the house felt like it belonged to someone else.

Maybe to us.

Bella tucked herself into one of the dining chairs, legs folded up, scrolling her phone with a thumb that barely moved. I leaned against the island, my own phone in hand, pretending emails mattered. The music had cut off hours ago. All that filled the room now was the hum of the fridge and the occasional creak of old pipes.

I'd been chewing on it all night. The words stuck in my throat like dry bread. Hard to swallow. Harder to spit out.

Finally, I set my phone down and forced it. "Can I ask you for a favor?"

Her eyes lifted, cautious, like she was bracing. "Maybe. Depends on what it is." The corner of her mouth twitched. "I won't be giving you another hug."

I almost smiled. Didn't quite make it. My chest stayed tight, like something cinched around it. "Actually…two favors."

She tilted her head, waiting. Phone loose in her hand now.

I rubbed the back of my neck, heat crawling up under my collar. Saying it out loud felt like giving up ground I didn't have to spare. "I want to put everything in your name until I can clear mine. My assets, accounts, what's left. Just temporarily."

The words landed heavy. Louder than John's TV. Louder than the fridge.

Her brows pulled together. She didn't answer right away. Just watched me, quiet, like she was working through the angles. What it meant for her. What it might drag into her life. Whether I was worth the risk.

My stomach twisted, bracing for the no.

Then she nodded. Slow. Certain. "Yeah. That'll be fine. We can go tomorrow. My first appointment isn't until two."

Relief hit hard enough to make me sway. My shoulders dropped. My lungs finally pulled in a full breath.

She didn't let me sit in it long. "What's the second favor?"

I hesitated too long, chewing on it while pride screamed to keep my mouth shut. But the words burned through anyway. I dragged both hands down my face, stubble scraping my palms. "This is so damn stupid. But...will you rent me a car? I need to be able to get around."

Her reaction was instant. "Shit, yeah." She straightened, eyes widening like I'd just pointed out something obvious. "I didn't even think of that."

No hesitation. No judgment. Just yes.

"After we get your accounts sorted, we'll get you a car," she added, already moving ahead. "You just need to help me get the car seat base into mine."

The knot in my chest loosened, air leaving me slow. My hands unclenched where they'd been tight against my knees.

It wasn't fixed. Not even close. But at least I didn't feel like I was sliding off the edge. And it was because she'd reached out, and held steady.

Chapter Sixteen

Under Bella's Name

Bella

Mornings always felt like a sprint. Shoes jammed onto tiny feet, jackets zipped halfway before somebody wriggled loose. Sam squealed, twisting like a fish, his arms slippery as I tried to catch the zipper with one hand.

Dean brushed past without a word, Lila's car seat gripped in his hands. He clicked it into the base with careful precision, each movement deliberate, like he'd practiced it in his head a dozen times before. No fumbling. No asking for help. Just steady.

Chloe and Alex clambered into the back row and immediately launched into battle. "I called left!" Chloe shouted. "No, you didn't," Alex muttered, already shoving her with his elbow.

"Knock it off. Both of you." I slid the door shut on their faces.

The stroller clanked as Dean hefted it into the trunk. By the time he slid into the driver's seat, his jaw was locked tight, shoulders squared like armor. Too much weight for this early in the morning. Too much chaos that wasn't his.

The car filled with the usual chorus. Sam whining through a half-song. Chloe's chatter sharp and fast. Alex grumbling like an old man under his breath. Lila's coos floated up between them, lighter, like she was singing her own tune.

By the time we dropped off the older two at school: Chloe skipping away, Alex dragging his feet like third grade was a personal attack, the car settled quieter. After Sam was dropped off at daycare, it was just the low rumble of the road and Lila's occasional squeal.

Dean's eyes never left the windshield. Hands locked at ten and two. I glanced sideways, searching his profile for some sign of ease, but found none. My voice felt too loud when I spoke.

"You know," I said carefully, "I can check if daycare has a spot for Lila."

For a moment, nothing. Just the tick of his jaw. Then: "That may not be a bad idea." His tone was flat. Mechanical. "She'll be safer at daycare than with me all day."

The words landed wrong. Not agreement. Not really. More like he'd already decided what he was worth, and it wasn't enough.

My fingers tightened on my bag strap. The unease slid sharp through my chest as we drove on into the day.

The bank smelled of stale coffee and too much carpet cleaner. A sterile hush that made every sound echo. Keyboards clicked. Phones murmured. People whispered like money was a secret they were afraid to say too loud.

Dean's voice cut through it, low but commanding. "I need to close all my accounts and transfer them to her."

The teller blinked, her eyes darting between his squared shoulders and my too-tight hands folded in my lap. "We can just add her to your accounts," she offered quickly, voice wobbling at the edges. "Then take you off. That would be simpler."

"No." His tone carried enough steel that she flinched. "Close them. Open new ones. In her name. And her name only."

Her nails clicked nervously against the keyboard. She wasn't used to this kind of certainty.

I leaned forward, softening my voice. "Maybe we could work with a personal banker?"

Relief lit her face. "Yes, of course!" She flagged down a man in a gray suit. "Dave, would you help this couple with their accounts?"

Couple. The word landed heavier than I expected. My throat tightened, but I didn't correct her.

Dave smiled, all polished charm. "Right this way."

Dean gestured me ahead, his hand hovering near the small of my back. Not touching. Just close enough to feel the heat. I slid into the smaller chair by the wall, leaving the wide-backed one for him. He filled it completely, posture stiff, every line of him wound tight.

Watching him there, shoulders squared like he was braced for interrogation, I wondered if this was what it felt like for him. Not a transaction. A trial.

The glass-walled office felt too bright, too exposed. Paper after paper slid across the desk, the steady scratch of pens filling the silence. Dave's voice carried in a smooth monotone: balances, transfers, closures, new accounts. All sorts of numbers tumbling out one after the other.

I told myself not to listen. To keep my eyes on my folded hands. But the zeros were impossible to miss.

Dean sat solid beside me in a wrinkled sweatshirt and worn jeans, his shoulders dwarfing the chair. His jaw worked tight, like he was holding something back with sheer force. And still, line after line of his life's worth rolled across the desk like it was nothing.

Loaded. The word stuck sharp in my chest.

I pressed my palms flat against my knees to keep them still. My stomach flipped. This wasn't a neighbor dropping off their mail to be collected while they vacationed. This was everything slipped into my name. Every cent. Every account. Trust so heavy it pressed into my ribs.

I couldn't tell if it steadied me...or made me want to run.

By the time Dave set the final stack down, my head buzzed with too much. My hand hovered over the signature line, and before I could stop myself, the words came out.

"Can I get a debit card, please? And I'd like to apply for a credit card too."

Too fast. Too sharp.

Dean's head snapped toward me. Surprise flashed in his eyes, quick and unreadable. But he didn't say a word. Not one.

Dave lit up with professional cheer. "Of course," he said, already typing.

When the PIN forms slid across, I pushed them toward Dean. "You pick them."

His brow furrowed as he bent over the paper. Every number he wrote looked deliberate, his broad hand moving with the same care he used to steady Lila's stroller. His fingers tapped slow across the keyboard for the online setup, each keystroke landing like it carried weight.

The fluorescent lights hummed overhead. Paper shuffled. And I sat there staring at his profile, wondering what it meant that he trusted me with this much of himself.

By the time we stepped out into the sunlight, my head spun. The air felt too bright, too sharp against my skin. I made myself smile, stepping a few paces toward the car.

"Well," I said, forcing a lightness I didn't feel, "thanks for all the money. Good luck with everything."

It came out like a joke, but my laugh cracked thin as I picked up my pace. He caught me in half a stride. His arm slid firm around my waist, pulling me back against the heat of him, his other hand never leaving the stroller handle.

"I don't think so," he murmured, laughter low against my back.

I twisted toward him, still pinned against his chest. "You know I wouldn't do that."

The space between us thinned to nothing. Traffic hummed at the edge of the parking lot, but the world narrowed to the weight of his arm and the stroller pressed steady between us. His eyes locked on mine. Heavy and unreadable, but holding something darker underneath.

"Thank you," he said finally, the words leaving him like he'd been holding them too long.

"You're welcome," I whispered, my throat tight. I tugged him into a hug, and he folded around me. Strong, steady, grounding. His grip never loosened on the stroller handle, like letting go of either of us wasn't an option.

Back in the car, I tore into the little white envelope they'd handed me, the plastic edge of the debit card catching on my nail. It felt heavier than it should've, like the weight of everything we'd signed was pressed into that one sliver of plastic.

I slid it out and held it toward him. "Here," I said, trying for another joke. "Now you can buy food for my kids." The words came light, but my voice snagged, nerves bleeding through.

Dean's chest moved with a quick huff of laughter. Not mocking. More like he saw what I was doing and let me keep the joke.

"And this one." I pulled out the second envelope, holding the credit card between two fingers. "Try not to do any shady shit with this one, okay?" My smile was crooked, tight. Safer to tease than admit what it meant to hand over everything he owned.

His mouth quirked faintly, but his eyes stayed serious. He slid both cards into his wallet like they were something fragile.

Then he started the car, the engine purring steady while my chest buzzed with the weight of it all. Papers signed. Numbers shifted. His life in my hands.

The rental lot shimmered under the late-morning sun, rows of cars lined up sharp, heat lifting in waves off their hoods. Dean crossed his arms, scanning the lineup like every SUV was guilty until proven innocent.

The clerk, all fake cheer, gestured toward a crossover. "This one's ready. Great mileage."

"Too small," Dean said, jaw ticking. He glanced at the stroller propped awkward against the curb. "She's got more gear than I do."

A laugh slipped out before I could stop it. "So, you're saying you need a truck for a baby?"

He shot me a deadpan look. "I'm saying I need something that won't strand us in a snowbank."

Fair enough.

We ended up at a dark SUV near the back. Oversized and shiny. Built for a family of six. Practical. Safe. Big enough to swallow the chaos of diapers, bottles, groceries.

The paperwork slid easy under my name. My license, debit, and insurance. Clean. Quick. The clerk didn't know, couldn't possibly know, what that stack of forms meant.

I signed the last page and pushed the keys across the counter. "You're street legal again," I said.

He looked down at them, then at me. "Thanks to you." Low. Quiet. Like it cost him to say it.

Outside, the heat from the sun clung to my skin while Dean wrestled the car seat base into place. Muscles tight, knuckles white. "These things were designed by someone who hated parents," he muttered.

I laughed, bouncing Lila on my hip. "Or maybe someone who hated dads. Moms figure it out faster."

He shot me a look over his shoulder, mock, not real, and yanked until the strap snapped into place. A smirk tugged at his mouth. "Done."

I eased Lila into the car seat, tightening the straps across her tiny shoulders. She blinked up calm, fists curled like the whole world wasn't shifting under her.

Dean straightened, wiping his palms on his jeans. "I'll run errands. Stock up." His tone was steady, but I caught the flicker under it. The control he was trying to take back.

"I've got a closing," I said, shifting my purse higher on my shoulder. "I'll be at the office the rest of the afternoon."

For a moment, we stood there in the sun between two SUVs, the hum of traffic rolling in from beyond the fence. The distance between us felt like too much, and not nearly enough.

“Well,” I said, forcing a smile I didn’t quite feel, “just don’t do any weird stuff with that credit card.”

He huffed a laugh, real this time, like it surprised even him. “No promises.”

I shook my head and turned for my car. “Be safe.”

“You too.” His gaze followed me until I slid behind the wheel.

In the rearview, as I pulled out, I caught one last glimpse of Dean standing steady beside the SUV, the stroller balanced in one arm, keys in the other.

For a half-second, it looked like it belonged to another life entirely.

Chapter Seventeen

No Trace Left

Dean

The rental SUV reeked of new plastic and whatever industrial cleaner they'd hosed it down with. Sharp. Chemical. Too clean. But under all that, what I smelled was failure. Bella's name sat bold on the paperwork. Her insurance. Even the gas in the tank wasn't mine.

I gripped the wheel, thumb dragging over the stitches in the leather. Gratitude should've been the first thing I felt. It was there, buried deep. But shame rode on top, heavy and sharp, grinding against my ribs with every breath. Forty years old and leaning on a woman who owed me nothing.

A soft coo floated up from the backseat.

Lila.

Her legs kicked at the seat, feet tapping the air like she had her own rhythm going. She gurgled at the toy bar overhead, eyes bright, humming to herself like the whole world was a safe place.

"You don't even know, huh?" My voice came out rougher than I meant. I caught her in the rearview, her tiny fists batting at nothing. "No clue your mom took off and left us behind."

She squealed, a bubble of sound that punched straight through my chest. Oblivious. Safe. Fed. Happy.

My hands tightened until the wheel creaked.

She deserved better than this half-life. And Bella. Fuck. Bella deserved better too. Better than cleaning up my wreckage. Better than carrying weight I should've been able to hold myself.

The brick face of the precinct came into view, solid and square against the sky. Same revolving glass doors, turning lazy like a mouth chewing people up and spitting them back out. My stomach dropped, heavy and sour.

I didn't pull into the lot. Couldn't. I parked two blocks out instead, engine cutting off with a shudder. I sat there, eyes locked on the building, chest tight.

Every car that rolled past made my pulse hitch. Every pedestrian felt like they lingered too long. Watching. My hand hovered over the keys, ready to bail. Run.

But I didn't. I climbed out, pulling a baseball cap low over my head, and grabbed the carrier from the backseat. Lila's weight settled into my arm, heavier than it should've been. Every step toward those glass doors was a fight. Instinct telling me to get the hell out. Duty dragging me forward anyway.

The smell hit first when I pushed inside. Burnt coffee. Paper stacked high. Dust curling off the edges. A faint tang of gun oil clinging to the walls. Phones rang sharp enough to cut. Printers hummed. Somewhere, a typewriter clattered, keeping rhythm with the noise.

Same as always. But standing there, Lila's car seat in my hand, I knew. I didn't belong in this place anymore.

The squad room hadn't changed. Same flicker of overhead fluorescents, same smell of burnt coffee and gun oil. A couple of the old guys looked up when I walked in. Men I'd sweated beside. Men who'd had my back in alleys and on raids. Their eyes caught mine for half a second before sliding away, like they'd seen a ghost. Like I wasn't one of them anymore. Just a shadow cutting through their space.

Lila's carrier bit into my hand, knuckles whitening. She stirred, a soft sigh slipping past her lips, and I adjusted her gently, trying not to show the strain.

That's when I saw Mark. Leaning in a doorway. Phone to his ear. His face carved tight. Figures. Worst timing as always.

His eyes flicked up, locked on me. Brows jumped, then dropped hard. He muttered into the phone, "Call me back," and shoved it into his pocket.

"Dean." My name landed like a verdict. His gaze swept over me, then to the carrier in my hand. "We can't find her."

The bottom dropped out of my gut as he led me into one of the side rooms we used to speak to family in.

"No transactions. No cameras. Not a single hit." He shook his head, jaw tight, shutting the door behind us. "She's gone."

The word burned. Gone. No trail. No crumbs. Vanished meant she'd learned how to disappear.

"Fuck," I muttered, shifting my weight, staring at the floor just to keep my knees steady. "So what? She could be anywhere?"

"Anywhere," Mark confirmed, quiet but sharp. "And she's not alone. Somebody's helping her. High up, if I had to guess."

My pulse hammered. I couldn't hold his stare.

He must've seen the panic building, because his tone softened a notch. "Look, I'll throw you something. A guy I trust. P.I. Keeps his mouth shut. He'll dig." He pulled a yellow legal pad from his pocket, scribbled fast, tore the corner off, and pressed it into my free hand.

I stared down at his scribble. A name. A number. It didn't look like much.

But it was more than I'd had walking in.

We met in the parking lot an hour later. Our cars idled nose to nose, sunlight flashing off windshields. Felt more like a drug deal than a favor.

I pulled the folder from my seat, the one that had been riding around like a stone in my gut, and shoved it across the console. Photos, numbers, scraps of a life I hated keeping but couldn't bring myself to burn. Vicky at her desk. Vicky holding a wineglass, laughing. Vicky smiling a smile I now knew was a goddamn lie.

"This is everything," I said, voice rough. "Last I knew, she was heading to D.C. on a red eye."

The PI flipped through it quick, eyes narrowing under the brim of his ballcap. His fingers lingered on one photo, then he looked back at me. "I'll dig. But you need to hear this. If she doesn't want to be found, you might never find her."

The words cut like glass. Sharp. Final. I swallowed hard, but it didn't go down clean. He wasn't wrong.

We shook hands. His grip was firm. Mine stiff. Too much weight balanced on too little. He slid the folder under his arm and drove off, taillights bleeding into traffic until there was nothing left.

I stayed. Engine off, staring through the windshield at nothing. The rental SUV smelled like fake citrus and failure. My reflection stared back, faint and warped in the glass. Bloodshot eyes. Jaw locked. A man I barely recognized.

If she doesn't want to be found, you might never find her.

The words looped. Over and over. Until they hollowed me out.

A soft gurgle rose from the backseat. Lila, batting at the toy bar overhead, fists flailing, giggling like the world was brand new. Oblivious. Safe.

I gripped the wheel until my hands shook.

None of it made sense. The woman I'd married. The woman who left. The way the pieces refused to fit, no matter how hard I tried to force them together.

Vicky wasn't just gone. She had help. Real help. My frozen cards. The fraud alerts. The joint accounts bleeding out one after the other. Precise. Clean. That wasn't random. That was surgical. Like watching my life carved apart with invisible blades.

I'd chased criminals who thought they were untouchable. Men with clerks in their pockets. Judges on their payrolls. Cops who lost evidence when it mattered. I knew the signs.

And now I was the mark. Boxed in. A rat waiting for the trap to spring.

Even the new card Bella had put in my hand had already pinged when I tested it. That told me everything I needed.

They weren't chasing numbers. They were chasing me.

My mind wouldn't stop racing. Every path I tried to follow twisted darker.

Biker gangs? Too sloppy. They never moved without a green light from the top, and the top didn't move without cash. Big cash.

So, who was paying?

The DA's office? No chance. Too many eyes. Someone would've spotted the leak.

The bikers themselves? No. Vicky was never theirs. She wasn't built for that life.

Which left something worse. Someone bigger. A man who liked a sharp woman at his side, ruthless enough to break rules for him. Someone she could barter with, use her looks, her smarts, any maybe even her body. Whatever currency she had left.

The thought churned in me until bile burned my throat.

"Who the hell are you working with, Vic?" I muttered, knuckles tightening on the wheel until the leather creaked. My fist snapped forward before I could stop it. Bone cracked against the wheel, the sound sharp in the cab.

Lila jolted awake, her thin wail ripping through the air.

"Shit." My chest seized. I climbed into the back seat with her, fumbling the buckle, pulling her out fast. Her little fists clutching my shirt like she'd drown without it. Her sobs hiccupped against my collarbone, damp warmth spreading through the cotton.

"I'm sorry, bug," I whispered into her hair, rocking slow, the motion pure instinct. Her baby shampoo clung faint and sweet to her scalp. The smell tore through me, memory and ache and guilt all at once. "I'm sorry you got dragged into this."

Rage, confusion, fear. They knotted up so tight inside me I couldn't untangle one from the other.

"She's out there," I said to the window, to the dark, to myself. My voice cracked. "And she's got help. Big help. I don't even know how to fight something I can't see."

Her weight shifted against my chest, breath evening out. My heartbeat calmed her, even if mine felt like it was splitting me apart.

"I'll keep you safe," I promised, clutching her closer. The words shook coming out, like they already knew I couldn't guarantee them. "Even if it kills me, I'll keep you safe."

But doubt crawled cold through the cracks.

When she finally drifted back to sleep in the carrier, I couldn't bring myself to turn the key. Couldn't sit still either. My leg bounced hard against the floorboard as I dragged the laptop out from under the seat. Balanced it across my knees, fingers trembling.

Hotspot on. Old passwords tapped out. Each keystroke felt like it might collapse the ground under me. My temples pounded with my pulse.

"Come on," I muttered. "Give me something."

The server page flickered alive. My breath hitched. Hands moved on their own, muscle memory from too many nights chasing leads that weren't mine to chase. Search bar. One name.

Victoria Hayes.

Not blank. Worse. Files sealed tight, red flags stamped all over them. Restricted.

That alone told me enough.

I dug deeper, sliding through back routes I'd built years ago. None of this should still be working. But it did. I'd designed them that way. For nights like this, when answers mattered more than air.

And then I saw it. A buried folder under DA Oversight.

Leave of absence. No memo. Just digital whispers: internal investigation. Words scattered through the metadata like broken glass. Concerns about prosecutorial integrity. Evidence missing. Witnesses unprepared. Cases collapsing under "clerical oversights."

My stomach pitched. This wasn't incompetence. This was surgical.

And the dates. Shit, the dates. The pattern started almost a year and a half ago.

I scrolled faster, jaw clenched until my teeth ached.

The first name on the screen hit like a knife in the ribs. Ramón Calderón.

I read it twice, hoping I'd misread it. But there it was, black on white. The bastard we'd chased for years. The ghost who always slipped through with one "mistake" in the chain of evidence. Lab results gone missing. Witnesses pulling out last minute. Reports with the wrong page, the wrong signature.

Every time I thought luck or slick lawyers saved him; he'd had his people cutting the holes. And now, Vicky was his latest tool.

My fingers froze on the trackpad. Heat crawled up my neck, cold sliding down my spine.

"What the hell did you do, Vic?" My own voice sounded rough in the empty cab.

I scrolled. More patterns. More cases collapsed in ways too neat to be accidents. She'd been trading outs, making sure his people walked light. Maybe even walked free.

And in return? Cash? Influence? Protection? Or worse. Muscle.

The gangs. Calderón had them lined up in his pocket like dominoes. If she'd leaned on him, given him what he wanted in court, he'd send them after me without a blink.

The thought curdled my gut. I shoved back so hard the laptop nearly slid off my knees. My chest burned, sour, like I'd swallowed acid.

The woman I married. The one I built a house and a life with. She hadn't just walked away. She'd been working for the enemy.

Every late night she claimed she was killing herself for justice, she was selling it to the highest bidder.

My palms dragged down my face, rough, shaking. The scream in me had no way out.

"How far back does it go?" My throat scraped raw around the words. "How much of us was real? Was Lila just another chip on your table?"

I slammed the laptop shut. The screen went black, and there I was staring back, eyes wild, jaw trembling. A stranger.

She hadn't just betrayed me. She'd sold me out.

I don't know how long I sat there, watching my reflection swim in the dark glass. Betrayal circled me like wolves, teeth sunk deep. How many late nights were lies? How many fights just smokescreens? How much did I swallow whole because I was too goddamn in love to see it?

The dash clock ticked forward in red numbers, each one another minute bled away. Shadows stretched across the lot until the SUV felt like a box sealing shut.

Then Lila's scream cracked it all. I jolted, knee slamming the wheel. She thrashed in the carrier. Fists tight. Face scarlet. The sound raw enough to slice me open.

"Okay, okay, baby girl," I rasped, fumbling the buckle. My hands shook like I'd never held a child before, but once she was against me, her heat seared through the cold. "I hear you. I'm here."

Her cries filled the cab, leaving no space for anything else. No room for my poison thoughts. Just need. Just her.

I tore at the formula bag, spilling powder across the seat and water down my jeans. Clumsy. Twitching. Still, the bottle came together. Warm enough. Cap tight.

She latched hard, pulling at it like she hadn't eaten in days. The sound of her gulping, the hiccups softening into hums, hit deeper than any bullet ever had.

I leaned back, eyes shut, clutching her small body tight. Her heartbeat fluttered against my chest, fast and steady, the only anchor I had left.

"Alright, bug," I whispered, kissing the damp crown of her head. The sweetness of her shampoo cutting through the sour in me. "We've got to get you home. Bella will be back soon."

When she calmed, I buckled her in slow, checking each strap twice like it was the only mission that mattered. The laptop went into its bag with a snap loud enough to make me flinch.

Back in the driver's seat, I turned the key. The engine roared, steady and alive, even if I wasn't.

I didn't have answers. Didn't have a plan worth a damn. Only her. And the vow I wasn't sure I could keep. I had Lila. That meant quitting wasn't an option.

Vicky wasn't just gone. She was in the system, pulling strings from places I couldn't reach. A license. A keystroke. She could choke me out without ever stepping into a room.

Heat crawled up my chest, shame folding into rage until I couldn't tell one from the other. Rage at her for gutting me piece by piece. Rage at myself for letting her. For being so goddamn blind.

The wheel rattled under my grip, the fury with nowhere to land.

Then from the back seat, soft babbles. Lila's feet drumming against the carrier straps like she was kicking out her own rhythm. That light, easy sound split me wide open.

I used to be the man who built houses from lumber and nails, who dragged killers off the street, who carried his own weight without thinking. Now I couldn't buy diapers without borrowing someone else's name. Worse. I'd dragged Bella into it. Her cards. Her insurance. Her kids under the same roof as me. If Vicky traced that? If she decided Bella was leverage? I'd painted a target on a family that deserved anything but this.

I shoved the gearshift into drive and let the streets swallow me. No plan. No destination. Just stoplights bleeding green to red. Brick and glass sliding past in a blur I didn't register. By the time I cut the engine on a side street, my hands were trembling so bad I had to breathe slow to steady them.

I climbed into the back again, unbuckled her. Lila's small body curled into my chest, heat seeping through my shirt. Her damp breaths soaking the edge of my collar. My arms tightened until she squeaked in protest, and I eased, rocking without thinking.

"I'll keep you safe," I swore against her hair, voice breaking rough. "Even if I lose everything, you'll be safe."

The words scraped raw out of me; a promise I wasn't sure I had the strength to keep. But saying them to her was the only thing stopping me from falling apart right there in the dark cab.

Chapter Eighteen

Music in the Kitchen

Bella

By the time we rolled into the driveway, my body felt hollowed out. Groceries sliding in the back. Kids bickering in one breath, laughing in the next. Sam's cheeks still sticky from whatever neon snack daycare thought passed for an afternoon treat. John's car sat parked in its spot like a warning sign. Dean's car was nowhere to be found.

I sighed as the older two dumped their backpacks and sprinted up the stairs for their iPads, blue glow washing over their faces before I even shut the door. Sam wriggled loose from my arms and toddled straight for the small couch, climbing up with his sippy cup like he owned the place.

Friday. I didn't have it in me to fight them about screens.

I dropped my bag on a chair in the kitchen, tugged my earbuds out of my purse, and let a riff of guitar pour in. The first sip of wine all week slid sharp down my throat, warm in my chest. Groceries lined the counter: half-smashed granola bars, bottles of Gatorade, like I had some kind of system. Dinner would be stir-fried beef with rice. Quick, filling, and enough for leftovers.

Knife steady on the board. Onion peel sliding free. Oil popping in the pan. I swayed with the music, the small rhythm shrinking the day to something I could hold.

Then a voice threaded through, muffled past my earbuds.

"Guys, I got some stuff for Lila to play with. Want to help me put it together?" Dean's voice cut through my thoughts. The words startled me. One bud slipped to my shoulder.

Dean stood in the entryway of the living room, car seat in one arm, plastic bags dangling from the other. Calm on the surface, but I saw the ringed shadows under his eyes, the jaw clenched too tight. He looked worn down to the bone.

"Yay! Baby play!" Sam squealed. His iPad clattered onto the recliner, forgotten. He tugged at one of the bags, chanting, "Presents! Presents!"

I couldn't stop the laugh that broke out, sharp and sudden in my throat.

Dean's mouth twitched into something softer. He handed Sam the lightest bag like it had been meant for him.

"I'll help," Alex said, pushing himself up before anyone asked. He grabbed the heavier bag, shoulders set, face serious like he'd just been assigned guard duty.

Chloe didn't move from her seat. Neither did John. Her eyes glued to the tablet; his to the TV. The glow lit their faces, both tuned out.

I turned back to the stove, knife heavier now, the onion sting sharper than before. My eyes blurred, and I told myself it was the fumes.

Dean settled cross-legged on the rug, instructions spread, plastic pieces spilling across the floor. Alex crouched beside him, snapping parts together with quiet pride. Sam clapped at every click, shouting, "Again! Again!" like they were building magic instead of a play gym.

Dean steadied the pieces, patient, letting them lead. When he finally laid Lila on the mat, she squealed so loud it cut through the whole house. Arms windmilling, legs kicking toward the toys overhead.

The sound snapped Chloe's head up. She slid off the couch, tablet clutched tight, but edged closer until her finger brushed Lila's toes. The baby's foot kicked back. Chloe giggled, bright and surprised, like she'd been caught off guard by joy.

"Sam, gentle," Dean murmured, low but firm. Sam froze, then stroked Lila's hand softer. Dean turned to Alex. "Keep an eye out, yeah?"

"Got it!" Alex puffed up like a soldier taking an oath.

And for a moment, the house didn't feel so heavy.

The onions hissed loud enough to drown my earbuds, so I almost missed it when Dean stepped into the kitchen. I caught him in the corner of my eye as he rolled his shoulders like he could shrug off the day, though the tight line of his jaw said otherwise. He leaned against the counter, close enough I could feel the heat of him. Not touching but there.

"More wine?" he asked, nodding at my half-empty glass.

I tugged the earbuds free, placing them on the counter. "Sure."

His gaze flicked down at the phone. "What are you listening to?"

"Nothing you'd like." The smirk came without thinking, because I could already picture him wincing.

"Try me," he said. There was a spark in his voice that didn't match the exhaustion written all over him.

I slipped one bud out and held it toward him. One tap and the bass rolled heavy through the kitchen: Cliché by Machine Gun Kelly.

His brows lifted. Then, to my absolute horror, he started nodding along. Stone-faced. "I like this one."

I barked out a laugh so sharp it bent me over the counter. "Liar."

He didn't crack. Just reached for the bottle, poured the last splash into my glass, then crouched at the little fridge. He came back up with another bottle, turning it in his hand like he was debating.

"That's the sweet stuff," I warned, still chuckling.

Too late. He'd already filled the glass to the rim. One swallow and his face twisted so hard I nearly dropped the spatula. He bolted for the sink, gagging loud enough that I doubled over with laughter.

"That's not wine," he sputtered, spitting foam down the drain. "That's liquid sugar."

"I tried to tell you!" My cheeks ached from grinning. I grabbed the glass and drained half with a dramatic hum, just to make him scowl. "More for me."

He shook his head, but the corner of his mouth tugged upward anyway. "You're insane."

"There's a Chardonnay in there," I pointed out, nodding at the fridge. "Or beer, if you want to be boring."

He grumbled, but the smile lingered. Crooked and warm, like maybe he'd forgotten himself for a second.

The air felt lighter, not thick with chaos or silence, just...easy.

Dean moved beside me, stacking plates and setting the island like he'd always known where everything lived. I stirred the vegetables into the pan, steam curling around my face. The scent of garlic and soy sauce cutting through the kitchen. From the living room, Sam's high voice narrated every noise Lila made. Chloe muttered at her screen. Alex corrected her like he always did. John stayed planted in the recliner, bathed in the blue glow of the TV, as if none of us existed.

I reached for the stack of plates out of habit, already bracing myself to serve everyone in the living room, when Dean's hand brushed mine. Just enough pressure to stop me.

"Guys, dinner's ready," he called, voice steady, carrying through the whole house. "Come get your plates."

I froze. The words weren't mine, and the room felt off-balance because of it. But I didn't argue.

Chloe wandered in first, dragging her feet but grabbing a plate without complaint. Alex followed, eyes darting to Dean with something quick and bright before piling food onto his plate. Sam needed help. Of course. Dean crouched, filling his little dish, handing off the sippy cup like it was second nature.

Dean poured the juice without asking, diluting it with water the same way I always did. He didn't even pause before sliding the pink tumbler to Chloe, the blue to Alex, the dinosaur sippy to Sam. I hadn't told him. He just knew.

"Alex, can you carry the cups?" I asked, my voice softer than I meant.

"Sure!" He balanced them all, proud of himself as he marched out.

John's plate sat untouched on the counter. I left it there. Not tonight, I decided.

Instead, I filled mine and slid onto the chair at the island. Dean sat beside me, steady and quiet, and for the first time in weeks, the kitchen didn't feel like a battlefield. It felt like maybe we'd reclaimed a corner of it.

For a few minutes, I let myself believe the quiet might last. Forks clinked against plates as the kids actually ate without complaint. Music hummed low from the headphone speaker. A rhythm I could've lived in forever.

Then John's voice ripped through it. "Where's my food?"

The fork froze halfway to my mouth. My stomach tightened hard, like someone had pulled a knot behind my ribs.

"Right here, come get it," Dean answered before I could open my mouth. Not sharp. Just flat.

The recliner groaned, then footsteps thudded across the floorboards. John filled the entryway a second later, red creeping up his neck. He grabbed the plate so fast the fork rattled against ceramic.

"Don't you tell me what to do in my house," he snapped, glare cutting past me like I'd wound Dean up myself.

Dean didn't blink. "The least you can do is come get your food when someone's cooked it for you."

My throat closed up. The air went brittle in an instant. John's sharp, accusing stare landed on me again. He slammed his plate down on the counter before he turned on his heel.

Upstairs, the bedroom door shut hard enough to rattle the frame.

Silence bled into the space he left behind.

I stabbed my fork into the rice, chewing hard. Jaw tight enough to ache. Irritation burned in me, messy and tangled. John for being useless. Dean for lighting a match in a house already primed to blow.

Dean's chair scraped faintly as he leaned against the counter, elbow braced, filling the quiet with his weight. I kept my eyes on the green bean I'd skewered, like chewing bland greens could keep me from saying something I'd regret.

Then his arm slid into my line of sight. The brush of his sleeve was careful, deliberate. My phone scraped lightly across the counter toward me, earbuds trailing loose. One still hung from his ear, catching a glint of light.

"Let's get the music back," he murmured, low, like the words were meant only for me. His thumb tapped the screen.

The bass pulsed back through the speaker, Steady, familiar, the same track from before. He let it fill the space, head bobbing lightly to the beat. The faintest smile tugging at his mouth like nothing had just detonated in this kitchen.

I let out a slow breath. Not forgiveness. Not relief. Just a loosening, like a valve cracked open.

From the living room came the rise of laughter: Alex cracking up, Chloe pretending not to join in, and Sam squealing over both of them. Normally the noise would've grated after a day like this. But with the music weaving through it, their sounds braided together into something softer, something almost warm.

Dean leaned back in his chair, quiet, letting it all wash over us. His presence didn't press, didn't demand. It just held.

And for the first time all evening, I wondered if maybe the night didn't have to collapse completely. Maybe, just maybe, this moment, this atmosphere could hold.

Chapter Nineteen

The Recliner

Dean

Guilt sat heavier than the beef in my gut. I knew what I'd done. I'd poked John, shoved right where I knew it would sting. Part of me had wanted it, the explosion. Watching him rot in that recliner while Bella ran herself ragged. Yeah, it ate at me until my skin itched. But the look on her face when he stormed off? That wasn't thanks. It wasn't relief. It was exhaustion, and maybe a slice of it aimed at me too.

When I offered to handle dishes, she flicked her wrist, already stacking plates.

"Go," she said, bumping me with her hip without even looking. "Play with Lila. I've got this."

I opened my mouth, fork still in my hand, ready to argue. But the slope of her shoulders was warning enough. Don't push. Don't make it worse. So, I didn't.

Lila fussed in her swing. Legs kicking like she was trying to launch into orbit. Fists swiping at the toys overhead. I scooped her up, her tiny body curling instantly into my chest, cheek hot against my shirt. The soft sigh she made rattled right into my sternum.

"Alright, crew," I called toward the living room, voices and iPad glow bleeding across the room. "Who's gonna help me play with Lila again?"

Sam's head popped up first, hair wild, eyes round. "Me! Baby play!" He scrambled down so fast he almost face-planted over his cup, laughing when he caught himself.

Alex tugged one earbud free, tilting his head. "What kind of play?"

"The toy kind," I said, nodding at the mat we'd pieced together earlier. "She needs teammates."

That was all it took. He slid off the couch, grin wide, and jogged over like it was his job.

Chloe didn't budge. Tablet clamped to her chest. Chin down and wall firmly in place.

Sam plopped cross-legged beside me, shaking a rattle with both hands. "Vroom vroom!" he yelled, like it was a race car instead of baby gear.

I couldn't help but laugh. "Easy, buddy," I said, crouching. "She's small. Try letting her grab it."

Sam froze, wide-eyed, then held it out slow. Lila latched clumsy onto the handle, fist tight. Sam's whole face lit up. "She likes me!"

"She's grabbing," Alex corrected, smirking, but his grin matched the pride in his brother's. He dangled the crinkly cube above her toes. "Bet she kicks this."

Lila squealed, legs pumping until the cube wobbled.

That noise cracked Chloe's armor. She slid closer, still pretending her tablet mattered more, and poked at Lila's toes. Lila kicked back, harder. Chloe giggled, quick and bright, before ducking her head like she hadn't.

"Good job, Lila," she whispered, quiet enough like it wasn't for anyone else to hear.

I leaned back against the couch, arms folded. Just watching. Sam's laughter, Alex's commentary, Chloe's secret smiles, all tangled with Lila's high-pitched squeals until the room hummed with a life I hadn't stepped into in years.

For the first time in too long, I didn't feel like an intruder. I felt in it. In this life I had once imagined for myself. And Vicky...

At some point, John drifted back out of the bedroom and sank into his recliner, eyes fixed on the TV like the rest of the world didn't exist. The low murmur of the game filled the room, broken only by the squeak of the kids' toys against the hardwood. He didn't look at us. He didn't look at me or at the mess of blocks scattered around our feet. His plate sat cold on the end table, steam long gone, a fork balanced on the edge where he'd left it an hour ago.

Sam's laugh burned out mid-giggle, dropped straight into whining. He rubbed his fists into his eyes and kicked at my leg, then shoved the rattle like it had betrayed him. Up, down, twisting sideways, no clue what he wanted. Just restless. Code was clear: bedtime.

From the kitchen, Bella caught it without even looking up. She let the rag slide off the counter and came over, sigh soft but heavy enough to carry.

"Come on, buddy," she murmured, scooping him off my lap as if she'd done it a thousand times. He melted into her, thumb already moving toward his mouth. By the time she slipped out of the living room, his head was tipped against her shoulder, lids sagging.

I stayed on the rug with Lila. She was still flailing at the toys above her head like she was winning something big. Chloe had migrated to the recliner, face lit blue by her iPad, head resting against John's arm. He was out cold, mouth open. Snores sawing through the cartoon voices blaring from her screen. An empty beer bottle sweated on the end table.

Bella came back, face tighter than before. She didn't glance at Chloe. Didn't glance at John either. But her jaw flexed as she passed, and I felt it anyway. The irritation coiled sharp. Still carrying what I'd stirred up earlier. Still pinning it on me. And I didn't blame her.

Words gathered in my throat: an apology, an excuse, something. But Lila squealed, high-pitched and demanding, and I bit it back. Wrong time.

"Alright, bug," I whispered instead, lifting her off the mat. She curled into me right away, cheek hot against my chest. "Your turn."

In the kitchen, I rocked her with one arm and reached for the formula with the other. The faucet hissed steady as I filled the bottle.

Bella reappeared, setting Sam's sippy on the counter. She stopped when she saw me scooping powder, one brow cocked.

"You got it?" she asked. Not skeptical, just worn thin.

"Yeah," I said, keeping it even. "I'll make her a bottle."

She held my gaze for a beat, unreadable, then gave a short nod and drifted back down the hall.

I leaned against the counter, bouncing Lila gently. Her fussing sharpened at the sound of water running, fists curling into my shirt like she thought she could climb inside me. By the time the bottle warmed, and I pressed it to her mouth, she latched hard. Her whole body loosening in relief.

The kitchen fell quiet with just her sucking and the hum of the fridge. John's muffled snores leaked in from the living room. All I heard was silence. Peaceful, even if it didn't belong to me.

I let myself breathe with it, holding on to the weight of her, the simple truth of keeping her fed, alive.

When Bella returned, I tried to lighten the mood, tilting my head toward the recliner where Chloe was curled into her dad, iPad glow washing her face. "Not fighting with Chloe tonight," I muttered, aiming for half a smile.

She didn't bite. She stopped wiping for half a second, her hand pressed flat against the counter. Then her eyes lifted to mine, flat and frayed. "No. On the weekends, she's his to deal with."

The rag started moving again, harder this time, like she could scrub a hole straight through the granite.

I shut my mouth. Didn't need a second invitation. Message was clear enough.

Later, when I laid Lila in the pack-and-play, she went soft the second her head touched down. One hand curled against her cheek, tiny breaths puffing steady. Her bottle slid from her lips, only half-finished, but she'd had enough. Out cold.

I stayed leaning over the rail, arms locked, staring at her chest rise and fall. Making sure. Maybe just needing to see that something in my life could still be that simple.

When I finally pulled myself away, the house felt different. Quiet. Too quiet. Not the kind that meant peace, but the kind that pressed in heavy from every wall.

Bella sat at the dining table, glass of wine within reach, her iPad propped up. Fingers tapped quick against the screen; her brows drawn into a sharp crease. The look of someone building a wall one keystroke at a time.

"What's up with you?" I asked, easing into the chair across from her.

"Work," she muttered without looking up. Her pink manicured nails clicked against the glass as she took a slow sip.

I pulled out my own iPad, fired it up. Files, screenshots, notes from the PI in my email. Every dead end staring back like a bad joke. Bank notices. Frozen accounts. Vicky's name stamped over everything like graffiti I couldn't scrub off.

The glow stabbed at my eyes. My temples throbbed. I typed a line of notes, deleted it. Tried again. Deleted that too. Nothing stuck.

Across from me, Bella scrolled, face washed in the cold blue light. I could see her jaw tighten every few seconds, like whatever she was reading was grinding her down grain by grain.

"Do you ever stop?" I asked before I could think better of it.

Her eyes flicked up, quick and sharp. "Do you?"

That shut me up. My thumb hovered over the screen, words blurring together until I couldn't tell one from the next.

By the time the frustration hollowed me out, I knew I'd lost whatever thread we'd had earlier. The small pocket of ease between us was gone, slipped somewhere between the dishes and the silence.

So, I quit pretending. Locked the screen, leaned back, and let the weight of it all press down.

The blank screen blinked back at me, smug as hell. Every search I ran circled the same drain. No new leads. No cracks in the wall. Just my own reflection in the black corners of the glass. My jaw ached from grinding; the inside of my cheek raw where I kept worrying at it. I squeezed the iPad hard enough the case gave a low groan.

Across the table, Bella scrolled like her life depended on it. The glow from her iPad carved shadows under her eyes, lit the tight line of her mouth. She tapped, typed, sipped what was left in her glass, then did it again. Locked in.

I stared too long. Waiting for her eyes to flick up, even once. For a spark of recognition that I was still sitting here. For proof the walls she carried weren't thick enough to shut me out entirely.

Nothing.

The knot under my ribs pulled tighter, sharp enough I had to swallow hard just to breathe around it.

"Goodnight," I said finally, pushing back from the table. The legs of the chair screeched across the tile, louder than I'd meant, like the sound was demanding an answer.

She didn't look up. Just hummed a distracted goodnight, more reflex than anything, and kept scrolling. Fingers moving. Eyes locked on her world, not mine.

I stood there for a beat longer, hoping she'd lift her head. Hoping for something.

Nothing came. So, I walked away. Left her with her glass, her screen, and the weight she carried alone. And now mine stacked on top.

And as I stepped into the hall, the thought landed brutal and clean, no room to dodge it: maybe she didn't have space for me in her world. Not now. Maybe not ever.

Chapter Twenty

BEFORE SUNSET

Bella

I didn't realize how late it was until the numbers on my iPad blurred. The glow stabbed into eyes that felt gritty, lids heavy, shoulders locked from hunching forward too long. Friday night, and instead of relaxing, I was still buried in listings and emails, chewing through tasks like the weekend didn't exist.

When I finally lifted my head, the house was silent. Too silent.

Chloe had slumped sideways on the recliner. Her iPad tilted against her knees, screen dark where the battery had given out. Alex sprawled on the couch, mouth open, arm dangling limp toward the floor like he'd just melted there.

I sighed, a long, heavy sound that scraped its way out of me. No point in waking them. I pulled a couple of throw blankets from the back of the couch. Draped one over Chloe's shoulders and tucked the other across Alex's chest. They stirred, small shifts under the fabric, but stayed asleep.

The kitchen felt dim, washed in the faint blink of the dishwasher's light. My half-empty wine glass sat abandoned by the sink, the lipstick smudge along the rim faded to a ghost of itself. I rinsed it clean, slid it into the bottom rack, and pressed the start button. The machine hummed to life, filling the silence with a low, steady rhythm.

One by one, I clicked off the lights until the house dipped into shadows.

Upstairs, my bed waited. Empty, but at least quiet. I climbed in without brushing my hair and without anything except the hope that maybe sleep would come fast enough to crush the weight still sitting heavy in my chest.

It didn't.

I lay on my side, eyes fixed on the faint glow of the alarm clock across the room. The green numbers changed slower than they should. My body sagged into the mattress, pulled down by exhaustion, but my mind spun in circles.

Dean had been quiet today. Distant. I guess I had been too. We'd circled each other all evening, careful and polite. Like two people carrying boxes through a narrow hallway, close enough to touch, but making damn sure not to.

At least he was all set now. A car. Accounts he could use. Even if it was really my name stamped on the paperwork. A way to move without leaning on me for every step. Independence was what he wanted. And well, I needed him to have it. I needed one of us to be steady. One of us to be okay.

The thought looped and looped, my jaw aching from the way I clenched against it. I flipped my pillow over, pressed my face into the cool side, eyes squeezed shut.

Eventually exhaustion dragged me under. But it wasn't peace. Sleep came heavy, and restless, like my body refused to loosen its grip on the tension knotted tight in my chest.

The weekend blurred. The kids barely lifted their eyes from their iPads except to poke at Lila's toes or shove a bottle into her mouth like they were performing some grand service. I didn't fight them on it. Screen time wasn't the hill I had the energy to die on.

I just kept moving. Laundry baskets scattered across the hall. Clothes sorted into piles; too small, too stained, or too worn to keep. Dust clung to my hands from under Chloe's bed. Sam's side of the room looked like a toy bomb had gone off with blocks and dinosaurs covering every inch. By evening the house smelled of detergent and lemon cleaner, and my lower back burned from bending too long.

John was gone most of Saturday. I didn't ask where. I don't even know when I stopped asking. The house ran smoother without him, and that was all that mattered.

After lunch on Sunday, with Sam and Lila both down, Dean leaned against the counter and nodded toward the door. "Let's get the big kids outside before they forget what the sun looks like. It's a warm day for March, might as well use it."

Alex groaned like we had suggested manual labor, but he laced up his sneakers and threw on his jacket anyway. Chloe dragged her tablet halfway to the door until I raised an eyebrow. She dropped it on the couch with a scowl.

Out on the lawn, they tossed a ball back and forth. Dean kept half an eye on them, jogging to chase down the wilder throws. I crouched on the porch, picking up planters after the winter and brushing dirt off the steps with my palm.

My head kept slipping into lists. The mower hadn't run since last summer. The chainsaw sat in the shed, broken. Bushes at the end of the drive blocked the view every time I backed out, and soon they'd be thick with spring leaves. The whole place looked tired, like the kind of house neighbors whispered about when they passed.

Maybe if I got on top of it this summer, trimmed the yard and fixed what was broken, it would look less like a battlefield. Maybe.

"Whatcha thinking about?"

Dean's voice came from the edge of the porch. He had the ball tucked under one arm, sweat darkening the collar of his shirt even with the chill in the air. Behind him, Alex was chasing Chloe in lazy circles. Both of them laughing between shouts.

"Nothing," I said too fast, dusting my hands against my jeans. "Just making a list in my head."

He didn't move, just tilted his head like he could wait me out.

"The mower needs fixing," I admitted. "Chainsaw too. And the bushes at the end of the driveway. Soon I won't be able to see when I pull out."

Dean chuckled, low and easy. "Those don't sound like 'maybe' things. Those sound like 'when' things."

I shrugged, eyes on the dirt under my nails. "Maybe."

The word hung heavier than I meant it to. I settled into the cold lounge chair and watched my kids move without screens in their faces.

The screen door creaked a while later, and Dean stepped out with Sam draped over his shoulder. The kid's hair stuck out every direction, his cheek still blotchy from sleep.

"He woke up asking for you," Dean said, lowering onto the step beside me. "Lila's still out."

I reached for Sam, but he turned his face deeper into Dean's shirt, chasing the warmth, thumb already tucked in. Dean smirked, patting his back like he'd been doing it his whole life.

I let it be.

We sat there, the three of us. Quiet on the porch while Alex and Chloe tore across the dried-up grass, their laughter carrying bright down the street. The sun pressed warm against my shoulders. Sam's weight steady against Dean, and for once I didn't feel the urge to get up.

For once, stillness didn't feel like failure.

Chapter Twenty-One

ICE CREAM BEFORE DINNER

Dean

Two weeks in this house and every night feels like the same loop with different meals, but the same rhythm.

Bella moves like she's running a drill. Bags down, hair pulled back, stove on before her shoes are even off. I hover by the counter, trying to wedge myself into the pattern, but she waves me off before I get a foothold.

"Go play with Lila," she says, hip bumping the drawer shut while she grabs plates.

"I can set the table," I offer, already reaching.

"I've got it." Her voice is even, not sharp, but final enough that my hand stalls midair.

And I would back off, pull juice from the fridge instead, pour it into cups the way I've memorized. Pink for Chloe, blue for Alex, and a dinosaur sippy for Sam. By the time I set them down, she's already sliding food onto plates like she's clocking in for another shift.

The kids sprawl on the couch, iPads glowing. John doesn't budge from the recliner, TV throwing shadows across his face. Not one of them moves until Bella puts food in front of them.

"Thanks, Mom," Alex says sometimes, soft, like he knows he's the only one who thinks to. Chloe barely looks up. Sam just digs in. John doesn't say a damn word. Just takes the plate she sets on the side table like it's owed to him.

I stand there, my jaw locked so tight it aches, watching her shoulders sag the second she turns away. She doesn't complain. Doesn't even roll her eyes. Just lets out that tired little sigh she thinks no one hears.

I dry the pans while she scrubs, try to cut Sam's food smaller when she's juggling too many things, but she still brushes me off. "Dean, it's fine. Don't worry about it."

"It's not fine," I mutter once, low enough that she almost doesn't catch it.

Her hands pause in the sink water, soap dripping off her fingers. She glances over her shoulder, eyes flat with exhaustion. "Please. Just—don't."

I swallow it down. Step back. Because pushing harder would only add to the weight already grinding her into the ground.

But sitting there, watching her carry it all while the rest of them just wait, it kills me. Sadness knots in my chest until it feels like I can't breathe. Anger burns so hot I have to press my nails into my palms to keep from lighting the whole damn house on fire with a single word.

And underneath all of it, the thing I can't shake is the hopelessness. Because no matter how much I want to take the load from her, she won't let me. She keeps me on the outside, reminding me I don't belong here, that I'm just passing through.

But standing by while she breaks herself? That feels like its own kind of betrayal.

By the time Bella pulled the chicken out of the oven, I'd already made up my mind. I wasn't letting her carry dinner alone tonight.

"Hand me that," I said, nodding toward the pot of rice. She hesitated for half a beat, then passed it over. One by one, I set the dishes on the table: rice, roasted chicken, vegetables. Steam fogging the air, the smell sharp and savory.

"Guys, dinner's ready," I called, picking up Lila and shifting her higher against my chest so I could feed her too. She rooted at the bottle, mouth open, fists batting until I steadied the nipple for her. "Go wash up."

I expected groans, bargaining for "five more minutes." Instead, I heard the shuffle of feet, the quick rush of water at the sink, and the thump of cabinet doors. Then they came back, sliding into their chairs without protest.

"What the fuck," John muttered, finally glancing up from the recliner, TV glow cutting across his face. "I am not eating at the table."

"That's fine," Bella said quickly, steadying Sam as he climbed into his booster.

"Nom nom," the little guy crowed, clapping when he saw the mound of rice. His grin made the tightness in my chest ease for a second.

I dropped into the chair beside Bella, balancing Lila against me, bottle steady in her mouth. She curled her hand into my shirt, sucking like the world depended on it.

"You don't have to wait for me," I murmured to Bella. She gave me a soft nod and slid into her seat.

Alex plopped into place, already piling rice onto his fork. Chloe lingered, then took the chair next to him, leaving a space open on her other side.

"Daddy, sit next to me!" she sang out, bright and hopeful.

John didn't move. His glare cut straight through the table, sharp enough I felt it in my jaw. "No."

One word. Cold. Final.

Chloe's smile collapsed. She dropped her eyes to her plate, fork dragging through the broccoli without lifting a bite.

Bella leaned in, her voice wrapping around the silence like a blanket. "Hey, Chloe-girl. You want chicken first or rice?"

"Chicken," she mumbled, not looking up.

Bella served her quick, filling the space John had left gaping.

I clenched my teeth, the words burning the back of my throat. Every muscle in me wanted to snap, to throw something across the room just to wipe that glare off his face.

Instead, I sat there, jaw locked with anger pounding steady in my chest.

Lila's bottle went dry, and her lashes already heavy, so I slipped from the table and carried her down the hall. Quick change, fresh sleeper, and a kiss pressed to her warm forehead. By the time I laid her in the pack-and-play, she'd curled her fist under her chin and sighed herself to sleep.

I was halfway back when I heard it.

"Where's my food?" John's voice cracked sharp through the house.

"Your plate is right there," Bella answered, even as stone.

"Daddy, here," Chloe said, her voice small, but hopeful, tapping the spot next to her again.

A hard exhale, then the word: "No." Something clattered, and then Chloe's sobs tore through the air, high and broken.

I froze just outside the entryway, my hand fisting at my side.

Bella was already moving, scooping Chloe into her arms. She didn't say a word, but the glare she cut at him from over her daughter's head was sharp enough I felt it.

John scraped food onto a plate like it was an insult, muttering loud enough for everyone to hear, then stormed back to the living room. The recliner cracked, the TV blared, and his voice followed. "Jesus fucking Christ."

I swallowed hard. My jaw ached with the effort of holding still.

When he stomped back in for a fork, Bella had Chloe settled again, smoothing her hair with a hand that shook once before steadying. Chloe sniffled, staring at her plate. Sam was oblivious, face buried in rice, humming to himself.

I stepped into the kitchen finally, keeping my voice steady. "You guys didn't have to wait for me."

No one moved. Plates sat untouched, except Sam's. They'd been waiting.

Bella caught my eye, gave me a small smile that didn't quite reach her eyes, then shook her head just enough to say, not now.

I let it go. After picking up the chair John knocked over, I slid back into my seat, pretending not to hear John cursing through the wall.

We started eating like nothing had happened. The scrape of forks, clink of glasses, and Sam babbling through a mouthful of rice. Chloe's blotchy cheeks still wet but calmer now, poking at her broccoli.

I leaned in, elbows braced on the table. "So," I said to Alex, "who's your best friend at school these days?"

He blinked, surprised. "Ethan," he said finally, chewing. "We play basketball at recess."

"Basketball, huh? Are you any good?"

He smirked. "Sometimes. I can't dribble, but I'm good at blocking."

"That's the fun part," I said. "Nobody likes getting blocked."

Bella glanced over at him, a faint smile tugging at her mouth before she went back to her plate.

I turned toward Chloe. "What about you, boss lady? Who's your best friend?"

She straightened; voice quiet. "Maya."

Bella's brows lifted like she hadn't heard the name before.

"What's Maya like?" I asked.

"She's funny. She has pink shoes. She shares her cookies with me."

"Cookies?" I grinned. "What kind?"

"Chocolate chip."

"Smart kid," I said, winking.

Sam banged his spoon against the tray. "Snack!"

"What's your favorite snack, Sam?" I leaned close.

He scrunched up his face, thinking hard. "Goldfish. And gummies. And...chips!" He slammed the tray with the last word.

Chloe giggled. Alex rolled his eyes. "He just likes everything."

I laughed too, shaking my head. "Fair. Can't argue with that."

From the other room, the recliner groaned again as the game announcer yelled at nothing. John was stewing. I could feel it, like static in the air.

But none of us looked his way. We just kept talking.

Bella asked Alex about his science project, and he lit up describing the model volcano again. Chloe showed me how she dipped broccoli into her rice like it was some five-star trick. Sam smeared food on his cheek until I tucked a napkin under my chin and copied him, which set him howling.

It wasn't perfect. But it was close to something that mattered.

And if it drove John insane? Good.

Plates sat half-finished, the kids shifting in their chairs, yawns breaking through bites. Bella set her fork down with a quiet clink.

"Alright," she said, voice gentle but firm. "You're excused."

Chairs scraped and silverware clattered. Alex and Chloe bolted for their iPads, Sam toddling after them with rice still on his cheek. A few minutes later their faces were lit by blue glow again, the house sliding back into its usual hum.

I stacked plates while gathering cups sticky from juice. Bella lifted the serving bowls, her wrist brushing mine as she passed them. No words, just a rhythm. Rinse, stack, wipe, close the dishwasher. For the first time all night, we moved together.

When the counters were bare and the sink finally quiet, she tugged open the freezer. A small smile tugged at her mouth. "We picked up ice cream today."

I cocked a brow. "Ice cream?"

She smirked, pulling out the tub. "Yeah. I figured they earned a treat."

Bowls clinked soft against the counter. Two scoops each, a quick drizzle of chocolate syrup, as sprinkles rattled against ceramic. The sweet, cold smell hit as she balanced them on a tray.

"Alright," she called, carrying them into the living room. "Ice cream for everybody."

The cheer that followed shook the walls. Sam nearly dove face-first into his bowl, chocolate smearing his cheeks within seconds. Alex dug in like he hadn't eaten dinner at all. Even Chloe cracked a smile, quiet but real, spoon tapping against the bowl as she went after the sprinkles first.

I leaned in the doorway, arms crossed, watching the three of them light up over nothing more than sugar. Bella sank onto the edge of the couch, her shoulders finally unclenching. Her laugh soft when Sam shoved a spoonful too big into his mouth and sputtered through it.

And tonight, the house didn't feel so heavy.

Chapter Twenty-Two

If He Disappeared

Bella

I left Dean in the living room with John and the bigger kids, steering Sam down the hall toward the bathroom. His little hand was sticky in mine. His hair damp with sweat from running laps around the couch after all that sugar.

The second the bathwater started, he lit up. "Shark's gonna get you, Mama!" He shoved the plastic shark across the surface, kicking his legs so hard water slapped the sides of the tub.

I gasped loud and dramatic, jerking my hand back. "No, not the shark!"

He dissolved into giggles, sliding under until only his eyes peeked out. "I'm hiding!"

"Not from that shark, you're not," I teased, tickling his ribs until he squealed.

We kept it up until his fingers wrinkled like prunes. By the time I wrapped him in a towel, he was humming to himself, eyelids drooping while I rubbed lotion into his legs. Pajamas zipped up and blanket tucked around him, he was half-asleep before his head even hit the pillow.

"Today was a happy day, Mama," he murmured, voice soft as a sigh.

My chest pulled tight. "Good. I'm glad, baby." I kissed his forehead, brushed curls from his face. "Love you. Sleep now."

"Love you, Mama," he whispered, rolling to his side.

The lull of his music filled the room, soft enough to melt into his breathing. I stood there a moment longer, letting the quiet settle in, before I slipped out and pulled the door shut.

Back in the bathroom, I rinsed out the tub and started the water running again. Steam curled against my arms, fogging the mirror, and filling the space with damp heat. Over the rush of the faucet, I caught voices carrying down the hall: John's sharp, low rumble. Dean's steadier reply.

The sound slid into the bathroom like smoke. My stomach clenched. I shut the faucet off and dried my hands.

"Chloe, bath time," I called, stepping back into the living room, pretending not to notice how quiet John and Dean got.

Her head shot up, iPad forgotten. She scrambled off the couch so fast she nearly tripped, bare feet slapping the hardwood as she bolted past me. If there was one thing Chloe loved more than clinging to John, or her iPad, it was bath time.

The door clicked shut behind us, but the voices kept rolling from the living room. Only John's rumble and Dean's even tone. The words didn't carry this far. Maybe that was for the best.

Chloe slid into the tub with a dramatic sigh, arms draped over the porcelain like she was settling into a throne.

"Don't drown in there, Your Highness," I teased, pouring water over her hair. Warm rivulets streamed down her back, and she squealed, tipping her head for me.

I worked the shampoo into her scalp, suds puffing up into a foamy crown. She giggled, shaking her head so bubbles slid down her shoulders.

"Snow!" she crowed, spraying foam from the soap pump into her palms, and clapping until it splattered across the tile.

I laughed in spite of myself, even as my knees soaked through against the mat. For a second, it was just her laughter, not the rumble of voices threading through the walls.

When the water cooled and her fingers pruned, she sighed again, resigned this time. I bundled her in a towel, rubbing her hair until it fluffed around her pink cheeks. Nightgown over her head, brush through her damp strands, and she was off, darting straight down the hall.

Her giggles reached me before I caught sight of her again, curled against John's side in the recliner. He didn't look down, but she beamed anyway, pressing herself closer.

I lingered in the hallway too long, listening. Then I exhaled and turned toward the couch. Alex was sprawled out, thumbs flying across his tablet with his brow furrowed like he could ward me off by sheer will.

"Bud," I said, leaning against the armrest, "bath or shower?"

"Neither." His eyes stayed glued to the screen.

I opened my mouth to push, but Dean spoke first from the chair. "Showers are better anyway. In and out in five minutes." His voice was easy, like it was just a fact of life.

Alex froze mid-game, thumb hovering over the screen. He looked at Dean, then back at me, gave the smallest nod. "Shower."

Relief slid out of me before I could stop it. I shot Dean a quick look, lips quirking. He didn't say anything, just nodded like it wasn't worth noticing.

"Alright," I said, nudging Alex's shoulder. "Grab a towel and clean clothes. Let's go."

He groaned, but he followed me down the hall. By the time he came back out, hair damp and skin smelling faintly of soap, the scowl was gone, replaced with quiet focus on his game again.

I brushed his shoulder with my hand as I passed, catching Dean's eye. "Thanks," I murmured.

Dean just dipped his chin, like it was nothing.

"Do you want to go shower too?" I asked, keeping my voice low.

"Yeah," he said, pushing to his feet. His size filled the space different than John's. Solid and steady, without trying.

I dropped into his seat once he disappeared down the hall, sinking back beside Alex. The game flickered on the TV, Alex muttering his commentary under his breath as he tapped furiously at his tablet.

I nodded along, but the noise blurred. My mind wandered. Back to the sound of Dean's voice steadying Alex, to John's silence brewing heavier in the corner, and to the fragile balance tipping through this house.

By the time Dean came back out, the living room had settled into a strange quiet. John was slumped in the recliner with his mouth open in the kind of heavy sleep that came with too much beer. Chloe was curled in his lap, tablet sliding from her hands as her head tipped against his chest. The game flickered on the TV, voices low but insistent.

Alex was the only one awake. His thumbs tapped quickly across his screen, eyes glued to the glow.

I stretched, setting my phone down. "Guess it's my turn," I said, patting Alex's leg as I stood.

Dean crossed the room at the same time, and we brushed shoulders in the narrow space between the couch and coffee table. The scent hit me before I could move past. Sandalwood and clean soap, warm and sharp, clinging to him like heat. His short hair, starting to grow out, was still damp. T-shirt sticking in places to the hard lines of his chest. Sweatpants slung low on his hips.

For one dizzy second, the house fell away. My skin prickled, heat crawling up my neck. I looked up, just long enough to meet his green eyes. He looked worn down, dark circles shadowing beneath them, but steady. Always steady.

I forced myself to move, padding down the hall before my thoughts could catch up.

In the bathroom, steam swallowed me whole. I twisted the knob and let the water pound against my skin, tilting my head back until it drenched my hair and spilled hot down my shoulders. Soap slid slick across my arms, bubbles swirling down the drain, but my chest didn't lighten.

Vicky crept in, uninvited.

She always arrived late.

Vicky Hayes. Back then still "the girlfriend," not yet the wife. Clicking her way across the sticky floors of the bowling alley in heels that didn't belong anywhere near a lane. The air smelled like nachos, cheap beer, and shoe spray, and she looked like she'd stepped out of a boutique catalog, not a Thursday night hangout.

Like she'd taken a wrong turn on the way to somewhere better and hadn't realized she could leave.

Her hair was perfect every time. Platinum blonde and glossy, twisted up like she was on her way to a cocktail party instead of league night. Lipstick just dark enough to look intentional. Not a smudge on her.

I used to wonder how long she sat in front of a mirror before showing up, how much time it took to look that untouched. Or if it just came naturally when you didn't actually do anything once you got there.

We'd already be a few frames in by the time she showed up. John would look up from the scorer's table, always polite, always that half-smile. Dean would whistle low, half admiring, half trying to show her off.

And she'd wrinkle her nose, her voice smooth but sharp. "God, it's freezing in here. How do you people stand it?"

You *people. Like we were a category.*

Dean would offer his jacket, puffing up, and she'd drape it over her shoulders like she was humoring a child. The rest of us: me, John, the rest of our team and even some of the regulars, pretended not to look.

"Want a drink?" John asked once, trying to be friendly.

She gave him that quick, dismissive smile, the one that never reached her eyes. "I don't really do beer."

Of course you don't. Wouldn't want to risk looking like the rest of us.

"Water's fine," John said, already half annoyed that she wasn't joining in.

She'd take a seat at the edge of the booth, legs crossed, scrolling through her phone while we bowled. She didn't cheer or laugh when Dean guttered three in a row. She didn't even flinch when John teased him for it. Just kept flicking her thumb across the screen, like we were all background noise.

Like Dean was background noise. And he never seemed to notice. Or maybe he did, and decided she was still worth it anyway.

At one point, I tried to draw her in. "Do you bowl much?"

She looked up, one eyebrow arched. "Not really my thing." Her eyes flicked from my lane shoes to my ponytail slicked with humidity. "But you all seem...comfortable."

There it was. Not even subtle.

I smiled anyway. Tight. "Yeah. It's kind of the point."

Comfortable. Like it was something to be embarrassed about. Like choosing to be easy in your own skin was a flaw instead of a luxury.

By the time she finally got up to take her turn, after Dean all but begged her, she held the ball like it was contagious. Walked up to the line, flicked her wrist, and sent it spinning straight into the gutter.

John bit back a grin. I didn't. "Wow," I said before I could stop myself. "Impressive aim."

Her head turned, eyes narrowing just enough to make it clear she'd heard the bite. "Well," she said, smile slicing across her face, "not everyone spends their Wednesday nights in places like this."

Not everyone.

I felt it land. Not just on me, on all of us. On the noise, the laughter, the cheap beer, the stupid little league that gave people something to look forward to at the end of a long week.

On the kind of life she'd never understand.

"Yeah," I said, quieter this time, but not softer. "Some of us like it."

She didn't respond. Just turned, her heels clicking against the floor like punctuation, and walked off. Dean followed her to the bar without hesitation. Of course he did.

John just watched them go, quiet, a muscle ticking in his jaw.

And I remember thinking, even then, even before everything fell apart, that she wasn't just out of place here. She didn't want to belong.

I remember thinking then, as I lined up for my next shot, that whatever world Vicky lived in that it wasn't one built for nights like ours. And it sure as hell wasn't one built to last. She'd always felt...wrong. Cold. Out of place. Like she wanted to be seen but never to belong. Like belonging was something beneath her.

I pressed my palms against my eyes, water beating down harder. Maybe she'd been like that all along. Maybe none of this was new. Dean's haunted stare or the wreckage trailing him. Maybe it had just been waiting.

Waiting for the right moment to crack open.

By the time I shut the water off, I swore I wouldn't give her another inch of my headspace tonight.

I wrapped myself in a towel, steam still clinging to my skin. After quickly getting dressed in capris and a tank top, I padded back down the stairs. Each step closer to the living room tightened my chest again. Back to the noise. Back to the weight.

When I came back into the living room, hair damp and slumped over my shoulders, the first thing I noticed was the recliner. Chloe wasn't curled up on John anymore. My stomach dipped.

"Where's Chloe?" My eyes darted across the couches, half expecting her tablet glow to give her away.

"She's in bed," Dean said, steady, like that was the most ordinary answer in the world.

Alex looked up from his game, grinning. "And now it's my turn." He slid the iPad into Dean's hands with all the seriousness of passing a torch. Then he hopped up, grabbed his toothbrush on the way up the stairs, and called, "Goodnight!" like he didn't need prompting.

I stopped dead in the middle of the rug, staring at the quiet around me. Ten o'clock on a Friday and no battles. No bargaining for five more minutes. No tears. Just...done.

"Seriously." I turned toward Dean. "What did you do to my kids?"

He shrugged, casual. "Told them they better be in bed before Mom got out of the shower."

"That's it?" My voice tipped somewhere between disbelief and amusement.

"That's it." Not quite a smile, but the crinkle at the corners of his eyes gave him away. His gaze lingering just a second too long, taking me in before he looked back down at the iPad in his hands.

Before I could answer, Lila's sharp, urgent cry cracked through the baby monitor. My body moved on instinct. "I'll get her," I said quickly, already crossing the room. He only nodded.

She was thrashing when I reached the pack-and-play, face blotchy, fists balled tight. "Hey, hey, sweet girl," I whispered, lifting her close. Her heat sank into me as I rocked her against my shoulder. Her sobs tapering into uneven hiccups as she settled into the warmth of my skin.

Back in the kitchen, I balanced her on my hip, one hand fumbling for the formula. Scoop. Shake. Test against my wrist. The bottle warmed in seconds and she latched with a desperate little sigh, her body easing as the milk pulled her under.

The lights had been dimmed while I was gone. Dean's doing, no doubt. Softer now, shadows stretching easy across the counters. Even John's snores from the recliner sounded dulled under it.

I sank into a chair, cradling Lila in the crook of my arm and tossing a blanket over us. Her tiny fingers curled into my shirt, her jaw working slower now, relaxed.

Dean leaned against the counter, arms folded, watching quietly. The tired lines carved into his face looked deeper in the low light, but his presence was steady. Solid. The house felt almost... peaceful.

Dean's eyes cut toward the recliner, to John sprawled in it, head tipped back, snores rattling through the room. His voice came low, steady. "How often does this happen?"

"Most nights for the last year or so," I said, easing back in the chair, propping a pillow under my arm and Lila. Her lips smacked greedily at the bottle, the rhythm pulling me into that familiar lull. "I fight the kids into bed, then I get everything ready for the morning too."

Dean's jaw flexed, the muscle ticking once before he spoke. "You shouldn't have to do everything by yourself."

"Maybe not." I tipped the bottle higher as I felt Lila's little fingers press into my chest, her lashes trembling as she fought sleep. "But I'm their mom. It's on me to make sure they're okay. Even if that makes me the bad guy sometimes."

He exhaled, a sound caught somewhere between a laugh and a groan. "For what it's worth, you don't run this place like a war camp." His mouth tugged into a small, crooked smile. Something rough around the edges but real.

When the bottle went slack in her mouth, I shifted her upright, patting gently until a burp popped out. Her head lolled against my collarbone, the soft powdery smell of baby lotion rising off her skin. She felt too light. Too breakable. I traced a finger over her tiny fist, quieter now.

"She's small for her age." A beat. "Takes after Vicky, I guess."

Silence stretched. Maybe I shouldn't have mentioned her name.

Then his feet scuffed against the floor, the faint scrape of wood telling me he'd stepped closer. His hand brushed the back of the chair, so close I could feel the heat of him at my shoulder.

"You deserve more than this," he said quietly. The certainty in his voice hitting deeper than the words themselves as he ran a finger across my shoulder.

My hand stilled on Lila's back. The air thickened, charged making my chest heavy.

He didn't move, not really. Just lingered there. His presence wrapping around me, close enough that every breath reminded me he was still right behind me.

"She's almost asleep," I murmured, though it wasn't the thing I meant to say.

Dean leaned in, just enough that his shadow fell across me. The space between us shrank to nothing. Then his hand shifted. Slow, deliberate. His fingers brushed against mine on the armrest, light as a question. He paused there, waiting.

I should've pulled away. But I didn't.

His hand slid over mine. Warm. Not a grab. Not a claim. Just a squeeze. Small, but enough to tell me he meant what he'd said. That he saw me. That he hated what I carried alone.

I stared at our joined hands, his large fingers wrapping easily around mine. Lila's soft breaths rising and falling against my collarbone. My heart pounded so hard I was sure the sound filled the space between us.

He could've done more. Tilted my chin. Closed the distance. But he didn't. He just stayed there. Restrained. Careful.

"You deserve more than this," he murmured again, barely above a whisper, like he was afraid the words would shatter if he pushed too hard.

I wanted to look at him. Man, I wanted to. Instead, I kept my eyes on Lila. On the tiny curl of her fist against my chest, pretending that was what anchored me.

His thumb brushed once across my knuckles before he pulled back. The absence was sharper than I expected, a sting I hadn't braced for.

Silence stretched until it felt like a wire ready to snap. Then his voice cut through.

"Hey."

"Yeah?" My voice came out quieter than I meant.

"I need to tell you something."

My stomach tightened. I knew the moment was over as I looked up at him. "Okay..."

He raked a hand down his jaw, eyes flicking past me before settling again. "Whatever Vicky did, she completely fucked with my identity. Even me being here is dangerous."

The words dropped heavy, and I held Lila tighter as her tiny fist pressed into me like she could feel the shift in the air. "Dean, you're scaring me."

"I need to make Marcus Dean Stone disappear," he said, sitting down, elbows braced on his knees.

I blinked, confused. "Who's Marcus?"

"Me." His laugh came short, humorless. "My real name. After my father. I hate it. And him. So, I've always gone by Dean."

Relief slipped out before I could stop it. "Oh. Okay. That's all?"

Even as I said it, I knew it wasn't.

He shook his head, leaning closer, voice low. "My friends at the station can wipe me clean, set me up with new papers, and a new trail. But it means changing how I look."

"Like what?"

"They said I should grow my hair out. Well, I guess I already started that," he said, running his hand through the short stubble on his head.

"I should wear brown contacts, so I don't stand out." He hesitated, almost sheepish. "The problem is, I've got a lot of grays in my hair now."

I bit my lip, fighting a laugh. "That's what you're worried about? Dean, they make dye for that. I can help you."

His eyes flicked to mine, open and vulnerable in a way that made my chest ache. "So, you think I should do it?"

"If it keeps you safe, yeah. Absolutely."

He went quiet, then I asked softly, "What about Lila? Does she get a new identity too?"

"It'd be safer," he admitted.

That answer settled heavy. Final.

"That's fine," I said. "Pick a new name for her too."

His gaze drifted toward the baby, her lashes fluttering against her cheek as she drifted deeper into sleep. "Luna," he said finally, almost shy.

"Luna." I repeated it, softer this time, the name sitting strangely warm in my chest. "I love that."

His shoulders eased, the tension loosening in his frame. "Then maybe I should put Luna to bed."

He slid her carefully into his arms, fingers brushing against me as he lifted her. His knuckles skimmed the side of my breast, so light he didn't even seem to notice. Heat shot through me all the same, sharp and immediate. My body stiffening before I could control it. I told myself it didn't mean anything. That he hadn't even felt it.

When he came back out, the air between us felt charged again.

"I think you need to sell your house," I blurted, sharper than I intended. "If Marcus is gone, everything tied to him should be too. You've already handled the accounts. All that's left is the house."

He let out a dry laugh. "Good thing I know a good realtor."

The tension cracked, and I laughed too, the sound rough but real.

After a while, I shut off the kitchen light and headed up the stairs. John's snores rumbled from the recliner, but I didn't bother looking at him. Dean had already disappeared into the guest room. The dishwasher hummed steady, the house otherwise quiet.

In my room, I slipped under the covers, the mattress sinking around me in its familiar grooves. Sleep didn't come easy. My mind spun.

That house. He'd built it, every inch shaped by his hands. Too modern for me. All glass and sharp edges, but it was what Vicky had wanted.

Of course it was. Vicky.

Her name still burned when it crossed my mind. How do you rebuild with someone who detonated your life and vanished into smoke?

I stared at the ceiling until my eyes blurred, the thought circling heavy and unrelenting, a weight I couldn't set down.

Chapter Twenty-Three

Before Victoria Hayes

Dean

The kitchen was dead quiet once Bella disappeared upstairs. John's snoring rattled from the recliner, uneven and loud. A sound that made my jaw clench. The fridge hummed, clicked off, hummed again. I sat at the island with a glass of water sweating against my palm, staring at the dull reflection of my face in the granite.

I should tell her.

Every piece of it. The frozen accounts. The PI's warnings. The DA file buried deep in the system. Calderón's name surfacing again and again like rot through floorboards. She had a right to know. She deserved to know what kind of danger she'd let into her home when she opened the door to me and Lila.

No, actually, it's Luna now.

The name settled strange in my chest. Too soft for everything circling us.

But I kept seeing her face tonight. The slump of her shoulders. The way she still carried everything and still managed to hold it together. I couldn't stack my wreckage on top of hers. Not now.

I dragged both hands down my face, fingers digging into my scalp. On the monitor, Luna shifted with a soft rustle, then silence. That tiny sound hit harder than any badge I'd ever worn, sharper than any oath I'd sworn.

Secrets pressed against my ribs, tight enough to choke me. Pride, fear. Maybe both. Saying them out loud would make them real, and I wasn't ready for that. I moved to the couch, hoping to loosen the tightness in my chest.

The ceiling shadows blurred while I stared too long, until the soft creak of a door cut through. Bare feet padded down the hall, paused like she was second-guessing, then carried on.

"I can't sleep," she whispered.

John didn't stir. His head lolled back, TV glow washing his slack face. She didn't look at him. She looked at me.

Before I could speak, she crossed the room and sank onto the couch beside me. Not at the far end. Not with space between us. But right beside me, her arm pressed to mine. A quiet sigh slipped from her chest, her head tipping until it rested against my shoulder. Like she'd decided I might do what the dark couldn't: calm her.

I pulled a blanket off the back of the couch to cover her bare legs tucked underneath her. I shifted without thinking, my arm coming around her shoulders. Reflex. She leaned into it, settling against me as if she'd been holding herself upright all day just to finally drop here.

I noticed her bare skin under my palm. I should've pulled away. I didn't. Instead, I traced small circles with my thumb, slow passes up and down her arm.

She was warm. Soft. Real in a way I hadn't let myself touch in too long. Too easy to forget what this was. Too dangerous to let it feel like anything else.

The air thickened. Charged. Each breath she let out brushing my chest. My heart thudded hard enough I was sure she could feel it.

I should've stopped. Pulled back. Said something. But I didn't want to.

The TV muttered low in the background, some late-night commentator I couldn't even follow. John's wet, rattling snores cut through it. The baby monitor glowed faintly on the table beside us. None of it mattered.

All I could feel was her. Bella leaning into me. Her head against my shoulder. Her arm under my hand. My thumb moving slow and steady. Like if I just kept that rhythm, I could quiet the weight pressing on both of us.

And maybe because I needed the touch just as bad.

She let out a soft breath, almost a sigh. I felt it against my shirt more than I heard it. My chest tightened, heat climbing up my throat.

"You okay?" I asked, voice low, careful not to wake anyone.

She nodded against me, a small, tired motion. "Yeah. Just... feels easier like this."

The words landed heavy. My hand stilled, then started again. Slower this time, tracing the curve of her arm. I wanted to tell her I felt it too. That being this close was the first thing that had made sense in weeks.

Then John snorted awake for half a second, coughed, and sank back into his guttural snore. The sound cracked through me like a warning shot. My breath hitched. Muscles locked tight. What the hell was I doing?

I stared across the room at him sprawled out, empty beer bottle on the side table, TV flickering against his slack face. Ten feet away. And here I was, with his wife leaning into me like I had any right.

My gut twisted. Once, not too long ago, I'd called that man my friend.

We were teammates on Wednesday nights at the lanes. Same cracked neon lights. Same beer-soaked air. Same terrible playlists looping from the jukebox. We weren't very good, but we made a show of it. Traded jabs over gutter balls, clinked glasses after half-decent frames, and laughed about nothing until our sides hurt.

Back then, I thought he had it figured out. John Turner: a steady job, fancy car, pretty wife, and a few kids who ran to him when he walked through the door. A house that buzzed with noise and warmth. He had the kind of life you measured yourself against. The kind that made you wonder where you'd gone wrong.

I used to watch him between frames. The way Bella leaned into his side when she laughed. The way his kids waved from the snack bar when she brought them by. And I'd think—that's it. That's what I want. Not the trophies or the paycheck. Just that easy kind of belonging.

Funny how time shifts everything.

Now when I think about those nights, about the glow of the lanes and the echo of pins falling, it doesn't feel like friendship anymore. It feels like a ghost of something I never really knew. Because the man I thought had it all was already losing it. I just couldn't see it then. Maybe he couldn't either.

And maybe that's what stings the most. Not that he fell apart. But that I ever believed he wouldn't. Maybe I'd been jealous from the start. Jealous of the life I thought he had. Jealous of her.

Bella shifted slightly. Closer, like she hadn't felt me go rigid. My hand was still on her arm, warm against her skin, holding on when I should've let go.

The guilt burned sharp. Hot enough I almost moved. But the darker truth pressed harder: I didn't want to.

Bella shifted against me, her head lifting from my shoulder. She'd felt the way my whole body had gone stiff.

"What's wrong?" Her voice was quiet, but it hit sharp, cutting through the hum of the TV and John's snores.

For a second, I almost said nothing. Let her rest her head back down. Let the moment pass. But the words pressed too hard in my chest.

"I've been digging," I said finally, rough in my throat, trying to shift my focus to anything but how close she was to me.

Her head turned just enough for me to see her eyes in the blue wash of the TV. "Digging into what?"

I rubbed the back of my neck, heat prickling there. "Into Vicky. Into why she ran, and what's been circling me since."

Bella straightened more, pulling back just enough that my arm dropped uselessly to my side.

"What did you find?"

I blew out a breath. "I don't think she just walked away. I think she's tied up in something bigger. I've known Vicky for a long time, and she's never chosen to take a leave."

"Right, not even after having a baby," she nodded, remembering the fight she witnessed about maternity leave when she came to visit Vicky.

"But there seems to be one constant name." I paused, not sure how much I should be telling her.

Her brows pinched. "A name?"

"A kingpin," I said. The bitterness scraped in my mouth. "Big enough to buy gangs, big enough to put a hit out on me with one call."

Bella's face shifted. First confusion, then recognition, then fear. "So, you think she's been protecting him. Covering for him."

"I think so." I nodded once, sharp. "Right before we got pregnant, things started changing. She pushed for the house, pushed for control. I thought it was about family. But I think she was already tied to him. Maybe even working for him."

She leaned away further, her arms crossing tight over her chest. "And those guys who came after you?"

"His muscle," I said flatly. "She had the power to freeze my accounts and screw with my credit. A lot of people owed her favors. But the boots on the ground? That's him. His people don't stop until they're told to."

Bella sat all the way upright now, putting space between us. Her knee bounced against the edge of the couch; her arms cinched tighter.

"So, what does that mean? For you?"

I swallowed; the words thick. "If I'm right, it means I can't just sit here and wait. If I stay visible, they'll keep coming. And if they find me here..." My eyes flicked upstairs where the kids slept, the monitor's glow faint against the wall. "...then you're in it too. All of you."

Silence pressed between us, her body inching further away like the truth itself had weight.

Finally, her knee stilled. She looked at me, steady now, her eyes no longer confused but knowing.

"Dean," she said, voice low and careful, "this doesn't sound good. This sounds like you and Luna may be in real trouble if she, or these people, ever find you."

The words sat heavy between us.

I wanted to tell her I had it handled. That I could keep her and the kids safe. That I'd never let Vicky's mess touch them. But the lie stuck in my throat.

All I could do was nod, jaw tight. The silence swallowing whatever promise I wanted to make.

Chapter Twenty-Four

BACK TO HAWTHORNE

Bella

The morning pressed down heavily before I even opened my eyes. I dragged myself upright, the weight of what Dean had told me the night before still sitting in my chest.

Vicky.

I never liked her. Too polished, too perfect, like she was playing a role and everyone else was the audience. The way she looked at Dean back then had always made my skin crawl, like he was a project to fix, not a man. I used to think she was using him for the house, for the picture of stability. But this? What if he's right and she really is trading favors? Protecting criminals? Pulling strings to put a hit on the father of her child? That wasn't just ugly. That was sick.

I moved on autopilot through the morning chaos.

Sam fought me, burrito-wrapped himself in his blanket until I tugged him out, grumbling and floppy. Alex needed two reminders to get dressed, and Chloe, of course, hated the shirt I picked. "It's scratchy," she whined, arms folded tight. I ended up bargaining her into another one just to keep the clock from beating me.

Toast. Lunchboxes. Water bottles lined up on the counter. Bookbags leaning against the stairs. The motions felt heavier than usual. Every small task pulling at me like I was dragging Dean's truth behind me, tethered.

By the time everyone was crammed into my SUV with their backpacks half-zipped, I felt strung thin. Chloe was still pouting and Sam was rubbing his eyes raw. After Dean clipped Luna into her car seat and climbed into the passenger seat, I forced a smile into the rearview mirror.

"Alright, let's go, team."

They didn't hear the strain. Or maybe they were used to it.

Dean's words kept circling underneath it all. Him saying he might have to disappear. The way his voice stayed calm, but his eyes told the truth. And Vicky, watching, waiting, pulling wires, somewhere out there.

The thought made me shiver.

As soon as I dropped the kids at school, I pulled my phone out, thumb hovering before I dialed. My sign guy picked up cheerful, like always.

"Hey, it's Bella. I need you at a property in Somerset at ten," I said, glancing sideways at Dean in the passenger seat. He was staring out the window. His jaw tight, lost in whatever storm was still rolling inside him. "Bring a trailer if you can. I'll pay extra."

"No problem. Which property?"

I hesitated. Saying it out loud felt like crossing a line. "Stone residence."

Dean's head turned. His eyes met mine, then slid away. He rubbed the back of his neck, looked back out the window.

"Got it. See you then," the guy said, and hung up.

I set the phone down, pulse still racing. That was it. No going back now.

The daycare was next. I carried Sam in while Dean unbuckled Luna. The name had already stuck, felt safer. The director met us at the door, paperwork ready. "We've got space," she told Dean with a kind smile. "We'll take good care of her."

He lingered when he handed her over. Kissed the top of her soft hair, his fingers tightening before he finally let go. I watched the way his shoulders dropped after, like he'd just given up something he wasn't ready to.

Back in the SUV, just the two of us, the silence thickened. The fields blurred past, empty road stretching long ahead.

"We'll meet him there at ten," I said, mostly to break the quiet.

Dean only nodded; eyes locked forward.

We headed home to switch into his rental car for safety. His call to the precinct already logged, a promise of backup. It should've reassured me, but the silence in that car weighed more than any badge could.

I pulled up his property profile on my iPad as he drove, trying to thread normalcy into the tension. "Built in 1982, right?"

"Yup." Clipped, flat.

"Five bedrooms, four bathrooms," I read, scrolling. "Finished basement with an entertainment center...what?"

"Yup." His knuckles whitened against the wheel.

I tried again. "Game room?"

"Yup." Each word mechanical, like he was already somewhere else.

I swallowed back more questions. He didn't need me poking at the pieces of a life already unraveling. Not when the last two times he stood in that house, he'd barely made it out alive.

"Never mind," I murmured, closing the iPad. "I'll print this later and let you check it."

His jaw flexed, but he stayed quiet.

The hum of the tires filled the silence, steady and relentless. I gripped the iPad tighter in my lap and forced myself to breathe through it. He was driving back toward the house he built with his own hands. The one Vicky had demanded, the one he thought would be theirs.

Of course it hollowed him out.

All I could do was sit there, let him drive, and not add one more weight to the load he already carried.

The silence pressed thicker the closer we got, like the air itself didn't want to be breathed in. I shifted in my seat, iPad shut tight on my lap, fingers drumming against the case just to do something. Words itched at the back of my throat with questions about what parts of the house meant the most, what piece would hurt him to lose. But I bit down hard. This wasn't about me digging. This was about him getting through it.

His grip on the wheel gave him away before anything else. Knuckles pale, fingers flexing and releasing like he couldn't keep them steady. His shoulders had gone tight too, locked in a way that made my own chest ache to watch.

"You okay?" I asked finally, keeping my voice low.

He didn't answer right away. His jaw worked, and then: "Yeah." Short. Clipped. A lie, but one he needed to hold onto.

The highway signs blurred past, then sharpened into ones I recognized. Markers that told me we were almost there. I glanced sideways. The tremor in his hand was small but there, like a current running under his skin.

He slowed as we hit the town line, eyes flicking across the corners like he expected someone to step out. I saw it too: the way shadows seemed thicker here and the way every street felt claimed. My pulse kicked, but I kept my mouth shut.

Then up ahead, a cruiser sat idle on the shoulder. No lights, no siren. Just there. Present.

Dean's breath left him in a rush, his hands loosening a fraction on the wheel.

"Backup," I said, half a whisper.

"Yeah," he murmured, eyes still scanning the road.

The tension didn't ease completely, but the edges dulled. He drove on, jaw still tight, the silence stretching again. Neither of us said it out loud, but it hung there anyway: whatever waited at that house was going to be tough.

And all I could do was sit beside him, trying to breathe through the same weight pressing down on both of us.

Chapter Twenty-Five

Everything He Built

Dean

The house swallowed the next two hours whole.

I took what mattered and left the rest. Clothes. Papers. Luna's things. A few boxes of tools I couldn't stomach leaving behind. Bella moved through the rooms with her phone and her clipboard brain switched on, snapping listing photos and making notes in that quiet, efficient way of hers. Neither of us said much. There wasn't anything to say that didn't hurt.

By the time we loaded the last tote into the trailer, the cruisers had multiplied outside. Black sedans still lingered at the curb, close enough to remind me this wasn't over, far enough back to avoid forcing a scene. Bella suggested hiring movers for the furniture and everything else, so I wouldn't have to come back. I agreed before she even finished the sentence.

Then I pulled the garage door down on the only version of my life I'd spent years trying to build, and we got the hell out.

One of the cruisers rolled ahead of us, lights pulsing against the late-day haze. I kept my hands on the wheel, steady only because I forced them to be. In the mirror, the sedans lingered behind the second cruiser, dark shapes sliding in and out of view like they were waiting for permission to close in.

Funeral procession. That's what it felt like. I just wasn't sure what I was burying: the house, the marriage, or the man I thought I was. Maybe all three.

Bella broke the silence first. Her voice was careful, almost testing. "How long did it take? All of it? The house, the custom pieces?"

My throat tightened. I cleared it, eyes on the road. "A little over two years. Every night after shift. Weekends. Picked up skills I had no business touching like wiring and plumbing. Learned by screwing it up, then doing it again until it was right."

She tilted toward me, waiting for the rest.

"I didn't know I could do it," I admitted, softer now. "Didn't think I had that in me."

"You made it beautiful," she said. No pity in it. Just truth.

The words caught in my chest, sharp as glass. "Doesn't matter. None of it was mine. Every choice was hers. Fixtures, colors, down to the damn drawer pulls. I just...made it real." My grip on the wheel creaked. "Thought I was building us a future. Really, I was just building her exit plan."

The cruiser slowed ahead, signaling the turn toward the highway. I followed, while the sedans hung back like shadows with teeth.

Bella stayed quiet a long minute, then murmured, "You did more than she ever deserved."

I let out a laugh with no humor in it. "Doesn't change the fact she burned it all down."

The silence that followed wasn't awkward. Heavy, yeah. But honest. For once, I didn't rush to patch it.

The highway opened wide in front of us, empty except for the cruiser leading the way. In the mirror, the sedans were gone, peeled off somewhere behind. My shoulders loosened a fraction, breath easing for the first time all day.

We drove like that a while, the tires humming beneath us. Then Bella shifted, turning slightly toward me.

"How did you meet her?" The question hit soft, but it carried weight.

It started in the courthouse, with fluorescent lights, stale coffee, the scent of sweat and nerves clinging to every hallway. I was there to testify. Assault with a deadly weapon for a career lowlife with a record longer than my arm. Routine stuff. I'd done it a hundred times before.

Except that day, she was there.

Victoria Hayes: Assistant District Attorney. Sharp suit, sharper eyes. She stood at the prosecution table like she'd been born to command a room. Blonde hair pulled back in a sleek twist, no fly-aways. No nerves. Her voice was cool and clipped. Precise. Every word deliberate. Every objection a clean slice through the air.

I remember thinking she didn't look real. Too polished for a place that smelled like dust and bad decisions.

When I took the stand, she met my eyes, unblinking. "Detective Stone," she said, tone smooth enough to settle a jury. "Can you confirm for the court that the suspect resisted arrest?"

"Yes, ma'am," I'd said, and she nodded once, like that was all she needed.

Afterward, she caught me in the hallway outside the courtroom. I was signing some paperwork, still half in my head, when her heels clicked across the tile behind me.

"You handle yourself well up there," she said, standing close enough that I caught the faint scent of her perfume, something cold and clean, like winter. "A lot of officers get rattled on the stand."

I shrugged. "Not my first rodeo."

Her lips curved, half amusement, half challenge. "I can tell."

She asked where I'd learned to stay so calm. I told her ten years on the force will sand down anyone's edges. She laughed, a soft sound, surprising after how serious she'd been in court. "Maybe I need to spend more time around cops," she said.

I didn't realize it then, but she was already working me over. Every word calculated. Every smile measured. I thought she was interested because of me. Because I made her laugh. Because I didn't flinch when she pushed. But looking back, I see it clearer: she liked control. And I was just another case she wanted to win.

We ran into each other again a few weeks later. Another trial, another arrest. She stopped me outside the courtroom that time too. A file in one hand and a coffee in the other. "Detective Stone," she greeted, her voice a touch warmer now. "I'm starting to think you're following me."

"Pretty sure it's the other way around," I shot back.

That earned me a smile that reached her eyes for once. "Maybe," she said, taking a sip of her coffee. "But I don't mind the view."

It started simple: lunch between hearings and late nights reviewing evidence. Even inside jokes over bad courthouse vending machine snacks. I told myself it was harmless. Professional.

Then one night after a long deposition, she asked if I wanted to grab a drink. We ended up at a bar near the courthouse. She ditched the blazer, let her hair down, and suddenly she wasn't the DA anymore. She was just a woman who laughed easy and leaned close when she talked. I remember thinking she looked softer under the neon light, like something only I got to see.

When she kissed me in the parking lot, I didn't stop her. And just like that, I was in over my head.

It wasn't love at first. It was fascination. Admiration. Maybe even a kind of awe. She was everything I wasn't: calm, deliberate, untouchable. I thought maybe being with her would make me more like that.

But even that first night, there were cracks. She corrected the way I told a story. She ordered for me without asking. And when I made her laugh, she looked almost annoyed, like I'd gotten past something she didn't mean to let slip.

I should've seen it then. I should've walked away before it ever got that deep. But I didn't. Because for a long time, Vicky Hayes made me feel like the hero I used to want to be.

And by the time I realized she didn't want a partner, but a project, it was already too late.

"Cases," I said after a beat. "I was still on the job. She was the DA. We kept ending up in the same rooms, chasing the same assholes. She noticed me. I wasn't used to that."

Bella's gaze lingered. "Did you love her?"

The blow landed clean. My jaw flexed before the words came. "I thought I did. Maybe I just liked being seen. Liked feeling needed. She was relentless, and when her eyes were on me, I felt like I mattered."

Her hand moved, brushing mine on the gearshift before settling there. Warm. Steady. My throat knotted.

"Were you happy?" she asked.

The painted lines blurred under the headlights. "Yeah," I said, low. "At least I told myself we were. But the last couple years...

it wasn't happiness. It was survival. Just making it through the next fight, the next demand, the next time she reminded me of what I wasn't."

Her fingers tightened, firm without pulling. "Dean," she said, quiet but sure, "you gave her everything you had. That's not on you."

I looked over. Her eyes caught mine, held there longer than they should've. The silence thickened. My pulse kicked hard, heat rushing through me like whiskey hitting the gut.

She didn't let go.

I wanted to lift her hand. To press my mouth to it, let her feel how much that small touch meant. But I gripped the wheel harder instead, every muscle wiring tighter. Because she was married. Because this wasn't the time.

Still, something cracked open in me just having her there.

The cruiser up ahead signaled and peeled off at the last exit. Suddenly it was just us, an empty stretch of highway. No flashing lights. No safety net. Her hand stayed in mine. I should've let go. I didn't.

The breath I dragged in scraped raw in my chest. Before I knew it, I eased the SUV onto the shoulder. Gravel crunched under the tires as the car settled into a restless quiet.

Bella turned, her eyes wide. Not afraid. Expectant. "What are you doing?"

"I don't know," I said, my throat tight. And it was the truth. I didn't know a damn thing anymore.

The air thickened, heavy enough to choke on. I shifted toward Bella, my free hand hovering over the console. Close enough to feel her breath, warm against my cheek.

"Dean..." she whispered, my name balanced between warning and invitation.

Her fingers tightened around mine, holding me there without moving an inch. My pulse hammered in my throat. One inch closer and there'd be no taking it back.

I wrapped both hands around hers, gripping like it was the only thing keeping me tethered. "Tell me to stop," I murmured, low, raw.

She didn't. Her eyes flicked to my mouth, then back up, and the pull was unbearable.

Then the rush of cars past us on the highway startled both of us.

Bella flinched, pulling her hand back to her chest like she'd just remembered how close we were.

I stared out the windshield, every muscle locked, the burn of restraint shaking through me. My heart wouldn't slow, but the moment had already slipped away.

I shifted the SUV back into gear. "We should keep going." My voice came out steadier than I felt.

She nodded, silent. Her cheeks flushed in the dashboard glow.

The highway stretched open again, nothing in front of us but the road. But the space between us was fuller than it had ever been.

I eased the SUV back onto the highway, the wheel steady under my palms.

Beside me, Bella shifted toward the window. Her reflection faint in the glass. Shoulders angled away. Silent. The kind of quiet that said everything without a word.

I gripped the wheel tighter, locking my eyes on the dark ribbon of road. My chest ached to even out, but every breath came rough. I told myself what I had to: it was too dangerous already. Too dangerous to want more, to pull her closer, to cross a line we couldn't uncross.

I repeated it mile after mile. Like a prayer. Like a warning.

Street signs flickered by as the highway bled into town roads. Bella stayed turned away, her silence pressing heavier than the night outside.

By the time her neighborhood appeared, I'd buried it deep enough to keep driving. Survival. That was all that mattered. Survival for me. For Luna. For Bella, even if she didn't know it.

I pulled into her driveway and killed the engine. My hand stayed on the wheel, holding still for one long beat. Then I reached for the door handle.

"Home," I said quietly, just to fill the space between us.

She nodded, eyes still on the glass. Not on me.

And that was it. The end of it. For now.

Chapter Twenty-Six

The Chairs in Her Kitchen

Bella

I couldn't tell you how I got the kids down. Sam must've mumbled about dinosaurs before I tugged the blanket over his shoulders. Chloe's lamp had to have clicked off after she passed out with her iPad still buzzing on her lap. John said something from the recliner when I brushed past him. Probably some half-slurred nothing I answered with a "goodnight" that meant even less.

What I do remember is the car. The crunch of gravel when Dean pulled onto the shoulder. The way his hand slid over mine, solid and warm, holding like it meant more than either of us dared to say. The tilt of his head. The way I leaned. The charge between us sparking close enough to burn.

And then the cars passing by, snapping me back, dragging me to my senses.

Now I'm here, staring at the ceiling. Twisted in sheets that feel too heavy, my pulse still running like I never left that road.

I should be relieved. Thankful, even, that the moment broke before anything happened. But I'm not. I'm raw. Stripped open. My skin still hums with the memory of his thumb brushing across my knuckles, his voice rasping low: *Tell me to stop.* And I hadn't.

The clock glares past midnight. John snores beside me, face mashed into his pillow. Oblivious. I don't remember him coming to bed. He doesn't stir when I sigh. Doesn't notice when I press both palms into my eyes like I can force sleep to come.

But it's useless. Every time I blink, I see Dean's bright green eyes. Searching. Right before we almost crossed that line.

I'm married. I repeat it to myself like a prayer. I'm married. I'm a mother. I don't get to want. Not like that.

And yet...want is all I feel.

Guilt sits low in my stomach, sharp as acid, but it tangles with something worse. Something that feels a lot like need.

By two a.m., I quit pretending I'd sleep. I slid from under the covers, bare feet brushing the carpet, and padded down the stairs. I told myself it was for water. Or to check the locks. Some excuse that made sense. Really, I just needed to move. If only to remind myself I was still in control of something.

Halfway to the kitchen, I stopped.

The guest room door was shut, but a thin line of light spilled under the crack. My pulse tripped. He was awake. Or maybe he wasn't. Maybe the lamp was left on. Either way, I stood there too long, wondering if Dean was lying on the other side thinking the same thoughts that had me pacing.

One step closer and I'd know. Instead, I turned, pressing my palm against the wall to steady myself. Water. Locks. Back to bed. Nothing else.

But the ache didn't fade.

The days blurred after that.

I threw myself at work like it was armor. Things I could control: listings, showings, contracts, phone calls. All crammed into every minute between drop-offs and pick-ups. The calendar filled faster than I could check boxes.

At home it was a different kind of marathon: snacks, homework, tantrums, dinner, laundry, baths, dishes. By the time the kids were down, it was always past nine, and I was still on my feet, packing lunches, folding clothes, or typing out emails with my eyes half-shut.

Dean saw all of it. The slammed cabinet doors. The piles of unfolded laundry. The way I muttered under my breath when I couldn't find clean Tupperware. He saw me sink into the couch at ten with my iPad still balanced on my knees.

And he didn't say a word.

At night, he was always at the kitchen island. Sometimes his iPad glowed in front of him, his fingers hovering like he couldn't decide whether to type. Other times, Luna was curled against his arm, her tiny fist clutching his shirt while he rocked absently.

I moved around him like I'd rehearsed it. Quiet. Efficient. Plates stacked, counters wiped, fruit cut into neat cubes for lunchboxes. The hum of the fridge and the soft click of cabinets over his steady breathing. It all blended into a rhythm I pretended was normal.

"Can you hand me that towel?" I asked without looking up.

He reached, brushed my hand as he passed it over. "Here."

"Do you want coffee in the morning?" My voice stayed low, even.

"Yeah. Thanks." His answer was clipped, but his eyes lingered too long.

I set the fruit in containers and snapped the lids shut one by one. "She ate three ounces," I murmured, nodding at the baby against his chest. "Think she'll sleep longer?"

"Maybe." He stroked her back with two fingers, watching her lashes flutter.

That was all we said. Functional words. Nothing more.

But the silence between the words felt louder than anything else. The car. His hand over mine. The pull I couldn't shake. None of it spoken, all of it alive in the space between us.

John didn't see it. Or maybe he didn't care. He was slumped in the recliner, beer sweating on the side table, sports flickering across his face until he was out cold before the ten o'clock news.

Sometimes a grunt if the kids were too loud. A bark if the food wasn't hot enough. Then back into his rut.

Dean saw. I felt it every time his gaze found me when I crossed the kitchen. The way his mouth started to open, like he might finally say what was sitting heavy between us, then shut again.

I didn't let myself stop moving. Because if I paused, if I let him catch me standing still, I didn't trust myself not to shatter.

By the end of each night, the house gleamed. Lunchboxes lined on the counter. Laundry stacked, folded and tucked away. Everything in its place. Everything, except me.

And every night, my thoughts always turned back to him.

We got Dean's house on the market the following week. I didn't let him anywhere near it again.

By the time I sat at the island with my laptop, the photos were already uploaded, bright and perfect. Dean was across from me, Luna asleep in the swing beside him, her tiny chest rising steady. He still held the bottle in one hand even though she hadn't touched it in twenty minutes.

I had Tina on speaker, her voice sharp and focused through the phone as she pulled up the draft on her end.

"Alright," she said, already in work mode. "Let me see what you've got."

I read the opening line aloud, watching Dean from the corner of my eye as I did.

"For Sale: Custom-Built Modern Colonial, 5BR/4BA, Finished Basement, Luxury Outdoor Living."

Tina hummed. "Strong. Clean. But you can push it more. This isn't just a house, Bell, it's a lifestyle sell. You've got high-end buyers here."

"I don't want to oversell it," I said, fingers hovering over the keyboard.

"You're not overselling," she shot back. "You're positioning. There's a difference."

Dean's jaw flexed slightly across from me, but he stayed quiet.

"Okay," I said, typing as she talked. "What are you thinking?"

"Lead with craftsmanship," Tina said. "Custom build, high-end finishes, designed for entertaining. Hit the emotional pull early, then back it up with the specs."

I adjusted the wording, reading it back. She cut me off twice, swapped phrases and tightened language like she always did.

We went back and forth for nearly an hour. Small tweaks. Word choices. Flow. Tina caught things I would've missed, pushed where I hesitated, and softened where I pushed too hard.

At one point she paused. "This is a good listing, Bella." Her voice shifted, just a touch. Less business. More her. "You okay?"

My eyes flicked to Dean, to the way he stared at nothing, bottle still loose in his hand.

"Yeah," I said, quieter. "Just getting it done."

A beat. Then Tina exhaled softly. "Alright. Send it to him before you finalize."

"Yeah. I will."

"Call me later," she added, already slipping back into motion. "I want to hear how it goes."

"I will."

The line clicked off. The kitchen felt quieter without her voice filling it.

"Here," I said, turning the screen toward him. "Tell me if this works."

The words glared back at both of us:

For Sale: Custom-Built Modern Colonial, 5BR/4BA, Finished Basement, Luxury Outdoor Living.

He leaned in, scrolling. Marble countertops. Double ovens. Bay windows. A master suite staged like a magazine cover. Every inch of the house captured, frozen, shining.

I watched his jaw flex. He didn't say anything.

"I could change it," I added quietly. "Cut the detail. Add more. Whatever you need."

He exhaled through his nose, long and slow, still staring at the screen. "It read nice," he said finally. His voice was flat, careful.

"Too nice?" I asked.

His mouth twitched, not quite a smile. "Too real." His fingers tapped once against the counter. A restless beat. "Seeing it like this...it is like looking at a stranger's house. Not mine. Not anymore."

I wanted to reach across the island, cover his hand with mine. To tell him it was okay to grieve a place even if it had been built on lies. Instead, I just nodded, throat tight. "Then it is ready."

He leaned back, eyes closing for a second before they found mine again. "Yeah," he murmured, rough. "It is ready."

And God help me, the way he said it didn't sound like he was talking about the house at all.

Dean finally cleared his throat, low and rough. "It is...accurate."

"That's all I needed," I told him, though I didn't pull the laptop back yet. His fingers twitched like he was about to reach for the screen, then stilled.

Luna shifted in her swing, letting out a sigh that sounded bigger than her tiny body. The moment broke.

I turned the laptop back toward me and hit save. One click. It was out there now. No going back.

Dean leaned back against the counter, mug in hand. His eyes flicking toward the window. "So," he said, voice casual, but I caught the flicker in his gaze, "Isabella Blake, huh?"

I smiled faintly without looking up from the stack of paperwork. "You saw the sign."

He huffed. "Hard to miss. Big, bold letters right next to my mailbox. I was half-expecting it to say, 'Bella Turner Realty' or something."

"That would've gone over well," I said dryly.

He chuckled, but his eyes stayed on me. "Why that name? I mean, I get it. It's still you, but...different."

I set my pen down and rubbed at the bridge of my nose, thinking. "Because it was different. It was the only thing that was mine. Really mine."

He didn't say anything. Just waited, the way he did when he knew I wasn't finished.

"When John and I first got married," I said slowly, "everything became 'ours.' Our house. Our friends. Our money. Our plans. Our life. Even my name. He didn't ask me to change it, but he acted like it was a given. Like being Mrs. Turner was just part of the deal."

Dean's jaw flexed, a muscle jumping near his temple.

"I went along with it for years. Until I started real estate. And when it came time to order business cards, I just...couldn't do it. I didn't want to see his name next to mine anymore." I shrugged, tracing the rim of my coffee mug. "So, I used my maiden name. Isabella Blake. It sounded clean. Professional. Separate."

"Separate from him," Dean said quietly.

I nodded. "Exactly. It was the one part of my life that didn't have his fingerprints all over it. My clients didn't know about him. They didn't know about the fights or the bruises on my confidence. When people called me Isabella, I could breathe. I could be someone competent and respected...unbroken."

Dean's mug hit the counter with a soft thud. He crossed the space between us and leaned his hip against the table. He was close enough that I could smell the faint trace of cedar soap and motor oil.

"You know," he said, voice low, "I liked that name. It fits you."

I looked up at him, eyebrows raised. "You liked the fake one?"

He shook his head. "It wasn't fake. It was the version of you that decided to survive. To start over. That wasn't pretend."

Something in my chest tightened. I wanted to look away. "I don't use it at home," I said softly. "It feels like armor. Necessary, but heavy."

"Then keep it," he murmured. "Use it when you need to. But don't forget you didn't have to wear it here."

My throat went tight. "I know."

He smiled then. A small, real, steady smile. "Still...Isabella Blake," he said, testing the sound again, like he was tasting it. "Hell of a name for a woman who could take on the world."

"Yeah," I said quietly, feeling the corners of my mouth lift. "It was the one I kept for myself."

I took one more look at the published listing. At the end: Isabella Blake Realty. And for the first time, instead of seeing something tied to John's past, I saw something that was only mine.

A week later, we were standing in his driveway with a moving truck coughing gas fumes into the air. The crew unloaded dollies and straps like they'd done it a thousand times. Dean signed their paperwork without a word. His jaw locked, arms folding across his chest the second the pen left the page.

They filed into the house. I followed with my clipboard ready, asking the questions he wouldn't.

"Do you want to store these things, or just sell them?" My voice came out too neat, too professional.

"Store what you can." His eyes stayed fixed on the hardwood; voice clipped.

I jotted it down. "Okay. Storage for the furniture and baby things. The rest we'll push through the estate sale."

He gave no answer, already moving down the hall.

The place felt hollow as echoes slipped off bare walls that used to hold...something. I couldn't tell if it had been laughter or fights. Maybe both.

The men hauled out a leather sectional, barely broken in. I muttered, mostly to myself, "This could've sold in a heartbeat."

Dean didn't look back.

I kept talking anyway, partly about business, partly to push against the silence pressing at my ribs. "The dining set's custom. We should sell it."

"These nightstands. Solid wood. They'll move fast."

"This rug? You don't find pieces like this in stores."

He walked on like he couldn't hear me. Blank-faced. Hands buried in his pockets. Eyes skating past each piece as though none of it had ever belonged to him.

But when the crew reached for the oversized wooden bed-frame in one of the bedrooms, he stiffened. His hand came up instinctively. "Careful with that." The edge in his voice froze them mid-lift.

Then he stepped back again, shutting down. Silent.

I didn't push. I didn't joke, didn't try to fill the space the way I usually might. Not after last time. Not after how close everything had come to cracking open.

So, I just scribbled notes and kept the paperwork moving, watching the house empty itself around him. Piece by piece. Memory by memory.

When we got back that night, the first thing I noticed was the chairs. Dean's solid wood chairs. Dark finish with carved backs catching the kitchen light. Lined up neatly around my table like they'd always belonged there.

He cleared his throat when he saw me staring. "Hope you don't mind. Yours are downstairs. These all match, and there's enough for everyone." His smile was faint, almost sheepish.

I ran my fingers along the polished edge. Smooth. Cold. "I didn't mind," I said. "They were gorgeous."

Dinner started the way Dean wanted it to, plates set out neatly and chairs pulled in close, with the smell of roasted chicken and buttered corn hanging in the air. He insisted the kids sit together.

Sam clapped like it was a show made just for him. "Yay!" he shouted, banging his spoon against the table.

Dean grinned, sliding him a plate. "Save that energy for the food, buddy."

Alex straightened when Dean leaned an elbow on the table and asked, "So, how's school going?"

That little flash of pride crossed Alex's face. "Good," he said, louder than usual, talking about his science project while Dean actually listened.

Chloe tried to sneak toward the living room, iPad already clutched in her hand. Dean caught her mid-step with one steady look: calm, quiet, but unyielding. Her eyes rolled as she huffed and stomped back to the table. "Fine." She plopped into her chair, arms crossed.

For a second, the chaos softened. The sound of plates clinking, the hum of small voices. It almost felt...normal.

Then John's voice cut through it from the kitchen. "I'm still not eating at the damn table."

The air stilled. Dean didn't look over right away; he just set down his fork and exhaled through his nose. "Come on, man. You could at least sit down with your kids."

The plate slammed onto the counter with a crack that made Sam flinch and drop his truck. The sound echoed through the kitchen. Sharp and final.

John came around the island. Face flushed. Shoulders tight. "I'm sick of this! You don't tell me how to run my house. You don't tell me how to raise my family!"

His words bounced off the walls, louder than the hum of the fridge. Louder than my heartbeat.

"John, please—" My voice shook, but I kept it even for the kids.

He snapped his head toward me, laughing. Bitter and humorless. "Please what? You think you can just undermine me in front of them? Make me the bad guy in my own damn house?"

Chloe pressed herself against my leg. Sam's lip quivered; eyes glassy. I reached for his hand, but he was frozen.

"John," I whispered, "they're scared."

He threw up his hands. He was pacing now, jaw tight, voice cracking with anger. "Yeah? Well maybe they should learn what respect looks like."

The silence that followed felt thick enough to choke on. The only sound was the scrape of the fork he'd thrown, spinning to a stop against the tile.

"Go cool off," I managed, steady but small.

He turned that glare on me, chest heaving. "In my house?"

I didn't answer. I just took Sam's hand, feeling his tiny fingers wrap around mine, and kept my eyes down until John stormed down the hall.

Dean was still at the table, body coiled but steady. "Then maybe you should start acting like you're part of this family," he said, voice low, cutting through the tension like a blade.

John spun, something ugly on his tongue, but Dean's stare stopped him cold. He muttered under his breath and disappeared up the stairs.

No one moved for a long time. The kids hovered near the table; eyes wide. I crouched to their level, pulled them in close, and whispered something soft I didn't even remember saying.

When the house finally went still, I didn't go after John. Later, when I tried, the door was locked. I ended up on the couch instead, a blanket pulled to my chin. The dishes sat untouched. The kitchen heavy with silence. Upstairs, Dean moved quietly, checking on the kids and turning off lights.

And for the first time, I let the quiet settle.

Hours passed. I must have drifted off, because I woke to soft footsteps and the faint whimper of a baby. Dean's silhouette glowed in the light of the monitor. Luna was pressed against his shoulder, tiny fists tucked under her chin.

He startled when he saw me sit up. "Didn't realize you were out here," he whispered.

"John locked me out," I answered flatly, like it was routine.

Dean's jaw tightened, arms cinching Luna closer. "Bella..." His voice was rough. "You deserved better than this."

I shook my head, pulling the blanket higher. "It isn't that simple."

"Yes, it is." His voice cracked. Just a little. The rawness in it cut deeper than John's shouting ever could. "You don't have to keep living like this. Don't teach your kids this was normal."

I looked away, my throat closing up. "Dean..." The word caught. "This is the life I built. For them. For me. I can't just throw it away."

Even as I said it, the words sounded hollow. Fear filled the space they didn't.

"It is easier to stay," I whispered. "Suck it up. For the kids."

His shoulders sagged. He kissed the top of Luna's head, his eyes shadowed in the glow. He nodded once, like he was giving up the fight.

Neither of us spoke again. The silence between us was heavier than the fight that sent me there in the first place. It hung in the kitchen that night, stretched across the couch when the kids were finally asleep, and followed me even into bed.

By the end of the week, his house was under contract. Well over the asking price. My inbox pinged with the signed agreement, the number bold at the top like a final verdict. The closing date landed six weeks out.

Six weeks and it would all be gone. Six weeks and Marcus Dean Stone would vanish, along with every inch of wood and tile he poured himself into. Along with the life he thought he was building. Six weeks and he'd have a new name. A new start. A clean slate with his baby girl.

I should have felt relieved. I told myself I was. But the glow of the contract on my iPad screen felt less like victory and more like a clock winding down. Six weeks, and I'd lose him too.

Dean walked in carrying Luna against his chest, quiet as always. Her tiny mouth hung slack, a string of drool glistening on his shirt. He shifted her carefully, lowering her into the swing in the corner. The faint creak of the straps was the only sound.

"She's out," he said, voice low.

I nodded, turning the iPad toward him. The movement was sharper than I meant it to be. "Congratulations, by the way. Over asking."

He drew in a breath, rubbing a hand over his face. "Doesn't feel like congratulations."

"Yeah," I whispered. "I get that."

He looked at me for a second longer, like he wanted to say more, but then just lowered himself into the chair across from me. His elbows rested on his knees, hands clasped tight, knuckles pale.

I poured the last glass of wine from the bottle. The glug of liquid echoed in the quiet. I lifted it in his direction. "Want some?"

He shook his head. "If I start, I won't stop."

The honesty in his tone made my chest ache. I took a sip instead, the wine sharp and warm on my tongue.

"You should be excited," I said finally, setting the glass on the table between us. "Six weeks and you'll be free. New name, new start. Just you and her."

His jaw worked. "Free, huh?" He leaned back, tilting his head against the wall. "Funny how freedom feels a hell of a lot like losing everything."

The words landed heavier than I expected. I swallowed hard, staring at the rim of my glass. "You'll have her," I reminded him softly. "That's not nothing."

His eyes flicked toward the swing. Luna stirred, let out a small sigh, then settled again. "She's everything," he said, almost to himself.

I didn't answer. I couldn't. My throat was too tight.

Because I knew he was right. And yet, selfishly, all I could hear was the countdown ticking in my head. Six weeks until the house closed. Six weeks until he disappeared.

I leaned back into the couch, the cushion swallowing me whole. I sat there, glass in hand, trying not to stare at Dean. Trying not to let him see the way my chest twisted.

Six weeks.

And the thought I couldn't shake. The one I didn't dare say out loud: Why did it feel like I was losing him too?

Chapter Twenty-Seven

What Silence Means

Dean

It should've felt like progress. Six weeks and the house would be sold. Six weeks and Marcus Dean Stone would be gone. Nothing left but paperwork and a ghost in some database.

I stayed at the island, jaw clenched, my hand still pressed flat against the closed laptop. It should've felt like winning. All I felt was hollow.

Every time I saw my chairs tucked under her table, something twisted in me. Chloe perched on one, legs swinging, half the time she wouldn't meet my eyes. Sam pounded both fists on another, babbling nonsense until Bella laughed so hard she doubled over. Alex sat taller when she praised him.

My chairs. My work. My hands in every cut and carve of that wood.

And yet they looked like they'd always belonged there. Like they were part of her kitchen. Her family. I wasn't supposed to want that.

I kept busy. Grocery runs. Dishes. Folding laundry I didn't even know how to fold right. Bella correcting me with a quiet shake of her head but letting me try again. Playing with Luna on the rug until her shrieks pulled Sam over or until he climbed into my lap demanding turns.

It filled the hours. It didn't settle the storm under my ribs.

And when I wasn't here, I was walking movers through the house, through the things I'd built, feeling like an intruder in my own memory. Marble counters I'd laid my arms across, now polished by strangers. Bay windows I'd measured ten times, sunlight spilling across empty floors.

All of it designed for a woman who didn't love me. Maybe never had. Who turned me into collateral damage the second it suited her.

Bella kept her distance. On purpose. I knew it. No music through shared earbuds anymore. No leaning too close over late-night coffee. She worked. She wrangled kids. She poured her wine like it was armor.

I let her. Because if I pushed, if I said the things rattling in my throat, I'd lose the fragile thread holding me safe under her roof.

But watching her...Watching her carry everything without complaint. Watching her curl up on the couch when John locked her out of her own room like it was nothing. Like it was routine.

It burned.

"Bella," I'd said once, too sharp, after John barked from the recliner.

She'd just shaken her head. Told me not to. That it wasn't worth it.

Not worth it. I hated him for it. And I hated myself for not doing something, anything, to stop it.

I told myself it was temporary. Six weeks and I'd be gone. Six weeks and she'd be rid of me. Six weeks to keep my head down. To keep Luna safe and keep my hands off the only woman who'd made me feel anything in years.

But every night in that guest room with half-painted walls, I lay awake listening to the dishwasher hum through the silence, knowing she was just on the other side. Close enough to touch. Close enough to ruin both of us. And too far away to ever have.

By the fourth night of pacing grooves into the same four walls of that unfinished guest room, I snapped. Luna had finally slept more than an hour straight, her tiny breaths soft in the pack-and-play, but the silence pressed in so hard I couldn't take it.

I slipped my phone from the nightstand, eased the door shut, and stepped onto the back deck. The boards creaked under me. Cold air hit my lungs, sharp and clean. Bella's kitchen light still glowed faint through the window, so I turned away and hit Mark's number.

He picked up on the third ring. "Stone. You alive?"

"Barely." My voice dropped low, like the shadows could carry it back inside. "Got a minute?"

"For you? Always. What's going on?"

I leaned into the railing; paint rough under my palms. "My house is under contract. Movers came through. Bella's...keeping me steady." I rubbed at the knot forming at my temple. "But it doesn't matter. I feel like I'm walking blind through a minefield."

Mark didn't hesitate. "So...you're still fucked."

"Yeah." The word scraped out of me. "My name was flagged. Every road felt like a setup. Vicky had disappeared, but I could feel her pulling strings. I just didn't know how far they reached."

He blew out a breath. "We've been checking. Jenna's been digging deeper. You want her in on this?"

"Put her on."

A shuffle. A click. Then Jenna's voice came through, steady as always. "Dean, what the hell are you doing still out in the wind? You should've left already."

"I couldn't. Not until I knew the whole picture. Not until I disappeared clean." My grip tightened on the rail. "What've you got?"

Paper rustled on her end. She hesitated before answering. "Her trail was cold. No bank hits, no cameras. But you're right—it's ugly. Internal Affairs is circling her cases. It looks like she's been shielding one of the state's biggest drug suppliers. I think that's your muscle. That's who ordered the hit."

The railing groaned under my hand. "I wasn't just paranoid."

"No," she said firmly. "You weren't. They want you alive, which is worse. If she's in bed with them, you can't assume you're safe anywhere."

The words knifed through me. I pressed my forehead against my arm, wood biting into my knuckles. "She was supposed to be my partner," I rasped. "My wife. I built her a damn house. I built her a life."

The crack in my voice carried before I could choke it down.

Mark came back on the line. "Dean, you've gotta stop looking at what she was supposed to be. Look at what she is. A ghost with a gang behind her. The best thing you can do for yourself, and that baby, is cut her off clean. Take whatever Bella's giving you and use it. But don't hang around longer than you have to."

I gripped the phone tighter, my thumb digging into the edge. Part of me already knew he was right. Hell, I'd known for months.

But another part, the one that sat in Bella's kitchen every night, watching her fold herself smaller while her husband snored in the next room, wasn't ready to walk away.

"Dean?" Jenna's voice slid back in, sharp, pulling.

I swallowed; throat dry. "I hear you," I said finally. The words came out low, rough. "I just didn't know if I can."

Mark didn't let me off the hook. "Then let me make it simple. We've got eyes out. Nothing was moving. No cards. No sightings. No chatter about her movements."

Jenna cut across him, her tone quieter but sharper. "It was like she doesn't exist anymore. And that's the part that should worry you most."

A muscle jumped in my jaw. I pressed my forehead into the railing until the wood bit into my skin. A woman like Vicky doesn't just vanish. Not without help. Not without a plan.

"Dean," Mark said again, steady, like he was trying to nail me to something solid, "stay sharp. If she surfaces, it'll be on her terms. And you won't see it coming."

The line clicked dead. I lowered the phone, listening to the crickets buzzing in the dark and the faint hum of the porch light behind me. The night air felt thick. Heavy.

No activity. No sign of her anywhere.

It should've been a relief. Instead, my gut twisted until I felt sick. Because silence didn't mean she was gone. Silence meant she was waiting.

And the longer I stood there in the dark, the more certain I became. She'd find me before I ever found her.

Chapter Twenty-Eight

The Name He Chose

Bella

I told myself to keep my distance. To stay busy. To stay sharp and keep the boundaries clean. But Dean made that impossible.

Within days, he slid into the rhythm of our house like he'd always been here. Some nights he cooked, some nights I did, and whoever wasn't at the stove ended up beside the sink. I'd walk in and catch him with his sleeves pushed up, arms slick with water and suds clinging to the dark hair on his forearms as he rinsed plates.

Sometimes he hummed under his breath, off-key, but steady. Like he wasn't the man who'd been chased out of his own life only weeks ago.

"Those aren't rinsed enough," I teased one night, nudging his hip with mine as I set more dishes beside him.

He shot me a look, the corner of his mouth twitching. "You're worse than the sergeant who used to inspect my locker."

"Maybe because I don't want soap in my kids' mac and cheese tomorrow."

That low, almost surprised, laugh slid under my skin before I could stop it.

The kids felt it too. They gravitated toward him like he was a magnet they hadn't known they'd needed. Even Chloe, who usually clung to John like her survival depended on it, found herself leaning into Dean's orbit. She'd hover at the edge of the kitchen until he noticed.

"Hey, Chloe-bug," he said once, crouching to her height with a wooden spoon in his hand. "You think this sauce needs more pepper?"

Her small shoulders lifted in a shrug. "Maybe."

He grinned, handing her the spoon like she was the expert. "Alright, you're the boss."

She giggled. Actually giggled, and I almost dropped the stack of bowls in my hands.

Alex followed Dean everywhere, like a shadow made of curiosity. "Dean, what's that tool? Why does the pasta water look white? Do you think I'd be good at basketball if I practiced every day?"

Dean answered every question with the same patience, never brushing him off. "That's a ladle. The water's starchy. It helps the sauce stick. And yeah, kid, you'd be great if you kept at it."

Alex beamed every time, shoulders squaring a little straighter.

And Sam. Sweet, clingy Sam, toddled over whenever he wanted attention, climbing into Dean's lap mid-sentence like it had always been his place. Dean would just steady him with one hand, keep stirring or folding or talking with the other kids, completely unbothered by the extra weight.

And then there was Luna. She tied all of us together without even trying. Every night, after the chaos of homework and dinner, we ended up on the living room floor, circling her like she was the center of our universe. Alex cheered when she rolled halfway over. Chloe shoved toys into her chubby fists. Sam clapped like it was the greatest show on earth.

Dean knelt close, pride etched into his face as he coaxed her on. "That's it, baby girl. Push harder. You've got this."

His voice softened in a way that made my chest ache.

Meanwhile, John barely moved from his recliner. Same routine: TV glow washing over his blank stare, beer bottle slipping lower until I couldn't tell if he was asleep or just gone somewhere inside himself. He never joined in. Never even looked up when the kids laughed loud enough to shake the walls.

And that left Dean and me. Alone in a way I hadn't been with anyone in years.

The moments stacked up. Quiet, but impossible to ignore. His hand brushing mine when he passed me a plate. The way his eyes lingered when I bent to help Chloe with her shoes. The low laugh he let slip when Sam announced he wanted to marry Luna because "she was the cutest."

We never said a word about it. Never acknowledged it. But the air between us told the truth anyway; charged and humming in the silence John left behind.

Every night, when I finally slid under the covers, the feeling wound tighter. A pull I hadn't asked for and couldn't shake.

Then the house sold. Faster than I'd thought it would. Cash buyer. No contingencies. A clean deal. No hiccups.

At closing, I sat beside Dean, the smell of copier toner and stale coffee thick in the small office. The underwriter slid the check across the desk.

Dean's hand didn't move. His jaw flexed hard, like he was bracing for a hit.

"This goes in your name," he said, voice flat.

My head jerked toward him. "Dean—"

His eyes stayed locked on the check. He didn't blink. Didn't even glance at me.

It wasn't just money on that paper. It was his entire life, shrunk down and signed away. And he was placing it in my lap like I wouldn't drop it.

He scrawled his name across the last page, snapped the folder shut, and pressed it into my hands. It felt heavier than it should've.

"We'll deposit it together," he said.

My throat tightened. I forced a nod, keeping my face neutral. Of course he'd come. Of course he'd want to. But if his name triggered something in the system, if even one bank employee recognized him, this whole fragile balance could shatter.

I clutched the folder against my chest, pulse hammering. "Alright," I said quietly. "We'll do it together."

But inside, panic spread like fire.

The bank smelled faintly of floor polish and printer ink. Too clean and too bright under the fluorescent lights. My heels clicked against the tile as I walked to the counter, Dean a half step behind me. His presence loomed, steady and silent, like a wall at my back.

I forced a smile for the teller and slid the check across the counter, my hands steadier than they felt. My heart hammered so hard I swore it might rattle the glass partition between us.

The woman on the other side glanced down, typed, then looked back up. "Good morning, Mrs. Turner. Just the deposit today?"

"Yes," I said, my voice calm. Polite. Normal.

Dean didn't say a word. His shoulders stayed squared, but his jaw was tight. I could see the vein ticking in his temple out of the corner of my eye.

The teller's nails clicked against the keyboard. "Everything looks good. You'll see it clear within two business days." She slid the receipt toward me with a smile that didn't reach her eyes. Too rehearsed to mean anything.

I nodded, tucking it into my purse with careful precision. "Thank you."

Beside me, Dean's hand curled into a fist. He never shifted or broke his stance, but I felt the tension pouring off him like static.

We stepped back from the counter, out through the glass doors, and into the sharp sunlight. Gravel crunched under our shoes as we crossed the lot.

Only then did he let out a rough, jagged breath, like he'd been holding it the entire time.

"Too smooth," he muttered, his eyes sweeping the lot, the cars and people, everything a potential threat.

"Dean, it went fine," I said softly, slipping the receipt deeper into my purse as if hiding it could make the money less real. Less dangerous.

"Maybe." His gaze kept moving, scanning the street like he expected someone to step out from behind a parked SUV. His shoulders stayed high, coiled tight. "But I don't trust it."

I stopped by the passenger side of my SUV, watching him. Sunlight caught the edge of his profile, hard and unyielding. But beneath it, I saw what he wouldn't say: fear and loss. All of it wound so tight he couldn't let it show.

This man had just handed me his entire life in the form of a check. Every hour he'd worked. Every wall he'd built. Every piece of himself, put in my name without hesitation. And he hadn't even blinked.

That night, the papers hit the kitchen island with a soft slap, the edges fanning slightly across the wood grain. Dean slid them toward me, his fingers lingering on the stack like he wasn't quite ready to let go.

"Dean," he said, voice even but quieter than usual. His eyes lifted to mine, steady, but heavy. "Dean Williams."

I pulled the top sheet closer, scanning the bold type at the header. The official stamps. The signatures inked across the bottom lines. Just like that, Marcus Dean Stone no longer existed.

The silence between us stretched until I finally asked, "That was it? Just...over?"

His mouth tipped into something close to a smile, but it didn't reach his eyes. "Clerks still remembered the guy who used to bribe them with glazed donuts and Boston creams. They made sure the wheels turned quick." He tapped the corner of the paperwork with one knuckle. "By late afternoon, it was done."

I touched the edge of the page, careful, like it might burn. "I thought about offering you my name. Blake. It would've given you a clean start."

"You did offer," he reminded me, his tone softening. "But that's yours. Everyone knows it's yours. It's on your signs and your license. If anyone went digging, it would lead straight back to you. Too risky."

He was right, of course. I'd known it the second he said it. Still, something in me ached hearing him say it so matter-of-fact.

"So... Williams," I murmured, rolling the word on my tongue. "Plain. Solid. Forgettable."

"Exactly what I needed to be."

He adjusted the carrier strapped across his chest. Luna stirred against him. A tiny sigh escaping her lips before she settled again. His hand pressed to her back, instinctively.

I stared at the man standing in my kitchen. The papers in one hand, his daughter pressed close in the other. He'd erased himself in the span of a single afternoon. A whole life gone, reduced to a stack of signatures and a name that wasn't really his.

And yet, when I looked at him, at the strength and loss carved across his face, all I could feel was that hollow pull in my chest. Because the more he disappeared from the world, the more I realized how much I didn't want him disappearing from mine.

Chapter Twenty-Nine

Not in This House

Dean

That night, the house was quieter than usual. John had stomped out for bowling, the garage door rattling behind him. The kids were sprawled across the living room floor, faces lit by iPads, the soft game sounds muffled by cushions.

Bella and I stood shoulder to shoulder at the island, sandwich fixings spread between us. She stacked bread and cold cuts into baggies for tomorrow's lunches. I sliced an apple, the knife biting into the skin with a crisp snap. My shoulders were wound tight, every breath shallow.

She noticed. I felt her eyes on me before she spoke. "Hug time?" she asked, her tone light but edged with something steadier.

I froze, the knife halfway through the apple. My throat worked once before I managed, "Please." The word came out lower than I meant.

She set the bread down and stepped into me, her arms sliding around my ribs. I dropped the knife, pulled her in, and everything in me eased and tightened at the same time. Her shampoo smelled clean, faintly floral. A scent that caught me off guard, dragging me back to a time when being held didn't cost anything.

Her palm moved across my back in slow, steady circles. I mirrored her without thinking. My hand broad between her shoulders, tracing gentle arcs like I could smooth out the weight pressing on both of us.

The hug should've ended after a few seconds. A polite squeeze. A release. It didn't. We held on. Too long. Long enough that my pulse jumped. Long enough that I knew we'd both feel it later when we tried to sleep.

Her face pressed against my chest, heat bleeding into me. Her breath fanned across my collar. My jaw brushed her hair without meaning to, and before I could stop myself, I dipped closer. The roughness of my cheek caught against her temple.

Her fingers slid up the back of my head and into my hair. Gentle at first, testing. Then firmer, pulling me toward her.

I turned, just a fraction. She pulled back, only a breath's width. And that was enough.

Our mouths met. Soft. Hesitant. Starved.

The kind of kiss that had been building for weeks, waiting for the smallest excuse.

Her lips trembled against mine, and for a second, I thought she might give in completely. Then she broke away. Her breath unsteady. Her eyes wide, like she'd been caught doing something unforgivable.

"I'm sorry," she whispered, already retreating, shaking her head. "I can't do this."

The cold rushed in between us as she stepped back. My arms fell, useless, the taste of her still on my lips.

I knew she was right. But that didn't make me want her any less.

The kitchen door banged open, slamming so hard the frame rattled.

John's voice tore through the air. "I knew it. I fucking knew something was going on here. Why else would you have him living in my house?"

Bella jerked away from me like she'd been burned, her lips parted, chest heaving.

I didn't move.

John stormed closer, face red, eyes wild, spit flying with every word. "This is bullshit. I want you out. Now."

I opened my mouth, but Bella cut across me, her voice sharp enough to slice. "First of all, this is not what it looks like."

Her finger jabbed into his chest hard enough to make him rock back. "Second, he's been under more stress than you can even imagine. Not that you've once bothered to ask your so-called friend what the hell he's going through. And third—" her voice broke, then came back louder, shaking but fierce, "—he has nowhere to go. So shut up and go to bed."

Her scream cracked against the tile, echoing down the hall, ripping the kids from their iPads in the living room.

John froze, jaw flexing, the vein in his forehead pulsing. For half a second, I thought maybe he'd back off.

Then his arm snapped up.

The slap landed with a crack that echoed through my bones. Bella's head whipped to the side, her hair flying across her face. A whimper came from the entryway. Alex stood frozen, one hand clamped over Chloe's eyes.

"You will never speak to me like that again," John hissed, looming over her, his hand still raised like he might swing again.

Bella flinched. Small. Instinctive. Her eyes wide with fear.

That was it. The last line. The world went red.

My hand shot out before I even thought about it. I grabbed John by the collar and drove him back into the wall so hard the cabinets rattled. His head thudded against the plaster, dishes clinking in protest. My forearm pinned him across the chest, muscles burning with the force I poured into it.

"You never—" the words tore out of me, rough and shaking, "—lay a hand on a woman. Do you hear me? Not her. Not anyone."

He bucked against me, trying to twist free, but he didn't have the strength. Not like this. His breath reeked of beer, hot and sour, hitting my face with every strained exhale.

Out of the corner of my eye, I saw Bella. She stood frozen, one hand pressed to her cheek. Eyes wide, shining but dry, refusing to let the tears fall.

The kids clustered behind her, scared out of their minds. Chloe's cheeks were wet with tears even though she hadn't seen the worst of it, thanks to Alex. That image carved deeper into me than John's rage ever could.

I leaned in closer, pressing harder, my face inches from his. "You've been coasting on beer and her patience. That's all you are. A waste of space."

My fist curled, knuckles aching to land somewhere.

"If you ever touch her again—" I shoved him harder, letting him feel the promise in my body, "—I will end you."

His eyes flickered, anger and fear warring for ground. My pulse thundered in my ears, drowning everything else out.

This wasn't just about tonight. This was every night I'd watched her drown while he sat there in silence. Every tantrum she wrestled through alone. Every plate she scraped clean while he cracked another beer. Every inch of her he wore down until she folded smaller and smaller just to survive him.

And under all of that rage was something sharper. The way I wanted her safe. The way I wanted to be the one she could lean on. The one she deserved.

His fight finally sputtered out. His hands shoved weakly at my arm, curses slurring together, but there was no strength behind it anymore. No edge.

I held him there a second longer. Just enough to make sure he understood. Then I let him go.

He staggered back, dragging a hand over his collar, muttering under his breath as he turned. He didn't look at Bella. Didn't look at the kids.

Just stomped up the stairs. The door slammed hard enough to rattle the frames on the wall.

No apology. No words. Just absence.

The silence that followed was louder than anything he'd said.

The fridge hummed. The baby monitor buzzed soft on the counter. Somewhere upstairs, footsteps paced once, then stopped.

Bella was already on the floor, arms wrapped tight around the kids. Chloe buried her face into her side, shoulders shaking. Sam clung to her leg, confused and quiet now, thumb back in his mouth. Alex stood stiff beside them, trying too hard to be steady.

I moved before I thought about it.

"Hey," I said, softer now, crouching down just enough to catch their eyes. "Alright. Let's get you guys to bed."

They didn't argue. Didn't stall. That scared me more than anything else.

I walked them up the stairs, one by one. Tucked them in. Checked closets, under beds, like it mattered. Like I could fix something with routine. Chloe grabbed my shirt before I stood up.

"He's not coming back, right?" she whispered.

My throat tightened. "Not tonight," I said, steady as I could make it. "You're okay."

She nodded, even though I could tell she didn't fully believe it. None of them did.

By the time I came back down, the house felt hollow.

Bella sat curled into the corner of the couch, an ice pack pressed to her cheek. Her shoulders were rounded in, like she was trying to make herself smaller.

For once, she looked small. Too small.

When I came back into the living room, I crouched in front of her, elbows heavy on my knees. My voice came out low, rougher than I meant."Let me see."

Her fingers hesitated, then she lowered the ice pack.

My stomach twisted. Her lip was split, swelling fast. A flush of red spread across her cheekbone where his hand had landed. I clenched my fists to keep from storming down the hall and tearing the door off its hinges.

"You're bleeding," I murmured, reaching without thinking. My thumb hovered near her chin before I gently tilted her face toward the light.

She flinched. Not from me, but from how careful I was. That nearly broke me.

"It's not that bad," she whispered, but her voice wavered, thin at the edges.

"It's bad enough," I said, jaw tight, the words grinding out.

Her eyes searched mine, steady even as they shimmered. We sat there, locked in silence. Nothing between us but the weight of what had just happened.

"Are the kids okay?" she asked, already turning away from herself, like she always did.

"They're okay," I said, lifting the ice pack again and pressing it back gently against her cheek. Her hand trembled, so I steadied it with mine. "Keep this on," I added, softer now. "It'll help."

She gave the faintest nod, her lips parting like she might say something more, but the words never came.

I stayed there, kneeling in front of her. My hand braced over hers, holding the ice in place while the silence settled around us.

And somewhere under the anger, under the adrenaline still burning through me, something else took root. Quiet and unshakable.

This didn't happen again. Not to her. Not ever.

Chapter Thirty

COVERED BRUISES

Bella

Dean stayed on the rug in front of me, one knee down, one foot braced. His hand held the ice pack steady when mine wouldn't stop trembling. His voice was low, almost like he was afraid raising it might break me in half.

"Why don't you leave him?"

The words hit harder than John's slap had. My throat locked, breath catching. The ache spreading deeper than my split lip.

"Because I don't want to break my family," I whispered, even though I feared tonight had done just that.

His eyes sharpened, unflinching. "Bella...if he laid a hand on you tonight, what's stopping him from doing it again? Or doing worse—to the kids?"

"He won't." The denial slipped out fast, thin as paper. I clung to it like it might shield me. "He never had before. He was just—" I swallowed, "—he was being protective."

Dean shook his head, jaw set hard. "Don't. Don't make excuses for him." His voice cracked, not angry, but raw. Stripped. "I've seen this before, too many times. You deserve better. You deserve to breathe. To be happy. To live without this constant tension pressing on you."

I tried to meet his eyes, but it burned. I dropped my gaze instead to the coffee table. To the ring digging into my finger. To the bruise I already felt blooming under my skin.

The silence was thick, suffocating. The baby monitor hummed faintly. Luna's small breaths buzzed through the static like background proof of innocence we both wanted to protect.

Finally, the truth broke out of me, ragged. "But I can't afford it."

Dean's brow furrowed. "What do you mean?"

Heat rose in my face. I hated saying it out loud. "He took out a lien on the house," I admitted, my voice splintering. "The payments are stupid high. We were barely scraping by with both our salaries. If I walked away...if I left him, then I lost the house. I lost everything. And the kids—" my voice cracked. "The kids needed stability. They needed a home."

Dean rocked back on his heels, pulling air into his lungs like it hurt to hold it. When he spoke again, his voice was steadier, softer. "Then let me help. I have money."

The tears pricked instantly. "No." The word was sharp, but it came from somewhere fierce inside me.

"It's the least I can do," he pressed, urgency creeping into his tone. "Call it rent for the last few months. You opened your door when I had nowhere else to go. Let me give something back."

I clutched the ice pack harder, pain throbbing through my lip. My words spilling like broken glass. "No. I won't take your money."

"Bella—"

"I said no," I snapped, but the sound fractured on the last syllable. My voice shook when I needed it steady, begged when I wanted it strong. "Because if I take it, then it means I failed. It means I couldn't take care of my kids myself. And I can't—" My chest heaved, hot tears spilling free. "I can't let them down like that. I can't let them see me lose everything."

Dean's face softened in a way that almost broke me more than John's blow had. His fight melted out of him, but his eyes didn't look away. Slowly, he reached up and brushed his knuckle across my cheek, catching a tear before it could fall.

The gentleness of it unraveled me. For the first time all night, I felt stripped bare. Exposed. Terrified. Because deep down, no matter how I tried to bury it, he was right.

Dean stayed with me on the couch until the ice pack lost its bite and turned damp and useless against my skin. Neither of us said much. The silence pressed in, heavy but not uncomfortable. Just the kind that came when there was nothing left to give.

His hand rested on my shoulder, steady and grounding, and I leaned into it longer than I meant to.

Finally, I shook my head, my voice breaking quiet. "You should get some sleep."

His jaw tightened, eyes flicking over me like he wanted to argue, to say he wouldn't leave me like this. But after a moment, he pushed himself up slowly, careful not to jar the coffee table where the baby monitor sat glowing.

"Goodnight, Bella," he said, low enough that I almost missed it.

I managed a nod, but the second he disappeared down the hall, the house seemed to swallow me. The shadows stretched wider. The walls felt closer. The silence thick with everything we hadn't said.

I tugged the throw blanket over myself and curled into the couch cushions. The springs groaned under my weight with a tired sound, like even the furniture was worn thin. I pulled my knees tight to my chest, making myself smaller, trying to disappear inside the fabric.

From upstairs, John's jagged, loud snores cut through the stillness. The sound crawled across my skin like sandpaper, reminding me exactly who waited in the bed I couldn't bring myself to climb back into.

Tears came hot, sliding down before I could stop them. I buried my face in the blanket, smothering the sound, desperate not to wake the kids. My lip throbbed, the bruise along my cheek pulsed, but it wasn't the pain that broke me open.

It was the shame. The fear. The endless excuses I'd fed myself for years, circling through my mind like a mantra I didn't believe anymore.

Eventually, exhaustion pressed me down. My eyes burned, my body heavy. I let it drag me under, the blanket damp against my cheek.

The morning came too soon.

Cartoons blared from the kids' bedrooms, the voices cutting through my half-sleep. My neck screamed from the couch cushion digging into it, the throw blanket half-slipped onto the floor.

"Mommy, why'd you sleep here?"

Sam's little voice snapped me upright. He stood beside me in his pajamas. His stuffed dinosaur tucked under one arm. His curls sticking up every which way. His wide eyes blinked at me like I'd done something strange.

"I...fell asleep watching TV," I said quickly, pasting on a smile. My lip cracked with the effort, sharp pain pulling a wince before I could stop it.

Sam frowned, tilting his head. "But the TV is off."

I smoothed a hand over his hair. "Must've turned off by itself."

Before he could press me, Chloe barreled down the hallway, iPad already glowing in her hands. She stopped short, her voice sharp and too loud for this early.

She looked at me but just shrugged, already tapping her screen again. But Alex lingered in the hallway, backpack slung over one shoulder, watching. His gaze flicked from me to the couch and blanket, then back again. He didn't ask. He just dropped his bag by the door and poured himself a bowl of cereal like nothing had happened.

In the kitchen, I yanked open the junk drawer, fingers fumbling for the concealer tube I stashed for emergencies. The mirror above the sink didn't lie. My lip was split, my cheekbone already purpling beneath the skin. I dabbed, blended, and smoothed until the worst of it blurred into something that looked like exhaustion, which wasn't exactly a lie.

When I turned, Dean was there in the doorway. Arms folded, shoulders filling the frame. His eyes locked on mine. He didn't speak. He didn't need to. The weight in his stare pressed heavier than words.

I looked away first, grabbing juice boxes from the fridge like my hands weren't trembling. "Busy morning," I muttered, steadier than I felt.

Dean didn't move until Sam's spoon clattered against the counter, spilling milk in a white arc across the surface and dripping down to the floor.

"I got it," Dean said, crouching before I could react. He wiped the mess with calm hands while Sam giggled at the splatter.

"Thanks," I muttered, sealing sandwich bags too hard, plastic crinkling loud in the quiet.

Chloe marched in with her iPad blaring some cartoon. Dean held out a hand. "Not at the table, kiddo."

She scowled. "Daddy lets me."

"I am not Daddy," he said evenly, no bite. Just fact.

For a beat she looked ready to argue. Then, with a huff, she set the iPad down and climbed into her chair, like she remembered last night.

From the counter, Alex watched. He didn't say a word, but I caught the way his shoulders eased, like someone finally said what he'd been thinking.

I rinsed the knife at the sink, hands shaking just enough that I shoved them under the stream of water to hide it. My chest was tight, every breath too shallow.

Then came the sound I'd been dreading: the heavy thud of footsteps dragging down the stairs.

John.

He stumbled into the kitchen. His hair sticking up in wild tufts and eyes squinting against the brightness spilling through the blinds. The smell of soda hit sharp as he cracked open a can, tipping it back and gulping half before even breathing.

"You're late," I said without thinking, the words slipping out like muscle memory.

His head jerked slightly, but he didn't look at me. He just waved his hand like he was shooing away a fly and lumbered toward the living room. The recliner creaked a second later, followed by the hiss of the TV powering on.

The silence that dropped over the kitchen was heavier than his footsteps had been.

Dean pulled out the chair across from Chloe and sat down like it was intentional. Like planting himself there could steady the room. His gaze caught mine over the table, steady, unblinking. One second, two. Too much for me to hold. His look said what his mouth couldn't with the kids right there: *You didn't deserve this.*

I snapped the last lunchbox shut harder than necessary; the sound sharp in the quiet.

"Shoes and coats, guys," I said, brisk and clipped. "We were leaving in ten."

Alex slid off his stool and crouched to help Sam into his sneakers without being asked. Sam clapped when the Velcro stuck. Chloe dragged her feet, rolling her eyes but moving anyway.

Dean stayed put, his elbows resting on the table. Quiet. Watching. I could feel the weight of his eyes tracking my hands as I shoved juice boxes into bags, as I smoothed the plastic wrap over sandwiches that were already perfect. Every motion too sharp, too fast. Part of me wanted to whirl around, to tell him to stop looking at me like that, like I was fragile glass. But another part clung to it, because at least someone was looking.

The drive to school was crowded with noise and silence all at once. Chloe kicked the back of my seat in rhythm until I snapped, "Knock it off." She crossed her arms, pouting at the window. Alex hummed under his breath; his backpack clutched tight against his chest. Sam babbled about dinosaurs, his toy T-Rex roaring along with him, oblivious to everything else.

Dean sat in the passenger seat. Elbow against the door and fingers flexing on his thigh. He didn't speak. He didn't have to, because the tension rolled off him, filling every quiet space the kids left behind.

"Chloe," I said, catching her eyes in the rearview, "show-and-tell today. Did you pack something?"

She lifted her iPad case like it was proof enough. I bit down on the words that wanted to follow.

At drop-off, I pasted on my smile, wide and easy, as Chloe dodged my hand when I tried to fix her hair. Alex muttered a quiet "bye" and kept his head down.

"Remember your math homework," I called after him, my voice bright enough to fool the teachers waving from the curb.

"Bella!" one of the other moms chirped as she passed, her voice too cheery for the hour. "You're amazing. I don't know how you do it with three."

I smiled back, hollow but practiced. "Lots of coffee."

She laughed and kept walking. No one looked close enough to notice the concealer caked on my cheek, or the way my lip tugged awkwardly when I smiled. They never did.

The second the kids disappeared through the school doors, my smile dropped. My shoulders sagged. I leaned forward until my forehead pressed the steering wheel. Just a breath. Just a second to let it out.

Dean's voice came quiet beside me, steady but rough. "You don't have to keep pretending."

"Yes, I do." My whisper scraped out of me as I reached for the ignition. The wheel was cool under my palms, the leather biting into my grip. "If I fall apart, everything falls apart."

He didn't argue. The silence that followed wasn't agreement. It was heavier than that. I felt it in the way he sat rigid in the seat. Jaw working. Hands flexing against his jeans. Anger. Not at me exactly, but at the whole damn mess. At John. At himself for being stuck here, maybe.

I put the car in gear, forcing my eyes on the road. Another day to survive.

The drive home blurred after dropping Sam and Luna off at daycare, with the faint smell of crayons and spilled juice boxes clinging to the air. I pulled into the driveway to drop Dean off. My chest was tight, every beat of my heart sharp against the bruise under my makeup.

"I'll be late," I told him, my voice clipped as I grabbed my purse. "Paperwork."

Dean only nodded, but his eyes followed me as I backed out, heavy enough to leave an ache in my skin.

At the office, I tried to make the day normal. Sat down at my desk to open my laptop and start pulling up MLS. Numbers glared back at me: square footage, number of rooms, lot sizes, sale prices, mortgage approvals. Words stacked in neat little columns I couldn't absorb. I scrolled, checked emails, and read the same sentence three times without retaining a single word.

The hum of the office usually kept me grounded. Phones ringing, printers spitting, laughter spilling from the bullpen, but today it all scraped at me like static, harsh and endless.

By noon, my coffee was still full, the surface cold. My lip throbbed every time I moved my mouth. My eyes burned, but I refused to let them spill over here, in front of anyone.

Tina appeared at the edge of my desk like she always did, quiet but impossible to ignore. "You've been dodging my texts," she said, setting her coffee down beside mine. Her eyes swept over my face, sharp and assessing in a way that made my stomach drop. "And don't tell me you've just been busy."

"I've been busy," I said anyway, forcing my tone light, eyes glued to the screen.

"Bella." Just my name. Nothing else.

I looked up.

Her gaze locked onto mine. Then flicked to my cheek. Then to my lip, noticing the way I kept angling my face away from the light. Her mouth tightened, something dark flashing behind her eyes before she smoothed it over.

"What happened?" she asked, quieter now.

I hesitated, fingers curling against the edge of my desk. "It's nothing."

"Don't," she said, cutting me off. Not loud, but firm. "Don't insult me like that."

The words sat between us.

I exhaled slowly, my shoulders sagging. "John and I had a fight," I said, keeping it clipped, controlled.

Her brows lifted just enough. "A fight," she repeated, like she was testing the word.

I nodded. Didn't say more.

Tina held my gaze a second longer, then looked away first, biting back whatever she wanted to say. I saw it in the tight set of her jaw, the way her fingers curled around her coffee cup.

"Come on," she said finally, straightening. "You're not getting anything done here."

"I have work—"

"You're staring at the same screen for an hour," she cut in, already grabbing her purse. "Lunch. Now."

I should've argued. I didn't have the energy.

We sat across from each other at a small table by the window, the place we'd gone a hundred times before. The smell of fried food and coffee hung thick in the air. People talked around us, forks clinking against plates with the low hum of conversations filling the space.

Tina didn't touch her menu. She just watched me.

"You need to leave him." The words landed flat and heavy between us.

I stared down at the table, tracing a scratch in the wood with my fingernail. "We're not doing this," I said quietly.

"Bella—"

"No," I cut in, sharper this time. "We're not doing this today."

Her lips pressed into a thin line. "Then when?"

I didn't answer. I reached for my water instead, taking a slow sip just to give myself something to do.

"The kids need stability," I said finally. The words automatic, rehearsed.

Tina let out a breath through her nose, shaking her head slightly. "Kids need safety more."

I looked up, meeting her eyes just long enough to feel it hit, then glanced away. "They are safe."

She didn't call me out. Not directly. But the silence that followed said enough.

A waitress came by, asked for our order. Tina answered for both of us without looking away from me. Same thing we always got. Routine. Easy.

"I'm fine," I said after a beat, softer now, like if I said it enough times it might become true.

Tina leaned back in her chair, crossing her arms. "You don't look fine."

"I didn't sleep," I said, shrugging like that explained everything.

Her eyes dropped to my lip again, then back up. "Yeah. I can see that."

I forced a small smile, one that pulled awkward against the split. "Can we just...not?"

She studied me a long moment, then nodded once. "Fine. Not today."

Relief slid through me so fast it almost made me dizzy.

We ate in pieces after that. Small talk. Work talk. Safe things. Listings or rates. A nightmare client she'd been dealing with. I latched onto it, let it carry the conversation somewhere neutral, somewhere I could breathe.

But every so often, I caught her watching me. Quiet. Calculating. Like she was filing this away for later.

By the time we stood to leave, she squeezed my arm, brief but firm. "I'm here," she said.

"I know," I answered, meaning it more than I wanted to admit.

No showings. No closings. No clients waiting for my smile. Nothing tethering me here.

I slipped my laptop back into my bag, signed the sheet on the corner desk without anyone glancing up, and walked out the side door. The air outside was damp, smelled faintly of exhaust and wet leaves. No one stopped me. No one noticed.

At home, the silence slammed into me harder than any noise. The house smelled faintly of baby lotion and last night's dinner. I didn't bother with my heels, just let them thud against the rug as I dropped onto the couch. My body curled in on itself, knees pulled tight, like I could fold away the ache in my chest.

The fabric was scratchy under my cheek, the pillow smelling faintly of Dean's detergent from the laundry he'd folded the night before.

My last thought before sleep dragged me under was bitter, sharp enough to sting: If this is what holding everything together looks like, I didn't know how much longer I could keep doing it.

Chapter Thirty-One

YOU CAN HAVE HER

Dean

John had been a ghost for days; gone before sunrise, stumbling in long after midnight, or not at all. When he did show up, it was to sink into that recliner with the TV mumbling until the beer dragged him under. Bella said he hadn't touched their bed since the night he hit her. Good. He didn't deserve to breathe the same air, let alone share her sheets.

But tonight, he came through the door earlier. And I couldn't choke it down anymore.

I leaned into the kitchen doorway, arms folded tight across my chest. "You know what? I've had enough of this shit."

He was bent over the fridge, hand already on a beer. His head jerked up, eyes narrowing. "Excuse me?"

"Your wife," I said, steady, "is a damn saint. She busts her ass every day. For you, for those kids. She cooks and cleans. She keeps this house running while you rot in that chair. And you?" I shook my head, heat crawling up my neck. "You're a waste of space."

The fridge slammed shut so hard bottles clinked inside. He straightened, shoulders squaring, face flushing red.

"You don't get to talk to me about my wife." He stepped closer, breath sour, fist twitching at his side.

"I do when you treat her like dirt."

That was it. He lunged. His swing wide and sloppy, easy to read. I slid aside, gave his shoulder a shove to send him stumbling past.

He came back around, eyes wild, another hook already cocked. I ducked under, came up with my fist before I thought better of it. My knuckles cracked sharp against his cheekbone. His head snapped sideways. His body pitching into the counter with a grunt.

For a beat, I braced for him to charge again. Instead, he froze. His chest heaving, eyes glassy with rage.

Then he laughed. A jagged, bitter sound that didn't belong to anything human. He wiped his mouth, stared at the smear of blood on his hand, and sneered.

"If you think she's so great," he slurred, pointing a shaky finger at me, "fine. You can have her. I've got no use for her anymore. Good luck with her."

He shouldered past me, heavy steps dragging down the hall, and a door slammed hard enough to rattle the frames on the wall.

I stood in the kitchen with the hum of the fridge and the stench of his beer, fists still tight, pulse hammering. The only thing louder was the thought echoing in my head. He'd meant every word. *You can have her.* The words still burned in my ears.

No. She wasn't mine to have. She wasn't anyone's. She deserved more than being tossed between a man who broke her and another who thought he could fix her.

I straightened slowly, forcing my fists to unclench. Blood tugged at the skin on my knuckles, tacky and stinging when I flexed my hand. Upstairs, the floor creaked with a soft, familiar weight crossing the boards. Probably her, checking on the kids. Normal sounds in a house that felt anything but normal.

And that was when it hit me. John was wrong. I didn't want to have her. I wanted her free. Even if that freedom never meant me.

I braced my hands on the counter, drawing a slow breath, trying to quiet the drum in my chest. Then I heard her footsteps on the stairs, careful and hesitant, like she already knew the air was off.

"Dean?" Her voice floated in, low, uncertain. She stepped into the doorway, hair tied back, one of John's old T-shirts hanging on her. Her eyes moved over me, quick, searching. Then they landed on my hands.

Her face tightened. "What happened? Are you okay?"

I turned my palms up, trying to make it look casual, even though my knuckles were raw and scraped. “Yeah,” I said, flexing my fingers like it was nothing. “Caught it on the counter.”

Her brow pinched, not buying it. She didn’t call me out, though. Her gaze drifted down the hall where John had vanished. Tension coiled tight in the space between us, heavy enough I could feel it in my throat.

I leaned back against the counter, forcing a shrug. “It’s nothing, Bella. Don’t worry about it.”

She pressed her lips together, that thin line she always wore when she wanted to push but knew she wouldn’t. Not tonight. Instead, she let out a slow breath through her nose and nodded once.

“Okay,” she said softly, and turned toward the stairs.

I watched her go, every step pulling tighter at my chest. John’s words still rang, bitter and sharp, but I swallowed them down. She didn’t need that weight on top of everything else.

I stayed there, alone in the kitchen, with the familiar hum of the fridge filling the silence, pretending it really was nothing.

Chapter Thirty-Two

THE PAPERS ON THE COUNTER

Bella

I didn't realize my hands were shaking until the pages slipped against each other, that papery hiss loud in the quiet. The seal at the bottom glared back at me, weighty and final. Divorce papers. My name typed clean beside his. The neat blocks of words spelling out an ending I'd been patching together with duct tape and denial for years.

The house. The car. The debts. All signed over as part of the agreement.

And right in the middle, the line that hollowed me out: joint custody. 50/50.

From the closet came the scrape of hangers. The door banged against the wall. I turned just as John yanked shirts from the rod, dropping them into a half-zipped duffel. His back was rigid. His movements sharp, almost careless, like he'd rehearsed this moment in secret.

"John—" My voice cracked before I even knew what I wanted to say.

He didn't turn. Didn't pause. "Tell the kids I'll see them this weekend."

The words punched the air out of me.

"You're just...leaving?" I stepped closer, the papers drooping in my hand.

He moved to the dresser, scooping another stack of clothes without looking at me. His face stayed blank, hard. "Oh, and don't worry. I pulled my checks from the account. Took my name off it. You can figure everything out without me."

The duffel zipped with a violent jerk. He slung it over his shoulder and brushed past me. His cologne stinging my nose, bitter and sharp, like he wanted me to remember he'd been here even as he walked out the door.

The slam rattled the frame. I stood barefoot in the hallway. The silence pressing against my ear. The papers limp in my hand. Relief should've come rushing in, but instead it felt like the floor had split, a fault line opening beneath me.

I don't know how long I stared at the door just past the staircase. My knuckles whitened on the edge of the papers. Long enough that I didn't hear the garage. Didn't hear the footsteps. Just saw a shadow stretch across the floor.

"Bella?"

I turned, blinking, and for a moment I didn't recognize him through the tears welling up in my eyes.

Dean filled the entryway, though even that name barely seemed to fit him anymore. His hair had grown out just enough to catch the light, silver threading through like stories he'd never tell. A beard lined his jaw, neat and clean. Glasses softened him, but the dark slacks and button-down made him look... older. Different. Like he'd shed skin and come back weathered, harder, but somehow steadier.

My throat tightened. The boy I'd met at the bowling alley all those years ago was gone. This man standing in my hallway had been carved out of fire and ash, like a phoenix.

I must've been staring, because he tilted his head, brows pulling together. "What's wrong?"

The papers crinkled in my grip. I couldn't get words past the lump in my throat.

He stepped closer, his glasses slipping lower on his nose as his eyes flicked to the pages like he could read them from here. "Bella?"

I swallowed. My voice was dry and brittle when it finally broke out. "He's gone."

Dean's expression didn't shift much, but something flickered in his eyes. He set his keys down on the counter with a quiet clink, then moved closer. Slow, like he thought one wrong step might shatter me. And maybe it would.

Dean's voice was low and careful, like he was stepping onto thin ice. "What's going on?"

I dragged my eyes up to his, throat burning. My hand shook as I lifted the stack of papers between us. "Divorce papers," I whispered. The words scraped out raw. "He pulled his paycheck from the bank. Took his name off the accounts. He signed over everything to me." My voice broke. "Everything, Dean. He said it's all mine to deal with. All of it. All the loans."

The papers slid in my grip as my body folded in on itself. The weight of it was too much. "I can't pay for all this," I choked out, clutching the stack of paper against my chest like it might hold me together. "Daycare, after-school, the mortgage, the loans. Oh my god! I'd have to sell a house every single day just to keep us afloat."

My knees buckled. Before I hit the floor, his arms were around me. Solid, and pulling me in. One hand cupped the back of my head, the other banded across my shoulders. His chest was an anchor as the sobs tore through me.

He didn't speak. Just rocked me slowly, gently, like he knew words would splinter me further.

I pressed my face into his shirt, the cotton warm and damp under my tears. I told myself it was comfort. Only comfort. But every nerve betrayed me. Every part of me wanted to shift closer. To climb into his lap. To press against him until there was no space left. To drown in the strength of his arms and the scent of his skin.

I didn't. I stayed locked in place, shaking while the storm inside me raged.

Eventually the sobs thinned, breaking into sharp inhales and ragged exhales. My cheek still rested against him, his shirt blotched where I'd soaked it. His hand moved in slow circles between my shoulder blades. Steady. Patient. Grounding.

"You're not all alone in this," he murmured, his voice rough but sure.

I shook my head against his chest. My words came out muffled, thick with panic. "But I am. It's my name on everything. My paycheck. My kids. My responsibility. I don't—" My throat locked tight.

"No." His voice cut through, firm but not unkind. He pulled back just enough to make me meet his eyes. Calm. Certain. "You're not. You've been carrying this weight by yourself for so long that you don't even see someone standing right next to you, ready to take half of it."

My lips parted, ready to argue, but nothing came.

He tugged me gently back into his chest, his arms tightening like a shield. "I know you don't want my money. Fine. Forget money. But you don't have to do this alone, Bella. Not anymore. Not with me here."

The sting of fresh tears pressed at my eyes. I swallowed them back, refusing to fall apart again. Still, my voice slipped out in a whisper, barely brushing his collarbone. "I don't know how to let someone help me."

His hand stilled at my back, then resumed its quiet rhythm. "Then let me figure it out with you."

The knot in my chest loosened just enough to let air in.

His palm settled at the small of my back. "Do you want another hug?" he asked softly, like he hadn't been holding me this whole time. Like he knew sometimes you needed permission to crumble.

"Yes," I breathed. One word. Barely there.

Something cracked wide open in me. He drew me tighter, his chest unyielding against mine, and the last of my restraint fell apart. Raw, shaking sobs came again, tearing through me. And he held me through all of it, saying nothing. Just anchoring me with the rise and fall of his breath until I could finally breathe with him.

Later, I couldn't have said how, we ended up in my bedroom. The lamp on my nightstand cast the room in soft amber light, shadows stretching across the walls. I curled against him on top of the comforter. My cheek tucked under his jaw. His arm slung heavy and protective around me. His shirt smelled faintly of cedar and soap. His warmth wrapping over me like a weighted blanket.

I tried to hold it in, but the tears came again. Hot and relentless. My chest hitched against him.

Dean said nothing, just kept rubbing his palm slow over my back. The rhythm steadied me even as the sobs kept ripping through.

"I'm sorry," I gasped against his shirt, hating how broken I sounded.

His chin lowered until his beard brushed my hair. "Don't apologize. Not for this."

That undid me. I cried harder. Until the tears finally ran out. Until the silence between us softened into something gentler, almost safe.

For the first time in longer than I could remember, a flicker of something more than survival stirred in me. A whisper that maybe things would be okay. Maybe, with him here, I wouldn't have to fight every battle alone anymore.

But the guilt came just as fast. What was I doing letting him into my bed like this? John's presence still clung to the walls, even with his things half-packed. The divorce papers weren't even dry on the counter. And Dean was supposed to be my friend. John's friend. A man with his own storms to fight.

Still, my hand had fisted into the fabric of his shirt without me realizing it, clinging. And the thought circled sharp and terrifying: maybe this was where I was always meant to end up. Right here. With him.

The thought made me both warm and sick at once. My heart hammered. My body caught between wanting to melt closer and bolt out the door.

Dean's voice broke through, vibrating against my ear, low and steady. "Why don't I get the kids? Give you a moment."

I nodded against his chest, unable to find words. My fingers released his shirt reluctantly as he eased me back into the pillows. The mattress felt too big and too cold without the weight of him beside me.

I listened as his footsteps retreated down the hall. Then his voice calling to the kids, softer now. Their small replies rose back to him, muffled. Proof that he could step into the noise of their world as easily as he stepped into mine.

Over the next week, that steadiness became something I leaned into more than I would ever admit.

There were hugs. Always offered, never forced. His arms open like a question, and me saying yes more often than I thought I would.

When the panic pressed too tight, when the stack of bills on the counter made my chest seize with dread, he didn't promise fixes. He didn't tell me to calm down. He just wrapped me up in a hug. His silence heavy and grounding, his breath steady until mine matched it.

And I hated how much I needed it.

I still struggled. Every day. To function. To believe I could keep this life afloat for my kids. But for the first time in years, someone else was carrying part of the weight with me.

And I couldn't decide if that terrified me or saved me.

Chapter Thirty-Three

The Spare Bedroom

Dean

I never thought hugging someone could feel like a lifeline, but that's what it had turned into. For her. And if I was being honest, for me too.

Every time Bella reached for me, it was her way of saying don't let me fall apart alone. Hesitant. Almost embarrassed, like she didn't want to admit she needed it. And every time I wrapped my arms around her, I answered the only way I knew how: I won't.

But holding that line...Fuck, it has been brutal.

Some nights I'd sit at her kitchen island, elbows propped on the counter, pretending to scroll my phone while she packed lunches. The tremor in her hands was small, but I caught it. Other nights she'd pour herself half a glass of wine, sit on the couch, and fold into herself. Shoulders hunched, staring past the TV like she was the only thing keeping the walls from closing in.

And I'd want, hell, I'd ache, to cross the room, tilt her chin up, and kiss every ounce of tension out of her.

Instead, I picked up the dish towel. Or slid another juice box into a lunchbox. Or rolled Luna onto her back until her giggles filled the room.

That was the deal I made with myself: be here, but don't push. She didn't need another man pressing into her life. She needed someone to take some of the weight off.

Still, when she leaned into me, her head against my chest, and breath stuttering until it evened out, I felt the hunger rise sharp in my ribs. Not just protectiveness. Not just care. But want. Need. The ache of knowing how easy it would be to give in.

And then Sam would come barreling in asking for his dinosaur pajamas, or Chloe would roll her eyes and demand her iPad back, and the moment would snap clean in half. I'd smile, scoop Sam up or ask Chloe about her day. Pretend I wasn't drowning in want for someone who wasn't mine.

I stayed in the small ways instead. Cooked when she was too tired. Cleaned when she couldn't move. Listened when silence said more than words. I became the anchor she leaned on without realizing, telling myself it was enough.

But it wasn't shrinking. It was growing. Every damn day.

Bella collapsed onto the couch with her legs tucked under her, a wine glass untouched beside her. I clipped Luna into the swing, set it rocking with one hand until her eyelids drooped. Her tiny chest rising and falling in a steady rhythm.

"Thanks," Bella whispered. Her voice was rough, like even the word cost her energy.

I sat down beside her, close enough that our knees almost touched. "She's easy compared to your three."

A small sound escaped her. Half laugh, half sigh. "Don't remind me."

We didn't talk after that. She shifted just slightly until her shoulder brushed mine, and for a second, I thought it was an accident. Then her head tipped sideways until it rested against me, warm and impossibly fragile.

I froze, every muscle wired tight, before I let my arm move around her shoulders. Slow. Hesitant. She didn't pull away. If anything, she leaned deeper, letting the weight of herself fall against me like she'd been holding it up all day.

My palm slid up and down her arm in slow strokes meant to comfort, but the heat under my skin was anything but simple. Her hair brushed my jaw. The faint scent of rose-scented shampoo curling into me, pulling me closer than I had any right to be.

She exhaled, soft and uneven. That hollowed me out. I wanted to turn enough to press my lips to her temple, to let her know she wasn't alone. Instead, I locked my eyes on Sam in the baby monitor, then shifted to Luna's tiny chest rising and falling across the room, holding myself still.

"Dean?" she murmured, her voice thick with sleep.

"Yeah."

"Don't go anywhere tonight."

My throat went tight. My hand tightened just slightly on her arm, grounding myself. "I'm not going anywhere."

And I meant it. God help me, I meant it more than anything. But sitting there with her curled against me, I didn't know how much longer I could keep myself in check.

She drifted off against me on the couch, her head heavy on my shoulder, my arm still around her. I stayed until her breathing turned slow and even, then eased her down, pulling a blanket over her so she wouldn't wake. I told myself it was safer that way. Safer than carrying her to bed. Safer than giving in to the pull of one more second where my body might betray me.

But when I lay down in my room, the ghost of her stayed with me. The warmth of her pressed into my side. The weight of her voice, soft and drowsy: *don't go anywhere tonight.* I turned that over and over until exhaustion finally dragged me under.

By morning, the house was alive. Sam's voice rang down the hall: "Mommy, cereal!" followed by a loud roar as he made his dinosaur stomp across the floor. Chloe whined about her hair. Alex argued about shoes, claiming one pair was too big, another too tight. The usual chaos of a weekday morning.

I pulled on clean clothes and stepped into the kitchen. Bella was already dressed for work. Her dark hair was pulled back tight, a travel mug in her hand. She didn't look at me when she slid another mug across the counter, just said quietly, "Here."

"Thanks," I answered, keeping my voice low, softer than the kids could catch.

For half a second, her eyes met mine. Tired. Guarded. Probably the same as mine. Something heavy lingered in that look, and we both pretended not to breathe it in.

Sam tugged on my hand, holding out a toy dinosaur. "Can you help him eat?" he demanded, pushing it toward the cereal box.

I crouched down, made the dinosaur chomp on the rim of the box, and Sam burst into a fit of giggles. Chloe rolled her eyes and flopped into a chair, muttering about her iPad.

"Shoes, Chloe," Bella said sharply, still trying to wrangle her own bag and coffee at the same time.

"I don't want those shoes," Chloe shot back, arms crossed.

"Then no iPad."

That did it. She stomped off to get her sneakers.

Alex stood in the doorway, shoes half-tied, glaring down at the laces. "They keep coming undone."

"I got it," I said, crouching again. I tied them quick, double knot, then gave him a pat on the shoulder. "Try that."

He gave me the smallest nod before slinging his backpack on.

Through it all, Bella moved like a storm contained in glass: snapping lids on lunchboxes and wiping down counters with quick, precise motions. At one point she leaned against the counter, thumb pressing into the crease between her brows like she could rub away the fatigue.

I couldn't stop watching her. Couldn't stop thinking about how natural it had felt last night, holding her against me. How much she needed it. How much I did too.

But the glint of her wedding ring caught the light, and my brain snapped the reminder into place. She's still his wife. No matter how absent John was. No matter what he did or didn't do. She was still his. Divorce papers or not.

I bit my tongue. Let her brush past me without a word.

When it was time to go, I grabbed Luna's car seat without being asked and carried it to the SUV like it was just part of the routine.

But inside, the truth was louder than ever: every day I stayed here, I was falling further. And every day, I was running out of reasons not to cross the line.

Chapter Thirty-Four

Let Me Help

Bella

By midmorning, I'd read the same sentence in a contract at least twenty times. The words slid across the page like water I couldn't hold. My inbox kept filling with new messages, piling on top of the old ones, but I couldn't bring myself to click a single one.

The phone rang. Once. Twice. I stared at it until the screen dimmed and the call went to voicemail. My chest clenched with guilt, then let it go just as quickly.

"Bella?" my assistant, Karen, poked her head around the doorframe. Her smile was practiced and professional, but her eyes flicked over me. "Did you get a chance to review the Jacobs file?"

"Yeah, I'll...I'll get to it." My voice sounded scratchy even to me.

She hesitated like she wanted to push, then gave a tight nod and slipped away. The door clicked shut, leaving me with the quiet hum of the copier down the hall.

I dropped my face into my hands and whispered into the dark space of my palms, "How the hell am I supposed to do this?"

The image came sharp and cruel: John in the bedroom doorway, divorce papers shoved into my chest like a grocery receipt. His duffel half-zipped with his shirts balled up and cologne sharp in the air.

I'll see the kids on the weekend. That was it. No fight. No apology. Just gone.

My hands trembled against my cheeks. Fifteen years. Fifteen years and he couldn't even look me in the eye on his way out.

And still I hated myself for being shocked. The late nights. The empty beer cans. The way he'd been gone long before he packed the bag. I'd seen it. I'd felt it. But knowing didn't make it hurt less.

I tried not to think about him, but Dean kept creeping in anyway. The way his hand had steadied me when I shook. The way he'd said my name like it mattered if I was okay. The feel of him holding me that night, arms locked around me like I wasn't carrying everything alone for once.

It scared me more than John leaving ever had.

Because I wasn't ready for this. My life was a wreck: finances strangling me, the kids orbiting me like I was the only thing keeping them together, and the house echoing with his absence. I had no space for whatever this thing with Dean was becoming.

But every night he was there. Cooking beside me. Folding laundry. Kneeling on the floor while Luna tugged his hair and the kids begged for his attention. Every night another piece of me cracked, because I liked it. I liked him.

The thought burned hot in my chest.

"I can't," I whispered, pressing my fingers into my temples until my eyes stung. "Not now. Not when everything else was falling apart."

My phone buzzed against the desk, sharp in the quiet. Tina's name lit the screen.

I hesitated, staring at it for a second too long before answering. "Hey."

"You sound like hell," she said immediately, no preamble. Papers shuffled on her end. Her voice half distracted, half locked in. "Did the Henderson file come through yet? I've got numbers that don't—" She cut herself off. "Bella. What's wrong?"

I swallowed. "Nothing. Just...busy."

"Don't do that," Tina said, sharper now. "Not with me. What happened?"

The words stuck, thick in my throat. Then they spilled out anyway. "He left."

Silence. Then, softer, "John?"

I nodded even though she couldn't see me. "Divorce papers. Packed a bag. Said he'd see the kids on the weekend and walked out like it was nothing." My voice cracked. "He took his money. Everything. Left me with the house. The loans. All of it."

Tina let out a slow breath. "Jesus, Bella..."

I pressed my palm flat against the desk, grounding myself. "I don't know how I'm supposed to do this. I can't afford—"

"You've been doing it," she cut in gently. "For years. Don't rewrite history just because he finally made it official."

I squeezed my eyes shut. "It doesn't feel like that."

"I know," she said. "But listen to me. You weren't happy, Bella. You were surviving. There's a difference."

Her words landed hard, settling somewhere deep I didn't want to look at.

"This might not feel like it yet," she continued, quieter now, "but this is your chance. To build something that's yours. Not his. Not 'yours together.' Yours and your kids'. You get to decide what that looks like now."

My throat tightened. "I don't even know where to start."

"You start small," she said. "One step. One bill. One decision at a time. And you don't do it alone. You've got me, okay?"

I let out a shaky breath. "Okay."

"And Bella?"

"Yeah?"

"You're stronger than you think. You've just been too busy holding everything together to notice."

The line went quiet after she hung up, but her words stayed.

The office quieted as the afternoon lull settled in. Phones stopped ringing. Printers stopped jamming. I pulled my laptop closer, flipped it open, and signed into the bank.

Numbers filled the screen. Mortgage, utilities, daycare, car payment, groceries. My life broken down into cruel, neat rows. Half the savings vanished with John.

I scrolled once. Twice. Until my throat closed. The deposit had landed this morning: the check with my name on it from the sale of Dean's house. At least the check cleared after John had pulled his name off the accounts.

Temporary, I'd told myself. I'd hand it back once he was clear. At least part of it was my commission from the sale, and it was the only thing keeping us afloat.

Enough to cover the mortgage. Enough for daycare. Enough to keep food on the table for the next three, maybe four months.

I traced the edge of the screen with my nail, the tap-tap sharp in the quiet office.

And then what?

After dinner, I tried to sit down in front of my iPad. The numbers blurred if I stared at them too long, so I kept clicking between tabs as I chewed the inside of my cheek raw. Mortgage. Utilities. Daycare. Car payment. The same columns of debt staring back at me, daring me to make them balance.

Dean's deposit sat there like a silent accusation. The money from his house, the one piece of his life he'd been forced to let go. That sale was the only reason I wasn't already drowning.

"If it had closed a week later..." I muttered to myself, pressing my fist against my stomach. I would've missed the payment. We'd be under.

The thought made bile rise in my throat.

I leaned back hard in my chair, arms crossed tight over my chest, glaring at the screen like it was mocking me. Fragile. That's what it was. One flat tire. One ER visit. One missed client, and the whole thing would topple.

Dean's reflection appeared faintly in the dark edge of my monitor before he spoke.

"You've been at that for hours," he said, voice low but steady.

"I needed to line everything up." My fingers flew across the keyboard as I opened a blank spreadsheet to type out balances and due dates like I could wrestle the chaos into submission.

"Bella." His hand came to rest lightly on the back of my chair. "When was the last time you took a break from the screen?"

"I am fine." I kept my eyes on the numbers, my breaths shallow, sharp. "If I could just get it organized, then—"

"Then what?" His voice softened, but it pressed anyway. "The math doesn't change just because you torture yourself with it."

My throat tightened. I didn't want him to see how right he was. "This was what I can control. I couldn't stop John from leaving. I couldn't stop you from..." I stopped myself, words tangling.

His brows drew together. "From what?"

"From being here," I said finally, too quiet. My arms wrapped tighter around myself. "From filling spaces you shouldn't be filling."

Silence stretched between us. He shifted, leaning against the edge of the desk, his arms crossing now too. "If you don't want me here, just say it."

"That's not it." The words burst out of me before I could stop them. My voice cracked. "That's the problem, Dean. I do want you here. But every time I lean a little closer, every time your hand lingers too long...I feel like I am betraying myself. Like I am betraying the kids. And still, I don't push you back."

His jaw worked, the muscle twitching, but he didn't speak right away. Just looked at me like he could see straight through the defenses I was clinging to.

I dropped my gaze back to the spreadsheet, blinking hard at the neat little rows of numbers. "I am battling the bills," I whispered, "and I am battling myself. And I don't know which one is going to break me first."

Chapter Thirty-Five

DEAN WILLIAMS

Dean

The last account closed with a sterile click of a mouse. Just like that, Marcus Dean Stone was dead. Dean Williams. That was the name now. A clean slate, on paper anyway.

But paper didn't tuck Luna in at night. Paper didn't scrape by another day in Bella's house without crossing a line I couldn't uncross.

The kids expected me at dinner. Luna expected me at three in the morning. And Bella...she tried not to look at me the same way I tried not to look at her. Neither of us pulled it off.

I should've been searching for a rental. Something small and forgettable. But instead I asked, "Mind if I move one of my beds over here? That little frame's killing my back."

Her mouth pressed into a line like she wanted to argue, but she only said, "If it helps you sleep, sure."

We dragged the queen frame down her hall together. Inch by inch, through doorways that were too narrow. She braced one end while I shoved the other. Her hair falling loose from its tie, cheeks flushed with effort. When the mattress finally dropped into place, it swallowed the wall whole. Too much bed for too little room.

The crib pressed against the opposite side; the dresser crammed in tight. No space left to walk, but it would do.

I tugged the sheets straight and lined up Luna's blankets. Bella leaned on the doorframe, watching with her arms crossed. Her face gave me nothing, but her jaw twitched once, the kind of tell she couldn't hide when something sat heavy on her chest.

"Better than that torture rack I was on," I said, rolling my shoulders until they cracked.

Her mouth curved, just a fraction, and then she turned away. No words. Just the sound of her bare feet carrying her back down the hall.

I stayed there, in a room that barely fit me, staring at the too-big bed and the too-small crib. Freedom, they called it. A new name, a fresh start. But standing there, I couldn't shake the truth clawing at the back of my throat.

I hadn't left. I couldn't. Instead of packing, I picked up my tools.

The bedroom came first. Too tight and too awkward, with that dead wedge of drywall where the staircase cut through on the other side. It gnawed at me every time I stepped inside.

I dragged in the tape measure, sketched on scrap paper, and started cutting. Shelves went up. Then a built-in closet. Basic, nothing showy, but enough to hold Luna's clothes and mine. By the time I set my drill down, sawdust in my hair and sweat drying on the back of my neck, the place finally looked less like a storage unit and more like somewhere you could breathe.

Bella leaned on the doorway, arms folded, watching me sweep the floor.

"You didn't have to do all that," she said.

"I did," I answered, not looking up. "We needed it."

Her mouth pressed into a line, like she wanted to argue, but she didn't.

And I couldn't stop.

The bathroom came next because the clawfoot tub and the half-finished walls screamed abandoned project. I gutted it. Hung fresh drywall, laid tile, built a shower stall that wouldn't leak, and put in a functional vanity. I even carved cabinetry into the alcove so there'd finally be storage.

One night she caught me unloading lumber from the SUV, receipts stuffed in my back pocket.

"Dean," she said, hand slipping into her purse, "at least let me—"

"No." I shook my head before she could finish. "Not happening."

Her brow furrowed. "You can't just eat all these costs yourself."

"I can. And I will. You've done enough."

She studied me for a long moment, then let the strap of her purse fall back to her side. She didn't bring it up again.

But I felt her eyes some nights, when I came in from the garage damp with sweat, tools clanking in my hands. She didn't say a word, just noticed. And I noticed her noticing.

Sometimes she'd scoop Luna into her wrap, sway her to sleep like she used to with her own babies, and let me crash without interruption. I never asked, but she knew when I was running on fumes. She always knew.

And every morning I woke to Luna cooing in her arms, coffee already brewing in the kitchen, I felt the same ache in my chest: this wasn't my house. This wasn't my family.

But I wanted to take care of them anyway. Even if it killed me.

The bathroom should've been enough. Fresh grout lines and cabinet doors hung straight. Done. But my eyes kept drifting, picking at the rest of the house like loose threads. Spaces that didn't work. Spaces I could make better for her.

The kitchen drove me crazy the most. Counters buried under appliances. Lunchboxes stacked in corners with bags of chips shoved wherever they'd fit. I'd watched her fight it every morning: one hand spreading peanut butter, the other swatting Sam's little fingers away. Her sigh carrying heavier than the kids' noise.

I started knocking on walls.

Bella came in mid-afternoon, brow arched. "Why does it sound like you're trying to break into the neighbor's place?"

I tapped another hollow spot and glanced back at her. "Dead space. They left a pocket behind the bathroom. Wasted."

She leaned against the counter. "And what? You're just going to...open it up?"

"Yeah," I said, already marking lines. "For a pantry. You need it."

She shook her head, half a smile tugging at her mouth. "You don't even live here."

"Luna and I do," I muttered, sawing through drywall. "At least for now."

A couple of days later, shelves lined the recess, deep enough for cereal, baskets, and the blender she always shoved out of the way. I brushed the dust off my arms and stepped back.

Bella stood in the doorway, lips parted, eyes sweeping the space. "Dean..." Her voice was quiet.

"Better than juggling everything on two feet of counter," I said.

She ran a hand along one of the shelves, and for a second, I saw the real smile. The one she didn't give anyone unless it slipped. It hit harder than I expected.

But I didn't stop.

The bare stretch of wall in the corner bugged me next. I cut lumber, sanded it smooth, and set a shelf at counter height. The coffee machine slid into place under the anchored hooks for mugs. Two of mine hung beside hers. The ones she'd teased me about for being chipped.

The next morning, she padded in with sleep still on her face, the kids dragging in behind her. Her eyes caught the nook, then flicked to me.

"You built me a coffee bar?"

"Built us a coffee bar," I corrected, handing her a mug.

She took it slowly, fingers brushing mine. No words after that. Just the smell of fresh coffee filling the air, the clink of mugs against hooks, the kind of quiet that felt like breathing again.

Because every nail, every cut of wood wasn't just fixing her house. It was the only way I knew to keep fixing myself too.

Nights had a rhythm now too. Dinner and dishes, then the shuffle of pajamas and toothbrushes. And finally the quiet once the kids were finally down. By the time I sank into the couch, she was there too, iPad on her knees, lamp humming low beside us. Sometimes we talked. Sometimes the TV mumbled. Sometimes it was just silence. Either way, it felt steady in a way I hadn't had in years.

John's ghost still lingered in the house, but she barely seemed to notice. Why would she? He'd been checked out long before he walked out. I'd seen it in the way she hauled groceries in with a toddler on her hip. The way her laugh cracked brittle around him. Even the way her kids looked past him like he wasn't even there.

And the truth was, they barely noticed he was gone. No questions. No tears. Just a shrug and a quiet, "Daddy's away for a while," before they went back to their toys or their shows or their routines. He hadn't called. Hadn't shown up. Not even a word about weekends like he promised.

Like he'd already disappeared long before he ever walked out the door.

With me, it was different. I couldn't sit like a guest and watch her break her back. So, I got up with her kids, packed lunches, folded laundry, and fixed what leaked or creaked before she even pointed it out. When Sam wanted to "help" with the wrench,

I let him, even if it meant bolts got stripped. Chloe sulked, so I pulled faces behind Bella's back until she cracked a smile. Alex cornered me with questions about school projects, and I sat at the table with him until we figured it out.

It wasn't about replacing John. I didn't want that. But I couldn't unsee what was missing. And I couldn't unfeel what it did to me to be the one filling it.

One night, when the kids were down and the TV muttered in the background, I said, "You know, I can start paying rent. Or at least groceries."

Bella didn't even glance up from her iPad. "That's not necessary. With all the work you've put into this house, it's the least I can do."

I shifted to brace my elbows on my knees, staring at the blue glow on her face. "Bella, I'm not here just to swing a hammer. You feed me. You let me put my kid to bed under your roof. That's more than a trade."

She finally looked up, eyes steady but tired. "Dean, you've rebuilt half my kitchen. You've carried more weight than John ever did. You think I don't see that?"

Her voice softened at the end, almost enough to undo me. I swallowed hard through my tight jaw. She made it sound balanced, like a couple shelves and some drywall erased the debt I felt just by sitting on her couch.

But it didn't. Not for me.

Bella set the receipt book down on the counter with that sharp exhale she thought I didn't notice. Her thumb worried the corner of the paper, forehead pinched as she lined up numbers that never seemed to bend her way.

"Everything good?" I asked, leaning against the fridge.

She didn't look up. "Fine. Just the usual." The pen scratched quick, irritated.

I caught the way her shoulders curled forward, like she was trying to fold herself small. It landed in me like a punch. I'd been sitting at her table, drinking her wine, eating her food, and she was still stretching every dollar until it squeaked.

"I could take care of groceries," I said. The words slipped out before I could make them sound casual.

Her head snapped up, eyes narrowing. "Dean. No."

I lifted my hands. "I didn't say I'd move in and start paying your mortgage. Groceries. That's all."

She shook her head and pushed the receipt book aside. "I am not taking your money."

"Who said anything about taking?" I crossed the room and opened the cabinet just to give my hands something to do. Half a bag of cereal, a couple cans of beans, a jar of peanut butter sitting on its last scrape, and an almost empty pack of cookies. I let the door fall shut with a hollow clap. "Looks like it could use a refill."

Her jaw tightened. "Don't."

"Bella." My voice caught rougher than I meant. "I can't sit here watching you bend yourself in half to cover it all. Not when I am—" I stopped, swallowed, tried again. "Not when I am adding to the bill."

She went quiet, watching me like she was waiting for me to blink first.

I broke eye contact by rubbing the back of my neck. "You can't argue with what you don't see."

"What's that supposed to mean?"

"Nothing," I muttered, forcing a crooked smile. "Forget it."

But I didn't forget.

The next morning, I sat parked outside the bank with the rental SUV idling low. Luna's carrier rocked in the back with every little kick of her heel, a soft rattle of plastic and cloth as she slept. I had Mark's number on the screen, my thumb hesitating. One call, maybe two favors pulled. Not clean, but not dirty either.

By afternoon, I had Bella's account info staring back at me in black text.

I set up the transfer through a tightly locked jaw. Not too much, just enough to make the numbers on her screen ease up without screaming that something was off.

The confirmation popped up. My chest loosened a fraction.

I twisted around in my seat. Luna's lips worked in her sleep, a tiny sigh fogging the carrier hood. I whispered, "We'll pay her back, one way or another."

The key turned under my hand. The engine grumbled to life, vibrating steady and heavy up through the steering wheel. I pulled onto the road, headlights catching the late-day haze, carrying me and my daughter forward. The stubborn weight of knowing I had to try.

Chapter Thirty-Six

THE PARTNERSHIP

Bella

The place buzzed with silverware scraping plates and the low hum of half-heard conversations. I'd argued about the bill when we walked in, but Dean just shook his head and waved me off, so by the time the calamari landed, hot and crisp, I'd let it go.

He leaned back against the booth, the vinyl groaning under his weight, and exhaled like something heavy had been sitting on him all night. "I needed to figure out how to make money."

Not casual. Not tossed off. More like a line drawn in the sand.

I tore a ring of calamari apart, dunked it in the sauce before popping half in my mouth. "Don't we all?"

His mouth twitched, almost a smile, but his eyes didn't budge from mine. "I was thinking of setting up an LLC to flip houses." He rubbed at the back of his neck, the gesture pulling his shoulder tight. "I'd want you as a partner," He paused. "You'd find the houses."

I froze with greasy fingers hovering above the plate. "Me?"

"You," he said, steady like he'd already decided. "You know the market. What sells. What buyers want. I know how to build it, how to fix it, and how to flip it. We'd be a team."

That word. Team. My chest tightened around it. Not me carrying every list, every bill, or every bedtime. Not someone asleep in the recliner while I drowned alone. A team.

I forced myself to chew slowly, though my mouth had gone dry. "Dean...that's—" I had to swallow. "That's a lot."

"Yeah," he said, leaning forward now, forearms braced on the table. His voice dropped. "It is. But it could work. We could make it work."

The way he said it made me want to believe him, even when I knew better.

I set my fork down and reached for my bag before I'd even thought it through. "I know someone who could help with the loan application. Tina. She's good. She knows which areas qualify for which loans." My iPad was in my hands, my thumb swiping before the words finished leaving my mouth. "We'd need to check timelines. Inspection contingencies. Probably line up a contractor's license—"

"Bella." His voice was low. I barely looked up.

I kept talking, half to him, half to myself as the glow of the screen lit my fingers. "I can set up a meeting with Tina. That's the first step."

When I finally glanced across the table, his water glass was still in his hand, untouched. He hadn't moved. Just sat there, watching me like the ground had shifted under both of us.

"You're going to love her," I said, flashing him a quick smile before my eyes dropped back to the screen. "She's brilliant with structuring deals. And there are a couple areas in town where the turnaround is insane right now. I should make a list. I can send you the numbers tonight."

The booth creaked when Dean shifted. Leather against leather with a small groan. "Bella—"

"Just a sec." I swiped open a note, already typing. "We would need to figure out cash flow for renovations, materials, labor, permits." My stylus tapped faster. "Tina will know who to call."

The calamari sat cold between us. He had his elbows propped on the table now, leaning in like he wanted to pin me with his eyes but wouldn't force me to look. I kept talking anyway. Couldn't seem to stop.

"If we time this right, we could escrow in a month. Two tops. Don't even worry about comps, I'll—"

"Bella."

The word cut sharper this time. Firm.

My hand stilled mid-swipe. For a second, the restaurant noise crashed back over me: a baby wailing across the aisle, the metallic clink of cutlery, garlic smoke drifting from the open kitchen. My pulse thudded at my throat.

Dean didn't move, just held me there with that steady weight in his stare. Not angry, not sharp. Just...patient. And it made me want to squirm. Like he was reminding me this wasn't a client pitch.

Heat rose up my neck. I lowered the iPad to the table. "I didn't mean—"

"You don't have to fix it all right now." His voice was quieter, but it carried. "I just wanted to tell you what I was thinking."

The waiter swooped in with our entrees, plates sliding between us with a bright enjoy your meal. I muttered thanks, grateful for the break, though the knot in my chest stayed tight.

I jabbed at the stir fry, broccoli crunching between my teeth. "I know. Sorry. I went into work mode without realizing it."

Dean picked up his fork, slow and deliberate. His eyes didn't leave me. "That's why I asked you. Because you see angles I don't. But it's more than that."

I frowned around a bite of rice. "More than what?"

"More than numbers. More than paperwork." His mouth twitched with a ghost of a smile. "I asked because I trust you."

The words hit harder than they should have. My throat dried out, and I had to force the swallow.

"Okay," I whispered, softer than I meant.

I pushed broccoli through the rice, chewing his words longer than the food. *I trust you.* It was too much to hold still, too much to sit with.

I cleared my throat, tugging the iPad closer as I slid right back into the only place I knew how to breathe. "Okay, so. Tina is usually at the downtown branch on Fridays, but sometimes in

Naperville. If I can catch her now, she might squeeze us in this afternoon."

Dean exhaled. Quiet, but steady. Not frustration. More like letting something go.

I didn't let myself notice the way his hand shifted on the table or the look on his face when I pulled my iPad closer. I typed fast, my nails clicking against the screen. "If we could get the pre-approval rolling today, you'd have a clearer picture of your budget," I said, not glancing up. "And with the market the way it is, you don't want to wait another week. The right property could disappear in twenty-four hours."

Dean started to say something, but I pulled my phone out before he could.

"I'll just send her a quick text," I said to the space between us, already typing.

Hey Tina, any chance you could meet with a potential client this afternoon? He's looking into starting an LLC and applying for financing for flips. We're free anytime after 2.

"Bella—" he tried again.

"Two work for you?" I cut him off, lifting my eyes just long enough to catch his expression. Half a smirk, half a frown.

He leaned back, crossing his arms loosely. "Sure. Two works."

"Perfect." I hit send before the hesitation could catch up to me and set my phone aside like I'd settled the matter. I grabbed my water glass, tipping it back in more of a gulp than a sip. The cold bit my tongue, but the noise of the restaurant swallowed it.

Forks clinked against plates. A server laughed at something near the bar. Couples leaned in close over shared appetizers. All of it gave me cover, just as my phone dinged on the table.

"2 p.m. it is." I tried to smile at him, but he was still staring at me. "See?" I said brightly, setting the glass down with too much force. "Already handled."

Dean shook his head, not saying anything, and turned back to his plate.

"You'll thank me later when you're signing papers on your first flip." My voice came out lighter than I felt.

His fork paused midair. He looked at me for a long second, eyes steady, then dropped his gaze to his food. "Maybe I already am," he said, low enough that I almost missed it.

I stabbed at my stir fry, pretending I hadn't heard. The metal scraped the ceramic bowl louder than it should have.

By two o'clock we were sitting across from Tina in her office, the faint smell of coffee and eucalyptus essential oil hanging in the air. Laminated flowcharts covered the walls, bright arrows pointing from one loan type to the next. Tina adjusted her glasses, her nails clicking softly against the keyboard as she pulled up reports.

"So," she said, peering over the frames at both of us, "you want to set up an LLC for house flipping. That's the short version?"

Dean nodded, his posture going straight like he was back at the precinct giving a statement. "Yeah. Buy, renovate, sell. I've got the skills for the work. Bella knows the market. I just need the financing."

Tina tapped a few keys and tilted her head to look at me like *why hadn't you mentioned this man before.*

"Okay. With flips, you don't want a thirty-year mortgage. Too slow, too rigid. You'll want something short-term and flexible. Fix-and-flip loans. Sometimes hard money loans, depending on the property. Higher rates but built for quick turnarounds. Six months, maybe a year."

Dean leaned forward, elbows on his knees. His interest sharpened. "And the requirements?"

"You'll need a strong exit strategy each time," Tina said, swiveling her monitor so we could both see a map streaked with color codes. "Lenders want proof you aren't buying a wreck without a plan. But—" her eyes flicked to me, then back to him "—Bella's track record helps. Credibility goes a long way."

I uncapped my pen and scribbled lines across my notepad, even though I knew most of this already. Safer to look busy than to meet Dean's gaze. Out of the corner of my eye, I saw him nod, not just at Tina, but at me. Like every word she said about me being an asset was true in his head.

"And as for where," Tina continued, pointing at the screen, "you've got options. In Aurora, there were a few up-and-coming neighborhoods. Smaller homes, decent schools, low entry costs. Naperville's tighter, but resale values were strong if you snagged the right property at the right price. Joliet's rental market was growing fast. Higher turnover, sure, but plenty of demand. A duplex there could do well. You could renovate it and hold for a bit until you find an investor as the area keeps trending up."

Dean rubbed his jaw, studying the map like he could memorize the colors. "What kind of budget for the first flip?"

"Two-fifty to three hundred minimum," Tina said. "And keep reserves for renovations. Don't tie up every dollar in the purchase price. First one's about learning the rhythm, not chasing a jackpot."

I nodded, jotting it down even though my hand had slowed. Rhythm. Plan. Numbers. Things I could control.

"Anything else?" Dean asked.

Tina glanced between us, something knowing flickering behind her lenses. "Yeah," she said, leaning back in her chair. "Don't go into business with someone you don't trust. This kind of thing—" she gestured between us, the file and the list of numbers, "—it'll test you fast."

My pen stilled. Dean didn't hesitate. "I trust her."

The words landed heavier than anything else said in that room. I didn't look at him. Just stared down at my notes, the ink bleeding slightly where I'd pressed too hard.

Tina hummed like she'd expected that answer. "Good," she said. "Then you've got a shot."

The meeting wrapped after that. Papers stacked. Next steps outlined. Another list added to the hundred already running through my head.

Outside, the late afternoon sun hit hard, bright enough to make me squint. The parking lot shimmered with heat, cars ticking as they cooled.

"We've got a real shot at this," I said, sliding my sunglasses on, forcing my voice into something steady. "If we move fast, stay organized—"

"Bella."

I stopped. There was something in the way he said my name. Not sharp. Not impatient. Just...grounding. I turned.

He stood a few feet away, folder tucked under his arm, eyes on me in that steady way that always made it hard to breathe.

"We're good," he said. Not about the deal. Not really. "You and me. We're good."

My chest tightened around the words.

"Yeah," I said quickly, nodding once. Too fast. "Of course we are."

But I was already reaching for my keys. Already turning toward the car. Already moving. Because if I stood there any longer, I might've had to feel it. And feeling it was the one thing I wasn't ready for.

Chapter Thirty-Seven

THE CLOSET COLLAPSE

Dean

Bella kept her tablet balanced on her knees the whole drive, fingers flying like she was trying to outrun me with keystrokes. She didn't look up once. Not when I shifted in the seat. Not when I cleared my throat. Not even when I tried, "Tina looked like she was having the time of her life with those loan programs. Think she was more excited than we were."

Nothing. Just the faint clicks of her nails and the glow of the screen reflecting on her face.

"Bella," I said after a minute, softer.

"Mhm?" She didn't lift her eyes.

"You always type that fast, or is this just you avoiding me?"

That got me the smallest flicker of a glance before she dropped right back to the screen. "I'm just...making sure I don't forget anything."

I leaned back, thumb rubbing the old callus in my palm. "Pretty sure Tina emailed us both a novel in the last few days."

"I like having my own notes," she muttered, scrolling. Her voice was clipped, but her jaw worked like she was holding back something sharper.

I let it hang there, watching the town slide by through the window. Houses with peeling paint, busted porches, kids on bikes, the smell of exhaust sneaking in through the vents. She rattled off numbers under her breath for loan types and property values, like she was reciting a manual, and I nodded at the right moments even though it all blurred together.

When I'd asked her to be my partner, it wasn't about loans. It was about her. About us.

But she'd pulled Tina into it, folded the whole thing into something safe and manageable. A project.

"Bella," I tried again, quieter.

"What?" She didn't stop scrolling.

"I didn't just mean business," I said.

Her fingers froze for half a beat, then started moving again. "I know."

I didn't push.

By the time we turned into the driveway, she was already talking through her calendar, lips moving, counting under her breath. I wanted to tell her to stop, to just look at me, but the words caught somewhere between my teeth and my chest. Maybe this was how she stayed upright with lists and screens. This was the armor she wore. For now, I let her.

Inside, she dropped her bag by the door and fired up her laptop without missing a beat. I unbuckled Luna, kissed the warm crown of her head, her little fingers catching in my shirt. Bella's keys clattered on the counter, the familiar hum of her laptop powering on filling the kitchen as the rest of the kids grunted their way up the stairs.

I didn't interrupt. I moved around her instead by helping Sam up the stairs, putting groceries into cabinets, spreading school forms across the table, and fixing a screwdriver on the loose hinge of the back door.

She didn't ask me to. She didn't have to. And that's the thing, I couldn't stand back and watch her burn herself out, not when I can see it happening in real time. So, I stay close to catch what spills over.

"Hand me the spatula," I say when she's juggling dinner and her phone buzzes on the counter. She passes it without looking, already mid-email, and I finish the risotto before it scorches.

When she leaves the laundry half-folded on the couch because a Zoom call dings, I drop onto the cushion and finish stacking towels as the kids climbing over me like it's a game.

Most mornings, she forgets her coffee on the counter. I press it into her hand as she's digging for her keys. She blinks at it, startled, then mutters, "Thanks," like she doesn't know how it got there.

Maybe she notices. Maybe she doesn't. I can't tell.

But I know this: I've spent enough years looking out for myself first. Right now, she needs somebody who doesn't push and doesn't demand. Above all she needs someone who doesn't fold when things get ugly. If her way through is grinding herself raw, then mine is standing steady in the background, making sure nothing else falls apart.

By the next week, we had an LLC with both our names on it. Dean Williams and Isabella Blake. Not Turner, but Blake.

Tina worked her magic. "I know a guy," she'd said, and by the time we drained our coffee at her office, the paperwork was already in motion.

Bella didn't hesitate or stall. She just pressed forward: this needed doing, here's how we did it, let's move. Watching her was like trying to keep pace with a current that never slowed.

That night, I came home to the glow of her laptop at the kitchen island. The kids were bickering in the living room, their voices rising and falling over who got the iPad. Bella barely flinched.

"Three beds, two baths. Built in the twenties," she said, eyes on the screen. "Half-acre lot. Needs a roof and some foundation work, but it's in the right zone for construction loans."

I leaned on the counter beside her, close enough to catch the citrus smell of her hand lotion still clinging to her skin. "You found that today?"

A small smirk tugged at her mouth. "I found six today."

Two days later, Tina had us back in her office, papers spread across the desk. She walked us through it all: what towns would actually approve rehab permits, where zoning allowed more than cosmetic work, which loans moved, and which sat forgotten in some banker's drawer.

By the end, the math was clear: a small business loan for fifty grand. Not enough to buy a place outright, but enough to get us started. The down payment would be covered, I'd have to front the materials and sweat, then we'd flip and roll it forward.

Bella scribbled furiously on a yellow legal pad. Her handwriting neat and fast, every line underlined like a command. Then she set the pen down and looked at me. Business in her eyes, but something else humming underneath.

"Let's make a deal," she said.

I cocked a brow. "What kind of deal?"

"One house at a time," she said. Her voice was firm, but steady. "At least for now. I didn't want you overworking yourself, or us drowning in debt. Slow and steady, Dean."

I stared at her, the words knocking something loose inside me. Vicky had never once told me to take it slow. With her, it had always been more, faster, better, now. "Alright," I said, sliding my hand across the counter. "One house at a time."

She grinned, faint but real, and put her hand in mine. Her fingers curled tight, like she wasn't planning to let go anytime soon. We could call it a partnership. But sitting there, her hand warm in mine, it felt like more than that.

We started with the cheap houses. Two, maybe four bedrooms. Ranches with sagging roofs. Foreclosures that smelled like basements. Colonials that hadn't been touched since Reagan. Work, sure, but with her walking beside me, rattling off square footage with her pen poised like a weapon, it didn't feel like work.

She jabbed the pen toward the kitchen of one place, avocado tile climbing the walls like mold. "Imagine trying to convince a young family this is charming."

I leaned on the counter, which groaned under my weight. "Retro chic."

She snorted, then laughed so loud it bounced off the empty walls. It hit me square in the chest. It felt like years back, before kids, before the wreckage, when I'd wandered through houses I couldn't afford, making fun of shag carpets and floral wallpaper, and joking about futures I didn't believe in. Only now it didn't feel like a joke.

We shuffled through another wreck, where the walls bowed and floors soft enough to keep me on edge. She tugged a closet door, and it nearly came off in her hand. "Oh my god," she said, stepping inside, laughter still spilling.

I ducked in after her, mostly to see if the frame would hold. The closet stank of mildew. The air heavy and stale. She turned at the same time I did, and suddenly we were chest to chest.

Her eyes flicked up to mine, the gold flecks catching what little light slipped in. I felt her breath before I felt her lips.

No one leaned far. No one had to. Then she was kissing me. Soft, fast, urgent. My hand went to her waist like it had been waiting there for years. Her fingers tangled in my hair, tugging me closer, and the kiss cracked open. Teeth, tongue, and with the kind of sound in her throat that could gut a man.

The door groaned against my shoulder as I braced us. Rotten wood gave way, and the whole damn thing collapsed. I went with it. Dust shot up in a gray cloud as I landed flat on the warped floorboards, the broken door under my back.

For a beat, silence. My ribs stung, dust in my hair. Her wide-eyed face above me.

Then she laughed. Shit, did she laugh. Bent over, hand pressed to her chest. The sound raw and bright.

I should've cursed. Should've been pissed at the busted wood under me. Instead, all I could think was how bad I wanted to grab her, drag her down into the dust, and keep kissing her until we both forgot where we were.

Her laughter thinned, softened as her eyes dipped to my mouth again. That look nearly undid me.

I stood, brushing plaster from my jeans, forcing a crooked grin. "Guess that closet wasn't built for two."

She straightened her clipboard, smoothed her blouse like nothing had happened. Professional mask, neat as always. No words. No glance. Just that careful armor she wore when things cut too close.

And me, still tasting her on my lips, pretending I hadn't just felt the world tilt.

We walked the rest of the house without saying a word. Her heels tapped against the soft spots in the floor as my boots dragging over warped boards. Every time our shoulders almost brushed, I shoved my hands deeper into my pockets to stop myself from reaching for her again.

At the entry, the busted closet door leaned crooked against the frame like evidence of my screwup. Dust still clung to my jeans. I cleared my throat, trying to cut through the heavy quiet.

"Well," I said, voice coming out rougher than I meant, "we broke the place worse than it was. Guess we've got no choice but to buy it now."

Her head tilted, eyes flicking to the closet, then to me. Her lips twitched like they wanted to curve, but she pressed them flat.

I gave a half shrug, waiting.

"Retro charm," she muttered finally, adjusting the clipboard against her chest like it could block out the heat between us.

"Yeah," I said. My laugh caught in my throat. "Adds value."

She shook her head, but the corner of her mouth betrayed her for just a second before she reined it back in. Then she turned, tugging the door open to the sunlight outside like that would erase what had just happened.

I followed, pretending I was fine as my pulse thundered. Pretending my chest didn't still ache from the way she'd fit against me,. That my scalp didn't still tingle from her fingers in my hair, and my lips didn't still carry the ghost of hers.

One clumsy kiss in a busted closet and I was wrecked. And I knew damn well there was no uncrossing that line.

Chapter Thirty-Eight

No Taking It Back

Bella

That night, the kitchen felt tighter than usual. The hum of the overhead lights pressed down while we leaned shoulder to shoulder over the island, the glow of my iPad washing both our arms in pale blue. Numbers swam on the screen, but all I could feel was how close his skin was to mine.

"It's been sitting a hundred and fifty-eight days," I said, tapping the listing. My voice came out steadier than I felt. "The seller's got to be desperate by now."

Dean leaned closer, his arm brushing mine, his heat stealing my focus. "And you're sure it's outside their borders?"

I dragged my finger across the map, zooming out.

"Definitely," he said, low and certain. He caught my hand before I could pull back, guiding my finger over the screen. "See? It ends here."

His rough, warm palm dwarfed mine. Calluses scratched gently against my skin. I should've been studying zoning lines. Instead, the heat of him climbed straight through my chest.

I looked up. His grip didn't ease. He lifted my hand, slow, until his lips brushed across my knuckles.

My breath caught. Rough stubble. Warm mouth. The kiss was nothing. And it was everything.

"Dean..." It slipped out of me, half warning, half plea.

He didn't move. Just held my gaze. The shadow of his beard cut his jaw sharper, older, harder. Hotter.

I didn't think. I grabbed the back of his head, my fingers tangling in the longer strands of his hair and pulled him down to me.

The kiss landed desperate. Hungry. His arm swept the iPad aside with a dull clatter, and then he was wrapping me up, chest pressed to mine, his hand firm at the small of my back.

I gasped against his mouth as his tongue coaxed mine. Every ounce of restraint we'd been pretending to hold shattered in an instant. Heat rushed everywhere: my face, my throat, my chest, between my legs. His grip anchored me like he couldn't stand the thought of me slipping even an inch away.

I broke off for half a breath. My lips burning. My chest heaving. He chased me immediately, kissing me again. Harder.

God help me, I kissed him back like I'd been waiting years.

Then the baby monitor cracked alive with Luna's sharp, insistent, merciless wail. Dean let his forehead drop against mine, breath hot. "Right on cue," he muttered, and pulled away.

The loss hit like cold air. My lips tingled; my chest stuttered. I pressed my palms flat to the cool countertop, trying to steady myself while he disappeared down the hall. I sucked in a shaky breath. My pulse was still racing like he hadn't left at all. Crap. What had we just done?

"I'll start a bottle," I called, though the words barely sounded like mine.

Crossing the kitchen, I couldn't trust my legs. I stopped at the chrome-gray formula dispenser gleaming under the lights. Sleek and expensive. Of course it was Vicky's. The perfect DA's wife with the perfect baby gear.

And here I was, my lips swollen, my breath ragged, still tasting her husband on my mouth.

My hand hovered over the machine's glossy buttons. I couldn't remember which one did what. The lights hummed above me as the chrome surface reflected my face back in pieces. Heat crawled up my neck, not from the formula warmer but from the name echoing in my head.

Vicky.

I stared at the damn dispenser like it had called me out. Aren't they still married? My throat tightened. How did someone disappear, change his name, and sell a house, while she was still out there somewhere?

And then there was me. I was the idiot standing in my own kitchen, making a bottle for their baby after kissing him like I'd been starving for him all this time.

I pressed my palms hard against the counter, eyes shut. What was I doing? What was I risking?

The buttons blurred as I jabbed at one, then another until the machine whirred to life. Water heated as the gears churned and the spout hissed. Too clean, too precise. Nothing like the clumsy, half-asleep bottles I used to shake together at three a.m.

By the time the cap twisted tight, Dean had settled onto a chair at the island. His arms made a wide, steady shelf for Luna. She curled there, tiny fists pressed against his chest, trusting him with every gulp of the bottle.

I sat across from him and flipped open my iPad. The glow painted my face while I pretended to scroll. Numbers blurred. Addresses slipped through me. All I felt was his nearness, the ghost of his mouth still pressed to mine.

Luna's sucking filled the silence with tiny gulps, the steady rhythm of her feeding. The fridge hummed. Dean tipped the bottle, patient, like nothing else in the world existed.

When Luna finished, he lifted her to his shoulder, rubbing circles against her back until a tiny burp popped out. She melted against him, already sliding back into sleep.

I kept my eyes locked on the screen. Pretending. Scrolling nowhere.

Dean's soft footsteps padded away, followed by the quiet click of his door. When he came back, he didn't sit. He planted himself at the end of the island, hands flat on the counter, eyes steady on me.

I finally looked up. Dark. Unreadable.

"Are we going to talk about it?" His voice cut the silence clean, steady but edged.

"The house?" I asked, eyes darting back to the glow of the listings.

"Sure," he said, mouth twitching. "But also, the other thing." He paused just long enough to make me squirm. "Actually, the other two things." His wink landed like a spark.

Heat rushed through me so fast I wanted to hide behind the iPad. My cheeks burned. Like I was sixteen again.

"That was a mistake," I blurted, dragging my finger down the screen without seeing a word. "You're married, remember?"

He barked out a laugh. Loud. Bitter. Sharp. It jolted me. "Married? Bella, she disappeared and hasn't returned any of my calls. Ring or not, that chapter is over."

"Still," I muttered, voice too thin, "we shouldn't have done it. Either time..."

His footsteps came closer. My chair scraped back as he nudged it with his knee, stepping into the space. His presence filled the air between me and the table. My pulse leapt.

"Tell me you don't feel anything for me," he said, catching my hands. He pressed them against his chest, heat searing through the fabric into my palms.

"Tell me you don't feel anything when I do this." His mouth brushed the side of my neck, then pressed, slow and deliberate. My breath hitched, catching in my throat.

"Tell me it's a mistake when I do this." His grip shifted to my ass, lifting me clean off the chair. In a blink I was perched on the edge of the island, thighs braced around his hips. My arms locked around his neck before I could think.

"Dean—" I started, but his mouth found mine, cutting me off. And holy shit, I kissed him back. I didn't resist. Not for a second.

His kiss deepened, insistent, pulling me closer. My stomach twisted, pulse hammering. I dragged him closer, answering him with a desperation I couldn't pretend away. Heat poured off him. His body pressed to mine, pinning me against the island's edge. The counter dug into the backs of my thighs, anchoring me in the wrongness of it. And the way it still felt inevitable.

"Dean—" I broke away just enough to breathe, his name spilling like a confession. "It's complicated."

He didn't let me go. His hands stayed locked at my back; his breath rough against my lips. "How?" His voice was low and feral, but his eyes searched mine like he needed the truth.

I turned away; throat dry. "The kids. The living arrangement. All of it..." My chest heaved against his, but my arms still clung to his neck as my body betrayed me.

He caught my chin with callused fingers, tilting me back toward him until I had no choice but to meet his gaze. The force of it stripped me raw.

"All I know is I want you," he said. His voice wasn't just desire. It carried something fragile, almost breaking. "I don't know where I'd be, where Luna would be, without you. And I sure as hell don't want to be anywhere else."

The words hit harder than his grip. My forehead dropped to his, my chest aching. "But what about the kids?" I whispered, my last line of defense.

"We don't have to tell them. We set rules. Protect them. Protect you." His hand slid down up spine, anchoring me. His mouth hovered a breath away. "But answer me first. Do you want this?"

"Yes." The word rasped out of me before I could stop it. "More than you know."

His mouth found mine again. This time deeper, more certain. My lips burned as I met him there, giving back the same desperate need I'd been holding in for far too long.

Then he lifted me effortlessly. My legs wrapped tight around his waist as my sundress went up with his hand clamping under my thigh.

"My room," I panted against his mouth, fumbling blindly across the counter until my fingers closed around the baby monitor. I clutched it in one hand as he carried me upstairs. His strides were sure. His mouth never leaving mine.

The door slammed behind us with his foot. My back hit the wall, hard. His hips pressed forward, pinning me there. His hands moved up my thighs, under my dress, fingers brushing the heat between my legs through thin fabric.

I gasped into his mouth, my hips lifting to meet him. "Dean—"

"Fuck, Bella." His teeth grazed my jaw, his voice rough. His fingers pressed, testing the damp fabric. "You're already soaked. Been wanting this as bad as I have?"

"More," I admitted, rocking against his hand without thinking.

He pushed my panties aside, his touch firm and unrelenting. My head tipped back against the wall, a broken sound escaping as he found exactly where I needed him as he pushed a finger past my slick folds.

"Fuck, you're tight," he muttered, his forehead pressing to mine as he moved me toward the bed. "I need you."

"Yes. Now," I breathed, fumbling at his belt with shaking hands. He caught them, guiding me as he shoved his jeans low enough to free himself. The weight of him pressed hot against my stomach.

"Raw," he warned, voice rough.

"I don't care," I said, dragging my dress higher. "I need you. Now."

His hands hooked under my thighs again, lifting me like I weighed nothing. Then he pushed in, one sharp thrust that knocked the air straight out of my lungs.

"Dean—oh fuck—" My nails dug into his shoulders, my body stretching to take him.

"Fuck," he groaned, his forehead dropping to my neck. He held there for a second, like he needed to feel it. "So good."

"Move," I gasped, rocking against him. "Please, Dean. Move."

He did. Harder this time, setting a rhythm that sent heat spiraling through me. My legs tightened around his waist as he drove deeper, each movement pulling me closer to the edge.

"Yes. Yes." My head tipped back, exposing my throat. His mouth found me there. Rough and claiming, leaving marks I'd feel later.

"Bella," he groaned, his voice thick with it. "I've wanted this, wanted you..."

The words pushed me further. I clenched around him, and he cursed, losing control of his pace.

"Dean. I'm—" The words broke as everything hit at once, my body arching as the release tore through me. I buried my face against his shoulder, shaking through it.

He followed with a rough groan, holding me tight as his body tensed and released with mine. His face pressed into my neck; his grip steady while I came down in uneven breaths.

We stayed like that, clinging to one another, both of us breathing hard like letting go might undo it all.

He was the first to speak, voice low, a little unsteady. "Sorry. I'm a bit out of practice."

"Same," I admitted, chest still rising and falling. My arms stayed looped around his neck. "It's been...three years."

He pulled back just enough to see my face. His eyes darkened. "What?"

I shrugged, trying to play it off even as heat crept up my neck. "Since I got pregnant with the baby...well, with Sam, who is not a baby anymore."

"Seriously?" His voice sharpened, disbelief cutting through it. His grip tightened slightly, searching my face like I might take it back. I pressed my lips together, shaking my head.

His jaw flexed, something like anger and something softer colliding in his stare. "That's unacceptable," he muttered, low and firm. "You've got a lot of time to make up for."

Before I could respond, his mouth found mine again. Slower this time. Deep. His kiss shifted. Less urgent and more consuming, until everything else faded out again.

Chapter Thirty-Nine

THE SHAPE OF HOME

Dean

I couldn't stop staring at her.

Her hair was tangled across the pillow. Lips swollen and parted. Chest rising fast like she'd just run a mile. She still had her arms looped around my neck, holding on like letting go wasn't an option.

"Dean..." she whispered, my name slipping out broken, almost afraid.

I pressed my forehead to hers, fighting to slow my breathing. My chest still heaved. My pulse still thundered, but I didn't want to rush her again. Not this time.

"Let me have you," I murmured, my voice rough in my own ears. "Slow. Properly."

Her eyes lifted to mine. Nervous, wide, but soft too. She nodded, just once, and that tiny motion unraveled me more than anything else could have.

I moved with her, slower this time, deeper with every inch, watching her face as she adjusted to me. Her gasp shot straight through me. Her nails curled into my shoulders, holding on.

"Ugh, Bella..." I groaned, burying my face in her neck, breathing her in to keep from losing control. "You feel perfect."

Her hips tilted up instinctively to meet me. I caught her mouth with mine, swallowing the sound that slipped free, and started moving. Not frantic. Not desperate. Just a steady rhythm, deliberate, that made her tremble beneath me.

Her hands slid into my hair, tugging, holding me there. "Don't stop," she breathed against my mouth.

"Not a chance," I murmured into her kiss, and kept moving, losing myself in the way she responded to every shift, every press.

I watched her come apart beneath me. The way her head tipped back, exposing her throat. The way her sounds grew sharper, more desperate. The way she moaned my name.

"Dean—Dean—" she gasped and hearing it like that nearly undid me.

I held it off, wanting her to feel every second of it, until I couldn't anymore. Release hit, not fast and desperate like before but slower, drawn out, like I was pouring every part of myself into her. Surrender.

I collapsed onto her carefully. My chest pressed to hers, my face buried in the crook of her neck. Her skin was damp with sweat. My lungs dragged for air, matching hers, both of us trembling in the aftermath. Her fingers traced the back of my neck. Soft and absent, but it damn near undid me again.

"Dean..." she whispered, quieter this time, like she didn't trust her own voice to say more. She didn't have to.

In that moment, I knew I was exactly where I belonged. She curled into me without thinking, like her body already knew where it fit.

No words. Just our breathing. Ragged. Matching. I should've felt guilty. Instead, lying there with her bare legs hooked over mine, it felt right. Too right.

Sometime after, I drifted off to sleep. Luna didn't care. Her cry cracked through the monitor around two in the morning, sharp and insistent. My eyes snapped open. My arm was still wrapped around Bella's waist. She stirred with a soft sound in her throat but didn't wake. I pressed a kiss to her shoulder before I could stop myself, then slid out from under the sheets. The cool air hit my skin, reminding me I was still naked in her bed.

Jeans and shirt, pulled on in the dark, each movement heavier than it should've been. Then down to my room. To my girl.

Luna was sideways in her crib, her face blotchy and fists knotted tight. She saw me, and her cry hiccupped into something smaller, arms lifting toward me.

"Shhh, baby girl." I scooped her up, pressed her tight against my chest. Her damp cheeks smeared against my collar. "I'm here."

She melted fast, her tiny body softening against me. I sat on the edge of the bed with her and rocked slow as I warmed a bottle in my hand. The quiet between her gulps left me alone with thoughts I didn't want.

What the hell was I doing?

I cared about Bella too much. Every time I saw her pushing herself to hold it together. Every time she laughed with the kids. Every time her eyes caught mine like maybe I was worth something...I sank deeper. Tonight, after that kiss, that touch, the intimacy...I was already gone.

But what if I dragged her down with me? What if Vicky's mess found her? Found her kids?

I could handle being hunted. I could handle disappearing. But them? No. Not them.

Luna gave a little sigh, her breath puffing soft against my shirt as her mouth slipped from the bottle. I kissed the crown of her head and held her tighter. She was my whole world. Always would be.

Upstairs, three more kids I had no claim to, and their mother, were slowly becoming part of it too. That truth scared me more than any bounty. More than any bullet.

Chapter Forty

Three Weeks

Bella

The morning felt off. Not in any way I could point to. The coffee still dripped in the pot. Dean still balanced Luna in one arm while she sucked noisily at her bottle, his other hand scrolling something on the iPad. But he wasn't with me.

He didn't drift to the counter while I cut fruit for lunches. Didn't offer one of his dry one-liners when the knife slipped and the strawberry squirted juice across the cutting board. It was like he'd folded himself inward, tucked away somewhere I couldn't reach. And it scraped me raw.

Sam slammed his juice cup on the table, Chloe whined about her hair elastic, and Alex dragged his backpack across the floor loud enough to rattle the table legs. Usually Dean would've stepped in, settled one of them, or cracked a joke. Just redirected the noise. Today he just sat at the island, eyes down. Luna cradled against his chest like the whole world started and ended with her.

Maybe it did. Maybe that was the point.

I shoved the packaged sandwiches into their bags harder than I meant to, the zipper biting my fingers. He didn't look up. Not once.

When the kids finally thundered out of the kitchen, the silence stretched between us. I caught myself waiting. Waiting for his eyes, for anything. But he kept his gaze fixed on the iPad.

My chest cinched. Maybe last night was it. His final conquest. He wanted me, he had me, and now it was over.

The dishwasher clattered shut, too loud. He flinched. Dean never flinched.

I almost said something. Almost. Instead, I told myself to bury it with everything else: bills piling in my inbox and the weight of running a house that always felt one step from breaking.

But the question kept gnawing anyway. Am I just a mistake he already regrets?

I retreated to the only thing that steadied me: structure, errands, numbers, planning, logistics. But first, I had to get the kids to school and daycare.

I slid my iPad across the counter between us while the coffee brewed. "The fixer-upper we saw. 175 days on the market. Nobody's touching it. We go fifteen under the asking price. They'll take it."

Dean raised one brow, skeptical. "You sure?"

"They're desperate," I said, tapping the numbers in like proof.

He didn't argue.

By the end of the week, the email pinged in my inbox: Offer Accepted. No contingencies. No inspection. Cash and closing in three weeks.

I finally let myself breathe.

I sat back in my chair as the iPad glowed on the table in front of me. Offer Accepted. My heart kicked hard, adrenaline still buzzing under my skin. I should've felt relief. Triumph. Instead, my hands trembled against the smooth edge of the screen. Three weeks. We had three weeks before we had to start turning a disaster into something anyone would actually want to live in.

Across the kitchen, Dean crouched over Luna's play mat. He made some ridiculous face that had her squealing, her little fists flapping the air. His low and warm laugh spilled across the room, filling corners I couldn't reach with spreadsheets. For a moment, I let myself believe it would all work out.

But deep down, I knew better. I could control the numbers, the paint colors, and the deadlines. What I couldn't control was him, or the way my chest kept tightening every time I looked at him.

I called Tina before the kids were even dressed the following morning. "We've got three weeks," I said as I paced between the sink and the fridge. "I need a full budget breakdown and contacts for supplies. Paint, trim, doors, flooring, appliances. The whole nine yards."

Tina laughed at my tone, a soft huff through the phone. "Bella, breathe. It's one house, not a full subdivision."

"It might as well be," I muttered, dragging a hand through my hair.

"Mm," she hummed, and I could hear the shift in her voice to the way she always clocked more than I said. "You sound... wired. What's going on?"

"Nothing," I said too quickly.

"Uh-huh." Papers shuffled on her end. "And this has nothing to do with the mystery man you dragged into my office?"

My steps faltered. "He's not a mystery."

"Right," she said lightly. "Just a guy you're starting a business with. Who looks at you like you hung the moon."

Heat crept up my neck. "Tina."

"What?" she pressed, teasing now. "I'm just saying, I've never seen you move this fast on anything that didn't involve your kids or a closing date."

I leaned against the counter, lowering my voice even though no one was listening. "This is business."

"Sure it is," she said, not buying it for a second. Then softer, "Just...be careful, okay? You don't have to outrun everything."

I swallowed, pushing past it. "Can you send me those supplier contacts or not?"

A pause. Then a sigh. "Yeah. I'll send you everything I've got by the end of the day."

By noon, I was already hunched at the island, typing formulas into a fresh spreadsheet: materials, labor hours, target resale value, profit. My fingers tapped fast, numbers lining up like soldiers.

Dean leaned over my shoulder, close enough that his shirt brushed my arm. His frame blocked the light, his breath warm near my ear. "You're insane," he muttered, shaking his head. "This place is going to eat us alive."

I stabbed the enter key harder than necessary. "Correction. This place is going to make us money. If we don't waste time. If we stick to the plan."

He chuckled, low. "There it is. The mom voice."

I shot him a look. "Don't start."

"Not complaining," he said, grinning as he straightened. "Just...I'm not sure I've ever seen anyone boss around a spreadsheet like that."

I rolled my eyes but didn't deny it. The truth was, I needed this. The kids were chaos. John was gone. Dean was a storm I couldn't name out loud. But a house with sagging floors and rotting drywall? That I could fix.

We drove past the property just before dark, headlights cutting across the peeling siding. The street was quiet,. Two little boys on bikes weaving slow circles and a mom hauling in groceries who gave me a quick wave. I lifted my hand automatically. The place looked rough, but the neighborhood felt safe.

I pointed through the windshield, already making a list in my head. "Siding's shot. Kitchen's a full gut. At least two of the bathrooms need total overhauls. Floors too. All of them."

Dean's hands stayed loose on the wheel. "Sounds like fun."

I glanced over. "You don't sound convinced."

One side of his mouth curved. "I'll believe you when I see it. But sure, let's save this wreck."

Later, after the kids were finally down, the kitchen island disappeared under my notes. Closing date circled. Tasks broken into weeks. Costs stacked against what we might make back. I smoothed the page flat as my pen tapped in time with the hum of the fridge.

Dean sat across from me with a mug of coffee. His eyes were half-shadowed in the warm light. Luna dozed in the swing beside him, her tiny breaths whistling soft and steady.

"This is going to be tight," I said, sliding the pen down the column of numbers. "If anything goes wrong, we'll be pulling from our own pockets. Again."

He leaned back, took a slow sip, then set the mug down with a quiet click. "Then nothing goes wrong." His tone was easy, but his eyes didn't move from mine.

I let out a shaky laugh. "That's not how houses work."

"That's how we work," he said. No grin this time. Just steady. Certain.

The words lodged in me, heavier than the spreadsheets. I wanted to believe it could be that simple. That we could muscle through this the way we'd muscled through everything else.

But three weeks wasn't long. And if I was honest with myself, it wasn't the house that kept me up at night. It was what might happen to us while we tried to fix it.

Chapter Forty-One

The Fractured Mirror

Dean

The second I forced the front door open, the smell punched me in the chest. Stale air, mold, wet carpet, and old smoke sunk so deep into the walls it was never coming out. Every bad rental I'd ever been called to as a rookie cop came rushing back. Only this one was supposed to be ours.

Behind me, Bella was already moving, iPad in hand, snapping pictures like she couldn't smell the rot choking the air. She looked like she belonged in a bright office not in this wreck with sagging floors and nicotine-stained ceilings. Her red hair neatly in a low bun, dress pants, neat blouse, heels clicking as she walked, sales pitch polished.

"Bathroom needs to be fixed first," I muttered, stepping over warped laminate. My boots stuck with every step. "Can't have a house without a working bathroom."

"Already writing it down," she said, thumbs flying over the glass.

I dropped to my knees and started cutting carpet. Knife through the backing, fingers yanking. Roll. Haul. The air filled with dust, dry and gritty in my throat. My muscles fell into rhythm with the kind of work that burned and settled all at once. Better to ache in my body than in my chest.

Halfway through, I looked up and caught Bella leaning in the doorway. Her iPad hugged tight to her stomach. Her eyes were on me in a way that felt too long, too needy. The second I met her gaze, she looked away and pretended to type. I let it go.

By noon I'd torn out the living room carpet and half the kitchen cabinets. My shirt stuck to my back, arms raw from splinters. Bella ordered sandwiches, and we ate sitting on overturned paint buckets. She kept her shoes on, careful. My socks were already black with dust.

"You don't have to kill yourself on day one," she said, unwrapping her sandwich, her eyes flicking over my arms like she couldn't help noticing the cuts.

I took a bite, chewed slow, and swallowed hard. "Better me than you."

Her frown lingered, lips pressing tight, but she didn't argue. Just sat there across from me in the ruin of that house, typing notes between bites, as if believing in the plan was enough to hold it all together.

The rest of the day blurred into noise. Hammer on studs, crowbar biting into plaster, the groan of old wood giving up. Every swing of the sledgehammer was Vicky's face. Every shattered tile was John's voice echoing in Bella's kitchen. Rage kept me moving, but when I stopped, it left me hollow.

I washed my hands in a cracked sink that spit more rust than water. The mirror above it was fractured down the middle, splitting my reflection into two strangers. Longer hair, rough beard, brown contacts, and glasses sliding down my nose. I didn't recognize him. Maybe that was the point.

Bella came up beside me, close enough that the citrus bite of her hand sanitizer cut through the mildew. Her shoulder brushed mine. "Don't burn yourself out," she said.

"Too late," I muttered, drying my hands on my jeans.

The house was broken. So was I. Maybe fixing one would fix the other.

For the next few weeks, mornings started early. Coffee down before it cooled, Luna and Sam in their car seats if Bella couldn't get them to daycare. Then straight to the house. Tools out. Sleeves rolled. Saw whining, nail gun cracking, hammer finding studs. By the time noon hit, sweat had bled straight through my shirt and my hands stung. I welcomed every ache. Work kept me steady.

Afternoons blurred into evenings. Room by room, the place came back to life. Bedrooms rebuilt square and clean. Beige walls in the living room catching sunlight instead of shadows. Each nail sunk deep felt like proof I hadn't lost all control.

And in between? Bella.

She didn't just leave me here grinding it out alone. Every few days her SUV crunched up the gravel drive. She'd climb out with her iPad, pretending she was only there to check progress, snapping photos, or asking for updates.

But it never stayed that way.

The first time it happened, she leaned against the unfinished kitchen counter, watching me cut the trim. "You're covered in sawdust," she said, smirking.

"Better than mold," I shot back, setting the saw down.

"Not by much." Her eyes lingered on me too long.

The next second, I had her bent back on the plywood slab, her legs wrapped tight around me. Both of us reckless and starved. After that, we stopped pretending it was an accident.

Then she showed up with a bag of sandwiches or coffee, pretending it was just to check progress. "Trim's up straight," she'd say, running her finger along the fresh wood, eyes flicking to me. Too long. Always too long.

"Gonna find something wrong if you keep staring that close," I'd mutter, and she'd smirk like she knew exactly what she was doing.

No excuses. Just hunger.

Next thing I knew, my back was pressed against a wall still tacky with paint, her breath hot in my ear, her hands tugging at my shirt. On the kitchen counter. In the half-finished hallway. Sprawled across a moving blanket I kept rolled up for my knees. Once in the back seat of my car when she didn't have long.

And then it ended the same way, with her smoothing her hair and tugging her blouse straight, right before kissing me quick like it didn't count. She'd walk out, and I'd pick up a hammer again, trying to steady hands that still shook from her touch.

I started carrying a clean blanket, folded over my tool bag. She had enough chaos. I wasn't about to leave her crawling off a dirty floor.

Work, sweat, Bella, repeat. The work steadied my hands. She kept me from coming apart. And I knew it couldn't last. Nothing like that ever did. But the rhythm set in fast.

By sunset I'd stand in the middle of a finished room, the shine of new flooring catching the last of the light. "Not bad," I'd mutter to nobody, roll up the blanket, and head out.

Still, the days bled together. Crooked frames rebuilt, trim sanded smooth, flooring and tile laid until my knees screamed. I'd lose hours inside the work, only to look up and realize Bella had been doing it all alone on her end: picking up kids, wrangling homework, cooking, cleaning and pushing through bedtime battles.

She never complained. Not once. But I saw the slump in her shoulders and the way her voice went flat when she thought nobody was listening.

The cushion from selling my place had bought her time, but it wouldn't last. Bills still stacked in her inbox. Groceries, school fees, gas, daycare. And every time I offered money, she shut me down. Pride. Fear. Both.

I couldn't sit back and watch her grind herself down while I rebuilt walls. Not after everything she'd done for me and Luna. I made myself a promise, standing in that half-finished house with sawdust sticking to my skin. I'd find a way to help her, even if she never asked.

Because the truth was simple. I didn't want her carrying this weight alone. And I'd do whatever it took to make sure she didn't.

Chapter Forty-Two

PAID IN FULL

Bella

The numbers refused to budge. I sat hunched at the kitchen island, iPad open, staring at the bills fanned out beside me like they were mocking me. The calculator screen still glowed red. The digits refusing to line up no matter how many times I punched them in. The commission from Dean's house was long gone to the bills. All of it eaten up faster than I wanted to admit.

The loan payment sat at the top of the stack; the due date circled in red. It felt like a blade hanging over my head.

I pressed my palms flat to the counter, my throat so tight I couldn't swallow. I'd built this whole life to be solid for the kids, proof that John couldn't break us. And here I was, staring at the possibility of not even making it through the month.

The back door creaked open. Dean came in, rolling his shoulders, his shirt clinging with sweat, sawdust still in his hair. He dropped his tool bag by the door and rubbed at his neck like the weight of the day had settled there.

I snapped my iPad closed before he could see.

"Problem?" he asked, voice quiet and careful.

I shook my head without looking at him. If I spoke, I'd crack.

He lingered for a beat, then exhaled slowly and crossed the kitchen to kiss Luna's head where she sat in her swing. I kept my eyes fixed on the bills, nails digging into my palms under the table.

The next morning, I logged into my bank account, panic still coiled in my chest. I'd planned to shuffle money from one corner to another. A magic trick with empty pockets, just to buy a few more days.

The screen loaded. I froze. The loan: paid off. All of it.

My brain stalled, refusing to process the zero. Then it hit, sharp and fast, stealing my breath.

Dean. Of course it was him.

I found him in the garage, sharpening and fixing the chainsaw—one of the tasks I'd been putting off for months. My throat was already tight before I opened my mouth.

"What did you do?" My voice cracked worse than I wanted as I stormed up the driveway.

Dean set the saw down casually and wiped his forearm across his forehead, as if he hadn't just detonated my entire life. "What needed doing," he said. "Loan's gone. You can cover the mortgage without it hanging over you. You'll breathe easier now."

"You paid it off?" My chest burned, hot and sharp. "Dean—no. That wasn't yours to fix."

He gave a short laugh, like he thought he could ease me with it. "Call it repayment. For the couch, for the dinners. For taking care of Luna and putting up with me. Back rent. Hell, hazard pay too."

"Don't joke about this." The words snapped out of me faster than I could stop them. My eyes stung, tears pressing up before I could shove them back down. "This isn't some game. You don't just swoop in and fix my life like it's a leaky faucet. This is my house. My mess. Not yours."

He didn't flinch. Just watched me steadily while my hands shook at my sides.

Relief sat in my chest, heavy and awful, warring with the anger. And I hated it. Hated that he'd seen me slip far enough to think he had to catch me.

"I don't need you to fix this for me!" My voice cracked sharper than I wanted, but I couldn't stop. "I've handled everything in this house for years. Every bill, every lunchbox, every broken appliance, every late notice. If I can't keep up, I'll figure it out. But you—" My finger jabbed toward him, trembling. "You don't get to decide that for me. You don't get to make me feel like I can't stand on my own two feet."

The silence after echoed louder than my shouting. My breath came in ragged bursts, my chest heaving with fury and humiliation twisting tight inside me.

Dean didn't move. Didn't look away like John used to when he wanted to dodge a fight. He just stood planted in the messy garage, jaw tight, eyes locked on me.

"Bella." The low way he said my name stilled me.

"You've been standing on your own two feet so long it's breaking you," he said, softer now, almost gentle, though his voice carried a weight that pinned me in place. "I watch you drown every night while you pretend you are fine. You take on everything, for the kids, for this house, and then you go to bed with tears dried on your cheeks like nobody sees. But I see it." His chest rose with a sharp breath. "And I can't stand here with the means to help and just watch you sink."

My throat ached so bad I could barely swallow. The denial sat on my tongue, but the truth pressed in harder. I wasn't fine.

He stepped closer, slow. Leaving room for me to shove him back. I didn't. His hand brushed my arm, steady, not forceful.

"I didn't do it to make you feel small," he said. "I did it because I couldn't stomach watching you fight battles you didn't have to fight alone."

The anger I'd been holding onto splintered. Not into shouting, but into something softer, something far more dangerous. The urge to lean into him, to let him shoulder even a sliver of the weight.

Guilt came first; sharp and mean. He had stepped in, paid a debt that was mine to fight. My failure, not his. Then anger piled on top. How dare he decide for me? Cut me out of the chance to prove I could handle it?

And under both sat frustration, a knot I couldn't untangle. What did I want?

The kids adored him. Sam shadowed him everywhere. Chloe listened to him when she barely looked at me. Alex lit up when Dean noticed the smallest victories. Dean had walked into this house and somehow brought a balance I hadn't even realized we were missing.

But he was also the reason John walked out. The catalyst that blew everything apart, no matter how necessary it was.

I shoved at him again, harder this time, just enough to make space. I needed air, needed to breathe without his scent wrapping around me, without the heat of his body undoing every boundary I was clinging to. He didn't push back, but the look in his eyes cut deeper than if he had.

"I can't think when you are this close." My voice cracked, dropping to almost a whisper. My arms curled tight across my chest, holding myself together. "I needed to figure things out. Alone."

His jaw flexed. He didn't move toward me, didn't even lift a hand. Just stood there, something storming in his eyes. Waiting.

"I appreciate it," I managed, guilt threading through the anger, "but you shouldn't have done that. That was my responsibility. My mess. Not yours."

The silence thickened between us. He didn't argue. And his stillness, his quiet, scared me more than if he'd exploded.

His lips parted like he might speak, but no words came. His hands opened and closed at his sides, like even he didn't know what to do with them.

I couldn't stay. Not another second. If I let myself falter under that gaze, I'd fold. And folding was something I couldn't afford.

I turned, my heart hammering with each step toward the house. I slipped into my bedroom and shut the door, pressing my back against it until my breath slowed enough not to give me away.

The silence of the house was piercing. Kids asleep, Dean somewhere in the house, and me locked in with the hollow ache of my own thoughts.

I crawled into bed fully dressed, yanking the blankets up to my chin. The ceiling blurred above me as I stared into the dark.

He'd lifted a weight off my shoulders. But in doing it, he'd dropped something heavier on my chest. And I lay awake under it all night, restless. The crack between us stretching wider with every hour.

Chapter Forty-Three

CHOOSING SILENCE

Dean

It had been three days since she shut her bedroom door on me, and I still felt it every time I passed the hall. The door was open now, but the lock was still there.

She moved through the house like always, packing lunches, wrangling Sam into shoes, juggling her phone while Chloe whined about her hair, reminding Alex about his homework, and making sure everyone was out the door on time. But her rhythm was sharper. Clipped. When she brushed by me in the kitchen, her shoulder angled just far enough to miss.

This morning, I set a bag of groceries on the counter. "Picked up milk. And coffee. We were low."

"Thanks." She didn't look up from the strawberries she was slicing, just moved the container aside so I could put the milk in the fridge.

That was it. We talked like that now. Groceries, pickup schedules, dinner, or the timeline on the flip. Never about the loan. Never about that night.

I couldn't push. She'd asked for space, and I was giving it, even if it felt like sawing my own arm off.

I just worked. I poured it all into the house: sanding trim until my palms stung, ripping out warped boards, hauling debris until my shoulders screamed, putting in new doors and floors. Sweat was easier than silence.

Luna didn't care about any of it. She babbled now, grinning with her two new teeth as she grabbed at my beard with sticky fists. She had no idea how heavy the air was between me and Bella.

After dinner, Sam climbed into my lap with chocolate on his cheeks, pointed at Luna in her mini highchair. "Baby sissy," he announced proudly.

I glanced at Bella. For once, she smiled. Not at me. At him. But still. It was something.

The nights were the worst. I lay in the dark with Luna's soft breaths rising from the crib beside me, counting each one just to stay calm. My head wouldn't quit. All I could see was Bella leaning against the counter, laughing at something stupid I said. All I could feel was her lips on mine the night she finally stopped pretending she didn't want it.

And now all I heard was silence.

Tonight, dinner was no better. She sat across from me, passing the salt without looking up. I tried. "Alex, how's math going? Still crushing those fractions?"

"Easy," he said, grinning. Chloe jumped in, talking about her teacher's shoes, when Sam smeared ketchup everywhere. The noise filled the table, but when I glanced at Bella, she just smiled at the kids. Not at me.

"Want me to cut that chicken smaller?" I asked Sam, already doing it. He giggled when juice sprayed out of his mouth, and I wiped his chin with a napkin. Bella's eyes flicked to mine for half a second. Then away just as fast.

Afterward, I gathered plates. "I'll wash," I said.

"Fine," she answered, sliding past me with the lunch containers. Her arm brushed close enough to feel the heat, but she angled away like it was an accident.

We moved around each other like strangers who'd practiced this dance too many times. She packed sandwiches, I scrubbed pans. No words. Just the hum of the dishwasher and the clatter of silverware.

When the house finally went quiet, I stood outside her bedroom door, hand half-raised. I could've knocked. Could've asked if she was okay. But I pictured her face tightening, her voice going flat, and I let my hand drop.

Back in the kitchen, I sat at the island, staring at the stack of bills she'd left in perfect order. I dragged my thumb along the top envelope, careful not to shift anything. My chest ached with the things I didn't say.

I wanted to tell her I missed the weight of her head on my shoulder. That I missed her laugh echoing in my chest. That I'd give anything to talk to her like before, about Vicky, about how fucked my head still was, without feeling like I was pushing against a locked door.

Instead, I stayed quiet. Stayed useful. And waited.

Chapter Forty-Four

ON BELLA'S PORCH

Bella

The driveway was still in shadow when I pulled in, earlier than usual. I killed the engine and sat there, listening to the tick of cooling metal. My palms left faint ridges on the steering wheel. Ten minutes, I told myself. Just ten minutes of quiet before the house swallowed me again. Before kids and dinner and bills and the weight of pretending nothing had happened between me and Dean.

I grabbed my purse, slung it over my shoulder, and made my way to the porch to pick up the packages that had arrived today. The air was thick and humid, heavy with cut grass and the threat of rain hanging low.

That was when I saw her. Vicky.

She was sprawled on my deck swing like she owned it, one leg draped over the other, rocking slow and lazy. Her smile wasn't a smile. It was sharp. Practiced. Cruel.

"Vicky," I said. My voice came out harder than I meant, but I didn't take it back.

"Well, well, well." She drew the words out slow, savoring them. She didn't stand. Just kept rocking. "Look what we have here."

The purse strap bit into my shoulder. "You have some nerve showing up here."

Her smirk widened. "Do I? Because from where I'm sitting, you're the one playing house with my husband. And my kid." She flicked her fingers toward the door like the whole life inside was Exhibit A.

Anger shot up hot in my chest. "You left." My throat burned, but I didn't stop. "What was I supposed to do? Stand back and let him die? Let Luna die?"

"Luna," she repeated, dragging out every syllable like it tasted foul. Then she groaned, long and theatrical. "Of course."

My keys dug into my palm, but I didn't move for the lock. No way I was turning my back on her.

"Long story," I muttered, quieter now, because the last thing I was going to do was hand her more than she already had.

The swing creaked as she leaned forward, elbows braced on her knees, eyes glittering mean.

We sat in the heavy air. Every slow rock of that swing felt like a taunt, her gaze pinning me in place. And all I could think was that I'd finally stopped running...only to walk straight into the Firestarter herself.

I didn't move any closer. My fingers dug into the strap of my bag until the leather bit back.

Vicky leaned into the swing like it was hers, nails clicking against the armrest in a steady beat. Her hair was twisted into some sleek knot. Her blazer was crisp and sharp, like she'd just stepped out of a courtroom instead of crawling out of whatever hole she'd disappeared into. She looked nothing like the ghost Dean had been haunted by.

"Oh, so you know." Her voice dripped sweet, poisonous. "About the hit. I wondered if you were blissfully ignorant or just pretending not to know who you were letting into your bed. Or rather...the danger."

My throat tightened, but the words cut out anyway. "You mean the man raising your daughter? Keeping her alive while you vanished?"

Her lip curled. "Alive? With you?" She laughed, low and ugly. "What the hell do you know about safe, Bella? You couldn't even keep your own husband in line. Dean's just another broken thing for you to patch up, and my daughter—" she spat the word like it burned, "—doesn't belong in this circus you're calling a home."

I took a step before I could stop myself, jaw clenched so tight it ached. "She doesn't belong with someone who abandoned her either."

Her eyes flashed, but she stayed seated. Calm. Too calm. That made it worse.

"You think you've won something. A man? A baby that isn't yours? Some ready-made family to plug into your picture-perfect fantasies?" Her voice dipped lower. Sharper. "Let me tell you. Dean isn't yours to save. He never was. He built his life for me. Everything else?" She tilted her head. "Temporary."

Heat clawed up my neck, my nails biting into my palm around the keys. I wanted to scream. I wanted to slap that smug smile off her face. Instead, I forced my voice even.

"Then why are you here, Vicky?" I asked. "If you've got all this power, if you really still own him...why are you sitting on my deck?"

For the first time, something cracked in her face. A flicker of doubt. Maybe fear. But it vanished just as fast, covered with that same sneer she wore like armor.

"Because, Bella," she drawled, each word dipped in poison, "I don't like losing."

She walked across the deck like she was on stage, deliberate and graceful. Every line of her body sharpened by the tailored jacket hanging from her shoulders like armor. She stepped closer until the boards under her heels groaned.

"You think you're different than me?" Her voice sliced through the warm air. "Dean always needed someone to save. Someone to fix. Right now, that's you. Don't confuse it for love."

The words burrowed deep. Sharp and cold. Because I didn't know if she was wrong. My arms folded tight across my chest, holding myself together.

"Go home, Vicky. Whatever home you still have. You don't belong here."

She laughed, low and humorless. The sound scraping against the siding of the house. Then she tilted her head, her eyes glittering like glass.

"Oh, Bella," she said softly. "You have no idea what you've dragged yourself into. Play house all you want. When this all comes crashing down, you'll wish you'd never opened that door."

The boards of the deck groaned under her heels as she shifted back, unhurried and calm, as if she hadn't just lobbed a grenade into the middle of my life. She lowered herself onto the swing again, one leg crossing over the other, the chain squeaking with each lazy rock. Waiting me out. Daring me.

My fingers clamped the railing until the wood bit into my skin. I didn't move for the door. Not with her perched there like a storm cloud about to split open.

"What do you want?" The words rasped out, raw, scraped thin from the back of my throat.

Vicky exhaled sharp through her nose, like I'd asked her to pass the salt instead of explaining why the hell she was on my porch.

"I want to talk to him, obviously. That's the only reason I'm here."

A knife twist. Because she wasn't wrong. He wasn't mine to guard. Not really. Legally, technically, on paper, he was still hers. Dean didn't belong to anyone. The reminder cut deep. Wife. Husband. All those words that still tethered him to her, no matter what she'd done. And me? I was what? A babysitter? A warm body? Maybe a stopgap? Maybe she was right. Maybe I'd let myself believe in something that never existed.

"I'll let him know you're here." My voice came out stiff, clipped. I turned toward the steps, desperate for distance before the crack in my composure widened too far.

"Have you fucked him?"

Her words sliced through the air, clean and merciless, hitting me square in the back. My foot froze mid-step as my breath strangled in my chest. Every muscle locked tight. I didn't give her the satisfaction of seeing my face. Didn't even blink.

"It's been a pleasure, Vicky," I said, spitting the words like poison. My middle finger flicked up over my shoulder as I stalked down the steps.

The metal of my keys dug hard into my palm, cool and sharp. I clutched them tighter, forcing my legs forward even as my chest seized around the weight of her question.

I didn't even make it inside the house. Didn't grab the packages. I turned toward the car instead, steps clipped, like if I hesitated for even a second, she'd sink her claws deeper.

The door slammed harder than I meant it to, rattling my whole car. My hands shook so violently I nearly sent my phone flying. My heart thundered in my chest, stealing my ability to think. My mouth was dry enough to crack.

When the call clicked through, I didn't waste breath. "She's here."

A beat of silence. Then, cautious: "Who is here?"

"Vicky." The name tore out sharp, clipped. "She's on my porch. And she said she wants to see you."

I heard the sharp inhale, the way his voice hardened instantly. "Well maybe I don't want to see her," he snapped, words slicing across the line like a whip.

"This may be your only opportunity to get some answers." I forced my voice steady, rational, even while everything inside me shook loose. "You really want to throw that away?"

The silence stretched long enough that I pictured him, his jaw tight and hand dragging over his face as he paced the floor the way he always did when cornered. Finally, his voice came low, rough, resigned.

"Alright. I'll be there soon."

I ended the call before my chest could betray me, before the ache rising in my throat could seep into the line. My hands locked around the steering wheel, knuckles bleaching white.

Through the windshield, I could still see her rocking on my swing like she'd grown roots there. Calm. Smug, like she owned the world she'd just set on fire.

The minutes dragged, heavy and cruel. Every tick of the clock dug the truth in deeper. She was his wife. His daughter's mother. She had the papers, the history, and the claim. And me? I was the babysitter. The housekeeper. The woman who warmed his bed when the silence got too loud. Not the woman he chose. Not the one he belonged to.

My chest cinched tight enough I could barely draw breath. Heat pricked behind my eyes, but I blinked hard, swallowing it down. I wouldn't let her see me crack.

Headlights swept over me from the side, washing me in white for a second before sliding away. His SUV turned onto the street, rolling slowly toward the house.

My stomach dropped, nausea twisting through me. He was here. For her.

I stayed frozen in the driver's seat. My hands locked on the wheel, body rigid like I was bracing for impact. I couldn't watch. Couldn't listen to whatever passed between them. Words, looks. History I could never compete with.

Because the truth pressed in, heavy and undeniable. To Dean, I was nothing. And to Dean, no matter what she'd done, Vicky was still everything.

I dug my nails into the leather wheel until it bit into my palms, and waited for the impact I knew was coming.

Chapter Forty-Five

TOMORROW AT NOON

Dean

I pushed the speedometer harder than I should have, my hand clamped on the wheel until my knuckles ached. Every mile narrowed into one thought: Bella. Her on that porch with Vicky. Vulnerable. Cornered.

I should have told her to call the police. Should have turned the car around, handled it another way.

But this. This was unfinished.

Vicky didn't just disappear. She left a mess behind. Questions. Threats. A target painted on my back that hadn't gone away just because I changed my name.

If I didn't face her now, it would follow us. Follow Bella. Follow the kids.

I needed to know what she wanted. I needed to end it.

By the time I swung into the driveway, Bella's car was already easing back. She didn't even cut the engine, just rolled the window down a crack.

"Kids," she said, flat as stone, her eyes fixed anywhere but mine.

Then she pressed the gas and pulled away, taillights fading down the street before I could even open my mouth.

And just like that, it was me and Vicky.

I sat there with the engine running, forcing my chest to slow its heave, then killed it. The door shut harder than I intended. The air outside felt too thick.

She was right where Bella said she'd be, rocking slowly on the swing, calm as a cat with a mouse cornered.

"Vicky." My voice came out sharp, clipped. I didn't step closer. Instinct told me not to.

She tipped her head, that smirk already in place. "Oh, come on. Are you afraid of me?"

Her tone slid under my skin like a blade. She knew. She could smell hesitation like blood in the water.

I planted my feet on the bottom step but didn't climb. Shoulders squared. Arms loose at my sides. Every muscle coiled tight.

"Fine," she drawled, tossing her hair back like the queen of something only she believed in. "We can talk from here."

"What do you want?" My voice was low, scraped raw, every word dragged across gravel.

She let out a soft huff, all false theatrics, and smiled that sweet, poisonous smile. "I've been good, thanks for asking. I've missed you."

The swing creaked. The sound grated down my spine.

"Cut the shit." My jaw locked so tight I tasted copper. "What do you want?"

Her eyes lit with satisfaction, like my anger was exactly what she'd come for.

Her pout slid into place like muscle memory. The same one she'd flashed across kitchen tables when we fought over money. The same look that had kept me tethered to her longer than I should have stayed.

"You sold the house," she said, dragging each word like it was some kind of confession, like I'd gutted her.

The laugh that ripped out of me wasn't a laugh at all.

"Couldn't exactly stay there after you sent people to attack me in my own home, now, could I?" My voice cracked sharp in the air, louder than I meant, but I didn't take it back.

Her smirk came back slow and deliberate, curling at the edges like smoke.

My stomach churned because I knew we weren't even close to the real reason she was here.

"Oh, that?" She giggled, light and girlish, brushing invisible lint off her designer jeans. "That was just to scare you."

"Scare me?" My voice hit harder and sharper. "My car had to be scrapped after they were done shooting out all the windows, Vicky."

She rolled her eyes. "Okay, maybe they got a little carried away."

Carried away. She said it like we were talking about someone knocking over a glass of wine at a dinner party. Fury shot hot through my chest, but I locked my jaw, refusing to give her the satisfaction of seeing me lose it.

"What do you want?" My words came out low and clipped. "I won't ask again."

She crossed her legs slowly, deliberate as hell, swinging one foot like she had all the power in the world.

"For starters..." Her smile widened, sharp and hungry. "...I want my daughter back."

The air shifted. My fists clenched so tight my nails dug into my palms.

"And," she added, tone casual, like it was just another line on a shopping list, "I want the money from the sale of my house."

"That wasn't your house." The words tore out of me, rough as gravel.

Her eyes lit at the bite in my voice, like she'd been waiting for it. She leaned forward, her perfume cutting through the damp air.

"Give me my daughter and the money, and I'll lift the bounty off your head. Especially now that I know where you live. All it takes is one little call."

Her head tilted. Lips parted into that same smile that used to reel me back in every damn time. She thought she had me cornered. Thought I'd fold.

But she didn't know me anymore. She didn't know what I'd already lost. And she sure as hell didn't know what I'd do to protect my little girl.

Something snapped.

I was across the deck before I even knew I'd moved. My boots pounding the planks, fists clenched so tight my knuckles ached. Heat roared through my chest, hot and violent, and I stopped just short of her, close enough to see her smirk falter.

"You think you get to walk back into my life and negotiate after what you did?" My voice shook the air between us, low and raw, each word tasting like iron. "Your antics nearly got me killed, got our daughter killed. And you want to sit there and talk about money?"

Her eyes widened. She leaned back into the swing, chains rattling against the hooks.

"Dean—"

"No." My voice cracked like a gunshot, cutting her off. I jabbed a finger so close her lashes fluttered. "You don't get to say my name like that anymore. You don't get to pout, or smile, or act like I'm still that dumb bastard who built you a house while you tore me down piece by piece."

Her mouth opened, but nothing came out.

"You want money?" My breath came hard, chest heaving. "You want power? You already sold yourself for it. You're rotting with it." I stepped closer, crowding her, pinning her in place with nothing but fury.

"But Luna, our daughter, she's not your bargaining chip. She's not your meal ticket. She's not your fucking possession. You will never touch her again."

For the first time, I saw the crack. A flicker of nerves in her eyes. She darted a glance past me, like she was checking for exits.

"You...you're scaring me," she whispered.

"Good." My voice came out sharp as broken glass. I leaned down until we were eye to eye, my breath harsh in the space between us. "You should be scared. Because the man you used to control, the one who took your shit and kept coming back? He's dead. And if you, or the people you crawl to, ever come near me, or Bella, or my daughter again..."

I lowered my voice to a whisper, steady and cold.

"...you'll wish you were too."

The swing creaked as she scrambled to her feet, smoothing her blouse with hands that shook. She reached for that old smirk, but it twitched at the edges, betraying her.

"Dean..." she said softly, almost pleading. That careful tone she used to use when she needed me to be pliant. "You don't mean that. You've always been...intense, but not cruel. You'd never hurt me. Not really."

Her voice was bait. But for the first time, I didn't bite. I laughed: sharp and jagged, the kind that cut on its way out.

"You're right, Vicky. I'd never lay a hand on you. But don't mistake that for weakness. Don't mistake me for the man who bent himself in half to give you everything you ever demanded."

I leaned back against the railing, shoulders squared, holding her there with nothing but my stare.

"That man's dead. You killed him the second you sold me out."

Her throat worked as she swallowed. I caught the flick of her eyes toward the yard and the street, like she was checking if anyone was watching. Like maybe she hadn't come alone.

"You already torched everything we had. So, what's this? A victory lap? Or are you just here to squeeze the last drop out of me before you crawl back under whatever rock you came from?" I held her there with my stare. "Why are you really here?"

Her chin jerked up, like she was trying to drag the old arrogance back into place, but it slipped.

"I just..." Her voice cracked before she caught it. "I miss her. She's still my daughter. I deserve—"

"You don't deserve a goddamn thing." The words tore out of me, sharp enough that she actually flinched.

"You left her. You put her in danger. You put me in danger. You even dragged Bella's kids into the crosshairs." My voice dropped, colder now. "Do you even hear yourself? Or are you so far gone you can't tell the difference between a child and collateral?" I shook my head once. "And her name is Luna now. Thanks to you."

She backed up, fingers catching the porch post like she needed it to stay upright.

"You sound insane," she whispered, but her voice shook.

"Maybe I am." I stepped in close. Close enough that the floral sting of her perfume mixed with the sour tang of my sweat. "But the difference? My insanity comes from protecting my family. Yours comes from selling yours out."

Her painted mouth opened. Shut. Opened again. Nothing came out. I dropped my voice, calm in a way that made her flinch harder than my yelling had.

"You ever show your face here again, you ever send your friends circling this house, I won't call the cops. I won't call Mark. I won't call anyone." I held her gaze, steady and unblinking. "I'll handle it myself. And you don't want that, Vicky. Trust me."

Color drained from her face. She fumbled with her purse strap, heels clattering down the steps. For the first time since I'd known her, Victoria Hayes didn't have a single clever line left.

I stood there. Chest heaving and pulse pounding like a war drum in my throat. Watching her retreat, I felt the shift hit hard enough to almost buckle my knees.

I wasn't afraid of her anymore. But she should be terrified of me.

At the bottom of the steps, her heel caught in a crack. She spun back, eyes wide, her composure stripped bare.

"Dean...wait." Her voice cracked, desperation leaking through. "Just...one chance to explain. Tomorrow. Meet me, and I'll give you everything. Answers. Proof. Whatever you want."

I stayed on the deck, arms crossed tight. Every muscle locked down.

"Why the hell would I give you another chance to play me?"

"Because it's not just about you anymore." Her voice wavered, but the words carried weight. "It's about her. About Luna."

She edged closer, like proximity was still her weapon. Like she thought I'd fold just because she breathed the same air.

"You think you've got her safe, but you don't. You need me. Just tomorrow. Noon. The old park off Route 16."

Her words lodged in me like shards of glass. Sharp and impossible to ignore. Every instinct screamed to tell her to go to hell, to never let her near us again.

But that seed she planted, about Luna, about danger, dug in deeper the longer I stood there. My jaw ached from clenching.

"Fine," I ground out. "Tomorrow. Noon. But if you screw me around, Vicky..." I leaned forward just enough for her to see the fury burning in my eyes. "...that'll be the last time we ever speak."

Her nod came too fast. Too desperate. Like she'd just rolled a lucky hand.

"Good," she whispered, clutching her purse strap so tight her knuckles went white. "You'll see. You'll see I'm right."

She finally turned for real. Her heels clattered down the steps, up the driveway, and into the street where she'd parked out of sight. Fumbling with her keys, she slid into her sleek little car and peeled away like something was chasing her.

The silence she left behind pressed heavy against my chest. My fists still trembled, adrenaline crawling under my skin.

But the worst part wasn't the threat. It wasn't her face, or her voice, or even the memory of what she'd already done. It was that I'd said yes.

Tomorrow, I'd sit across from the woman who betrayed me. Tomorrow, I'd walk straight into whatever trap she thought she'd laid.

And I hated myself for needing it anyway.

Chapter Forty-Six

The Recording

Bella

When I walked through the door with the kids, the first thing I saw was the bottles. One empty, one half-drained in his hand. His shoulders were tight and his jaw locked, like he'd been holding himself together by threads all afternoon.

"Sorry I took so long," I said, setting Sam's little backpack by the door. "I swung them through McDonald's. Figured you might need some time."

He didn't answer with a smile. Didn't even glance up. Just reached for Luna, arms wrapping around her like he'd been waiting all afternoon for something to hold onto.

"You okay?" I asked carefully.

His eyes finally cut to mine, storm dark. "No." The word came flat, clipped. Then softer, but still rough at the edges: "But...not right now."

I bit back anything else and nodded. He sank onto the couch, Luna wriggling against his chest, small hands tugging at his shirt like she wanted to bounce. He just held her tighter, face buried in her hair, like letting go wasn't an option.

Whatever happened, it was bad.

The evening crawled by under the weight of it. The kids ate their happy meals, and I pushed them through showers. The usual squabbles muted by the storm rolling off Dean. He didn't interfere, didn't even move. Just rocked Luna until her little body finally went limp in his arms.

With the house quiet at last, I was stacking dishes in the sink when I heard him behind me, Luna's baby monitor in one hand, phone in the other.

"Bella."

I turned, towel still in my hand. He stood there with his phone out, jaw rigid, eyes hollow. "You need to hear this."

I took it from him, the glass screen cool against my damp fingers. He tapped play.

Vicky's sharp, brittle laugh flooded the kitchen. "Oh, that was just to scare you."

Dean's voice answered, rough and furious. "Scare me? My car had to be scrapped after they were done shooting out all my windows."

"Maybe, they got a little carried away," Vicky drawled, like it was nothing. Then her tone slid colder.

A couple moments later, she continued: "For starters, I want my daughter back. And the money from the sale of my house."

Dean's voice cut back, low and lethal: "That wasn't your house."

"Give me my daughter and the money, and I'll lift the bounty off your head. Especially now that I know where you live. All it takes is one little call."

The room tilted. My stomach knotted so tight I could barely breathe.

The recording cut.

I stood there frozen, towel balled in my fist, my pulse thundering so loud I was sure he could hear it too. The kitchen hummed with nothing but the refrigerator, the silence pressing in. My fingers shook around his phone, slick with sweat. I couldn't make words form.

Because it was real. Every shadow he'd carried. Every glance over his shoulder. Every lock double-checked. It wasn't paranoia. She said it herself. A hit. A bounty. And she knew where we lived.

My kids were in this now.

"So...what now?" The whisper scraped out of me, thin and raw.

His eyes lifted to mine, hollow and desperate.

"I don't know," he admitted, voice shredded. "Part of me just wants to hand her the money, maybe even give her Luna. Just to protect her. Protect you. Protect the kids." His jaw clenched, but his voice fractured. "But—"

The word splintered. His shoulders collapsed. And then he was crying. Hard. Messy. Helpless.

The phone clattered onto the counter as I moved, pulling him into me, his head burying against my chest. My arms locked around him, fingers threading into his hair, holding on.

"I'm so scared something will happen to you," he choked, fists twisting in my shirt. His sobs wrecked the quiet. "All because of me. No, because of her. I can't lose you. I've lost too much already, I can't—"

"Hey, shhh." My lips pressed to his temple, my voice shaking into the damp strands of his hair.

"I'm right here." I stroked his back, his head, like maybe I could anchor him. Like maybe I could believe it myself.

"She threatened you," he gasped, dragging his face up to mine. His eyes were red, blotched, broken. "She threatened you, Bella."

"I know." My throat burned. "I heard."

"You're not safe," he rasped. "And I did that. By being here. By dragging this into your life."

I caught his face in both hands, forcing him to meet me, to see me. "No. You didn't do this. She did. Vicky did this. Not you."

He shook his head, disbelief etched deep. My chest ached watching him unravel like this.

But through the fear, a thought cut sharp.

"She admitted it. On that recording. Dean, that's leverage. If she slipped once, she could slip again. If we can get her to say more, maybe we can end this."

He stared, some flicker of hope fighting through the devastation. Then his voice cracked again.

"And what if we can't? What if I put you and the kids right in the line of fire?"

I held his face tighter, steadying both of us.

"Then we fight smarter." My voice steadied, even if my insides were shaking. "Together."

We sat in silence so long my legs went numb from perching on the armrest, half draped over him, half bracing myself against the chair. His tears finally dried, leaving his face hollow, his shoulders slack like he'd been emptied out. Neither of us spoke. His breath hitched unevenly; mine barely lifted my chest. Words felt too fragile, like one wrong syllable might snap the thin thread still holding us together.

At last, I eased back, my voice rough. "I'll get the kids settled."

He didn't argue. Didn't even look up. Just sat there, elbows digging into his knees, while I moved through the house.

Sam mumbled into his blanket when I pulled it up around his chin. Chloe sighed about brushing her teeth but didn't fight, too heavy with sleep. Alex barely noticed me. His iPad slipped from his hands to the mattress as his eyes closed.

When I returned, the house was quiet again, except for the refrigerator's hum and the faint creak of the chair. Dean hadn't moved. Same spot, same posture. His head hung so low I half expected it to drop. The beer he'd opened hours ago still sweated on the table. Untouched, a ring of condensation spreading beneath it.

"You didn't move," I said, soft enough that my words barely reached him.

Slowly, he lifted his head. His eyes were rimmed raw, his face carved deep with exhaustion. He only shook his head once. A small, fragile motion.

I stopped in front of him, my hands fidgeting uselessly against my thighs. I didn't know if I should touch him again, if either of us could take it.

"You should lie down," I whispered.

He just stared, hollow and unblinking, like sound itself cost too much. I lowered myself beside him. Our knees brushed, and I left them there like an anchor in the space between us.

After a long stretch of quiet, I finally murmured low, "Come to bed with me."

His eyes flickered, searching mine like he was waiting for me to take it back. I didn't. Without a word, he rose. I took his hand and led him up the stairs, his palm rough and trembling in mine.

We didn't sleep. Not really. We didn't kiss. We didn't even try to speak. He curled around me, his arm banded tight at my waist. My hand rested over his chest, pressed to the thunder of his heartbeat that refused to calm. The dark hummed with everything unsaid, with fear sharp enough to cut.

I lay awake listening to him breathe, both of us dreading what came next if he didn't give Vicky what she wanted.

Chapter Forty-Seven

The Last Meeting

Dean

The next morning, I cornered Bella before the breakfast chaos started, before Sam began whining for cereal and Chloe started hiding her socks.

"Take the kids to daycare today," I told her. My tone came out sharper than I wanted, but I didn't pull it back.

She studied me for a beat. Her head tilted and eyes searching for something I couldn't give. Then she nodded once. No questions.

Before her SUV cleared the end of the street, I was already halfway down the highway. The recording felt heavy in my pocket, like it was heating through the fabric, ready to burn me from the inside out. My stomach twisted with every mile.

Mark met me in the back lot of the precinct, away from the eyes inside. I didn't waste time with greetings. I pulled out the phone, thumbed the screen, and let clips of Vicky's voice spill through the speaker.

"Oh, that was just to scare you."

"My car had to be scrapped when they were done shooting out all my windows."

"They got carried away."

"For starters, I want my daughter back..."

Her poison poured out, steady and smug, until the recording clicked off.

Mark's jaw tightened. He didn't speak, but the look on his face said enough.

"I know what my legal options are," I told him. My own voice sounded like it belonged to somebody else: flat and practiced. "But that won't stop her. She's already got things in motion. You and I both know it."

Mark didn't disagree. He just stared out over the cracked asphalt, silent, thinking through the pieces. We didn't need to say the whole plan out loud. Not here. Maybe not ever. The less Bella knew, the safer she was.

When I left, the weight in my chest hadn't lifted. But at least it had shape now. A direction. This ended with me. Not her. Not Bella. Not the kids.

The park hadn't changed much since the days Vicky used to drag me here after dark, whispering about adventure like we were kids breaking rules. Now the cracked asphalt paths and rusted shelters felt wrong, like ghosts left behind.

I hauled myself over the chain-link, boots scraping the metal. I used to be faster at this. Lighter. Now the weight dragged me down.

She was waiting by the old picnic shelter, leaning against the railing like she owned the whole damn park. Arms crossed; lips pulled into that half-smile that always meant trouble.

"You came," she said, all smug confidence, like she hadn't been sure I'd show.

I didn't waste words. I pulled out my phone, thumbed the file open, and let her voice spill into the empty air. Her laugh. Her bargaining. Her demand for Luna and money. Every sick syllable.

Her smirk slipped fast. "What the fuck—"

"You've got two options." I stepped closer, my voice steady even as rage vibrated through every muscle. "One, you sign paperwork. Relinquish every right to Luna. Clean break. She stays with me." I lifted the phone higher, the screen glowing like a flare. "Or two, I turn this in. And you know damn well what happens when this hits the DA's office."

Her eyes narrowed, calculating. "You wouldn't."

I stepped in close enough that she could feel the heat rolling off me, close enough that she saw the way my jaw locked.

"You sure about that? You threatened my daughter, Vicky. You threatened Bella. You dragged her family into this. You think I'm just going to let you walk away from that?"

Something flickered in her eyes. Doubt. Maybe fear. For the first time, the upper hand felt like it was mine. Then she laughed. Short. Cruel.

"She's not your daughter."

The words hit harder than any punch I'd ever taken. Straight through the chest. For a second, I couldn't breathe. The world narrowed to the sound of her voice cutting me open.

"Of course she is." My fists clenched, nails biting into my palms. "I've held her. Fed her. Rocked her to sleep. She smiles at me like I'm her whole damn world."

Vicky leaned in, lips curling. "No, Dean. She's not."

Her voice dropped, quiet and precise, like she wanted to make sure every word landed.

"I was sleeping with someone else for months before I got pregnant."

The ground tilted under me. My stomach lurched.

"He didn't want anything to do with me, or her, once I told him," she went on, smooth like she was reading from a script. "He tossed me aside. So, I convinced you she was yours."

Her shrug was casual. Vicious. "Not that it took much."

I staggered back, sucking in air like I'd been gut-punched. Luna's laugh, her cries, the way her tiny hand curled around my finger, and the way she tucked herself against my chest. It all slammed against that one phrase: *not yours.*

"And then," she said, relentless, "I worked a few of the other guys too."

Rage and heartbreak twisted together in my chest until I couldn't separate them. My voice scraped out, raw.

"You used me. You used her."

Vicky tilted her head, not even blinking. "Don't look so shocked. It's what you're good for."

The words dug deep, sharper than any blade.

"I did it to protect you," she added, softer now, almost reasonable. "The hit was only meant to scare you. They weren't supposed to hurt you."

My head shook before I could stop it. *Not supposed to hurt me?* Glass shattering. Bullets screaming past my ears. Shadows outside my house. Flashes of survival stitched into my skin.

"And now," she said, crossing her legs like we had all day, "I'm free. You are too." Her smile widened, triumphant. "So just give me my daughter. And money to start over."

My tongue felt heavy, my chest locked tight. She had just stripped that word, *daughter*, out of me minutes ago, laughed while she did it. Now she wanted me to hand Luna over like she was a bargaining chip?

"You hear yourself right now?" The words ripped out of me, hoarse, strangled.

"I hear survival." Her eyes gleamed, flat and cold. "That baby is my way to start fresh. You can't give her what she needs. Not with your mess. Not with *her*." She jerked her chin toward Bella's house. "I can. I'm her mother."

Her mother.

My pulse slammed against my ribs, hard and fast. I was the one who made the bottles. The one up at two in the morning, rocking her through fevers, singing lullabies in the dark until my throat burned. I was the one she reached for. The one she called home.

And Vicky sat there, calm as stone, telling me none of it mattered.

My hands wouldn't stop shaking. Not fear. Rage. The kind that built behind your ribs until it felt like your bones might splinter.

I didn't answer her. I just stood there, fists locked so tight my nails cut into my palms. One twitch, one wrong move, and I'd break.

Vicky mistook it for weakness. Of course she did. She leaned back against the bench, casual, twirling a strand of hair like we were catching up over coffee.

"You've always been stubborn, Dean. Always thought you could muscle through anything. But this? This is bigger than you. Give me my daughter. Give me the money. We both get to live our lives far away from one another."

Her voice was just noise. All I could see was the smirk on her face, the same one she used when she knew she had me cornered. The one she wore when I thought I loved her.

Inside, everything was chaos. She lied. She played me. And Luna. *My* Luna. What the hell did that make her now? What did that make me?

The fury pressed against my ribs, demanding a way out. I choked it back. If I let it loose, I wouldn't be able to stop. I stayed silent. Let her keep digging.

Her smirk faltered. Just a fraction. Her eyes darted. Sharp and recalculating. Maybe she finally realized this wasn't the same man she'd left bleeding years ago.

Still, I didn't speak. Not yet.

"Why are you telling me this?" The words rasped out at last, low and hoarse. Tight.

Her smile sharpened, mean. She slipped a hand into her jacket. When it came back out, it held steel. The gun looked too big in her hand, but the steady, certain way she gripped it told me she'd thought about this moment. Maybe even dreamed about it. Her eyes lit up, sick with it.

"Because," she purred, stepping in, "if you won't do as I ask, I'm going to have to kill you and go get my daughter back myself. From Bella. And I might as well enjoy destroying you first."

The barrel leveled with my forehead.

I didn't flinch. Didn't blink. My heartbeat thundered so hard it rattled my teeth, but I kept my chin up, my gaze locked on hers. If this was how it ended, then so be it.

I gave the smallest nod. Like I accepted it. Like I'd always known it would come to this.

And then—

BANG.

The shot cracked the air wide open. Deafening. The echo rattled through the trees. Her eyes went wide. Shock wiped the smirk clean off her face.

My chest was still rising. My heart was still hammering. But the gun wasn't pointed at me anymore.

Chapter Forty-Eight

DRIVING HOME

Dean

Gravel tore through my jeans as I hit the ground, my knees screaming. My ears still rang, louder than the shot itself. My chest heaved like every breath scraped the inside of my ribs raw.

"Did you get all that?" My voice came out hoarse, aimed at no one and everyone. I couldn't pull my eyes off the body in front of me.

The communications earpiece crackled. "We got it, Dean. Every word. It's over."

Over.

The word didn't register. Not with her eyes still wide. Glassy and vacant. Not with her mouth frozen mid-sneer, like she'd been about to spit out one more lie. I could still hear that laugh, the smug one that crawled under my skin, the one that told me she thought she owned me. It echoed in my skull even though her voice was gone. Silenced.

I'd seen plenty of bodies. Too many. Written the reports, zipped the bags, knocked on doors to tell mothers their sons weren't coming home. But never like this. Never someone I once kissed goodnight. Someone I thought I loved.

Because once, I had. I'd loved her enough to build her a house with my hands. Tried to build a life. And now I'd made the call that ended hers.

My stomach lurched. I pressed my palms into the dirt to steady myself, but they shook anyway. This wasn't justice. It wasn't clean. It was blood on my hands. My choice.

Bella's face flashed behind my eyes. Her kids' faces. Luna's smile. What the hell was I supposed to tell them?

Branches cracked behind me. Boots moved in fast. Heavy and sure. Five men stepped out of the tree line with their rifles slung and vests catching the faint light. My old squad. Ghosts of a life I barely recognized. Mark at the front.

"You did good work here today." His hand clapped my shoulder. Too solid. Too heavy. I nearly buckled under it.

I couldn't answer. Couldn't look away from her. Vicky. The woman who once shared my bed. The mother of the baby I thought was mine. The woman who signed off on my death.

"We'll take it from here," Mark added. His tone softer now, like he was talking a rookie through his first bad scene. "Why don't you go home and rest?"

Home.

The word rattled in my chest like a spent casing. Empty. Hollow.

Gravel dug into my knees until the ache burned up my thighs. I forced myself upright on sluggish legs, every muscle heavy like I'd been carrying bricks. My balance wavered, but I didn't look away from the body.

"You're clear, Dean," Mark muttered, already on his radio. Static crackled as he called in containment.

Clear.

I didn't feel clear. I felt buried.

By the time I stumbled into my car, my hands shook so badly I nearly dropped the keys. The steering wheel was ice against my palms. My chest locked tight. My lungs refusing a full breath.

There wasn't anywhere else to go. No one else to call. My thumb found her name on instinct.

The line clicked. "Hey. Are you okay?" Bella's steady, soft voice cut straight through the static in my head.

Nothing came out. My throat sealed shut.

"Where did you go?" she pressed, sharper now, concern threading through every word.

"She's dead," I forced out. The words scraped raw, bitter on my tongue.

Silence. Then her voice again, smaller but solid. "Are you okay?"

"No."

The dam split wide. My chest convulsed. Panic and sobs tore out, jagged, unstoppable. My forehead dropped against the wheel as my vision blurred until the dash swam. My whole body shook like I was coming apart at the seams.

I heard her inhale sharply on the other end. "Dean, listen to me. Where are you?"

Her voice caught me. Kept me from sinking all the way under. My fingers dug into the phone like it was the only thing keeping me upright.

"Physically… I'm fine," I rasped, though my pulse hammered, and my skin felt slick against the wheel. My chest burned. My throat felt like glass.

"But I'm not okay," I whispered. The words broke on the way out.

"Can you get home?" she asked, gentler now.

"Yeah. I think so."

"Good. I'll meet you there."

Her certainty anchored me.

"You want me to stay on the line while you drive?"

"Yes. Please." My voice cracked, but I didn't care.

The line stayed open. Her breathing was steady in my ear, filling the silence I couldn't. She didn't push or ask questions. She just let me know she was there. Every so often, she said my name. Soft. Like a lifeline.

The road blurred through tears. My chest seized with sobs that wouldn't stop, the steering wheel slick under my palms.

I cried harder than I ever had, ugly and broken, as I emptied myself out until I was hollow but still trembling.

And through it all, she stayed. Not filling the silence. Not hanging up. Just...there.

Home.

The word didn't mean walls or a roof anymore. It meant her.

ACKNOWLEDGEMENTS

Thank you to everyone who supported this wild dream of becoming an author.

To my husband, thank you for being my number one supporter and promoting my book before I was even ready to share it with the world. Your encouragement gave me the confidence to finally let this story leave the editing stage.

To my son, thank you for seeing how much books and reading mean to me and telling me, “Mommy, you should write a book.” You have no idea how much that meant to me.

To my dad, thank you for sharing your lifelong dreams with me and reminding me to follow mine. I would not have had the courage to do this without you.

Ashley, thank you for bringing me back into the world of reading a few years ago and for letting me share my dreams of writing without judgment. Your support helped me feel brave enough to finally share my ideas with someone else.

Christine, thank you for being my very first beta reader and for introducing me to the terrifying world of letting other people read my work. Even though you did not beta read this book, your encouragement helped give me the confidence to finally let this book see the light of day.

Cody, thank you for constantly checking in throughout this long and scary process. Your enthusiasm, encouragement, and positivity helped carry me through some of the hardest parts of this journey and made me believe I could actually do this.

Hailey, thank you for being the first person to read this story. Your excitement and early messages while reading gave me the confidence to believe I might actually have something special here.

And finally, to Vicki, Ambur, Hash, Chanelle, and everyone else who supported this project while it was still a work in progress. Thank you for believing in me before I believed in myself. Your feedback, encouragement, and willingness to take a chance on this story helped shape it into something so much stronger.

— Emme Rosewood

ABOUT THE AUTHOR

Emme Rosewood writes stories that live in the quiet spaces between safety and truth, where love is complicated, choices carry weight, and nothing is ever as simple as it seems.

By day, she works in academia, leading in the sciences and teaching students to think critically about the world around them. By night, she writes emotionally grounded suspense and romance that explore the cost of protection, the illusion of control, and the people we become when everything we thought was safe begins to fracture.

She lives in Maine with her family, where long winters and quiet moments make room for stories that refuse to stay buried.

Learn more at www.emmerosewood.com

THANK YOU!

Thank you for reading.

If this story stayed with you, if the characters lingered a little longer than expected, I'd love to stay connected.

Join my reader list for exclusive bonus scenes, early access to upcoming releases, and a deeper look into the world of The Cost of Safety.

Sign up here:

www.emmerosewood.com

Or scan the code below.

Loved the story? A quick review on Amazon or Goodreads helps other readers discover the book and supports future stories in The Cost of Safety series.

ALSO BY EMME ROSEWOOD

The Cost of Safety Series

Book 1: No Safe Space

Love was never supposed to feel like survival.

Book 2: The Price of Silence

Every story has another side.

Book 3: After the Gun

Surviving was only the beginning.

Book 4: A Place to Land

Some people become your home.

For release updates, bonus content, and exclusive reader extras, visit:

www.emmerosewood.com

SNEAK PEEK FOR BOOK 2

The Price of Silence

The envelope hit the table harder than it needed to. A flat, papery crack against the stone. It skidded once, catching the weak glow from the under-cabinet lights before settling crooked against the ceramic bowl of oranges Dean had brought into the house that morning because they were "on sale and looked good."

I didn't turn.

Water pounded against the stainless-steel sink hard enough to make my fingers ache. I had been holding my hands under the stream too long. The skin across my knuckles had gone pale and tight, veins faint blue beneath the surface. Lemon detergent foamed in a slick halo around the drain. The smell crawled into the back of my throat. Sharp citrus layered over damp stone and the dry grit of sawdust still trapped in the grout.

Outside, rain slammed sideways against the dark kitchen window. Wind rattled the siding in long, restless bursts. Somewhere down the block something metallic kept clanging loose and hollow.

It was well past midnight. Dean was asleep upstairs. The baby was asleep upstairs. And Ramón Calderon was standing in my kitchen.

I let the water keep running. Let it fill the space. Let it cover the sound of my pulse starting to misbehave.

"They're asking questions," he said. His voice was quiet. It always was. Ramón never wasted sound. People leaned closer when he spoke like that. A faint accent still threaded beneath the polished English he wore so carefully, softened by years of boardrooms and courtrooms but never fully gone.

I stared at his reflection in the glass above the sink instead of turning around. A darker shape behind me. Broad shoulders under a rain-soaked jacket. Dark hair slicked neatly back despite the weather. Water dripping steadily from the hem onto my floor. Gold flashed once at his wrist when he shifted. Expensive.

He hadn't knocked. He hadn't asked if he could come in.

I reached out and shut off the tap. The silence that followed wasn't real silence.

The dishwasher hummed beneath the counter. Ice clicked somewhere deep inside the freezer. From upstairs came the soft mechanical rush of the white-noise machine Dean insisted on running every night. It sealed the second floor in a cocoon of artificial calm.

Unless someone decided to break it.

"About what?" I asked. My voice sounded steady. I held onto that.

Ramón gave a low laugh. Not amused. Not kind. Just patient.

"Don't." The word settled into my spine.

I dried my hands carefully on the dish towel. Folded the damp cotton into a neat square and set it beside the sink like the gesture itself might buy me time. Only then did I turn.

The envelope sat between us. Internal review letterhead. My stomach dipped before my brain caught up. I knew the crest before I picked it up. My thumb traced the raised seal automatically, feeling the shallow impression in the paper as if pressure alone might change what was inside.

Thunder rolled close enough to make the window tremble.

I broke the envelope open. The words arranged themselves into meaning faster than I wanted them to.

Financial irregularities.

Evidence handling discrepancies.

Formal request for clarification from the Office of Professional Accountability.

Chain-of-custody inconsistencies flagged for immediate review.

Three case numbers. They rose off the page like teeth. I knew every one of them. Not the way most attorneys knew files. I knew where they had bent. Where timing had shifted. Where paperwork had been nudged just far enough out of alignment to matter later.

If later ever came.

My eyes locked on the third number. For a second I was back in the evidence locker. Fluorescent light buzzing. Coffee bleeding across a requisition form because someone had bumped my elbow. Ramón's voice somewhere behind me telling me everything would be fine.

Everything was never fine.

I became aware of him moving. One slow step closer. Rainwater hit the tile again with a soft, steady tap.

"You didn't tell me this was coming," he said. Something in his voice had changed. The softness I used to mistake for restraint was gone. This was something else. Something colder.

My thoughts jumped upstairs without permission. To Dean sleeping on his side. One arm curved toward the crib even in his dreams. The baby breathing in those small uneven sighs that still made my chest tighten.

If Ramón raised his voice...If he decided to look around...If he took one curious step toward the staircase...

I smiled. It hurt. "They send letters like this all the time," I said. "Most of them mean nothing."

Ramón didn't smile back.

I let the page fall back onto the table. The paper made almost no sound. Somehow that felt worse.

Ramón had settled against the counter like he was composing himself for an audience. One hip resting on the edge, arms loose at his sides. Charcoal shirt open at the throat. Cufflinks catching the thin band of yellow light under the cabinets every time he shifted.

He always looked finished. Pressed. Groomed. Untouched by the kind of work that left blood under fingernails or bruises along the ribs. Except for the smell. Cologne first: dry cedar and something faintly sweet.

Under it, the scent I had learned to recognize before I even knew what it was. Metallic. Oily. Like coins rubbed warm between your palms. Like the inside of a gun that had just been cleaned.

"They're circling you," he said. "And if they keep circling, they'll find me."

"You're being dramatic." My voice came out level. I focused on that instead of the way he had positioned himself between me and the doorway without seeming to try.

"No." His mouth curved. "I'm being practical."

I slid the letter back into the envelope. My pulse felt wrong. Too even. Too measured. I should have felt the hot rush of adrenaline and the hollow in my stomach that meant run.

Fear belonged to private moments. This wasn't one of them.

Instead my body did what it always did when danger stopped being theoretical. It went quiet. Still. Watching.

"You won't be collateral," I said, flipping my long blonde ponytail over my shoulder and adjusting the thin silk pajamas I was wearing.

Ramón pushed away from the counter. He never moved fast. He didn't need to. The room seemed to rearrange itself around him as he crossed it. The soles of his shoes whispering over the hardwood Dean had refinished one winter with a rented sander and three YouTube tutorials. I had sat on the stairs and watched him that whole weekend. He had looked so proud when the final coat dried.

Ramón stopped close enough that I could see the shadow of stubble along his jaw. Close enough that if I leaned forward an inch, I would touch him.

"If this opens," he said quietly, "your husband gets dragged into it first."

My mouth dried instantly. He saw it happen. Of course he did. Ramón never missed the small betrayals.

"Phone records. Financials. Case access. Every conversation you had in the dark and called work." He lowered his head slightly, voice narrowing until it felt like something sliding under my skin. "You think they won't subpoena him?"

Dean in the courtroom appeared fully formed before I could stop it. The wrong suit. Navy. Bought for a cousin's wedding. Too tight across the shoulders because he refused to size up. A tie sitting crooked because he never noticed until someone reached across and fixed it. Shaved head. Bright green eyes that looked wrong whenever fear touched them. Square jaw clenched hard enough to pulse.

Hands that belonged on a pry bar. On a steering wheel. Wrapped around the railing of a crib. Not flattened against polished wood while men in gray suits asked questions they already knew the answers to.

Last Saturday he had been on his knees in the hallway, swearing softly because one length of trim refused to sit flush. He had come to bed hours later with sawdust stuck to his scalp with dried sweat and a smear of white paint at the base of his throat.

I had wiped it away with my thumb while he slept. He had built this kitchen. Built half this house.

"And custody," Ramón added. The word moved through me like cold water poured slowly down my spine.

Not prison. Not charges. Not headlines. Custody. The kind of word that let strangers decide whether you deserved to keep your child.

Upstairs, the white-noise machine shifted pitch for a second before settling again. My heart followed it.

Ramón watched my face as if he were reading something written there. "You see," he said softly. "Now you understand."

The baby monitor crackled on the counter. The sound sliced straight through the room. A soft rustle followed. Then a small sigh. The kind that sounded almost like disappointment. Like she had expected comfort and found only air.

My entire body went alert without moving. Ramón's eyes lifted toward the ceiling. For one second I saw something naked there. Not tenderness. Not curiosity.

Assessment.

Then he looked back at me.

"If you're indicted, they question everything," he said. "Judgment. Stability. The home." A faint shrug. "Environment."

My fingers closed around the carved back of the nearest chair. The edge dug into my palm hard enough that I welcomed it. Pain was clean. Pain had rules.

I knew what instability looked like on paper. I had read enough social worker reports to understand how a life could be reduced to bullet points and quiet conclusions. I knew the language teachers used when they called after hours because no one had come to pick you up and the secretary had already shut off half the lights.

I knew what it smelled like too. Stale cigarettes soaked into winter coats. Milk turning in refrigerators that had lost power. Mold pushing its way through drywall in rooms where windows had been painted shut for years.

"You wouldn't," I said.

Ramón smiled. Wider this time. Patient with my refusal to learn. "You still do that."

"Do what?"

"Talk to me like there's a version of me that cares about fairness." He moved before I could react. Reached across me in one smooth, unhurried motion.

My phone lay beside the sink. He picked it up like it had always belonged to him.

"Give me that."

He didn't even acknowledge the words. His thumb tapped once. Light bloomed between us. Her face filled the screen. Curled into Dean's chest in the rocker. One tiny hand splayed across the worn collar of his T-shirt. Mouth slack with sleep. A damp curl stuck to her temple where she had sweated through another restless night.

Ramón studied the photo longer than necessary. Too long. "She's beautiful," he said. "Looks like you."

Something inside me snapped tight. I tore the phone out of his hand. Hard enough that the heavy ring on his finger scraped across my knuckles. Pain flared. Sharp and clarifying.

"You don't get to threaten me with her."

His gaze lifted. Mild. Almost entertained. "You're not in a position to make rules."

"Get out."

"Not yet." He straightened one cuff with his free hand. The movement was absurdly meticulous. Corporate precision imposed on a kitchen that still held renovation dust in its seams.

"Make the audit disappear," he said. "Move whatever needs moving. Bury whatever needs burying."

"And if I can't?"

He didn't hesitate. Didn't soften. Didn't pretend. "Then I make sure I don't go down alone."

The monitor hissed again. For the first time that night, I wondered how long it would take Ramón to reach the staircase if he decided to. For a moment I imagined grabbing the bowl of oranges on the counter and hurling it at his head.

Not because it would stop him. Because I wanted the sound of ceramic shattering and fruit skidding across stone. Something loud enough to split the careful composure that had settled over the kitchen like dust.

Instead I stayed where I was. Stillness had always been my better weapon. Ramón's mouth twitched as if he could see the thought pass through me.

He turned toward the hallway. Each step quiet. Controlled. The walk of a man who believed every space already belonged to him. As though he had stopped by to drop off paperwork instead of a threat that could dismantle an entire life.

At the doorway he paused. "Fix it, Victoria." Then he was gone. A door closed behind him, somewhere deeper in the house. Not slammed. Just shut.

The kitchen expanded around me the moment he left. Too much counter. Too much ceiling. The black stone island gleamed under the strip lights like still water. Dean had driven two towns over to a warehouse that smelled like cut granite and forklift exhaust because I had pointed at a darker slab and said I liked that one better. He had stood there with dust on his boots and cold coffee in his hand and said, Then we'll make it work.

We.

I pressed both palms flat against the island. The stone still held the night's chill.

Dean had wanted this house for the yard. For the oak out front that turned gold every October. For the extra bedroom upstairs that could be a nursery and an office and maybe, someday, another child if timing cooperated and luck didn't run out. He had said this place felt like somewhere people stayed.

Stayed.

The word sat wrong in my chest. Nothing stayed when I was growing up. Not apartments. Not jobs. Not power. Not men.

My mother packed our lives into trash bags because boxes and tape cost money. My father disappeared for three days once and came back with gas-station flowers and blood dried along one knuckle, expecting gratitude for his return.

I left at seventeen with two duffel bags and a hundred and forty dollars sewn into my coat lining. Slept in a dorm that smelled like radiator heat and bleach. Ate ramen over a legal pad and learned how to build something that couldn't be taken away. Respectability had always felt conditional. Earned one careful layer at a time.

Even if the finished version fooled everyone.

I chose Dean because he was solid. Dean was the first thing in my life that had ever felt structurally sound. He showed up. He fixed what he said he would fix. He stayed where he promised he would stay.

I chose this baby because she made the future feel permanent.

The monitor hissed again. A small thump against the crib rail.

My eyes closed. If they dug, they would drag all of it into the light. Dean. The house. The rocker he had sanded down because the old finish smelled like mothballs and disappointment. Questions would become records. Records would become opinions. Opinions would become strangers deciding what kind of mother I was allowed to be.

No.

If Ramón talked, everything split open. If Ramón disappeared...Everything stayed as it was.

The thought arrived fully formed. Clean. Efficient.

That was the part that made something twist low in my stomach. Not the thought, but how natural it felt.

I opened my eyes and reached past the bowl of oranges. The kitchen light clicked off. Darkness dropped fast.

The dishwasher kept humming. The monitor upstairs kept breathing. Outside, wind moved through the oak leaves with a dry, restless scrape.

I stood there until shapes rebuilt themselves. Silence wasn't natural. It was made.

And I had always been very good at making things look exactly the way they needed to look.

Made in the USA
Coppell, TX
28 June 2026

82442646R00270